THE FANGS
OF WAR

The Blood and Steel Saga
Book I

E J Doble

Dedicated to seven-year-old me,
and all those who believed this could happen.

A promise made, is a promise kept.

Val Azbann

THE ICE
S

Casantri

EAKER

City of the Sun

J.B
'21

Prologue

The End Has Come

On a silent shore, in a distant land, the world was coming to an end. Within the folds of a low-hanging mist, streams of black smoke billowed across the skyline, the embers of orange and crimson streaked through each fold, reaching off from the south like prying hands. Debris clung to the waters, sloshing with the patient ripples of waves; slick mosaics of oily blood stained an otherwise pristine white beach. The lifeless flesh of the many dead bobbed among them, eyes rolling and bellies bloating like the undulations of a great sea serpent. It was an otherwise pristine serenity, agonised by the scream of distant violence – that the world was coming to an end.

And yet no one seemed to know why.

Watching the thick plumes blanche the sky above, with the hollow screams of the dead and dying echoing out across the shore, a figure shrouded in shadow knelt in prayer at the water's edge, hands opened in its lap to sense the air. Water splashed across its knees; wind lashed the black cowl of its face, hidden away from the machinations of the world like a mother sheltering her child from a storm. Unseeing, yet omnipresent – a fixed point in a shifting world that was slowly falling apart.

To its side, the broken boughs of a small fishing boat lay crippled across the sand, the mast snapped clean in two, a great gouge drawn across one edge to spill whatever goods lay inside. Arrow points lanced its hull, splintering wood panels in every place, the bloodstains of fallen souls painting the vessel's interior in shades of purple and grey. It had escaped the carnage of a far-gone land with the wind still cast from its sails – carrying off the shadowy figure, as fire drenched the walls and towers of a city asunder, lay bare by an ancient enemy who had come with scores to settle and the wounds of ancient past. The figure had cast off, gazing skyward as the volleys rained down and the anarchy ensued, and watched with the joy of inevitability as the world ruined itself once more. Then it faded from sight out onto the great sea, carrying the ultimate prize.

The final piece of the end that would come.

In a slow yet constant motion, the shadow rose to its feet, turning to the thick barricade of skeletal trees that marked the shore's upper edge, sprawling either side as far as the eye could see. Robes billowing in the sea's cold whisper, it studied the body lay dormant at its feet, stirring slowly in an unconscious bliss with no recollection of the reality beyond. How poor it looked, led there: the saturated folds of red-green robes cocooning a frail body; the hunched back and twisted legs wracked with age and infirmity; the gnarled bones of arthritic fingers circling in the sand like a child; the hollow face, gaunt as a ghost and carved with wrinkles as if borne of the bark of a tree. A half-dead man of a half-dead people ground to dust and bled to the bone with nothing to show for it left – only the wretched stench of a by-gone power, its time long overdue.

As the thought came, life seemed to stir, and a deep humanity washed over his pale features. A flutter of the eyes; the mutters of cold words through cracked lips; a twist of the face as the wind cut through from the sea. Eyes opening, blurring – the suddenness of the world rising to meet him, peering up to black-grey clouds and the haze of a delicate mist.

Into the eyes of a shadow, looming over like a vulture.

"*Your time has come.*"

A jolt of motion; the stir of fear painted pale across his face. "Who are you? Where… where am I?"

"*I am but a servant,*" the shadow rumbled, quiet as a whisper. "*And I am here, for you.*"

"What do you mean? Who's servant?" Gaze wandering, crossing the seas lapping at his side, the dense swell of trees towering off to the right. "Do you have any idea who I am?"

"*It matters not, for the gods smile to you — that is why they sent me. I saved you from attack… from a death unworthy of your stature.*"

"Attacked?" A pause, trying to make sense of the sheer darkness in the shape that loomed above. "By whom?"

"*The black coats… from the north. They come with tidings of war… the heir apparent has returned to her throne. The world is coming undone as we know it.*"

"What are you saying? This doesn't make any sense. I…" The wrinkles snapped and twitched over. "Who are *you*?"

No words followed; silence ebbed, and the darkness made no motion. Only the tug of the wind, its whistle in his ears — the distant voices punctuating the skies above. Their screams, many screams, and the fire churning in the grey to the south.

Almost like the world was dying…

Pulling away, the shadow lifted its gloved hands without a word spoken, peeling back the cloak about its skull to reveal what lay beneath.

What came was skin, pale as dragon-fire. Branded below the eyes, black and bloody like a raven's. A pale scalp like the moon, a great trench cutting through one side like a mountain ravine. Sliding deep into the skull, through the brain itself, a rotten knot of flesh coiled within. A dislocation from all things human — a wound, that in all sense, would've seen any mortal man dead. And with it, the realisation that what he lay eyes upon was not of the mortal kind and not drawing the same breath as he then did. That this was no ordinary man wrought in shadow and cast from a storm into fire; this was a being of the unknown, of a kind once-forgotten.

It was a thing of blood and terror — an arbiter at the world's end.

"What *are* you?" he muttered, the ache in his heart drawing close to giving in, beholden to the shadow figure that loomed high above.

"I am a redeemer, come to pay the due of the Mother and her kind," it thundered, the skies seeming to swirl at its head. *"I am here to end the world as we know it so that it may be reborn again."* A hand lingered within the robes at its side. *"And my redemption, at all accost... begins with you."*

A blade appeared in its hand.

"Your time has come."

The blemish of fire across the skyline erupted with red flame; the mist curdled and bent all-around with flourishes of a frightful coursing wind. A rupture, like the snap of cracking branches, and an electric pulse struck through the clouds high above. Saltwater splashed the old man's cheeks. He clutched at cold sand tainted purple by his blood; he could do nothing but pull away, his legs twisted and broken, arms little more than stumps at his sides, eyes heavy and lungs ailing and the terrifying shadow of the creature approaching at his back.

Sudden pain, exquisite across his thread-bare skull, and he was dragged up from the earth by a knot of grey hair with no life in his limbs left to give.

The end of all things come.

With a rush of power, seething like dragon's flame, the shadow cut across its robed body and struck the man's head from his shoulders. A single, swift motion of absolute demise – the reckless abandonment of life that followed as the body collapsed in a heap across the dark figure's steel boots. The passage from fear to nothingness. The sky growing still, the wind but a murmur catching at its ear –a blooded trophy in its grasp, a stump dripping blood across the sand like a tap. An end to a great many things, and a testament to the bloodshed that would come.

The shadow cast the severed head to the sands.

"To death, a deed is done."

It turned slowly, little more than a glance to the body at its feet, and paced slowly back to the broken boughs of the fishing boat that had brought them all that way. Its gaze drifting across its innards, skimming over the useless goods therein – catching for but a moment the dull shimmer of metal buried between, fallen from the robes of the man now-dead.

The shadow speared a hand within, pulling cargo aside – drawing the object into the light: an acknowledgement for the world to see.

A crown, perfectly golden in the soft glow and desperately empty in its mass. Adorned with ruby and emerald gemstones, ornate carvings running up the spine of every pinnacle at its peak. The beauty it held, in that quiet moment – all the death it had wrought in the end. The last remnant of an ailing civilisation on the cusp of war, sat plainly in his hand.

The shadow smiled. "*The King is dead.*"

And the end of the world had come.

PART I

A Song of Greed and Glory

†

Chapter 1

Live and Let Die

They had come in the night.

They had come on the backs of brutish galleons lined with cannon and steel, coursing over delicate waves while the moon's eye lay shut. They had swung down from the north, a dozen or more of them, igniting shot and unloading fire across the quiet walls of Casantri's harbour. There had been no warning, no sign of their coming. The first they had known of the enemy – those set watch at the harbourside – was when the initial steel rounds had buffeted the walls of their towers and sent them crashing down into the sea. Carnage ensued; the apocalypse dashed the harbour in hues of grey and gold fire. Screams echoed over the high outer walls, the crackle of broken ship hulls snapping through frozen winds. The enemy kept coming, the battle raged on, and steel struck through the skies under starlight – it was only as the sun mounted the shimmering waters to the east once more, that silence dared return, rough-shod and wary. It was only then that those who had sheltered in their homes dared venture outside, and when they did so they looked upon the harbourside where the enemy had come.

To find it was only death that remained.

Stood at a pontoon overlooking the blood-slick waters below, General Cavara watched as a lifeless body slapped against the pillar at her feet like driftwood, the deathly-pale gaze of half-rotten eyes staring back up to her and through. In the beyond, there were many others like it: bloated forms hung limply from shattered debris. Stretching off to open waters, she saw the upturned hulls of ruined enemy ships lay tossing in their slumber. Several still roared with flame, snapping at the beleaguered contents within, pillars of smoke raising skyward to blemish an otherwise perfect blue sky. A scene of hell, if she'd ever known one – certainly not far from the mark.

Stood there, reeling against the pungent swell of death in her nostrils, Cavara watched the lame body at her feet for a while, the abysmal waste of life hanging in the water, and sighed heavily. It wasn't even her soldier, and it wasn't even her business, but she still had a sense that someone somewhere cared about that weird floating blob of flesh pinned to the wood under her feet. Perhaps a wife or a child or a friend or a colleague. Someone, somewhere, who cared. Or maybe nobody, in the end – maybe there were none to care. Perhaps she was the only one to look at that soggy carcass in the water and feel a touch of humanity, rather than looking upon them as just another soldier among the ranks, serving for king and country.

Whatever that meant, anymore.

Blood spilt and an enemy defeated, Cavara hummed quietly into the wind. *Yet with so little left to show for it.*

Turning slowly, the general peeled away from the harbourside and looked back across the outer walls, jumping between the squat houses and broad streets nestled within, ascending the slow rise to the palace keep sprawled at the crest of the hill, towering pinnacles of shimmering bronze spearing upward through the sky. Much remained unchanged in the city-proper, untouched by the night's attack. But, as one drew steadily closer to the sea, the cracks began to appear, from huge knots of stone split through on the outermost walls to massive storehouses across the dock smouldering in flame. Smoke ate every inch of the sky over there; a grey haze hung lazily over the cold city air. From the pontoon, she observed a bustling, burgeoning capital wallowing in its wealth and power – but in another light, she saw a nation with its tail tucked between its legs, surveying the devastation of a long night cast in shadow with no answers come to bear.

What's the point? She rolled her tongue and spat into the sea. *All this greatness and grandiosity... yet caught with our arse out at the first sign of danger. Dozens of our own, dead in the waters of our harbour – an enemy come and gone leaving only violence in their wake.* The body seemed to slap harder against the pillar at her feet; Cavara ground her teeth and sighed.

What's the point?

As she turned back to the waters, she traced a familiar face pacing with a wide gait across the harbour's edge towards her, a self-important stare directed her way that sent an immediate bubble of sickness through her stomach. Facing the open sea, a disdainful snap of dread eating at her thoughts, she tracked his approach along the pontoon behind her using the clatter of his polished steel boots, marking several other soldiers also keeping pace next to him. Imagining his steely, disgusted eyes and the snivelling, snarling sneer he always wore, the grating of his voice and the snap of his commands as if drawing a knife down glass.

As if this miserable day couldn't get any worse...

"General Cavara... just the woman I wanted to see." He drew up alongside her, awaiting a response that never came, peering out over the waters as she did with a curious eye. "Something interesting in the water, general? Other than the bodies and blood, that is, of course."

"No sir, nothing to see... just daydreaming," she said meekly. "That's what we're meant to do, isn't it? Pretend all this ain't real and be done with it. Look to the body but not the blood spilt."

"As it should be, yes." She caught the edges of a wry smile out the corner of her eye. "We'll make a sergeant of you yet, general, if you start thinking like that."

"A kind offer sir, truly... but I think boot-polishing and arse-kissing are best left to the professionals. I wouldn't want to step on your toes."

17

Sergeant Revek of the First Imperial Division of Provenci screwed his nose up and spat into the water. "I think you'll find a job of such prestige holds greater power than boot polishing, general...."

"Oh? Do you get to open doors for the rich too? Good for you."

"If I'd come here for your childish antics, Cavara, I'd have put myself in the stocks and given you the shit to throw myself," Revek growled. "But as it so happens, that isn't the case."

"Everyone needs a past-time, sir," she mused.

"Everyone needs *respect*, too." The venom tippled the end of his tongue, but the fangs would not bear – reprimanding subordinates the morning after so much blood had been shed was not a mistake easily undone.

And best you remember it. "So what do I owe the pleasure, sergeant?" she said, turning to face him at last. "Have you come bearing answers to what caused all this mess?"

"Not so much what caused it," he rumbled, "but more so what we have now lost because of it."

She frowned. "I don't follow."

"This information comes in the strictest confidence – and I will have you buried in a gutter before high-sun should it get out – but it was discovered this morning that the king was not in his chamber to be spoon-fed breakfast... wasn't anywhere in the palace at all, in fact."

"So, where is he?"

Sergeant Revek inhaled at length and pulled a hand through his hair. "A contingent of the forces that attacked last night... the savages from the north; the creatures of Tarraz, one and all... were reported to have entered the palace, and in the confusion of the attack made off with the king as cargo on their longboats. This was just hearsay to begin with, but as the king is nowhere to be found... we can assume they were *successful* in that directive, and that our monarch is currently somewhere along the north coast... and probably not alive."

Her stomach abruptly sunk through the floor; the air seemed to dissipate in her lungs. Around her, the blood and bodies sweeping in with the tide didn't seem quite so serious anymore. "The king is *gone*? You... how has this *happened*?" she exclaimed. "Why has any of this happened to us?"

"That's what we have yet to discover... and that's why we're here now."

He said nothing more; Revek twisted slightly and gestured with his hand to the soldiers at their backs.

When Cavara turned, she studied the limp shape of a bloodied man in prison slacks dragged by his arms towards them. His face was a swollen rot of purple bruising, his eyes little more than tiny slits. Lacerations were carved across his chest, staining the white cloth shirt an ugly shade of pink. As he was drawn to the edge of the pontoon, sliding to his knees before the morning sun, the prisoner passed gaze to the general with the small of his eyes, and she saw in there the pleading thoughts of a dead man drawn to the end of it all.

"We dragged him from a flagging ship capsized at the edge of the harbour," Revek exclaimed, sneering down at the poor wretch bent low at his feet. "The longboats had used them as cover in their retreat... we were hoping this one knew a thing or two about the business that night, but he has so far proven... *incapable* of offering us what we want." The foul smile reappeared. "Perhaps today he'll come to his *senses*...."

A wave of the hand and the soldiers cast the prisoner to the ground – suddenly free of restraint, he made a half-hearted attempt to scrabble towards the pontoon's edge, perhaps in the belief that the Icebreaker Sea would be more forgiving than the sergeant at his side. With unassuming reflexes, however, Sergeant Revek unsheathed his sword and lunged forward to hold it at the man's neck – the prisoner ground to a sudden halt, swallowing sharply, a whimpering plea escaping quiet lips at the freedom so close yet so far.

"Now where do you think *you're* going, hm?" Revek grinned, grabbing the victim by the scruff of his hair. "We aren't finished with you yet...."

Dragging him down a small flight of stairs to a platform at the water's surface, the man broke out into spasms of distress, desperate breaks to writhe free of the sergeant's grip. He fought weakly and only received a backhand across the face for his efforts. The sound resonated like a bell-chime, and the red mark that formed on his cheek moulded with the rest in moments.

"Now, you may have thought last night in the cells that I was being a bit cruel to you," Revek growled, drawing him closer, "but I can assure you I wasn't. I gave you a just torture, in many respects. You see, I had to provide compensation for the damage you caused to my city and my people. I had to exact pain in equal measure. So perhaps it would be *wise,* that you consider exactly what you're doing, attacking the most powerful coastal fortress on the western waters expecting to get away with it unscathed. It'll save you a lot of pain, hm?" He stared into him, through him, the grey-steel pellets of his eyes pressing deep. "Because pain, you understand, can be quantified – and I intend to do *just that.*"

Cavara watched the contortion of fear that came beneath the bruising – a strangled plea came as a reply, claiming he knew nothing more.

"Oh, but you do, *you do,*" Revek snapped. "You knew about the longboats… you knew about the plan to infiltrate the palace. You knew all of it… and I *know* that you know where the king is now. I know… and you will tell me *everything.*"

More unintelligible words wailed from the man's mouth. Cavara stood planted in her place, teeth rolling against each other in agony, the soldiers at her side tapping their fingers. *This is how things are done,* came the bland and dutiful thought. *This is how things got done. This was how we get justice.* She sighed.

Doesn't make it right, though—

"You lie!" Revek stormed, a squeamish thing that strained the chords in his throat. "You know! Every one of you knew… that was why you came to this place. That was your purpose. You *know…* and mark my words I will bring you *misery* until you tell us what you've done...."

Striking down, Revek plunged the prisoner's face over the platform's edge into the blood-curdled water below. An eruption of frothing pink ooze tore across the surface; hands pounded across the wood planks behind. From deep beneath his skin, veins pumped into life across the sergeant's straining face. Teeth gritted. Growled. Clenched furiously. The man below bucked and kicked like a startled stallion, agonising as air slowly seeped from his body and light began to fail. A hollow scream suddenly cried out from beneath the oil-slick surface.

The sergeant grinned above at his slow demise.

Revek drew the prisoner back, thrashing wildly as he came, and angled the dumbfounded gaze his way. "Do you have anything you wish to say?" the sergeant barked.

The man said nothing, only mumbled aimlessly, tears at the corners of his eyes, the cesspit liquid seeping into his wounds.

Revek drove his head back under the water. More bubbles erupted. His bound hands slapped harder again like the oars of a river raft.

The head reappeared, pleading to speak its peace.

"Spit it out then," the sergeant said.

A voice emerged, heavily accented and gravelly. "The plan was to get him... as far along the coast... as possible," the man spluttered, "to have him...." The thought trailed to a close.

"What?"

"To have him killed." A look of uncertainty passed across the man's broken countenance. "He is most likely already dead."

Revek gave a solemn nod of confirmation, no other emotion making a pass.

"He's *dead?*" Cavara exclaimed, stunted in shock. "*Actually* dead? Why?"

"He is dead," the prisoner spat, a snarl appearing as he turned to her, "and it was deserved, for what your *people* have done to my homeland. Mark my words, when she returns and this world bleeds again... we will come for you all—"

Revek drew his blade across with a single sweep and slit the man's throat, blood cascading into the already-swarming waters below. The body was released, sliding disjointedly into the scum below, life leeching from broken eyes as it sank slowly beneath the surface.

Another body, gone in an instant.

"That's enough of that," the sergeant grumbled, sheathing his blade and rising slowly, offering a flick of his hair with all the pointless bravado he could muster. He ascended the steps, up onto the main pontoon, but found his path blocked as General Cavara stepped ahead of him, a thunder brewing in the dark of her eye.

You have some answers to give yet, sir.

The sergeant frowned. "What do you want? You've heard what he said. *He's dead.* We move on. We follow procedure, and send out a search party in the coming days to retrieve the king's body. That's all there is to it... now *get* out of my *way*."

"That was not *all* that needed to be said, and you know it," the general challenged. "What did he mean by *'our people'* and his homeland? What was he talking about?"

"It is not your business...."

"As a general of the army seeking information after an attack on our capital, I think it is my business." Heat rose in her neck.

"It's on a need to know basis—"

"Look at the fucking waters, Revek!" she bellowed, spearing a finger out to the wider harbour – catching sight of the body still at the pillar below. "Look at the dead! *Hundreds* of them. Men have *died*, because of what's happened in Tarraz, whatever that may be – and that prisoner was proof. Something has happened, something some people deserve to know. Do you think whatever he was about to say won't become common knowledge soon enough? People want answers, sergeant... *I* want some answers. And as a general, I'd like to know what kind of mess the military – of which I am a *part of* – has gotten itself into." She paused, blinking slowly. "So please, go on."

The look that appeared on the sergeant's face could've melted steel. A wave of anger bubbled at its edge, grating the sides, begging to be let loose and tear her head from her neck. Begging to, and yet never being able to – the eyes of the soldiers at her back watching him, a slight glint of fear wrestling in their gaze. That procedure took precedent, and so long as the law was watching, he would have no choice but to abide.

"Leave us," he gestured to the guards, who turned and paced a dozen steps back down the pontoon. Revek returned to Cavara, still looming large above.

"Explain," was all she managed in reply.

He sighed at tremendous length, bones clicking in his jaw. "They *found out*," he said cryptically.

"Found out about what?"

"The money... all of it. Our finely-tuned plans in Tarraz that would've made us rich... it all came to light a few nights ago. And to say the least, they were *none too happy* that we've been robbing them for the past four years under the guise of taxes, and given them nothing of any use in return...."

That money that was never supposed to be found. She remembered hearing about it in a report four years before, smothered in small print at the base of a long scrawl. That their territories to the north – the vast former nation of Tarraz, stretching from the lowland hills of their border to the coastal fortress of Val Azbann, administered by government puppets for a handsome sum – had eroded over the twenty-five years from mismanagement and neglect. The report had been bleak in its estimation: the region would be ungovernable within a decade if nothing were done; the tribes were too divided to fend for themselves. *Our exercise in arbitrary madness should come to an end.*

Yet, as expected, nothing was done.

Nothing, that was, until the taxes came in. Cavara ground her teeth, recalling the arguments she had made against it. *To fund projects in the tribal lands... developments in the main cities... a goodwill gesture from an absent father.* A guise, she knew: nothing more than a false promise to cover the true purpose behind it all.

Rearmament, she spat, the word heavy on her tongue. *To start the whole useless affair again...*

"So the Tarrazi found out, after four years, of the inevitable," Cavara muttered, shaking her head. "Who woulda thought?"

"I know you feel strongly about this ever since it started... and I know this also then upsets you to hear," Revek said with unusual deliberation. "But how you feel, and what you see here now, is not what's important at the moment."

"Will it ever be important, sir? To any of you?" Her voice crackled like embers, singeing the tongue. "You and your superiors were *ignorant* to the fact that playing games with your enemy will always end in tragedy... and what you see here, is a tragedy. The tragedy of people, who put faith in a king who yes, in the end, *got what he deserved.*" She speared a finger out into the harbour. "Look at it, sir, and tell me whether deep within yourself you believe this was all worth the few extra coin you robbed from the Tarrazi to fund *an invasion force....*"

"Keep your *fucking voice down,* general," Revek boomed, snapping suddenly. "I don't *care* what you think of me or my support of what happened. I don't care *one bit* that this is the cost of that decision – soldiers are soldiers, they do, and they *die.* But I will tell you, that it is *my duty* to this city and its people to seek a reasonable settlement for what happened and begin preparations for what comes next. We have to deal with Tarraz and what this catastrophe means, before anything else, or this will happen one hundred times over and *nothing will change.*" He prodded his metallic chest-piece. "I am Head of Imperial Strategy in the Grand Council. I have managed the rearmament program for years now in secret. What I am *not* is a street cleaner, or some urchin left to clear this mess up – I am certainly not the man to pass flowers over the dead still clogging the harbour. My duty is to the people who live in this city and die defending it, that is all. Once they are dead, they are *dead,* and died doing what they were born to do. That is *all.*" He paused, eyes twitching. "Now, do I make myself *clear* on that, general?"

Cavara found the fight rage within her, but with a sigh saw it recede just as fast. *This is no fight we need here,* came the solemn reply. *It would solve nothing in the end – only cause more grief.* She gave a single nod, once only, and met his eye with a scowl.

Not yet, at least.

"Good... I'm pleased we're in agreement." Revek's face twisted from a sour pink to a sullen grey. "There shall be a meeting of the Grand Council tomorrow to discuss any questions you may have and work out a feasible way forward. All are expected to attend." He turned to her poignantly. "*Do not be late.*"

"I wouldn't dream of it, sir," came her reply. Cavara stood to one side and watched as Revek skulked away back towards the harbour.

"Oh, and one more thing, general," he said suddenly, twisting like a serpent to address her. "With the death of the king comes a reorganisation of leadership and rank. Upon the king's death, it is the Imperial Commander who takes up the mantle of Governor, and the army is brought in to maintain order... and that makes me your new commanding officer." A sly grin appeared. "And I shall not hesitate in reassigning those worthy of holding the rank of general... and ripping out those who *are not.*" A crooked glare met its mark. "And mark my words, General Cavara... I will make you *suffer....*"

The sergeant turned his back to her; Cavara watched the vulture hobble his way back towards Casantri, and felt the walls of reality begin to close in.

The king is dead. The tendons in her heart plucked like the strings of a harp. *The army takes power.* A knot of sickness ballooned in her stomach. *The dead line the waters of our capital.* Beneath her feet, the same blue-skin bloated body knocked against the wooden pillars. The hollowness ruptured within her, black as the smoke rising from the smouldering wreckage of the toppled ships in the bay.

The drums of war rise, once again.

25

†

Chapter 2

Where the Blood Begins

The halls and passageways of the palace were empty that morning, the echo-chime of his steel boots dancing along the walls and spilling out of open windows to the quiet skies above. The silence was daunting; every noise was like a piercing cry. Trepidation fell taut across every doorway and coving, the numb fear of the violence that had descended upon the harbour below coursing through the streets like a serpent. The fear of what had happened, of what it all meant.

The fear of what was yet to come, and by who's hand the axe would fall.

Within the palace, Sergeant Revek paced the long corridor to the throne room with a deep-set premonition on his mind. *This is what we've been waiting for*, he cooed softly, the swell of air in his chest and the weight of his stride carrying him forwards through the sunlit expanse of enormous stone blocks and finely-woven red carpets. *This is the power that has alluded us for far too long.* Across both walls, in the tiny alcoves lined with ornate pillars, the domineering statues of armoured knights stood high and proud on their carved plinths, the red-green painted metal of their shields shimmering brightly. His toothy grin widened, looking off to the doors at the far end.

To get what I deserve, at last.

Wedging his shoulders together, Revek heaved the doors apart slowly, passing from a realm of light into one of swelling shadow, drawing them to a close behind him once more.

Within the cold confines of the throne room, the sergeant found himself reeling at the height of the ceiling stretching above, supported by interlocking columns of ancient wood entombed in a complex array of spiderwebs, some as broad as sails. Crossing left, he found high windows lay blanketed in thick curtains, sealing off the midday sun with only a ruminating glow to show for it at the edges. Twisting then right, in a black-grey gloom across the far wall, he spied the threadbare standards of ancient tapestries rippling softly in the dark, depicting the tales of long-past glories in threads of gold and green.

Revek found his nose curl at the sight of them, a wrinkle of disgust coiling in his mind. *Former glories, left to grow tired in the shadows.* Glories he had been told as a child; taught in military camps as a junior; studied in the field guides as a general and then sergeant. *Watching, all the while, as those self-same glories fell to rubble, at the hand of an impotent king with one foot in the grave.* The concessions; the treaties signed; the lies of prosperity as the vaults were run into the ground. *And now the old fool lies dead, without responsibility or concern, and the nation is in turmoil.* He ground his teeth, sighed gracelessly into the void. *And now we're left to pick up the pieces.* The grin reappeared – at that moment, his eyes turned to the back of the room.

And here to serve its new leader.

The first thing the sergeant came to, was a high-backed throne of oak darker than any he had ever seen, with carved rings curling out at its edge to gauge the impression of rolling waves. Before it, a bleeding mass of silk and fur spilt over the tiles like an open wound, rising over the arm of the chair and snaking out of sight behind the massive bear-like form of a man. Adorned in a hulking suit of armour of obsidian metal, that accentuated the thick swell of black across his jaw and the traumatising gaze of heavy grey pupils sunk deep into his skull, as Revek approached he seemed entirely captivated by the figure. A man he knew he should hold no fear of, for they had been

27

colleagues of the army for near a decade – yet who, sat in that massive oak throne with a maw of shadow shrouding his stern complexion, the sergeant found himself short of breath and weak at the legs as he approached, only mounting enough courage to grace him with a bow at the last moment.

"Supreme Governor Alvarez," Revek said, mustering whatever remnant of courage he could find.

"Sergeant Revek," the man on the throne boomed. "About time you and I talked again. Please, stand."

Revek rose to full height, the unbroken gaze of the new Governor holding him once more. "You wanted to speak with me?"

"Yes. On a few matters, in fact." The bear-man rose from his seat to a ferociously intimidating height, the throne little more than a stool at his back by comparison. "How fares our army, sergeant? I'm sure you've addressed them all by now…"

Revek bristled – *they are* my *army* – but said nothing of it. "In good spirits, sir," he replied. "They were pleased with the result last night, and at the enemy slain, even with the loss of life."

"This is good… very good."

"Although we will need to try and recover as many vessels as we can and get them to the dockyards in the next few days. We took some heavy casualties when they first attacked and many of our ships lay beleaguered up the coast."

"Do what you must, sergeant. I entrust your judgement to see these things tended to."

"Thank you, sir."

"Hm."

Revek found a coldness in his chest, the bear-man's face easing into a look of disgust before him, as he wondered if he had wronged the man on some matter, or if there was something he had said—

"The matters I wished to discuss with you," Alvarez rumbled suddenly, "are highly sensitive… I hope you know that."

Revek snapped back to attention. "Of course, sir."

"Because they concern communication we've had directly with

our informants in Tarraz."

The edge of his mouth twitched. "Shouldn't that information come to *me* to report to *you*, as commanding officer?"

"When we formalise power, yes." A warning glance shot his way. "Remember, the masses don't know what's happened yet. They don't know I sit on the throne, or that I draw the sword and sign the laws. They don't know you are now my second-in-command. And, to control the changeover of power successfully — without starting a miserable *bloody* rebellion — we must keep things as they were for now." He arced a finger back towards the throne. "As far as is concerned, the king still sits in that chair, rotting his way to oblivion, until we address the full council tomorrow. Are we at an understanding about that?"

Revek ground his teeth. "Completely, sir."

"Good. Now, to the matter at hand..." With a huge paw, Alvarez reached within the folds of his robe and plucked a folded wedge of paper out, handing it to Revek to read. "We received this from a scout in the early hours of this morning, amidst the fighting. Came straight from Tarraz... poor bastard had to dodge crossbow fire just to get over the border. It's a mess if ever I've seen one."

And that's no underestimation, Revek thought, studying the scrawled ink across the page in his hands, blotches of rainwater and blood splattering like blisters at the edges. He recited every part as it came, and found each to be more damning than the last. '*A gross loss of life, as hundreds of Provenci officials are publicly executed in the Tarraz capital*'... '*what seems to be a nation-wide revolution against the puppet government*'... '*tribes have come together to form a new leadership, led by an unknown*'... '*all other diplomats have been expelled*'... '*borders have been reinforced and closed off*'... '*an old enemy has returned*'. A bubble ballooned in his throat; Revek found no words would come. The corruption had been unravelled, and the country had erupted into revolution right on their doorstep overnight. Then they had manned the oars, attacked Casantri by sea, infiltrated the palace and kidnapped their dying king as revenge. A demonstrable act of treason;

anarchy and humiliation of the highest order – reading on, it was the last line that held the sergeant's gaze the longest.

'We have lost control'.

"Quite the read, isn't it?" Alvarez said, sighing. "The fucking *savages.*"

Revek was still found wanting for a reply. "It's anarchy…"

"It's more than anarchy. They've ripped up everything we've worked to secure for *twenty-five years* and bathed it in blood. I always knew those foul creatures and their backward morals couldn't be trusted… and here we are. Caught as bystanders, watching our vassal state tear itself to pieces. It's more than anarchy, sergeant. It's *chaos.*"

Revek withdrew the letter. "Does it pose a military threat?"

"They shelled our harbour and killed dozens of our soldiers, sergeant – yes it is a *military threat.*"

"Beyond an act of revenge, I mean."

Alvarez seemed to stiffen. "Do you mean to suggest that what happened last night goes *unchallenged?*" he said coldly.

"Not at all, sir. I simply… looking at it militarily… would question whether there may be any further attack. That would decide whether we man the borders and double the guard, or kick the bastards in the teeth for what they've done." Revek tried to recover more ground. "It um… this report says nothing about border *raids*, only *reinforcement* of border towns—"

"Reinforcement is a precursor to aggression. Why reinforce a border if you didn't intend to invade?"

"Because we may want to take back what's ours."

"We *will* take back what is *rightfully* ours, sergeant. Don't play games about that." There was a wild glint in the Supreme Governor's eyes then – the look of a starving predator, baying for blood, finally laying eyes on its prey for the first time. A look that spoke volumes of the bloodshed that would undoubtedly come. "This is no simple sleight, sergeant," he continued venomously. "Treat *everything* as a military threat. Take no chances on that. No one attacks the greatest nation of the Icebreaker Sea and gets away with it. *No one.*"

Revek nodded once, once only. "Aye... sir."

A few moments passed, moments more, as Revek watched the dark machinations smooth over in the Governor's eye. Whatever had overcome him, and run with uncontrolled anger through his mind, subsided as fast as it had come; Alvarez rolled his tongue across the roof of his mouth and exhaled loudly out his nose. "Did you get anything else out of that prisoner we dragged off the burning ship?" he enquired suddenly, lifting his gaze again. "Did he know anything of the king's whereabouts?"

"We didn't get anything out of him last night, so I took him to the harbourside this morning to... *test the water*, shall we say." Revek grinned, relishing the memory. "It certainly got him talking."

"And?"

"And the attack last night had no intention of succeeding. From his explanation, it was designed more as a distraction so they could infiltrate the palace keep and make off with their cargo."

"An awful waste of life and ships to achieve so little."

"I believe that was their intention, sir... to achieve their ultimate goal no matter the cost."

"Barbaric..." The word echoed through the chamber like a drumbeat. "Did he say anything more?"

"The prisoner explained that they intended to seize the king from the palace and take him along the coast to the north... to find a quiet bay, and..."

"And what, sergeant?"

"... and execute him, sir."

"Well..." The bear-man nodded, presenting an expression of surprise, but with the corners of his mouth twitching upwards with every second that ticked by. "Isn't that a *shame*."

Revek grinned. "Yes sir... truly, a *shame*."

"Then it is confirmed... the king is dead, and he has died at the hands of the Tarrazi savages – those who dare stand against us, and rally their forces, and attack us with such violent disregard." A single nod; a set of pearlescent white teeth shimmering in the low light. "An act of *war*, no doubt."

"Without question sir," the sergeant beamed.

"That being the case, we must yet proceed with caution. With the king's untimely demise, the last thing we want is carnage in the streets. We need to see off his death tactfully…"

"A palace funeral, perhaps, sir?"

"Nothing of the sort," Alvarez spat.

Revek swallowed. "Of course."

"We will find the body, wherever it may be, and we shall let the masses see their dead king and be done with it. He's gone now, and war beckons… whatever legacy he demands of himself matters nought now." A pause. "Not that I'd ever tempt it anyway…"

"Excellent, sir."

"I would like you to direct the search party. I want two generals and a handful of men, on whatever ships we can spare, heading north in two days to retrieve the body and return it to us here." Another pause. "In fact, let that General Cavara lead it. I feel she's up to the job."

She deserves nothing of the sort. "Of course, sir."

The huge figure wagged a finger his way. "Don't squabble over it, either. I know you two have your differences."

I hope she dies. "Wouldn't dream of it, sir."

"Good." Alvarez turned to the throne, gazing up at the vast curtains draped behind it. "Now, I must beg your leave, sergeant. The Mother has summoned me to her counsel… we must talk of these matters more."

"Of course." He bowed, not sure who to, and turned hastily towards the doors, hoping to escape the awkward confines as fast as he could, as if the weight of the world were bearing down—

"Oh, and sergeant?"

Revek stopped, swore under his breath; turned to face him.

"Ready the men to march within the coming days," he said gravely. "Casantri does not kneel to the whim of *savages*."

My time has come. Revek gave an exaggerated bow, a curling smile like a crescent moon gracing his thin face. "I shall see to it immediately, sir... hail to Provenci."

He turned back to the door.

And hail to me.

†

Chapter 3

Do Not Speak Their Name

The doors fell closed with a shudder of metal – Alvarez stood alone in the vastness of the throne room, with only the shadows dancing across the walls like waves to keep him company. To his side, he heard the faint ripples of civilisation drift up and knock against the panes of the palace windows, detailing in their tiny sounds the hive of activity that flourished across the vastness of Casantri below – the great capital of imperial power grown tired in its old age.

The former kingdom now in his grasp; the first thunder of the coming storm.

So it begins. He nodded slowly, a touch of satisfaction easing across his face for a moment. *The imperial army, come to power.* A roll of the shoulders – he inhaled slowly. *A new Governor, set to rule the ailing nation.* Spinning on his heel, Alvarez turned towards the throne and gazed up to the vast black curtains that lay sealed shut behind.

The Mother herself, calling to her new champion.

He had heard the stories, told in the barracks below when he had been but a young palace guard: tales of the god-like beings who inhabited the capital palace of the four nations of the Icebreaker Sea, known as the Mothers of destiny and human will. That they were secretive, unforeseen deities, only seeking counsel in a nation's one ruler – that their power was absolute, and that any soul who dared try to access their counsel beyond the chosen leader was never seen or heard from again. Curious soldiers made fools of in their naivety, entering the chamber never to be found. Many rumoured as to what happened, to those unworthy of entering that chamber, but Alvarez had time and time again simply shook his head and smiled. For he knew that the Mothers acted merely as a conduit to greater knowledge – the only point of access to a greater being, unseen and yet always present. The one who lay shrouded in legend, said to live at the heart of the Icebreaker Sea. The one who commanded all things and controlled the balance of the world.

The All-Mother herself.

As the thought came, and he gazed up at the broad curtained veil where the Mother was said to reside, he found a whispering voice rise and fall patiently in the base of his skull. For several days it had called to him, at first little more than a faint hum, but since that morning he had found its tune grow sharper, as if reciting a melody in an ancient tongue that he knew nothing of at all. It was a summoning, he knew – her summoning, although before that day there had been no purpose behind its subtle sweet song.

But if the king is dead, and the leadership has passed onto me, he mused with a searching eye, *then the summons are to her next champion.* That as the city recoiled from a vicious attack, and the throne lay empty once more, the Mother had cast her gaze out to who came next.

And it is I she found, stood waiting.

He knelt before the throne, eyes closing, the thrum of the Mother's cry echoing out through his ears.

"*Proveto densi anis, priventi ata tori,*" he muttered, the dead language rolling poetically over his tongue. "I answer the call of the Mother; may my fate rest in her hands."

With an abruptness that hit with the impact of falling stone, the call in the base of his skull was suddenly extinguished, and a wave of pain struck through his spine like a snapping blade. The room fell dark around him; the ceiling spun and his eyes twitched like a breaching dam. Every fibre in his system convulsed as if it were trying desperately to stay awake, fighting the subconscious as it drew slowly back into the shadows. Trying with every ounce to keep awake.

Or perhaps, trying to stay alive.

In the pulsing expanse before him, a shadow lunged suddenly from the veil, swelling outwards into a revolving cloud of dust and dark matter, arcing overhead in an impossibly-black swirl as Alvarez slipped back and fell across the stone at his feet. Coldness ruptured within him, crystallising in his veins, puncturing his soul like a knife. It was all-encompassing, eclipsing every bead of light that dared enter the chamber, swallowing the life from the world as his vision cleared and he swayed laboriously to his feet.

"Mother Katastro..." he muttered breathlessly.

"*Child,*" a voice boomed from the vortex above, reverberating through his eardrums like the tiny cracks of bell-chimes. "*I've been waiting for you for some time now.*"

"For some time, Mother?"

"*Yes, child. It is a fate which brought you here to me... and it is a fate alone that dictates where you are now.*"

"I don't follow, Mother... if you could—"

"*Alvarez.*" The sound of his name on her voice conjured a breach of sickness deep in his stomach. "*So dutiful, yet so naïve... always lusting for power and more. These things, the king was not.*"

"'*Was not*', Mother? So it is true?"

"*It is true. The king is dead... as destiny foretold.*"

Alvarez frowned. "He knew that he would die?"

"*All who rule shall know their fate... such is as destiny permits. The king knew, but simply chose never to believe.*" A silence; the shadow swelled above him. "*I would hope you are not like him, child... fate is a cruel mistress, but also an undeniable truth in all things whether one likes it... or not.*"

"I would not dream of it, Mother—"

"*For I come to you not with the good tidings I have otherwise met with your forebears – there are... many great things wrong in the world, that must take*" precedent at this time."

Alvarez nodded with concern. "Do you speak of the war, Mother?"

A long, punishing silence, ebbing out into the void. The shadow held no gaze, yet he found its eyes gouge into him then. *"I speak of the end times, child,"* it thundered eventually. *"I speak of the end times for us all."*

"What do you mean by *'us all'*? What is happening?"

"The balance of the world is breaking, child. Our power, residing with the All-Mother... I sense it is failing with time. We have not heard her commands for many nights now."

"What does that mean?"

Another grave pause. *"It means she is dead, my child... and with her gone I fear I, like my sisters, shall follow."*

An unusual weight doused the Mother's voice as it caught in his ear, something verging on sorrow. Alvarez looked up and into the vortex above, dancing from shadow to shadow, and found the floor seemed to fall away at his feet. That war was coming, and the end times were upon them – *and the Mother is dying before me, and there is nothing I can do.*

"You cannot *die*," the Governor spat. "I need to know, I... I need you. This nation, *our people*, need you. We are on the brink of war, an enemy on our doorstep... you cannot *die* and leave us to slaughter—"

"This nation needs leadership," the voice growled, a snap like a crackling storm arcing through the chamber above. *"It needs strength, virtue, courage. It does not need me. I am a vassal of the All-Mother. I can see destiny, and what the future entails. I am but a soothe-sayer... you, and you alone, are this nation's leader, not me."*

Emboldened by her words, Alvarez breached the rise in his chest and exhaled at length. "Then what must I do, Mother? What must I do, if you are to die... to save all this? To *keep my power?*"

The void snapped before him – he almost made out a smile.

"You must seize it."

"What does that mean?"

"You have power, yes, but you have yet no strength... no blood to your steel or bite to your command. It is not yours to keep this power you possess... it is yours to take it, to feed that urge which you so desire."

A glimmer of blood-fuelled pride swelled in his heart. "So I am to go to war then?"

"To war, my child... your destiny lies in Tarraz. It is there you shall find this power you so long for."

"There is nothing in Tarraz, Mother. Nothing but brutes and savages, creatures of a bygone age who need correction. There is nothing but worthless blood and reforged glory in that land—"

"So bold, yet so naïve," the voice tempted as it lurched closer. "You know that is not true, deep inside. You know what awaits you in that land." A pause, as if it were studying him. "You've known for twenty-five years... what lies waiting for you in Tarraz."

"You know nothing of that," Alvarez spat, a furnace roaring through his system suddenly.

"I know all, my child, for I am the Mother of destiny and will... you just fear the reality that brings—"

"She is dead."

"It is not so."

"I saw it with my own eyes. I saw her cast from that wretched cliff in the midst of battle, a sword through her stomach—"

"... escaped into the mountains, has lived in exile all these years – you know it's true." The shadow swung gently backwards, up towards the curtains again. "You fed lies to your superiors back then," it continued, "and now that you hold the reins of power you still feed those same lies to yourself. Destiny has foretold that she lives... and that the rise of Tarraz shall come again."

Alvarez struck a finger out toward the void. "You lie."

"I am the Mother of destiny and will—"

"I scoff at it – this is lies."

"This is the truth... fate, as the prophecy foretold."

"To hell with your fucking prophecy..."

"You cannot abandon destiny—"

"*I am master of my own destiny!*" Alvarez roared. Spittle flew from his mouth, his voice crackling with anger. Rage boiled like a tempest in the rounds of his eyes, flaring red fire through his mind. "This is my *power*, and this is my *will*... you said it yourself: I am the ruler here, not *you*. Do not distort that with your *lies* and this ruinous *fallacy* that that bitch still lives. She is *dead*... twenty-five years stand as testament. Do not dare offer any pretence otherwise... this destiny is mine and mine *alone*."

The shadow shifted slowly, slipping still further back towards the curtained veil.

Silence ebbed; the anger rattled through his bones but found no direction to exert its force. The Mother loomed large ahead, uncaring, a master of a world that fell apart all around it.

"*Whatever you claim to control,*" it rumbled slowly, shaking the dust from the walls, "*does not matter. The Iron Queen of Tarraz yet lives...*"

It slipped through the gap; the curtains fell still.

"*And destiny shall prevail.*"

†

Chapter 4

It Comes From the North

It took a good few tugs to prize her axe from the man's skull, blood cascading from the wound as she tore her slippery hands away and took a draw of cold air. She didn't even have time to register, let alone time to care, before the next brute charged at her, steel swinging wildly in his hand.

She dived to the left, swung right, clattered against the man's breast-plate mid-stride. A short-sword turned for her: her axe handle knocked it aside, using the blunt end to jab at the man's face. Poked him in the eye, forced him to stumble. She swung the axe again, this time hitting home, connecting with flesh and bone as she severed the forearm in two and sent the hand spinning off into the grass. Colour left the brute's face; she had never seen an uglier shade of white. Another swing and she cleaved him across his throat. A jet of blood arched through the sky like a fountain; the man's wretched eyes rolled to the back of his head.

He collapsed moments later – and even before he had hit the floor, Savanta was turning and running towards more chiming blades, in search of her next kill.

In the open stretches of the grassland before her, sparse pockets of trees forming here and there, the enemy were stretched thin but still charging on. As she scanned the near horizon, there were already more bearded figures in thick metal plates storming into the tree-line to her left, where fighting still seized through the shadows like spasms of flame. Looking down to her sides, she found to some satisfaction that few of the dead around her were her own. A whisper of a smile caught her face.

It looks to be a good day after all.

Savanta made for the trees, where the clatter of metal and the screams of the dying accelerated the blood craze she found coursing through her veins. More of her people came into view, the red and green sash across their shoulders rippling in the light winds. A few were scattered in the bushes to her left locked in bitter fighting. To her right, more of the enemy came into view between the trees, some she found armed with the thin wooden shapes of crossbows. As the realisation came, one let fly a piercing bolt that whistled through the low-lying branches just next to her, and pierced one of her men in the mouth, shattering his jaw.

A squeal, and he was cut down moments later.

Savanta ground her teeth, seething, and charged for the firing line – a few suddenly-fearful faces turned to her, readying weapons and firearms.

A bolt let fly and Savanta sidestepped, twisting to watch the tiny metal ball barrel past her chest. A second snapped against her axe-blade, the debris impaling a nearby tree. A third, fumbled in the hands of a younger man, crackling through the branches above her head. A fourth——

Found an axe in his skull before the crossbow snapped, a last silent breath drawn on blooded lips.

Aware of the others around her, Savanta dodged another shot and reclaimed her axe, stodgy pink brain-matter still wedged along the blade as she circled back round. Another swing and she cracked a man's crossbow down the middle, draw wire snapping against her bared and bloodied hand. She hissed with the sudden pain – the man stumbled back, defenceless, as Savanta swung again, ever intent to kill, to strike another on her tally of a good day's work——

Another blade slid through, knocking aside her weapon as she spun on her heel, spitting and wild-eyed and——

Staring into the eyes of a titan-like figure fastened knee-to-neck in metal plates, face awash with black paint and thick scars, grinning like a butcher set to slaughter.

Savanta struck out fearfully – the huge figure snapped it aside with his own weapon as if it were little more than a strand of grass. Lunging forward, she shrieked as his massive hand coiled around the back of her head and snagged a huge knot of her hair.

She didn't even have time to register, let alone time to care, before the huge man lurched forward and smashed his head through the bridge of her nose.

A shot of pain blanketed her face, fuzzing and swelling as her eyes spun, the forest before her fading and forming with each blinkered moment. Suddenly she was falling back, landing across the leaf-litter below. Blood leaked across her mouth, bitter on her tongue. She spat, watched it land on the boot of the butcher who'd put her there, and looked up to see a blade falling towards her and the mad lust in his eyes.

So much for all the hard work—

A glint of metal like a shooting star, and an arrow rifled through the man's shoulder before the blade had a chance to move. He squealed like a pig, pulling away, reaching for the shaft now embedded in his collar—

Sensing the opportunity as the man reeled with agony, Savanta flicked a knife from her waist and propelled herself to her feet, spearing upwards towards the canopy—

The knife lodging up through the man's throat.

Blood exploded from his artery, streaming down the blade and across Savanta's arm. His eyes seemed to ignite for a moment, the man's huge paws scrabbling for the hilt as life slipped away.

When Savanta finally let go, the mass of muscle sagged to the ground and buckled into the mud like a felled tree. Silence suddenly ebbed out through the forest grove, the clash of steel drawing to an end, a grand symphony of bloodshed meeting its final moments.

Looking out to the faces of her people beyond the trees, Savanta took a long draw of cool air and sighed at great length.

Only to find a bubble pop in her nose and the sudden return of pain that followed, as she ground her teeth and rolled her eyes and screamed out into the green.

"How'd you manage that?"

They had taken shelter around the base of a great oak tree, where shafts of the midday sun struck through breaches in the canopy above, and rustling leaves and twisting branches caught the chill western winds sweeping down from the mountains. A few of her people were busy recovering the dead nearby and finding them places to be buried; others prepped their weapons, grinding whet-stone across the fine steel; a handful sat tending wounds along the northern edge, at the invisible line that marked the border between Provenci and the southernly reaches of Tarraz. The aftermath of carnage dancing among the trees; the growing swell of mourning plucking at everyone's hearts.

"It was an unfortunate incident," Savanta replied, pinching the bridge of her nose and spitting into the earth, "between a large man's forehead and my face... an incident where, by some miracle, I actually came off better."

Markus, her second-in-command, gave a wry smile. He was twice her age, greying around the edges with deeply wrinkled cheeks and mellow brown eyes, hair woven into a top-knot bound with a length of red cord. "I can see that," he mused, studying the blooded swell. "Although, I don't know that I've ever seen someone's nose grow *inside* their skull before."

"Fuck yourself," she scoffed, but couldn't help but laugh too. They had worked together for nearly a decade – from a small collection of mercenaries roving the countryside into a scouting unit of the imperial army organised to defend against raids. That they had been side by side, through sweat and steel and dirt and blood, clashing blades and cutting throats and ambushing wagons, for most of her life. And now, looking into the jovial, conciliatory gaze of Markus then, she saw there a weathered face of a dutiful honest man – and more so, her oldest friend.

"Don't think you'll be able to smell with that thing much anymore," Markus added. "Not that there's much to smell around 'ere, that is, besides damp leather and mud."

Savanta released the pressure on the bridge of her nose and found, with some satisfaction, that the blood flow had stopped. "I fear much the same... although we did well today, I'd wager. How many were lost in the fight?"

"Of our number, the last count was six... although considering the enemy totalled near three dozen, I'd say we had a very good day, aye."

"Wish my nose could say the same..."

"Don't fret, you'll recover... you might look even more like a troll than you already do, but I'm sure you'll manage."

"Fuck yourself."

"You're very welcome," he said with a warm smile. "Speaking of trolls, do you remember the last time *I* got an injury like that? About a year or so back along the eastern hills..."

She pondered. "Vaguely, something about that..."

The greying man clasped his hands, reminiscing the tale. "We were sent in to clear out a troll that had been terrorising local farms and breaking their mills – so we found that cave under the waterfall, along the eastern hills in that small opening. And I went in... assuming it would only be about four foot tall and no great bother... and—"

"Got hit across the stomach with a club the size of a small building," Savanta finished, shaking her head at the memory. "Yes, I do recall. And I remember it because you were *insufferable* for days on end after."

"I had just been hit with a club the size of a small building, mind," Markus scoffed. "Not only that, but I also had a gouge across my stomach big enough to be a landmark... still got the scar, come to think of it."

"It's not a bad thing... what is life without brushing shoulders with imminent death?"

"Wouldn't fancy an easy life?"

She screwed her nose up. "What, as some housemaid in a grand estate, or a local baker cooking fresh bread for the young? Over my *dead body* would I."

"Well, it nearly was... had my arrow not intervened."

"Yea... I was meaning to thank you for that. It would've been quite an unsatisfactory way to die."

"Is that so?" He nodded sarcastically. "And what would be a good way for the great Savanta to greet the gods, then?"

She looked to him with contentment in her gaze. "That when I die, I will get to look the bastard in the eye and know for a fact that, at that moment, I am staring down the devil himself..."

Markus smirked. "For nothing else will suffice?"

"Nothing else will suffice—"

"Captain!"

The voice came from ahead of her. Savanta shifted her gaze between the nearest trees and found one of her scouts approaching, stumbling through the grove with a sweat-streaked face.

"Aye?" she called

"We've found something... ma'am," the scout spluttered.

"Found *what?*"

"People, ma'am... lots of them. Coming from Tarraz—"

Savanta was on her feet and moving before she had a chance to finish.

"What am I looking at here?"

Squinting through the spyglass, Savanta traced the horizon line and tried to make sense of the vast, shifting black mass that had manifested there. Like an ant colony, it seemed to swarm over the grassland in tight clusters, weaving in and out of each other in some pattern that she found impossible to follow.

"They appeared as the fighting ended, ma'am," the scout explained. "The bulk of the force has remained in place, but we've tracked several small groups break off from there and disperse along both flanks. The scouts have been ordered to watch their progress from the trees. We don't wanna be snuck up on out here..."

No, we do not...

As she spoke, Savanta tracked a small cluster of figures peel off from the main hive, marching left across the plain. They seemed different than the rest: their armour was lighter, and they carried with them large sacks slung across their backs, the awkward metal contortions of tools poking from the top like spears. Their motions were purposeful, highly disciplined – as if there were a place to go and a job to do. She questioned why, and what they intended to do, but when several heavily laden carts emerged from the central mass and followed the path of the first, a ball of thread began to unravel in the back of her mind.

"They have building supplies... although I somewhat doubt they're building houses," she exclaimed, retracting the spyglass and lying it at her side.

"What could they be doing?" Markus asked to her right, stationed with his own spyglass.

"It could be anything... but with that kind of military presence, and that quantity of material being carted to the border, whatever it is, is within our jurisdiction." She rolled her tongue. "And it doesn't look good by any stretch of the imagination..."

"What do you advise?"

She gave a long pause. "We have to warn the capital."

"But the capital's been attacked," the scout queried. "The reports said as much... why would they waste personnel coming all the way out here just to keep an eye out? Surely that's our job?"

"Our job is to patrol the border and stop raids... *not,* as far as this seems to be, to assess an army as a precursor to *war.*" The final word drew a few concerned looks at her back. "As much as I love cutting down ugly bastards with a hatchet for a living, we ain't the soldiering type... and we ain't about to start now."

"What shall we do, then, ma'am?"

She drew a hand through her hair. "We scout out this area for a good place to make camp and maintain watch of the enemy with regular reports to the capital. We leave nothing to chance: if they spot us and start charging, I want no one being a hero, alright? We're scouts, not soldiers."

A few murmurs came as a response, muted acknowledgements as the realisation of what lay before them began to kick in.

"Good... scout?" The woman next to her met her eye. "Send a message to Casantri, tell them what's happening here and what our plan of action is. Say we await further orders." Savanta pulled closer. "And don't mess this up, or the entire north will descend upon us with fire and hell and we'll be nothing but ruins in weeks. Understood?"

The scout said nothing, drawing away as she got to her feet and ambled off into the forest, back towards the capital, an expression of terror wrought like cast-iron across her face. Savanta smiled.

No pressure.

†

Chapter 5

The King is Dead

The amphitheatre they had been summoned to with the council's call was an impressive sight to behold – one that would have found even the gods humbled by its grandeur and eminence. A high domed ceiling bled with marble in glittering waves of pink and lilac; a rim of polished stone stained through with black dye to give the impression of wispy smoke; massive columns wider than the trunks of oak trees supporting the curved walls, which were themselves carved with depictions of great and noble figures whose names had long been forgotten. At the base, rows upon rows of red-cushioned seats spilt slowly inwards in a great horseshoe of polished wood, opening to a platform at the very base with an orator's stand squat neatly in at the centre. At its back, wooden pillars supported the royal box planted into the wall across the far side, adorned with the red-green curtains and broad-rimmed shields of imperial showmanship. Had she had a moment to spare, beyond the anarchic cacophony of voices that thundered all around as state officials discussed the orders of the day, Cavara would have taken ample time to study the finer details of the marvellous structure, its beauty and wonder by all counts.

Time, she found with some distaste, that would not be spared of all the noise that surrounded her.

"Can't hear myself think," she muttered, shifting in her seat.

"That's not surprising," General Broska said at her side, rubbing his huge paws together. "This place isn't designed for *thinking*..."

He was a rotund man, round of the face with a swell of greying brown hair pushed back across his scalp, exposing a knotted brow bridging two potent blue eyes. Every word he spoke came with mellow, warm tones rumbling from the depths of his great stomach, which seemed to bulge out before him like a sack of grain. As far back as she had known, Broska had been a larger man than most – and despite the apparent quality of his leadership and geniality of his speech, that had also mired his position in the army for several years gone. The threats of resignation that had wavered his way – *the ridiculing tests they put him through to declare him unfit for service.* Part of her wondered if then, in the presence of so many of those same disingenuous officers who had made their attempts to have him dismissed, he felt uneasy in his own skin. Yet, as he sat there with a broad smile and a perceptive gaze crossing every inch of the amphitheatre above, Cavara found herself impressed by a man who seemed nothing if not in his element.

"Sadly, this is a place designed only for big words and hot air," Broska added, "and I can assume we're gonna be getting a lot of the latter today."

"You're right about that much," she replied.

"Even for a nation in crisis, some things never change."

"You've heard then?"

"Heard?" He scoffed. "Half the bloody nation has heard. It's the only thing anyone seems to be talking about... and no one seems to have any answers."

"Well, I wouldn't get your hopes up about finding any of those answers here."

"Are we here to be lectured and lied to once more?"

"Lectured, yes... lied to, I'm not sure." She shook her head. "All I do know is, whatever it is, it'll be painted as the only choice we have and nothing more. It's how it always works: you can plant the same tree a hundred times over..."

And the roots will still grow to the same bastard depth they always do...

49

A gavel sounded from somewhere above them; the inconsequential mutterings of the officials in their seats drew to a steady halt. A call to order beckoned suddenly from within the shadows of the royal balcony, and all eyes turned there to see what came next.

Moments later, Sergeant Revek strode out into the light with a self-effacing sneer that Cavara found her mind wretch at. Strapped in a shiny suit of armour with the standard of *commander* stamped against his breast, he rested a hand on the balustrade and pulled from his side a fold of paper to read for the opening address.

As if it couldn't get any worse...

"Ladies and gentlemen, esteemed nobles of Casantri, thank you for coming at such short notice, and at such a grave time for this nation," Revek muttered, a droning sound in the back of her skull. "The attack on our capital's harbour last night was a grave tragedy to this nation, and it was only thanks to courageous leadership" – *you stood on the outer walls of the city and used the harbour like a dart board* – "and the profound effectiveness of our military that the attackers only caused minor damage to the harbour itself and the outermost walls of this city. A commendable effort, certainly. We can confirm the attackers, the brutal savages from Tarraz, were unprovoked in their assault... and that this is an escalation of violence that we did not want to happen." *Bullshit.* "However, that is not to suggest that we escaped the battle last night unscathed, for what this nation has lost is a grave tragedy in itself." A delicate pause. "We regret to inform those gathered here today, that the king was kidnapped during the assault, and is believed to have been killed somewhere along the northern coast in the early hours of this morning."

The response was muted, a raindrop in the sea. A few muttered prayers passed between those around her; a few turns of heads to read the room – nothing to suggest that their king had died, and that war was coming, and there was nothing they could do about it.

"*Do they not care?*" Cavara whispered.

"*Not as much as they should,*" Broska replied. "*Our king has been murdered, and they respond as if it's just lowering the price of bread...*"

"In the light of this information, there have been several questions raised over what happens next," Revek continued. "There are no heirs to the throne, and reinstituting a new monarchy is forbidden under our written laws. The king's body has yet to be recovered, and we are in a difficult position with Tarraz that many of my equals fear will lead to an open conflict in the coming weeks. Therefore, as is proper at this time... I shall hand over proceedings to the highest appointed individual in Provenci: Commander Alvarez of the Imperial Army."

A ripple of discontent passed through the officials gathered below, as Revek stood to one side and the bear-like mass of Alvarez materialised out of the shadows. Draped in a black robe that consumed the balcony front like a river of clotted blood, he was a domineering presence that, with a raise of the hand, silenced the quiet concerns of those below him. Cavara sensed the tension of the room — as if the gods themselves had peered down to watch what happened next.

"A time of great crisis is upon us," he boomed, "and in such times, there are a great number of stones unturned, and questions unanswered. So, it is in my interest, and the interests of the collective, that I answer these questions *decisively*." He paused. "With no heir apparent to the throne of Provenci, it is constitutionally binding that I, as the Commander of the Imperial Army, become the Supreme Governor and de facto leader of Provenci in the king's place, following his untimely death." Even under his watchful gaze, the murmur of dissenting voices was apparent. "I understand there may be those of you with *concerns* about military rule, but I shall state here and now that I shall ensure fairness and liberty in the transition of power. The councils shall remain as the elected advisory body and take command of the day-to-day runnings of the capital. As the barons of the villages are no longer vassals to the king, security in the countryside will be maintained by armed militia, and the const- ruction of new military camps will begin tomorrow at dawn. This is the extent of military control at this time."

"*Said as if these measures are trivial,*" Cavara muttered.

"*Anything short of martial law is trivial where the army is concerned, you know that as well as I do,*" Broska mused. "*At least we get more security in the villages now.*"

"*Security against who?*"

"On another note," Alvarez continued, "we also understand the need to retrieve the king's body, as it is believed he has been killed somewhere along the northern coastline. Whether the killer has taken the body or hidden it, we are unsure, but procedure indicates we must at least attempt to locate the king's body at the earliest convenience. Therefore, an expedition along the coast has been authorised at the command of General Cavara" – she looked up, taken aback – "who shall be joined by General Ferreus and another of her choosing. They are requested to find the king's body and return it to Casantri, for it to receive an appropriate ceremony and then for the ashes be cast into the harbour."

"*You,*" she whispered sharply.

"*What?*"

"*You're coming with me; you'll be my appointee. I refuse to travel alone in the company of Ferreus unless they want me to spear the bastard on the front of the ship.*"

"*I'm unsure if that—*"

"*No excuses. You are my choice.*"

Broska found he had no reply.

"And on a final, and perhaps most serious note," Alvarez proclaimed, "is the immediate issue surrounding Tarraz." The attention seemed to rally in the room around her. "We have learnt that Tarraz has recently undergone a revolution, the likes of which have not been seen since The Collapse twenty-five years ago. What this looks like now as a society and as a threat to us, we are unsure. We intend to send a number of our scouts into the former territory in the coming days, in the hopes of assessing what is currently happening there. As for our position militarily, our newly-appointed Commander of the Imperial Army, General Revek, will receive several large battalions of soldiers from the rearmament training program in the mountains, arriving tomorrow at dawn." A long pause. "Retaliation for what happened last night must be decisive and absolute, and it is only a matter of time before such action is taken. Let it be made clear: we will have our *revenge*."

Alvarez turned and disappeared into the shadows without a word more, and the floor around them erupted with chatter. Chiming in Cavara's ears, came words of good faith and those of lost hope, words of understanding countered by those of fear, optimistic sentiment followed by cynical mistrust. Grinding against each other like gears, with the Supreme Governor's cronies watching on from the balcony with seditious grins. As if they saw nothing wrong with the chaos.

As if they'd hoped for it all along.

"I'd hazard a guess and say you weren't expecting that," Broska said.

"Expecting what?"

"To lead an expedition to find the king's body. Thought they might've given it to someone of lower rank instead."

"Alvarez wants me out the way while he's reorganising things is what it is," Cavara acknowledged. "It's a strange little paradox, you see: he knows I'm a nuisance and have far too many opinions for my own good, but that I'm also too good of an officer to slap a demotion in my face. If Revek had his way... I wouldn't even be here. So rather than face that possibility, what better way to keep me quiet than send me on a ship to some remote coastline out of the way?"

Broska smiled. "Who thought Alvarez had a heart."

"Alvarez doesn't have a heart, my friend... nothing of the sort." Cavara stood, straightening her chest plate, scanning the balcony high above — watching Revek slip away into the shadows, wondering what nefarious deed he would tend to while eyes were not watching, all at the hands of his new master. "Alvarez has no heart — what he has, is *an agenda*. A set of possibilities in the back of his mind, tracing back decades, waiting for the opportune moment to seize it. And what did he get, in the end, from all that patient lust?" She watched the officials at the balcony shake hands, and slink off out of sight behind the rest. "A million ways to spill a man's blood..."

In a war with no winners.

†

Chapter 6

Good Soldiers Follow Orders

Under the cold shadow of a great pillar in the backrooms of the amphitheatre, Revek was plotting his masterpiece. It was an intricate puzzle, with so many pieces hung idle for so long finally realised upon the death of their king. Thrust into power, he found those pieces begin to fall into place: the border was secure, the image was clearing. A reality he'd conjured up some years before as a glory-hunting soldier just starting out in the world, finally began to make sense. But certain parts remained elusive, and the masterpiece remained agonisingly unfinished. He knew that it would take great lengths to bring his vision to life – knew the watchful eye of the law would have to cast its gaze elsewhere for but a moment if all was to go to plan.

Because he had a plan, after all.

He always had.

From a nearby corridor, an ominous grey-haired figure approached him, helmet curled in the fold of his arm like a sleeping cat. The scars dissecting his face appeared most harsh in the low light, exaggerating already-mangled features with unpleasant intensity. The hollow craters of his two pin-point eyes pierced everything they met, holding and never quite letting go. He was old, ruthlessly feared, and had a reputation that outranked and outlived Revek by several decades at least.

And that made him precisely the man Revek needed – the final piece, in a grand and gruesome masterplan.

"You summoned me, commander?" General Ferreus inquired with a deliberate bow of the head.

Commander… now that does sound good. "Yes, I did general," Revek replied. "On a matter of utmost secrecy, I shall make you aware. This business goes no further than you, myself and a handful of your company when you depart for the expedition, do I make myself clear?"

"Completely sir."

Revek fished a note from the folds of his armour and thrust it into Ferreus's hand. The general frowned, a mass of scar tissue, and unfolded the order to read. There was little indication of his feelings – which Revek supposed was good, considering the nature of what was written – and upon reaching the end Ferreus produced little more than a slow nod and a scratch of the head.

"Commander," he grumbled slowly. "Are you *certain* about this?"

"I've never been more certain in my life," Revek spat, heat rising across his neck. "This has needed to happen for years, and now I am the commander of the Imperial Army the whim is mine and mine *alone*. This will be done… and you are the man to do it."

Ferreus grunted. "You make a dishonest man out of me, commander. I see that you want this under wraps."

"There is nothing *dishonest* here. These are your orders, and I am your commander. And good soldiers *follow orders*. Do I make myself clear?"

"Yes, sir… understood."

"Good."

"But may I ask," Ferreus inquired as Revek made to leave, "what is to be done when this is all over?"

The commander's eyes glistened. "You leave no trace, general. You leave no *sign* you were ever on that godforsaken sandbank. I will have no one disobeying me, *no one*. I am in charge here." He speared a finger at the general. "Follow your orders, leave no trace. Got that?"

"Yes sir," Ferreus mumbled as Revek stormed away. As he looked down to his hands, he found he had been given what amounted to a bloody knife — a knife, it appeared, from which all the coming bloodshed would begin.

†

Chapter 7

Sealed Lips, Slit Throats

T he drawstring makes all the difference… if it ain't wound tight enough on the ends, your alignment's all off. Makes it bloody hard to hit a target. Needs to be tight as anythin' to get the most accurate shot, trust me."

"That's why I prefer the crossbow: still get the same range, but with greater strength and consistency than any bow could give. The only problem is how long the damn things take to load…pellets are so small, can't seem to handle 'em properly."

"At least they don't snap like arrows – miserable day when a man lands on his arse and finds his arrowheads all snapped off."

"Aye, guess you 'ave a point there."

On a rocky outcrop overlooking the sprawl of countryside under the moon's hollow glow, the two lookouts had watched for some time as the near horizon had bloomed with orange flame, swelling like a wave across the green-grey grass below. As the sun had ebbed over the western mountains, and the blue-black sky had bled out overhead, a dense, interlocking barricade of chopped wood had been laid out like a brown river by the new Tarrazi forces who had come from the north, preparing the base for a border wall. Wherever they looked, it seemed to swarm with blackcoats, near impossible to make out in the night beyond the shimmer of their armour and the minute flicker of their encampment fires. The enemy had worked deep into dusk, but much of the work had only been rudimentary thus-far: greater attention, the scouts had found, had been paid to the construction of the enormous watchtowers that now dotted the border line, metal behemoths diced with arrow-slits and a crown of metal thorns twisted at their peak. Structures that could, from their high-rise vantages, pinpoint a man from a mile away. Could probably end a life even faster. Several times, the scouts had found themselves wondering how safe it was out on the outcrop near the trees, with the blood-orange eyes of the nearest tower studying them from afar. Watching and waiting, as night fell.

Silence across the great plains below.

"Although, snappin' arrows can't be as bad as spillin' pellets," Crossbow said, shaking his pouch at his waist. "If you drop these somewhere, be damned if you're finding 'em again."

"I see your point, arrows don't go missin' as easily," Archer said. "And you can reuse 'em, wiggle them out a man's throat and load up another. Can't say the same about pellets."

"Aye, but here's the thing, I ain't gonna argue with you over the stopping power on an arrow: that bastard hits like a train." Crossbow pulled up his sleeve to reveal a small crater on his bicep. "Felt like the thing was gonna rip my arm out its socket when it hit. But I will say, the impact of these little pellets— *especially* bolts, with the pointy ends? You know the ones – can cut a man down far quicker than they arrows you got there."

Archer wagged a finger. "That's if you hit *skin,* my good friend. No doubt if a bolt snaps into your exposed leg or chest or whatever, that thing will burrow through and kill at least three men stood behind as well. But when we're fightin', the men ain't running at us bare-bodied, ay? They got leather hide undercoats, chainmail, body armour, steel linings. Pellet would bounce right off 'em... a bolt might make a dent but it'd lose all that power." He drew an arrow from his quiver and examined the tip. "These arrowheads are made of pure steel, sharp as a viper's fang. I've seen these things rip through chainmail like butter. I can't say a crossbow could do the same."

Crossbow screwed up his nose and spat into the grass. "I'd question whether a bolt's accuracy would make up for it. We might not breach the armour as you say, but we sure as hell hit the exact point we aim for – lot more reliable than an arrow does."

"Then let's test it," Archer suggested, lifting his bow from the ground.

"How so?"

"We find a target…" He gazed out to the open grassland sprawling at the foot of the small hill, which seemed to thicken into waist-high plumes the further out one gazed. Suddenly, Archer stuck a finger out. "Ah, there! Do you see it? The lil' rabbit just above that grass verge, about thirty feet away."

Crossbow did see it: a small smudge of grey shuffling between several mounds of earth, tearing at the ground with a paw absently. He shrugged. "So be it… the rabbit is our target. What are we testing?"

"So, I'll be testing for stopping power: I've gotta hit the bugger and kill it outright. As for you, you claim that crossbows are more accurate… so you've gotta aim for the head and meet the mark, whether it's dead or alive." A pause. "Either way, that rabbit's our breakfast, so best we don't fail."

Crossbow smirked as if the challenge were an easy one, handling his wood-barrelled weapon in deft hands. "Very well… you first, then. A clean kill."

Accepting the challenge, Archer pulled a knee up to his chest and steadied the bow in his hands, the arrow pinched between two fingers. He made a quick judgement of range and wind; lifting the bow delicately, fractions of fractions, he lay his eyes on the target shuffling through the dust below, and let fly.

The arrow struck the rabbit in the side, just above the front leg. A snap chimed through the crisp air – the tiny creature, pinned to the grass verge, squealed sharply before lying still.

Archer grinned, waving a hand. "You see… *impeccable* firepower."

Crossbow, unconvinced, studied the rabbit intently, before a wide smile appeared across his face. "It ain't dead."

"What?"

"It *ain't* dead."

"Yes it is, it clearly is..."

"It's still wriggling! Look at it! I can see the poor bastard crying from 'ere. You didn't kill it."

Archer looked off dismissively, only to find the small creature still writhing awkwardly with a haunting glow in its eye. He sighed, sliding his bow back into its holster. "Very well... put it out of its misery, then."

Crossbow, grinning arrogantly, tightened the string of his weapon with a crank of small gears. Securing the pellet in its holster along the main shaft, he cocked the weapon against his shoulder like a comforting instrument and drew it up to his eye. Down-sight, the squealing rabbit continued to buck and writhe in pain – a poor sight of a creature longing to be free of its misery.

Crossbow found himself happy to oblige.

A shot, and the tiny rodent's head snapped back into the dirt, its unblinking eyes gazing up to the pale moon as it fell slowly from the world at last.

Archer nodded at his side, somewhat impressed. "An excellent shot," he exclaimed.

But Crossbow only felt a swell of horror overcome him, sketched across his face like the poor rabbit's below.

"What's wrong?"

Crossbow turned to him. "... that wasn't my shot."

Frowning, Archer turned to inspect the treeline behind—

An arrow whistled past Crossbow's ear and a gush of blood erupted from his friend's skull moments later. The flight feathers continued to quiver, even as Archer's corpse spilt over the edge of the rocks and clattered down the hill beneath to where the rabbit's body now lay.

Crossbow himself turned around moments later, fumbling for

another shot. Watching the trees, the bushes, the rocks and grass banks and broken crags: found nothing. Made a complete turn, in time to see a massive figure in black armour bearing down—

The snap of a sword hilt against his temple.

The cold void, beckoning him into its arms.

He was awoken by cold water and the bitter taste of his own blood. A quick flush of panic, a deep breath of air. Shackles about his neck, a cotton bag across his face constricting airflow. The world spun, flickers of yellow and black thrashing past his eyes. And then the sound of a blade sliding from its scabbard, and the invitation of an end.

A string cut by his neck, and the bag disappeared moments later. A vastness of blaring orange light consumed his vision. Shimmering across metal plates, scaling high into the watchtower above. Surrounding him, the shadows of enemy blackcoats, towering over him like the gods. His chains fell heavy at the sight of them. He was at their mercy now.

"We found him and his friend on an outcrop of rocks near the border," one of the shadows explained. "We shot the friend... brought this one here for interrogation. Reckon he's a Casantri spy?"

"No, he doesn't have the look of one," another muttered. "He's a scout alright, but Casantri didn't send him to spy on us. I reckon he was out here anyway." An obsidian-armoured hand grabbed him by the jaw and hoisted him up to eye-level with frightening ease. "I reckon he's a scout with some friends hiding nearby."

Now in full view, the Tarrazi leader's face was a mesh of tribal scars and blackened paint, with an asphyxiating, slate-grey stare and a cobweb of black veins extending around an earless skull.

"Reckon he'll talk?" the other figure asked.

"If he knows what's good for him." A grin of pointed teeth struck a deep cord with the scout, as if he could smell the fear on his own breath. "He'll talk."

"I am hiding nothing..." he pleaded. "Please, I... I don't know anything..."

"Then what were you doing, on an outcrop of rock with another scout, in clear view of our forces? Not a place an idle man would be."

"I was not idle... and I am a scout. But I ain't hiding anyone... I was assigned by a nearby village, called Wincheg. They... they called me out 'cause they were worried about the noise and stuff at the border. I was just doing a routine check... to report back tomorrow. I... there is nothing else to it..."

"Where is this village?"

"About twenty leagues to the south from here, amongst small hills."

"And what would your report entail?"

Crossbow flinched. "I'd... I'd tell 'em there was no problem, that no one had crossed the border, so there... was nothing to worry about. Please, I... I'm telling the truth, really."

"Hm." The blackcoat rose to full height, releasing his grip on the scout's jaw. "It is certainly a convincing story..."

"Now please, let me go... I've done nothing wrong... please, I've done nothing—"

A hand snapped out and cuffed the scout across the side of the head with enough force to barrel him over and spill across the metal-plate floors below. He groaned, a wheeze escaping bruised lips.

"Don't grovel to me like a peasant, speak to me like a *man*," the blackcoat spat. "Although even that doesn't hide the lies..."

"I *haven't*..." he spluttered. "I haven't *lied* to you..."

The Tarrazi leader dropped to a crouch and scowled viciously. "We dragged another of your kind out of the woods earlier today. Same dress, same excuses. But when we stuck a knife between his fingers and started sawing away at the skin, he started talking... he told us he was one of a handful of scouts, overseeing the retreat of Casantri border patrols from this area. Said they were long gone by now." A long, painful pause. "And then *you* show up..."

"I hail from Wincheg, and so do my scouts. Whatever business this other man has... it's not *me*... it's nothing to do with me... I serve my village, not the patrols... please, you must understand..."

"Oh, I do." The blackcoat stood. "And you're gonna prove it to me..."

With a flick of the hand, two more blackcoats emerged from beyond the watchtower. Crossbow watched with a sudden lance of horror as another prisoner was brought before them in heavy shackles, beaten to a pulp and swollen purple under the harsh light of torches.

Thrown to the floor opposite him, he had never seen quite so distinctly into the eyes of a dying man. A bloodshot, hollow gaze, full of fear and desperation. Wanting to speak but fearing the words that would come. Fearing the enemy who surrounded them. There was a deep tiredness, most of all. No soul nor fight left. Only the touch of death, whispering delicately in his ear.

"This" – the blackcoat twisted sharply and punched the prisoner, a splatter of blood across the metal floor as his head snapped round – "was the scout we dragged out the woods earlier today that I spoke of. Miserable wretch, isn't he?" The other blackcoats gave a ripple of laughter. "And he wears the same slacks as you do... how *interesting*. It is no matter, though... because this man means nothing to you, scout, does he? He's not one of yours. So his death... untimely, but necessary in all this... will be one like any other."

Drooling blood, Crossbow could find no words of solace for the dying man, wide-eyed and fearful before him as life slowly slipped through his fingers. The scout drew away from the prisoner and looked up instead to the charred face of the blackcoat, his expression pained but blank.

"Hm... a shame." The Tarrazi leader unsheathed his sword. "Such a waste of a poor wretch's life..."

Grappling the bruised man's blood-matted hair, the blade drew across his neck with such exacting abruptness. A gut-wrenching slice of skin, arteries burst, and blood began to cascade across the metal floors. A disposal of life, so callous: the body was thrown to the floor, dragged out by the blackcoats. The Tarrazi leader, without so much as a breath out of touch, cleaned his blade and sheathed it once more, grimacing at the blood now pooled at his feet.

"You people are *savages*," Crossbow muttered, heart-wrenching, teeth grinding together. "Fucking *savages...*"

The blackcoat took a step closer. "Savage is relative," it mused. "To a herd of cattle, the long march to the slaughterhouse is at the hands of savages. The man wielding the blade, ready to gut the beast when it arrives, is the savage. The cattle may despise the savage... but the savage does not care. Why? Because the savage does not think the cattle have the capacity to *suffer* in the same way." That same suffocating stare fell upon him again. "I am *sorry*, truly, that for so long your people have enjoyed being the butcher. Watching the cattle come for slaughter. *Relishing* that we, a once-proud people, did not have the capacity to *suffer* under your rule." He speared a finger at the pool of blood. "And now we finally have our chance at freedom, to get *revenge* for all the years of suffering your people have caused... and you call *us* the savages?" The blackcoat grinned. "Your people are naïve... your days of slaughter are at an end. Provenci shall fall... and you shall *die with it.*"

The scout's eyes bulged, and at the chime of an unsheathed blade, the blackcoat cut across his neck with a single stroke of steel. Crossbow's body collapsed to the side, head rolling awkwardly and cracking against the metal floors beneath, smothered in its own blood. The Tarrazi leader offered little more than a disappointed grimace as its condolences, wiping the blade clean on the dead man's coat and ordering the soldiers to dispose of the next body. It was just another of the enemy dead.

There would be many more to follow.

"Officer," the leader exclaimed to another figure at his side. "We need to round up the other scouts who lurk nearby... we can't afford to have any Casantri spies rooting around along the border." He peered out through an archer's slit in the watchtower, out onto the expanse of shadow-shrouded trees just beyond. "Burn the wood down. Barrage the deeper parts with artillery fire. Send out search parties to find the bodies. *No one* gets out alive." A gaze to the floor, and the red ooze pooling at his feet. "And get this mess cleaned up, *now*!"

†

Chapter 8

Bad Dogs, Broken Leashes

The waters had taken on an abstruse shade of purple as the light had receded across the sky. The blood-clotted waters had diluted, debris floating off into the vastness of the Icebreaker Sea, carrying the tales of what happened the previous night off to distant shores. Bodies had been fished out in an endless stream, bloated and pale, half-massacred by lampreys and other blood-crazed beasts lurking in the murk below. What was originally horror, gave way to discomforting normality. The skies had cleared of smoke, giving way to a bulging summer sun. Flocks of seafaring birds speckled the skies once more. The harbour returned to its dull, clattering monotony, but the dark stains of death still hung low over the waters like a phantom and plucked at the minds of onlookers as the day had turned to dusk.

Now, under the eye of the moon, Cavara gazed across the gloomy dockside and took a long swig of the midnight air. Even in the depths of night, with Casantri slumbering soundly off to the side, the harbour remained ever purposeful and alive. For the dock workers, days spent barking orders to subordinates and making repairs in the shipyards were exchanged for nights of loading cargo and arranging trades over drinks and bartering tongues. Lamplights shimmered aboard the many docked vessels, the low thrum of business talk broken occasionally by light-hearted laughs and shakes of the hand.

Then the lights would shift like fireflies from the boats into the labyrinth of storehouses behind, and the night would grow eerily silent again. It was business as usual in the blood-curdled waters of Casantri's harbourside, always conducted at the most sinister times and in the most delicate manner.

As if there is nothing wrong with the world.

But there was an immensity wrong, and she couldn't tell if it was ignorance or denial that kept the world spinning as normal. Continuing to load the ships, resupply the cannons, shake the hands, sign the papers. Knowing that if they ran out of ink, the waters were so slick with blood that they could use it as an alternative just as easily.

And why not? Business as usual after all. The might of the Imperial Army would keep them safe. *Isn't that how it's always been?* Cavara scoffed, the stench of rot and decay receding to find unmitigated arrogance and excuses in its place. *The army is a scapegoat to everyone's problems. Come the war, and they'll find their trust grossly misplaced.*

"Which one is ours?" Broska said, sat beside her, taking a long swig from a flask at his side. "All look the same to me."

"Second one over," she replied, "or so I was told."

"The three-mast? Impressive. Didn't think they'd give us such a grand vessel for an expedition."

"Probably because of our intended cargo."

Broska snorted. "Even in death... the old bastard needs a bloody big boat to take him places. Who would've thought?"

Aye, who would've thought. Cavara felt the wave of nausea in her chest at the reminder of the king's death. It was a brute reality now, one she was fully acceptant of, but the discomfort prevailed. And it ached angrily in her chest. *Because even that is yet to be resolved.*

"Are you not drinking?"

"I rarely do," Cavara muttered. "I prefer a clear head... makes me feel saner, especially with everything going on."

"Do you worry about your assignment, and being sent away from the city?"

"You think they'll close the door on the way back and never open it again?"

"Not quite." Another swig. "I think you'll open the door again, and wish you never had."

"That I fear what the place will become in my absence?" She nodded. "That even though I have no control over the nation's fate... I will feel guilty as it tears itself apart over war and its many sins..."

"You will feel guilt, and I know deep down inside you fear it."

"How so? Or is this the drink talking."

"This is me talking, I assure you," he mumbled with a smile, slightly slurred. "That being said, there's something I've been meaning to ask you... for quite a while now. About those fears."

Cavara frowned slightly. "Go on."

"Do you remember when we had those union riots in the city, what was it... three years ago? Back when they burned one of the barracks to the ground and marched towards the palace demanding better pay."

"I recall." *Although at times I'm not sure I want to.*

"I've always wondered why you did what you did that day. And then, I suppose, why it caused so much anarchy after that... whether you wanted to step back into the army after that, or would've rather buried and be done with it."

She bristled suddenly, skin crawling, the memory hot and heavy in her mind. "You mean why did I refuse my duties to the Imperial Code, and was then put on military trial by those who wanted me dismissed from the army, only for the king to step in personally to clear my name?" The words were pointed, sharp on her tongue. "Why I came crawling back to them, fearful of what my *duty* really was?"

"I..." He seemed lost for words, suddenly aware of the twisting frown now curling at her lips and the dogged stare that burrowed through him. "Yes... precisely. I'm sorry if—"

"... you've overstepped a line?" Cavara paused, ground her teeth, a screaming sensation across the back of her eyes – and then a sigh, realisation and sadness eating away at the pain. *What am I saying?* "No, you haven't," she said softly. "You've asked an honest question about something I've been told I must be ashamed of." She looked at him. "And were you a dishonest man, I'd have stabbed you in the throat for uttering those words. But you aren't, Broska. You're a good man, and... perhaps it's about time I came to terms with my reality too." A slight chuckle. "Besides, looking at that flask in your hand, you won't remember it come morning anyway."

Broska produced a nervous smile. "Ah, well, you know me..."

She smiled. "Yes, I do."

Visible relief reclaimed him, the smile widening. "But anyway, please, go ahead...."

"Very well. I guess I should start with, um..." A deeper breath, a dramatic pause. Her throat was rattling. "I... can remember most of all..." She struggled for the words, liquid across her tongue. *Come on, get on with it.* "I can remember when the rioters were marching up the main street to the palace. It was dusk. Glinting metal and torches lined the street. I stood with the other generals on a wooden barricade hastily erected further up."

"And I was kept out of way on patrol."

"Where I'd have rather been." She scratched her hair distastefully. "I couldn't *stand* being there, watching my own soldiers brandish clubs and long-poles, screaming at our own people as if they were criminals. Revek – stood there with that self-certain *arrogance* of his – ordering men to advance with no restraint. No other general getting a word in, even though we were his equals. He just espoused that shit about honour and the '*might of the army*' and sent the men marching in ranks down the street towards these peasants with torches. Unarmed demonstrators. Common people, as common as you or I, being advanced upon by fully-armoured, battle-trained units of the army ready to beat these people to the ground. And why? Because *they could*."

"... what happened then?"

"They collided... like lead-shot through a wood-plank wall. The first row of soldiers clattered into the rioters and knocked them to the floor. Those rioters behind trampled the first who had been beaten down and swung their torches. Those who tried to crawl away got beaten with the clubs. And... then more and more bodies piled up. They clashed, surged together like great waves. I saw older men crawl away with bloody battered wounds spouting blood. Women with their faces smashed in. A quiet face, carrying little more than a sign requesting better pay... with a crack in the back of his skull, face down, dead." She felt cold rise within her. "People were dying, Broska... innocent people. And we stood by, watching, giving orders far too quiet to be of any use, 'cause... well, we didn't believe what we were seeing."

"And enough was enough," Broska said. "And you were the only one who said it."

"I was the only one who *did* something. I wasn't about to let our people die like that – and I wasn't about to let Revek have his *moment* over it, either." Her fist clenched, her tone harsher, more deliberate. "So I marched down that street, shoved my way through the jostling crowds of soldiers, clambered over bodies to the front line, and screamed for the anarchy to stop. I told them this was wrong, told them their lives were not worth petty beatings by supposedly honourable men. Told them the fighting would end, the blood would stop. That their pleas would be heard by the Council and the king even if I had to deliver it to them personally. Just to stop the fighting." She sighed longingly. "And then the crowds dispersed, and the soldiers stood aside..."

"And Revek marched up and ordered your arrest there and then... for disobeying orders and subterfuge of the Imperial Code." Broska teetered with disbelief. "By the gods... talk of a vendetta. The bastard may as well have just put a knife in your back then and there. Is mighty dishonourable putting your ego before your morals."

"Well, if you have no morals and placate it with your ego... you shit out someone like Revek one day," Cavara grumbled. "And you know the worst bit? He got *nothing*. Brutalising civilians protesting in the streets with clubs, killing dozens… and no one ushered a *word* against him. They did *nothing*. And they did nothing, because Revek is guarded by Alvarez, and in turn by high command, and in turn by the army *itself*. I tried to bring justice for it, sought counsel with the king several times about it… and marked as a *traitor*, Revek ran me into the *fucking* gutter for it." Her voice crackled; a lump formed in her throat. "I thought I'd lose everything…"

Broska bowed his head, gazing into the waters beyond. "I'm sorry."

"Ain't anything much, Broska… sure ain't your fault."

"All the same," he muttered. "It doesn't give much hope for what's happening now… what with those same people leading not only the army, but the country too."

"My father used to say that bad men were like dogs on leashes… it ain't about trusting the dog, it's about how strong the leash is."

"Bad people will always be bad?"

"He was a cynical man."

"If only he'd ran for office… we'd all be saved."

He chuckled. "That we would."

Cavara managed a smile at that, catching the warm glow in his eye. "I… know it was the drink talking, but… thank you for hearing me out." She looked to him with a warm gaze. "I've feared that story for so long, because of how they treated me. It's good to get it out finally…"

"I'll always help where I can, Cav, you know that," he replied. "But never fear how you acted, never fear your morals. Rules are designed to regulate bad people, not good ones. A good person, like you, should always stay true to their beliefs, rather than play the puppet. It isn't worth it otherwise." He stood, stretching his back, gazing off to the full moon dancing in the sky high above. "We need people like you now more than ever, Cav, making the right calls and standing up for themselves. And if anyone tells you different…" – he speared a finger at the harbour below – "…the proof's in the water."

Broska moved off into the dockyards, drifting from sight as Cavara stared off into the void of the harbour stretching out to the quiet distant sea. The peace of it all, despite the hell that had been and gone; the subtle ripples of waves, saying everything would be okay. She inhaled the salty air, and smiled.

The proof's in the water.

†

Chapter 9

Falling Sun

Savanta awoke to smoke and screaming. She coughed, felt a weight in her lungs like sludge. Through the blur, as she peeled open her eyes, the world was consumed by a suffocation of tar-black smog that not even the moonlight could penetrate through the canopy above. It was stifling, intoxicating, burned the eyes and stung the throat like cheap drink. Wrapped in a blanket covered in leaves, in the alcove of an oak's massive roots, what had been her hiding place she now slowly realised was to become little more than a shallow grave.

She thrashed about for some moments, trying to unravel the blanket that cocooned her. Breaking free, she lunged to her feet and felt the raw, unbridled heat envelop her. Every tree, every branch, every leaf above her was shrouded in shadow. A world of desolation; the smoke consumed everything. Savanta stumbled about trying to find another face, something familiar in the din of grey and black. Her lungs burned, mind and vision strangled by the deprivation.

Where is everyone?

A few more steps. The ground was bare and bone-dry, crunching underfoot. Screams howled through the bushes, human and animal alike. They echoed, chiming in her ears. Made her feel so exceedingly small and alone. Like a child again, wandered far from home, in a place she didn't belong. Yet the humble landscape of a quiet woodland as a child, was a damned sight more inviting than the hell-hole she found herself in.

A whistle, growing closer, and then a colossal snap overhead.

A thud, something landing nearby.

Savanta stumbled, panicked, gazed up to the skyline to a falling tree.

Falling down towards her.

A shadow to her left, connecting with her side, shunting her to the floor as the tree made impact. World spinning. Thought she'd go under again. Sleep through the chaos, until the chaos saw to her end. She'd know no different. It'd be welcoming, right about then.

Except she was hauled to her feet instead, and found fate had far more convoluted plans for her.

"We gotta move, now!" Markus bellowed, dragging her up and starting to run. "C'mon!"

"What's happening? Where are the others?"

"Captured, interrogated... probably dead. Savages started burning the fucking wood down. They've been barraging with cannon-shot since midnight. Most of the men have got out but... some of 'em didn't. Some of them met the flames. Couldn't do anything about 'em."

Shit. Men dead, burnt to crisp. Bare-boned bloodless corpses covered in ash and fallen trees. Never buried. Never remembered. *Lost to the night, at the mercy of our enemy.* "How many dead?"

"At least seven."

"Seven? We've lost over a dozen men in a *day!*"

"And we'll be next if we don't get out of this fucking place... now move, c'mon!"

They continued to run, battering through stretches of brush and bracken shrouded in the thick, cumbersome air. Vision slipping in and out, the world an enterprise of colours. Broken shadows of black, hazes of grey and deep brown. The occasional emerald green shimmer of leaves stifled in the dark. Nothing out of the ordinary. Nothing, that was, until a phosphorescence of orange clutched at her fears and illuminated the woodland beyond. Savanta's eyes wandered off to the right, through the smoke and mirrors, frightfully following the ominous glow. Before she knew it, she was peering through a gap in the tree-line coated in a maw of orange flame, racing through the branches over-head towards them.

She shifted her attention back to running and found pockets of raw flame spilling across the woodland floor ahead. Impact craters from cannon-shot formed great clefts in the soil. Flying over one, she spied for but a moment a twitching bird sprawled inside, wings snapped, eyes wandering, waiting for the flame to engulf it and end the suffering. Soon to be extinguished altogether.

The screams continued to echo all around.

"Oil canisters!" Markus said, dragging her attention back to the path ahead. As he spoke, a sound of splattering liquid slapped through the canopy above, and then erupted with fire as it blanched the earth below. Forward lay in flames – as did the right, and at their backs. It began to surround them, engulf them, seeking only to snuff them out.

"Getting mighty hot around here!" Savanta exclaimed. "How far are we from the grassland?"

"Should be getting close now! Just keep an eye out—"

High above, a familiar sound. Splashing liquid. Raining fire. Savanta gazed up frightfully and saw it consume the skies above. Orange and red and yellow and gold, all the colours that at that moment were anything but beautiful, spitting down toward them.

No!

She shoved Markus, who tripped and collapsed several feet away, face first in the dirt.

He turned back to her, trying to race to his feet, screeching at the peak of his lungs – saw Savanta had saved him, and that for her there was no other path.

Savanta felt the searing pain as burning oil splashed across her cheek and jaw, trickling down her neck. A piercing scream, exploding with pain, melting away at her face like a furnace.

Collapsed to her knees, began scooping dirt across it, stifling the horror. Still the oil burned, through tissue to bone, raw skin prickling with inextinguishable terror. She fought and screamed, crackling voice against crackling fire ripping through the trees above. It wasn't enough. It wasn't enough. It just kept burning. It wasn't enough. It wasn't——

Savanta's mind faded, the sky orange anarchy. To think she would never meet her maker. Never stare the bastard in the eye, as she'd always longed to – to die by a sword of a master fighter, pierced through the heart to a slow and beautiful end. Instead, she would slip to nothingness in an ash-smothered void, purged by the flames, gazing across the heavenly sky, realising how much of a waste it all was.

As life became nothingness, a shadow passed across her, and the trickle of water pitter-pattered in her ears. Bundled in the shadow's arms, she moved to the sky, and the darkness swamped down to meet her.

Markus broke from the tree-line drenched in sweat and plastered with ash, staring off into a sprawl of grassland nothingness, trying not to vomit at the smell of burnt flesh. His arms ached, heartbeat thundering through his skull like a crescendo. A swamping hell consuming him.

The plains stretched on, unending.

Where now?

In the distance, he spied the desperate flicker of lights, and the rigid impressions of houses that called to him with soft words. Just past this tract of land, set away from the terror of the walls and their cannons. Safety, or close enough to it. A place to get help. A place with no fires, no ash, no oil, and certainly no screaming dead tearing at his heart. A direction with a glimmer of hope.

He started running again.

The world seemed to orbit around him, as if he were there but never really part of it. He didn't know where the rest of the company were. Some of them had made it out alive, escaping the blaze – but for how long that remained the case after that, he wasn't sure. None had waited, certainly none had followed. He assumed they had the same idea as him: get to a village, get to safety, wait out until morning. Do anything to survive. Upon arriving at the village, Markus hoped to be greeted by familiar faces.

Hopes that began to wane, however, when the still night was dashed by yet more sounds of screaming.

Off to his right, torches shifted like a predator's eyes across the grassland. A hobbling survivor manifested from the dark, making a desperate escape toward the village. Moving too slow, far too slow to survive, with inevitability raising its ugly head behind, crossbow loaded and levelled.

The figure shuddered suddenly, struck by the flying bolt. A scream, shrieking into the night, and they disappeared from sight. The torches bounded over, black armour shimmering under the pale glean of the moon. They studied the body. Kicked it once.

Put another bolt in the back of its head for good measure.

They're hunting us, Markus realised. *It's not enough that they're burnin' us out. That wasn't the aim. The aim was to have no witnesses.* His legs became desultorily numb as he continued to barrel forwards. The distance from the village became acutely greater, the clouds that much higher in the sky... the roving blackcoats that much closer. *That means the rest of my men are dead.*

And I'll be next.

Markus charged on, but the adrenaline that had carried him that far began to wear thin. The saturated leather armour fastened across his chest became heavy and destitute. Matted hair prickled across his face, adding to the intensity the ash already caused. Air rifled through his lungs but couldn't replenish him an inch. He gazed down for a moment at Savanta's scar-ridden, bloody expression as she navigated quietly in a cold void, and felt a wave of jealousy at how peaceful she was.

How terrified he was by it all.

A shout in his right ear, followed by a whistle of a crossbow bolt skimming the sky overhead. Perhaps impending doom should've helped him, should've given that extra spur of momentum. But it didn't – for all intents and purposes, his body had given in. Bolts whistled all around, but the air was growing thinner. The village lights were little more than dull blurs ahead, spotted with shadows moving towards him. His ankles rolled numbly, feet struggling for purchase. Markus stumbled forward suddenly, his unconscious cargo collapsing into the thick grass.

Like a meteorite, he crashed hard into the dirt, felt his shoulder dislocate against hidden stones, and produced a disconsolate rumble in reply. Looking up as the world blackened, he just hoped those little shadows running towards him would kill him and make quick of it, so he wouldn't have to agonise over a twisted arm.

And an utterly soiled dignity, at that.

They'd spotted Markus as soon as he'd emerged from the tree-line, his sweaty swaying carcass spilling out onto the plain with one of those piercing looks only a dead man could make. He carried a cargo that, through the spyglass, they could guarantee would never make it to the walled village on its own. Markus could hardly bear his own bulk and armour, let alone whoever was bundled unconscious in his arms. It had played out before almost like some romantic piece of theatre, save the flashing lights and grand opera.

And the impending dread of getting shot by a blackcoat... aye, that too.

They'd made haste almost immediately, as the gates drew open and a swamp of light drenched the otherwise-black beyond. They charged out into the gloom, towards the fire-stricken woodland on the horizon, and had watched as the torchlight rounded on Markus and the faint whimper of crossbow bolts whistled through the night

79

air.

Death drawing in, ever closer.

A second later, and Markus collapsed into the grass – a ripple of fear spun out between the advancing rescue party, and it was only the shifting grass and the wave of a wounded hand that gave them any glimmer that he still lived at all.

To their left, the enemy seized on the moment, bounding over the grassland in a frenzy. The rescue party did likewise, covering ground in determining strides. Swords itched in their sheaths; crossbows twitched in curled fists. Other lights began to dot the horizon as more of the enemy were alerted to the commotion from the border. The lead scout found the heat escape his chest, and the fear eat through him – then a great rallying within, a voice breaking through.

"*Fire at will!*"

The call didn't feel like his own, but as the words spluttered from his mouth the crossbowmen drew to a halt, knees dug to the soil, weapons raised, and loosed a small volley toward the advancing foe.

Alerted by the snap as the weapon fired, the blackcoat company dropped to the ground. Bolts whistled overhead, peppering the grass, to be forgotten in the next moment. Precious time gained while the enemy lay absent.

Perhaps there is hope after all...

Looking back to the front, the scout found that the blackcoats rose fast from the earth and were mobilised once more with crossbows trained on their approach. They didn't stop to aim, levelling the weapons mid-run and loosing a disjointed volley across the grass. Whistling through their ears and smacking the dirt around them, a sigh of relief came and went as no voices cried out at death's door and they pressed ever onwards into the dark.

A second volley fired from those at his back, and the dark shadows of the enemy dropped again. One did so as more of a stumble, legs buckling rather than bending.

And they paid the price for it, too.

A bolt smacked into his exposed shoulder, a howl of pain as he went down, pirouetting like a ballet dancer. The others gave him not a whimper of remorse before they were up and moving again.

A whistle, and the enemy landed a second volley, this time at the crossbowmen stationed behind. A howling shriek echoed through the scout's ears, followed by the gargling of a pierced artery and blood exploding from the throat—

Time was running out.

Approaching the bodies strewn unconscious in the grass as the enemy drew in to do likewise, the scout made the executive choice to hit the nearest blackcoat first and deal with the rest later.

Diving left, he charged into the enemy with his sword raised and speared the blade deep into the man's shoulder. A brief melee as the two wrestled to the floor, the blackcoat squealing through their helmet like a pig. They barrelled through the grass, all teeth and sweat and blood and fury. But it wasn't enough for the blackcoat. The whites of its eyes grew heavy, blood streaming under the armour in great rivers. It drew still, let go.

Died a moment later.

Turning back, the scout found the other runner had Markus over his shoulder and was already high-tailing back to the safety of the village's distant glow. A sigh of relief at one saved – gone like a whisper, the moment next.

The scout stumbled through the grass, aware of the enemy breathing down his neck with their torches nearby. Scouring the ground at his feet, he near tripped over the fallen cargo as it appeared under the moon's eye, catching sight of its face—

Oh, fuck!

Without a second thought, he'd hoisted Savanta's body over his shoulder and broke out into a desperate sprint, frightfully aware of the clattering armour approaching from the north in droves. He ran, legs ablaze, back to the glow of sanctuary. Shoulder rattled; skull rattled. A shadow world swung side to side as he charged on towards his fellow runner, and the two crossbowmen wedged in the grass still landing volleys at whatever enemy remained.

As the world spun and his breathing became heavy, his grip of mortality beckoned. How desperately fragile his fleshy corpse was, running across that field, knowing any one of the crossbow bolts whistling all around could puncture him like a balloon, and he'd break out in a blood-curdled mess across the grass below with nothing to show for it. Spilling his cargo… leaving the only person he'd ever felt any honour following abandoned to the enemy. The only person who knew what to do when crisis struck and blood was spilt. The only leader he'd ever had in life, at times most dark and demeaning. He'd give his life, he knew, to save her skin from the enemy just then. Because had it been him, no matter the odds… *I know she'd do just the same.*

It gave some energy to his step, some strength to the charge, some hope that those walled gates were not really so far away. He skimmed past the last crossbowman, who jeered with relief and followed quickly behind. He caught up with the other runner, a sweaty grin across his face as he too charged on. Crossbow bolts whistled all around but none met their mark.

The walls materialised; hope was within reach. They fell under the dull glow of torchlight, the gates peeling open like an invitation with the gods. They were there now, so desperately close—

A bolt rifled into his leg, snapping his shin. He fell almost immediately, Savanta spilling from his shoulder. He hit the ground hard, a shockwave knocking the air from his lungs. The hope and warmth abandoned him to cold and frightening darkness, with the enemy at his back and the gods laughing high above.

The others looked back into the darkness from the walls, all a daze of lights and shadows evaporating in his vision.

"Take her!" he roared suddenly, pushing Savanta closer.

The crossbowman stood before him, face awash with horror, stood dumbstruck and motionless.

"Take her now*!*"

Behind, the bellow of the blackcoats grew louder, approaching fast. Crossbows began to snap and shudder.

"GO!"

A surge of shadows behind, and men suddenly spilt from the village gates, volleys of arrows raining down from the walls. The enemy behind him stalled, crossbows snapping in retaliation. Iron rain speared the skies overhead.

The end had yet to come.

A few brave faces scuttled out towards Savanta's stricken body, hoisting her onto their shoulders and breaking off to the village beyond. A glow of relief managed to pierce the veil of pain swelling in the lone scout's heart. Perhaps they would be saved after all—

A bolt hit him square in the back of the head.

Death was instant.

†

Chapter 10

The Savage Land

Alvarez stood at the tower on the western edge of the palace keep, surveying the world beyond through the hollow echoes of night. It was a vantage point, like the nest of a great eagle, overlooking a vast kingdom of grassland plains and the yellow-grey specks of tiny townships nestled amongst the trees. Its propensity, from the walls at his feet to the distant mountains stood like sentinels in the distance. Provenci.

My fiefdom.

Gaze shifting along the horizon, to what seemed like a world away, there was a delicate orange glow ruminating amongst the trees at the border – a stain of harsh colour, like a hearth burning bright on winter's day, that spoke volumes to him of times to come and the embers of the resonant end. Of the bitter conflicts, and rivers of blood – the unmaking of one nation at the redemption of another. Even though it was many hundreds of leagues away, dim in the dark of a dirty night, those fires marked the beginning of something new, something sinister and malevolent.

War has come… at long last. A shimmer crossed his pupil.

My destiny.

"You asked to see me, sir?" came a skittish voice behind him, drawing the chamber door gently to a close.

"Yes, sergeant, I did..." He rounded, taking in the scrawny, misconstrued shape of Revek in the half-light, who produced a quaint bow. "Do you see what's on the horizon at this moment?" the Governor asked.

The sergeant leered awkwardly to see past Alvarez, the enormity that was the man, and squinted as if it was difficult to see. "That's a lot of fire, sir." Revek swung back to two feet. "If I were to have a guess, I would assume it's deliberate."

"You want a fucking medal, sergeant? Of course it's deliberate." The sergeant shrunk down, all the banter and showmanship shrivelling away like a prune. "Reports from my scouts say those *savages* have lined the border with enough artillery to pop holes in Casantri if they so wished. Watchtowers, metal barricade walls, armed militia." He paused, turning back to the great window. "And as if that didn't insult enough... they've now started burning the woods down too. For all our pomp and bravado here in Casantri, in our tall towers and pretty palaces... we can sure be made to look the fools by these *animals* and their pointy sticks and their seething ignorance to the way the world works. I'd burn their entire country to the ground given half the chance. Those bastards need to learn who they're dealing with, who holds the *power* here..."

"They've long laboured in their poor freedoms, sir... expecting much and giving little."

"So *ungrateful*... so *careless* in their way of life. To think the king almost *pitied* them when he stood where I am, looking out to that distant place. Time after time, he chose reconciliation over a show of force... time after time, those savages became yet bolder. And all the while we paid the price." He waved a hand to the tall window. "And look now, where that has *got us*..."

"A shame, sir, truly—"

"It is no shame, sergeant: it's a *disgrace*. And now they amass their forces at our border, and light fires to keep us on edge..."

"No match for the might of the Imperial Army, sir," came the stoic but flawed reply. "Let us show them a thing or two about civilised order."

Alvarez shook his head, the hundred bitter motions of his mind turning over in that moment. "There's the thing sergeant, even after all these years you're still too *nice* about it." A half-turn, face a burning mass of murder. "I don't want you to go to them and teach them *civilisation*... fire a few pot-shots, make a few skirmishes and call it a day. That is conventional, sergeant, and frankly, I'm getting pretty sick and tired of what *conventional* means around here. It's won us nothing and cost us everything. We want *power* now, not statistics. I don't care for a good day's work... I care for a *lesson learned*."

Revek looked to him as if his skull were ripping open. As if a malicious presence had consumed him. As if a phantom coiled about his neck and made his eyes bulge and his tongue flick like a serpent. But there wasn't. There was none of it. He was just another man at the end of the day. But the hunger that paced like a caged animal behind Alvarez's eyes, that twitched across his fingers, that drew a wandering hand closer to the hilt of his blade, was something altogether beyond the primal instincts of man. It was cold, and calculating, and ferocious.

And it wanted *power*.

"What... will you have me do, sir?" the sergeant said cautiously.

"You will do what has needed to be done... for many years now, *sergeant*." Alvarez clicked his jaw – something close to a grin ebbed across his complexion. "You will take a handful of your closest people, and convene with the new divisions of the army currently marching from the north. When you reach them, you will tell them the plans have changed. You will command them, and you will march to the border where the fire rages, and you will put a hole in whatever this pretty little barricade is they've erected. You will kill *anyone* you find there, and you will continue to march on through the rubble and ruin of that foul place, until you reach the first village you find" — torchlight flared in his eye — "and you will *raze it* to the *fucking ground*. Burn everything, kill everyone... *no* exceptions."

"Sir... I... that's *genoci*—"

"I don't *care* what you call it!" Alvarez roared, the walls trembling around them, shadows dancing in the cold gloom. "I don't *care* what it looks like! We are here for power, sergeant... we are here to show the savage land who is in *control here*. We are *not* here for diplomacy and civilisation... those same wasted words that brought us so much ruin before. You will *burn* those villages to the ground and you will *kill* anything that moves within them... because I will *not* be *humiliated* by *savages*!" Spittle flew from his mouth — a few moments of rage came and went; Alvarez tried to rein in a silhouette of composure. "You will do as I say, sergeant, and you will do it without questions asked... do *I* make myself *clear?*"

A hesitation, an unwillingness in his broken stare — Revek gulped, fingers twitching, finding nothing but submission in the end, as a good dog always did. "Yes, sir," he muttered soundlessly.

"Good," the Governor growled. "Now go and tell your strategists to load their horses and ready the cavalry. You leave at dawn."

Revek turned back to the door and left in silence — Alvarez turned back to his tower window, gazing studiously at the distant horizon still hollowed out by the orange glow of flame. *They will come to learn the cost of insubordination, of testing the mightiest nation in the Icebreaker Sea with petty skirmishes and forest fires.* By his hand their walls would come down, their villages would burn and their people would die. A flicker of rebellion would be snubbed out under his boot, and he would live to see the day again and again. Power, *his* power, and the rightful greatness of Provenci, would be restored.

Alvarez grinned into the shadow.

War has come...

†

Chapter 11

At What Cost?

Markus awoke from a fever dream thrashing at his bedsheets as if being strangled. Eyes peeling open, he shot upright, heart racing. Expecting attack, or escape, fight or flight, or something. But the reality was more of a shock to the system than even the fever dream had been.

"Where the hell am I...?"

He had been stripped to his base garments and washed over with water at some point, face no longer plastered with ash and dirt. Someone had tended to the slices and scabs across his palms as well until they looked almost humiliatingly smooth. Looking around, a fraction of light passed through a single high window at the opposite end of the room – an unbarred window, he noted, meaning that wherever he was, he wasn't being held as a prisoner. It didn't answer his questions, nor settle his racing mind, but there were at least the reassurances that a bloody death wasn't awaiting him outside.

Or not one they want me knowing about, at least.

An attempt to roll out of bed ended with ferocious agony shooting through his thighs, as if someone had speared needles through them. He thought better of it, and used his hands to manoeuvre his stiff lower half around, buckling his knees with gritted teeth until feet touched the cold stone beneath. He produced a deep sigh, swearing under his breath – cursing that he felt so decrepit. That his calves hurt and his back ached and his skull rattled like a bell-chime, the ebbing strings of a headache plucking slowly therein. He swore again. Reached over to the small cup of water, found his ability to grip objects had receded to that of a small child, and instead proceeded to volley the thing across the room, clattering against the iron door at the far end and rolling despondently to a quiet corner. Even the noise managed to sting his eardrums, and he swore a third time.

Limbs are gonna start falling off at this rate.

A few moments' passed, and Markus was alerted to the sound of sliding locks and shuffling feet ahead. Mind spinning, he immediately anticipated a fight – but the searing headache that lanced between his eyes put that thought to rest almost immediately. A twisting latch rang sharply in his ear; the door peeled open—

The bruised and unshaven face of one of his scouts appeared from the light beyond.

"Oh sir, thank the gods you're alive!" the man blustered, sliding into the room and closing the door behind. "We thought you'd been struck by a bolt when you collapsed out there in the mud."

"With how much pissing agony I'm in, I may as well have been," Markus grumbled.

"We tried to clean you up as best we could."

"I can see that." With some disgust, he studied the transparent sheen of liquid across his palms. "Got hands like I work in a brothel."

"And a beautiful face to go with it, sir."

"Fuck yourself." He smiled, then winced at the pain, and groaned with displeasure as the headache thundered to life again. "But yes, anyway, where's..." A shudder went through him, the room tilting slightly. "Wait, where's Savanta? Is she okay? I... I collapsed, I remember, and then everything went dark, and she'd rolled off into the grass nearby and..."

"It's alright sir, she's alive," the scout reassured. "We managed to salvage her, same as you. She's being treated in the room next door."

A quivering sigh, as if he were deflating. "That's good, that's... but what about her face? Has that..."

"The medical officer of the village spent most of the night tending to her. I haven't seen yet but... they said they did everything they could, and that certain... more *drastic* measures had to be taken to make sure she could talk normally. You'll have to see for yourself... she's requested that no one other than the doctor and you may enter."

"Then by her standards, I'm already running late." Markus shifted his weight, felt the indiscretion nick at his bones, and lowered himself again. "Help me up, would you? An old bastard like myself has gone all stiff."

The scout shuffled over and curled an arm around Markus's shoulder, dragging more than assisting him to his feet. Bones crunching, Markus clicked his tongue with indignation and leaned against the bedside table. "I'm good now, I'm good... just needed to get to my feet is all. Get some sensation going again."

"Need anythin', sir?"

"Water 'n' some food if you got it, please – fucking *starving...*"

The scout gave a curt nod and skittered out the room like a bug, which left Markus ample time and space to resuscitate his limbs.

Just take it easy. Shifting weight off his left leg, he squirmed his toes and rolled the ankle to test how forgiving they were, pleased to find the pain was limited. A flicker of confidence, he coiled his knee up to his chest slowly, grinding his teeth as the joint snapped around like a grinding cog. The pain subsided; a deep breath followed. Markus proceeded to extend the leg out with great ease, and as his foot hovered over—

His knee crackled intensely as the joint locked, and a surge of pain squealed through Markus's body. He squawked like a frightened bird, other leg buckling with the movement. In a few moments, he'd slipped from the bedside-table, and collapsed half-sprawled across the straw bed like a drunkard, graceless and regretful. He swore loudly, hammering against the bedframe.

Something tells me I'm gonna be here a while.

*

The sun had reached full height, spearing across the cold stone chamber in great shafts, before Markus had found the courage to crack his joints, button up his stained leather overalls, and pass over to the room's door as if wading through a waist-high swamp. He could walk now at least — *but with none of the dignity I would've liked.* Every step creaked some ancient mechanism within him. Every roll of the shoulders crunched through his back like snapping wood. *Just over forty winters to my name... and I move as if I've seen double — such is the life of a busy man with the world on his shoulders.* He wheezed a breath.

Shit, I feel old.

The door peeled open and he entered the corridor outside, a vast stone expanse with five other doorways along its walls. As Markus emerged, so too did the medical officer whom the scout had spoken of: an older lady in black robes, tentatively writing reports on a board in the crook of her arm. From afar, she looked more like she was there to mourn the dead than save the living.

"You should be having rest, my good sir," she said with a hint of disdain. "You made quite the escape last night."

"Certainly feels like it," he replied.

"That man who was in here earlier, the one who came to visit... he thought so. Quite admired you..."

"Well, he's a good lad—"

"...And corrected me quite clinically when I said you were a fool for running that far carrying a load entirely unsuitable for your *age*."

Markus clicked his tongue. "Hm."

"But I was never big on heroics as it was: it's my job to advice against them, you see. Puts more people in here, with sliced legs and broken ribs, squealing like pigs. And I've seen my fair share of them, I tell you."

"Apologies for my... *vulgarity*, then."

"Oh not at all, you certainly weren't the worst of those I've treated through here." She paused, a hawkish smile twitching the wrinkles across her face. "Certainly made your friend in there laugh." She pointed her ink quill to the door opposite.

"She in there?"

"She is... believe she's still awake, too. Although I couldn't quite tell if she was admiring your heroics or not."

"Why's that?"

"See for yourself," the officer muttered, her voice growing colder. "But I should warn you... we had to apply some more... *unconventional* forms of healing for her. It was the only way we could preserve her face without leaving it exposed. Was the only way of saving her... although she hasn't altogether taken to that fact too well..." The words drifted off. "You'll see what I mean. Now, please... go see her. She said she wanted to see you first."

"Thank you," he said morbidly, trying to smile, but lacking any of the warmth and composure to make it seem genuine.

The officer floated off into another room, disappearing with the chime of a metal latch – leaving Markus to drift slowly toward the door, the thought of *'unconventional methods'* souring at the tip of his tongue, wondering what kind of fate had restored his friend locked away in the room beyond.

With a pale hand, he eased the door open slowly and entered the realm of shadows within, dull slices of sunlight from a curtained window exposing the few features of the room with a disconcerting aura. The bedside candle had been snuffed out; the sheets had been torn away and spilt across the cold stone underfoot; the faint aroma of cooked flesh still hung like melancholy in the air.

And then he lay eyes on the hunched shadow at the end of the bed – a hollow husk, unmoving and unafflicted by his presence, gazing off vacantly to the far wall that flickered with dull hues of yellow sun. The only sign it was even alive was the occasional rasping breath, forcing its way through a shattered nose cavity. An unnatural sound, uneven, shouldering a great many burdens of pain. Standing there at the door, Markus wanted to call her name, gauge some response, offer some comfort. What he'd done for near a decade now, as her accomplice – *as her friend*. But there was something so cosmically unnatural about her then, the quiet disposition so out of character and beyond his understanding. He didn't really know what to do, what to make of it, how to——

"Markus."

The voice made him jump. "Savanta," he mumbled, a pit of concern knotting in his stomach. "Is... everything okay?"

"Come and sit," came her cold reply.

Pulling the collar away from his neck, he obliged the command somewhat reservedly. As he crossed the room, a patter of discomfort gnawing at each stride, she remained coated in shadow, unmoving at his approach and only shifting slightly when he sat at her side. Markus remained there a while, eyes to his feet as if it were sacrilege to lay eyes upon her. A silence stretched out between them, an anxious sickness bulging in his stomach like a tumour. The discomfort of it – that unnatural edge that held the air taut and snapped like splinters in his lungs. Waiting, in that bitter darkness, until he had no other option but to ask the obvious question.

"Sav... what's going on——"

"I refused to retreat when we first saw 'em," she whispered suddenly. "I decided to make camp, instead of sheltering in a village somewhere further away. I... I heard members of our company, good men... *innocent* men... being burned alive while they slept. I heard their screams, every emotion. All of it." There was a hint of anger at the tip of her tongue. "And here I am, safe in this chamber, carried here by good men who are now dead. *Our* men. Knowin' that I caused 'em to die. I was the reason so many suffered, 'cause of my choices." She turned to him suddenly. "So what happens now... is I have to live with the consequences of those choices."

The shimmering metal plates where her cheek had been drew his eye first. Welded together with black rivets, it seemed to form almost naturally against the concaves of her face. Nothing about it indicated the 'unconventional', as the officer had said – that was, until Markus studied the bindings of her skin more closely.

Whether a trick to the eye or the work of a masochist, what remained of the seared flesh had been intricately woven into the metal plates and bound with a strange tar-like substance, slowly solidifying across her face. For a moment, in the realm of shadow, he almost convinced himself it was natural, almost every-day. But looking into Savanta's hollow human gaze, and all the emotion and premonition therein, he couldn't stomach looking at the near-mechanical complexion and trying to humanise something that was very obviously not.

All he saw there instead, was pain.

"I see," was all he could muster in the end, a despairing glance to the floor and the spilt sheets at his feet.

"It's an ancient practice, that gave me this." She tapped the metal woven to her cheek. "The black stuff at the edges is difficult to find, stops the metal rusting up. Stops infection too, apparently."

"Thought you and I agreed not to get involved with all that witchcraft. We got reservations."

"Reservations don't mean anything when your life's on the line... no matter how undeserving."

"It ain't undeserving, Sav. I sure as hell don't think any less of you for it. You made a choice... there was nothing we could've done."

"Had I made the better choice there could've been... had I listened to the others before they burned alive in that godforsaken hell-hole, things would be very different now."

"We're dealing with the beginnings of *war* here," he pleaded. "War complicates it all, muddies the water. There ain't one straight decision in times like these. You can't blame yourself for being a leader."

"No. But I can blame myself for dismissing consensus, the one thing in all this mess that's always worked for us. Consensus would've said to retreat yesterday... ain't much of a leader if you disregard that."

"Ain't much of a leader if you disregard *duty,* either."

"Duty to *what*, Markus?" she spat. "Duty to our men, who now lie riddled with crossbow bolts and burnt to a crisp? Duty to protecting the border, now overrun with blackcoats? Duty to this nation – this *miserable fucking* nation... over what? Lines on a board? Statistics? Profit? Duty to *what*?"

"To the company—"

"The company is *dead*, Markus!" Savanta roared suddenly, silence spilling out between them like a slit throat. It hit him like a gut punch; pierced him sharper than any sword could've. Hit him in ways not even his ignorance could plaster over, or the inner optimist could alleviate. It hit him because it was true, most of all: *the company are dead*. "It's gone... we're all that's left," she muttered, a gloss over her eyes. "They're dead by my choices, dead by my hands... there is nothing *left*."

"We can start again..."

"And watch war 'muddy the water' and kill another two dozen? You may enjoy marching with the company and spillin' blood, Markus, but I sure don't when I'm the one who feels like they're rotting inside, when yet another of our men hits the mud with no answers."

"What were you expecting, Sav?" he challenged. "This is our *job*. This is what we signed up for."

"I didn't sign up for a *fucking war*! What part of that don't you understand? I am not a soldier, I do not march in ranks and see aimless slaughter for the pride of a nation. I am not that. I am a scout, a spy. I fight a few raiding parties here and there, make a bit of profit on the side. Lead a group of honest men who just want to do their bit and get paid for it." A hand pounded against her chest. "I am a *scout*, not a *soldier*."

Markus ground his teeth. "And when war finally comes, then what? When it finally sinks its fangs into everything you know and love, and the blood starts pooling around us... then what? Ain't any place for a *scout* when that beast rears its ugly head, Sav. We have to serve the nation in whatever way we see fit, and with war coming..."

that's even more so."

"When war comes I will make sure I do my duty, Markus… but it won't be at the front line clad in the finest armour spilling the guts of every poor bastard who gets near." She stood suddenly – Markus found his chest tighten at the sight of a short-sword lingering in her hand. "It will be my own way… and that starts today."

Markus found one hand lingering at his waist, at the knife satchel tucked neatly away, listening to what amounted to the ravings of a mad-man spilling from the mouth of a friend. "What does that *mean?*" he mumbled.

"It means I ain't got a duty to anyone anymore… no one except myself. And I quite fancy guttin' the bastard who caused me to have this." Another tap at her metal cheek. "Feel like some redemption is in order." She walked around the bed, made for the door.

Markus found himself on his feet. "Against *whom?*" he boomed, stalling her progress to the exit. "Gonna cut down the sorry fool on that artillery wall who launched the oil into the trees? Gonna spear the commander through the eyes for giving the order to burn it all down? Gonna dish out all these *heroics,* harping on about needless bloodshed because you can't even *look* at yourself anymore—"

"Shut your *fucking* mouth!" Savanta turned sharply, sword levelled at him with every sinister intention one could muster. "You know *nothing* of what I want. This is about right and wrong and a lot of dead people in between. Redemption for the company, as much as myself. So no, you and your eclectic *wisdom* are wrong: I don't *care* for who launched the stuff, I don't *care* for who gave the order. I'm like this now and there isn't a thing I can do about it. That is not where the blood stops… you know that as well as I do."

"Then what is this? What do you plan to do?"

She lowered the sword slowly. "I'm gonna go skin the bastard alive who started all this. Whoever's leading that mass of savages out there… I'm gonna serve my country, and do some *heroics,* by cuttin' the head off whatever snake started this war… and then I can have my *redemption.*"

A shudder of disbelief, and Markus heard the chime of metal as his knife slid from its holster. "You're gonna march straight through the enemy... into the *heart* of Tarraz, in the middle of a war... and you think you're going to kill whoever started all this, and led to the demise of our company... for *revenge*? Are you *insane?*"

"It's what I deserve for my *suffering,*" she spat.

Markus raised his knife to her. "I can't let you do that, Sav..."

She scoffed – humanity and reason seemed to abandon her. "What are you gonna do, bleed me into seeing reason? Lock me up and throw away the key, to keep the memory of a dead company safe? Go on then... I'd like to see you *try*."

And part of him wanted to. For the anger simmering beneath his skin, it seemed a fruitful compromise. A perfect metaphor to mindless bloodshed, that Savanta so ardently refuted yet so passionately thrilled in the moment of. To undo whatever lies she had suddenly been feeding herself about right and wrong, duty and reason, the lives of others and that of her own. To make ends meet, and make her see reality again. To realise this plan she had was just a long-winded march to self-destruction.

But the more significant part of him, which echoed like a kindred spirit in his soul, knew even so that he couldn't. That this wasn't right, that violence for once in his pitiful life was not the answer. That he could never seriously brandish steel against one of the very few people in life he'd ever looked dead in the eye and called friend.

And now, we're all that's left.

He sighed, the blade wavering in his hand. "Whatever's got into your head, Sav... I hope you see through it someday. 'Cause call me a coward or a saint, regardless of my reservation... I ain't gonna raise a weapon against a friend." He sheathed the knife and slumped back down at the bedside. "But I also can't just sit by and watch you go out and kill yourself seeking redemption. That ain't right."

"You know I'm set on this," she said, anger beginning to boil over. "There is no other way."

"I know," Markus said.

Looking into the rounds of her eyes then with a knot in the depths of his chest, he imagined that his ma stood there, brittle with age. Living in the cold mountains, he remembered the words she'd said to him the night he'd left, about duty and kinship – a stubborn arrogance about him like overcast clouds as he trudged down towards the market and paid her no heed. He remembered the snow front that had swept through, as he sat at the open fire of an inn drinking merrily while his ma fought the elements at home alone. He remembered coming home the next day to find the house had collapsed entirely, and inside was nothing but ice and broken frame. How he had dug through the debris, tears welling at his eyes, until he pulled a wooden beam aside and found his ma's frozen face staring back at him, with nothing but disappointment blanketing her gaze. How his reckless abandon had killed her, more than the elements ever could. How the frustration was not at the roof being weak or the fire being weak… but at his own weakness, to protect the things he cared for most when crisis came.

And so he sat there, a great silence between them, a crisis revelling behind Savanta's eyes, and felt nothing but guilt well beneath him.

"I'm coming with you," he said at last.

"*What?*"

"If I can't convince you to see reason and reconsider… then I'm also not letting you just march off into Tarraz alone. We've been at this for too long, spilt too much blood for you to just go off without me at least having my part to play."

"I can't allow that, Markus…"

"That's not yours to make, Sav." He looked to her, a pain in his gaze greater than any wound. "This is *my* fate. *My* choice. I respect you Sav, and more'n that, I care about you. I've abandoned things before and seen those I care about die because of it. My duty may be to the nation or the company or whatever… but my duty of *choice,* lies with you." He paused. "So I'm coming with you, whether you like it or not… and only Tarraz now awaits me."

Savanta had a hollow look about her – whatever she thought to say, could not materialise. The world spun; shadows and the glow of the sun danced across the wall before her; her words still would not come. The understanding, the guilt, the regret and recon-sideration and reassurance that Markus had hoped for, never happened. There was only silence, disdain — *what has become of you?*

"I leave at midday," she muttered coldly, in the end. "And if you're coming, be ready at the gate for then."

Then she left, and the door closed, and Markus found the gaping void at his feet had opened even wider. He collapsed across the bed, clutching at his chest — the knowledge of a thousand sins tallied in his mind, knowing that come the morning he would be condemned. That entering Tarraz, against the tides of war, to strike at the heart of the serpent who commanded all things, was a sentence to death in itself. All for duty — *all for what?*

Head in his hands, Markus began to cry.

†

Chapter 12

Loose Ends

As the fog began to lift, and the relentless onslaught of crashing waves slowed to delicate tedium, the dull grey smudge of the northern shores manifested on the horizon, and their destination honed into view. Drawing closer with the sails billowing above, the indistinguishable shape began to prickle with trees, the grey leeching out into stretches of pale sand and green vegetation. Wave by wave, the coastline expanded across, until its greatness ventured from north to south in an unbroken line of sandbank.

Holding to the deeper currents, the great vessel that had carried the expedition thus far drew to a halt and dropped anchor – a screech of winches, wholly unnatural in a place of such serenity, and three longboats dropped from the deck into the surf below. Following behind down the thin stretch of rigging, the generals and their units clattered into the boats and steadied the oars, cutting loose from the main ship out into the broad shallows of the bay. Departing, in search of an ancient relic.

The broken body of a now-dead king.

"How far out are we going, ma'am?" one of the oarsmen asked, a fresh spray of seawater prickling his face as the oars ground over and over.

"As far as we need to until we find the body," General Cavara exclaimed, riding the waves as they came with steady feet.

"And if we can't find 'im?"

The thought had crossed her mind, but she didn't show it. "We search along the next sandbank... he'll be here somewhere."

"Right y'are, ma'am."

Looking down at them, Cavara found the obedience of the men as discomforting as it was dutiful. That they lived to serve, to fight, to take orders and march in line – for king and country and whatever else fancied it. She'd been there once, she knew, but had never given any obedience to those she found didn't deserve it. *Waste of time and effort, and got you nowhere at that,* she cooed. *As soon as you lose a bit of back-bone to the army, you lose yourself.* An instrument of war – statistical data on a map. A waddling sack of flesh and armour, just like the rest. Cavara glanced across the six men huddled together in the longboat before her, swinging at the oars with straining arms, and scratched her head in bemusement. *Ever onward, as obedient as dogs.* She shook her head.

As senseless as them too.

"Ferreus is making good headway," one of them called up to her. "Reckon he got the strongest lot of men to man the oars."

"He likes a good strong man to keep him happy, don't he?" another blustered to a ripple of laughter.

"Nice strong pair of hands to keep him up at night, ay?"

"Not the only thing that they'll be keeping up!"

Cavara stifled a laugh as the boat rumbled with glee, looking off in the direction of the lead longboat. She should've told them to watch their tongue, she knew, for talking about a superior officer in such a way. Should've led by example, drawing lines and maintaining order despite personal differences. Something like that.

Yet she found no love lost for General Ferreus, and from that no interest in reprimanding her soldiers for having a jest. She had seen little of him within the army itself – such was his position as an administrator, more so than an officer of the field – but she had heard enough beyond that to fill volumes in the palace vault. Stories of prisoners beaten to a pulp in the dead of night; entire barracks given lashings for negligent behaviour on guard; one child beaten to death with a baton for stealing bread at the market. Even as she stood there watching, the general paced back and forth along the body of the other longboat like a predator, swaying with the waves, cuffing men across the back of the head if they slackened their resolve before closing his hands tight behind his back once more. Whereas Cavara found total obedience discomforting, it was evident Ferreus deeply relished the power it gave him. There was no grey area to him – no space for humanising those destined for violence and war. If you were a soldier, you were a fighter first and a citizen last.

They will die all the same.

"Reckon this whole business is a bit of a longshot, really…" one of the oarsmen muttered suddenly, arms straining red under his metal guards. "Who even knows if the poor bastard's body is left?"

"Could've been buried, or eaten by something," said another.

"They'd leave the robe though, I'd guess. I wouldn't fancy chewing through all that fur."

"But that still ain't a body… it's an accessory. We're more or less on a treasure hunt, if that's the 'precious cargo' the Governor wants us to fetch."

"They could've left the crown, perhaps? That's worth somethin'."

"To a black market merchant maybe. If the bastard who's killed him has any sense, they'd have taken the crown to make a bit extra for their troubles."

"What do you think, ma'am?"

Cavara tilted slightly at the question, as all eyes turned to her and awaited a response – she wondered what to do, what to say, what face to put on in front of them, then decided on honesty as a first.

"I think we're here on orders, to do a job," she said bluntly. "It ain't a question of whether it's a waste of time or not – we're just here to get it done." The faces around her sunk slightly, that good-hearted joy evaporating as they turned back to the oars and rowed on. Cavara found her stomach curl, watching their despondency –

deciding instead to crouch down amongst them and call their attention back. "Although I will have to admit... *it's a bastard long way for a bag of bones, ay?*" she added with a smile.

Smiles returned; laughter broke out among them like mischievous children, as she received salutes and *'yes ma'am'*s and the invigorated sway of the longboat as it swung forward across the surf.

Looking up suddenly, she found that Ferreus had turned at the noise of laughing, and now studied her with a cold disgust from the other longboat just ahead. Disapproving, calculating... but ultimately weighing nothing: she was head of the expedition and he was not; she ordered the men and he listened to her, just like the rest of them.

Ever onward, she mused, waving a mocking hand. *As obedient as dogs could ever be...*

She had rarely seen the king in the flesh, throughout his many long years of reign. There had been times where he had made appearances: at royal ceremonies, waving to adoring crowds with a bone-brittle hand and sleeping eyes; at military pageants, sheltered from the blazing sun on the calvary fields for fear he may shrivel and decay; or at assemblies in the amphitheatre, outlining a new military reform that ended up ground to dust. Beyond that, the king was very much a figment of one's imagination: on the backs of coins or the banners of brewer's houses. Almost god-like, to be powerful and loving and present but never seen or understood. As if his face as much as his reputation could never be tarnished.

So, when Cavara looked up at the king's head speared on the end of a wood pike, mouth agape displaying a row of yellow teeth, eye sockets hollowed out by crows and hair ripped from his scalp in great ribbons, she wondered if in all their wisdom and disobedience the gods were laughing high above, gazing upon the dead pretender with glee.

"God is dead," General Broska muttered from beside her, head held low, "and we have killed his king."

"We've killed nothing," Ferreus grumbled, the sharp ridges in his face seizing up with the cold. "The gods took no part in this, and neither did we. Some treacherous bastard in Tarraz must answer for this... not us."

"He should've been the one to answer for all this," Cavara said, pointing up to the severed head. "Should've answered for it a long time ago."

"And now he's here... rotten flies n' all."

"What should we do, Cav?" Broska inquired.

"Yes, what should we do, *ma'am,*" Ferreus added with his usual sly disdain.

Cavara rolled her tongue over the roof of her mouth. "I want one of you two to get his head off the spike and bag it up, see if you can make it look less like a... well, less like a corpse; I want the other to grab the robe in the sand over there and search for any other clothing that may have been lost... and I want you both back at the temporary camp as soon as that's done."

"Jobs for the lackies, surely, *ma'am?*"

"Not at all, General Ferreus... necessary work in fact." She paused, a twist of a smile appearing. "And even if it were, you'd be the first on my list to mop up the mess." She turned from him, felt the eyes bore into the back of her skull, and began walking back to the encampment nearby.

As much as you deserve, you wretch.

Behind, Ferreus gave a disapproving glare to Broska who turned to begin work on the king's head – the grey-haired general waved a hand his way, dismissing any involvement in retrieving the king's clothes, and paced off towards the general moving off across the bay, the crunch of sand alerting Cavara to his approach.

"General! A word—"

"Didn't I order you to assist in retrieving the king's belongings to stow in the ship for our return?" she growled, rounding on him sharply.

"Yes… *ma'am,* only I have a *question.*"

"And what would that be?"

"I was wondering about what our plan of action was… from here, ma'am? What you intend to do once the cargo has been retrieved and *stowed away.*"

"The plan of action, general… is to cast off and away from enemy territory as fast as possible with the cargo on board, and complete the job we were sent here to do. Why are you bothering me with this?"

"Well, it's just… I would have thought perhaps the men would prefer to wait a while before sailing back… they have been at sea for a good six hours, after all," he tempted.

"With all due respect, we are within the borders of an enemy aggressor who no less than two nights ago attacked our capital and killed our king in one fell swoop. This is *not* the place to just be 'waiting a while'."

"The men wouldn't see it that way. There are no enemy patrols, no watchtowers, and no presence for a good hundred leagues in every direction. It's safe… and they've earned it."

"Nothing is *safe* about any of this. We were *ordered* to come here, find the body, and leave with it as cargo. So we are doing exactly that, with *no* deviation."

"I'm just looking out for the men's wellbeing…"

"*Wellbeing?*" she spat. "We have a war galleon and nearly two dozen men to protect, in enemy territory, and you decide to lecture a *superior officer* about what is best for their wellbeing?" The fire roaring behind her eyes smouldered with a deep breath. "We are leaving as soon as we've packed the cargo."

Ferreus nodded smugly at her, looking off to the open sea. "Good luck convincing them of that…"

"They will listen to a superior officer—"

"Superior officer don't mean *shit* in the field, general. Respect does… you may be a superior officer in Casantri, but I'm superior officer out here, whether you like it or *not*." He waved a hand arrogantly. "But by all means, try and convince 'em. What do I know, after all?"

Cavara skulked up to him and jabbed a finger at his chest plate. "You are whatever I fucking tell you to be, general. Don't try pretty-talking around that. Out here, you are under *my* leadership, *my* rules, and *my* decisions. If the soldiers don't respect me, they will learn to respect me... and they will find out, quite quickly, that I do not take shit from *anyone*. Not any of them, and sure as fucking hell not *you*." She drew away, teeth grinding like a chisel. "Now I will say to you again: we are gathering our things and we are leaving... and that is the *final word*. Do I make myself *absolutely* crystal clear to you, General Ferreus, or do I have to shovel orders down your neck like a *child*?"

"Yes, *ma'am,*" he mumbled.

Cavara nodded once, once only, and turned from him to march off towards the encampment once more, barking orders to the soldiers nearby to reload the ship for a return journey.

Ferreus found himself pinned to the spot, heat biting at his neck like a furnace, fist clenching and unfurling over and over until the knuckles gleaned white like the sand below. Watching her move off with a self-certain guile that swelled anger in his chest – watching a soldier pass her and approach him from the camp, looking between them oddly.

"All good, sir?" the soldier asked him. "Apparently we're haulin' out of here already. Is a shame that... would've wanted to rest a while longer, stretch my legs and keep watch."

"All will be fine, soldier... don't worry," Ferreus growled, his eyes not lingering far from the shape of Cavara just ahead. "Just a few loose ends to sort first..."

†

Chapter 13

It Changes Nothing

Cresting the ridge, surveying a broad horizon blanketed with light, Revek set his eyes upon the massive encampment that swamped the plains for as far as the eye could see, and felt the snap of pride engulf his chest. *Here it is.* He inhaled deeply, sensing the moment. *My greatest triumph.* Four years of work, ambition and plotting at every turn. A secret project of his own devising, marched down from the mountains with the drums of war – thousands upon thousands of soldiers, infantry and cavalry alike, to sweep down along the Tarrazi coast and rip through the lowlands in one defining stride. The great redemption, finally manifest before his very eyes. A new epoch in the history of their great nation.

And to Revek, it had been a long time coming.

Fifteen years I've waited for this moment, came the memory, rubbing his hands together. That he had been a poor fighter initially, a scrawny nobody, enlisted to the army to finally make something of himself as a young man. How he had been thrown to the front-lines of a civil war, in the depths of a great woodland as vast as a nation itself, to fight an enemy he didn't care about for a cause he had never heard of. How he'd schemed, and lied, and watched men march to their deaths while he played the humble coward and waited around for the slaughter to end. To march back to the martials in their grand military bazaars and espouse unmitigated lies about his courage and sacrifice and the desperate escapes from the enemy in the trees. How they lapped it up like reams of poetry, with no one to object because there was no man left alive to do so. How, suddenly, the scrawny nobody became the honest coward, and the honest coward became the master escape artist. That his lies won medals of honour, his schemes earning him military commendation. *From corporal to strategist, and strategist on to general* – the liar's bluff began to pay off. His scheming became even more intricate, the manipulation evermore complex. His men would fight and die with honour; he would stand at the rear guard and bleed their successes like a ripe fruit. Years stacked up, victories under his belt, blood on his hands yet never spilling a drop himself. The liar's bluff paid off. *And at a stroke of luck, in the end.* A dead king and a military government, a promotion to commander and war at their borders. An escapade built on lies; a stroke of luck to set the ball rolling. That the biggest lie of it all, had been that some thought war was not inevitable.

It was always inevitable, Revek thought, smiling, *because we designed it that way.*

"Now this is the kind of sight men sing songs about," Revek revelled to his fellow officers, mounted on horseback to either side. They, like him, were newly promoted men who had chided their way up the ranks, with as much boot-polishing of higher officials as any could muster without undressing themselves. They knew next to nothing about strategy, next to nothing about what they were walking into – were near hopeless leading men and even more so organising themselves. *But they're people of quality, is what matters.* He stroked the neck of his horse, who snorted approval his way.

And loyal only to me.

"It is a mighty sight to see indeed, sir," one blustered.

"A triumph," the other added.

"With an army of this size, we'll finally give Tarraz the boot to the grave for good…"

"They're savages through and through…"

"A long time coming sir…"

"Yes…" he pondered, looking off to the north where the tree lines still smouldered black and thick clouds of ash filled the skies. "…a long time coming *indeed*."

"A truly great time for a proud nation…"

"The least we deserve for our efforts…"

"A blessing that we're all here together for this…"

"An act of solidarity, sir…"

"Solidarity?" Revek scoffed, rounding on the man who had spoken. "Please, there is nothing further from it. There is no common view of the world anymore. Solidarity is pointless. We don't act in the interests of the old order, because they have failed us time and time again. We don't act in the interests of bureaucrats, because they dither over morals like children. We don't act in the interests of the masses, because once again they don't know what they want or what's good for 'em. So, I'll tell you who's interest we work in, and it ain't anything to do with solidarity. We work to our *own* means and our own morals, to seek out our *own* interests with some good old-fashioned blood and steel violence, y'see? We act in our own interests, because it's the military who runs this place now, no one else." *With yours truly at its helm.* "So no, officer… it's not an act of solidarity. What we act upon, is the control of our *destiny*." He speared a finger to his heart, as if anything was beating there that really cared about the bigger picture. "And *destiny* shall prevail—"

†

"—*whether you like it or not.*"

Alvarez found his frustration deepening, gazing up at the expressionless mass of shadow coiling about the room like a serpent. He'd debated whether going to see Mother Katastro would offer him any solace for his woes. Whether he could finally remove the burden of destiny and lead his nation in its most desperate hour. To take control, reassert that power at its highest level, so even the gods could see his achievements and recognise destiny was his own. So he had gone to her, this ancient dying creature, to proclaim he was the leader of the greatest army the world had ever seen, and would crush Tarraz and secure the throne and become a great ruler of men.

What he found there instead, however, was only disappointment.

"Your destiny remains the same."

"That's not possible," he growled. "What of the army? The artillery? We're a nation reborn, and you still claim things are *the same?*"

"I foresaw it. The army changes nothing."

"We have out there in the field the largest imperial force the world has ever seen, with advanced field artillery and reserve siege weapons in their dozens… at least a sixth of their number will be returning to the capital to enforce martial law and act as my *personal* protection. What part of *that* is the same?"

"The part that you fear, will not change by your hand…"

"I fear *nothing* of what comes next." He speared a finger at the swirling shadows, faceless and benign. "You hear me? Nothing."

"You lie. You feed a narrative you yourself don't believe."

"What have I to fear? We have more men, better tactics, better equipment, and we shall be the ones to bring the fight to them. We have the old maps, we know the terrain. There is no place for fear in that."

"Would a fearless man command genocide?"

Alvarez's face dropped like an axe to an executioner's block. The room darkened, an eclipse of the darkest day where even the sun's eye would dare not cast its gaze. "They are savages…"

"Then why slaughter them like pigs? If they are savages, you should fear nothing of them. They're below you, are they not?" Mother Katastro seemed to swirl closer to him, tiny licks of the shadowy mass curling about his arms, lancing beneath grooves in his armour. *"Unless you jump at shadows, in denial of the truth…"*

"Enough!" Alvarez challenged, dissipating the dark cloud that spiralled above him. "I can do as I please. I am the ruler here, I am in charge. If the enemy must die in their thousands, so be it. I will protect what I've earned with every last drop of Provenci blood if I so have to. Mark my *words.*"

"*And what words are they? One's of the war hero… or that of a tyrant.*"

"Dress it up however you like, I am in control here."

"*Destiny would say——*"

"Destiny means *nothing.*" He took a defiant step forward, challenging the dying creature that taunted him so. "I shall order the men from their capital, out to the fields, to burn the villages and kill the savages and flay their armies like skinning a sacred deer. There will be no chance of enemy spies reaching the city, no access to me except by my closest staff. We will triumph, and destiny will be mine…"

†

…and it will be our finest hour.

Revek led the procession of horses through the canopies and barrack tents of the camp, to the captivated glances and rumbling cheers of the soldiers. They seemed to stretch on for miles, unending, the thin dirt track just wide enough for the stock of the horses. Amongst the green-and-red lined canopies he spied the rounded carriages of merchant caravans hoping to sell their wares; the blacksmiths and their newly-designed portable furnaces, chiming against steel and spouting thick blooms of black smog into the clear blue skyline; caravans draped in thick curtains, with the unblemished skins of loosely-clad men and women hanging from the doors, offering services whichever way one swung. Revek looked upon it all, the shifting mass of the world around him, from atop a great stallion of the finest pedigree, with the banner of Casantri held in the crook of his arm and the sun glaring across perfect polished armour strapped against his chest. That he was a good image – that he represented not the bloodshed to come, but the glory that followed. *As it has always been.* He grinned.

Because I've earnt it, haven't I?

111

Ahead, a larger tent emerged from the mass of cloth that the dirt path weaved around like a small island. There were guardsmen at the door, heavily clad in thick chain armour, covering the entrance with interlocking spears. Revek dismounted and waved entry; in unison, the two guards raised their spears and the supreme commander slipped inside like a ghost.

The interior lay gaunt, beside a vast wooden table at the very centre strewn with maps and scouting reports. Stepping in, Revek passed a cautious eye over the seven other figures in the room, as he approached the central table and placed his helmet down there. They were four women and three men, fresh faces in the army's higher ranks, quiet and meek and nothing of the arrogant bravado of the old guard. That they possessed instead that uncompromising, stern gaze of professionalism, the slight tilt of the head when he caught their eye, the straightening of backs and rolling shoulders. To don the vestige of power – to be astute in the presence of their commander.

I like them all already.

"Afternoon all," he introduced. "I hope I was not intruding."

"Not at all, commander," the woman opposite replied. She had a lean face, jagged lines across one cheek where a vicious scar had healed – she met his eyes levelly, but not inviting insubordination. "We were awaiting your arrival."

"It's good to have someone of your skill at the helm," another said to his side. A stout man, bald like a musket-ball with a thread-bare face puckered with broken veins. "We appreciate your support."

"A pleasure," Revek mused. "I assume everything is in order as instructed, and the men have been briefed?"

"Everything is in order, sir..." the stout man muttered. "But we have not received any news by which to... *brief* anyone."

"We were hoping you could enlighten us," another lady, fair-haired with a nose like chipped stone, explained.

Where the hell are my scouts? I shouldn't be briefing lackies like this. "I see." Revek rolled his tongue, looked to the table, lancing a finger at a map of the northern border. "This point here... has recently been attacked by Tarrazi militias, who are as we speak fortifying their border with steel walls, watchtowers and artillery platforms."

"We assumed that was what the fires were," the blonde added.

"Precisely so... now, as you can perhaps imagine, the boss is none too happy about this modest humiliation, and has thus decided to make our plans a touch more... *decisive,* shall we call it?"

"How so?"

By burning them to the ground. "We have been instructed to engage the enemy at the same position that the fires were started, and rip a hole in their new border defences. That includes *unrequited violence* against any and all enemy forces posted along that same border that we encounter."

"Kill anything that moves, do you mean sir?" another bearded face inquired.

"I'd have put it more poetically... but yes, to that effect." The commander's finger continued to trace into Tarraz territory. "From there we reach the main access road and move north to the hill regions, razing any settlements we find..."

"I'm sorry, sir," the rotund figure interrupted, "but what do you mean by '*razing*'? I know of razing crops to force people to move away from the roads but... are you suggesting we also go about raising *settlements* that we find?"

"And you heard me correct, general... I shouldn't need to *repeat* myself," he said coldly, snarling his way. "We find villages, we burn houses, we destroy crops... we *kill* anyone we find. Any individual left alive feeds the cause of the enemy, and by that measure, any mercy to their savage kind will *not* be tolerated."

The cavernous tent became decisively smaller and less comforting as the words fell from his mouth. Eyes wandered, panicked, to other faces equally concerned, uneasy, shifting on their feet. The disgust was palpable, the disagreements bitter on the tongue. Revek watched them all, waiting for the first move, the first head he'd have to bite off to make his intentions known for all present.

"So, genocide, effectively," the blonde said pointedly. "The

Supreme Governor wants us to engage in genocide——"

"What the Supreme Governor wants is *results*... you can call it what you want, but results are the aim. We can't have the enemy slipping back through the border or damaging trade routes..."

"And peasants with sticks are our concern in that?"

Revek ground his teeth and glared at the officer. "*Anyone* could be our concern in that – Alvarez stressed the importance of *security*."

"From us, more like..."

"If I'd asked for insubordination, general, I'd have spoken to the whores in the brothel *outside!*" Revek growled, slamming his fist on the table – the room snapped still suddenly. "I don't care what you think about it. I didn't ask and don't want it questioned. We have a job to do, and a leader to serve. There is a *war* coming, if you didn't realise... and we must do our *duty* to this *nation* for its *people*. Am I understood in that?"

What followed was punctuated by silence, heads hung low, weak smiles and nods of affirmation with none of the certainty Revek dictated. Lost for words, almost in mourning, but with one thought in mind that rang true.

†

"*Is this the legacy you want?*"

Alvarez peered through the dust-coated window of the antechamber, engrossed in his thoughts. Beyond, the slate-tiled rooves of tight-packed city houses were glistening with fresh rain, sprawling down the slope of Casantri to the outer walls. To his right, the vastness of the Icebreaker Sea – to his left, the sprawling green plains and vast forests of Provenci, burgeoning towns and pocket settlements speckling like paint over a canvas. It should've been an image of peace, a sight to settle his fettered fears, but Alvarez saw the rot that was already growing: a harbourside still churning up bodies and debris like a fountain. To his left, thick grey plumes of smoke rose from the burnt carnage of a forest fire. And, just beyond that, a black smudge winding along the border, like inviting a child's ruinous brush to the otherwise perfect painting. An ire rose within him, surging like sea currents, desperate to seek some vengeance. Vengeance that he was willing to slaughter innocents to achieve, no matter the cost.

"That is the legacy I am burdened with," he said as his reply.

"*A burden… or a choice?*"

"Not to me. It never has been a choice. It's a legacy I must have… that the king was too weak to seize for himself."

"*You misplace the legacy of power for the choice of peace.*"

"Peace?" he scoffed, fist clenching up to a ball. "Peace solves nothing, when the rot sets in and the world crumbles around you…"

"*You are mistaken…*"

"All that peace has brought is misery and disobedience. The borders weaken, the coffers bleed dry. The people demand more, seek more of us in power. It's an insult, to let them in on the lives of those who have worked so hard to get to the top. Were we not strong once? A strong people, with a strong leader. Balance… beauty… *power*. We must do away with the rot and return to that great place, for the greater good…"

"*Of whom?*"

"Do I not deserve this?" he growled. "Have I not worked my life for this? Tireless years of dedication, service, leading brave soldiers at the front lines for near two decades… and not a whisper of influence for my duty to the crown? I stood by that wretched fool's side for my entire *life* and gained nothing but critique and bad blood. I was a servant, a *slave* to that crown. That filthy vestige of righteousness. That I was never as good as he once was, that whatever I did was a pale comparison to that old fool on his crumbling throne. The *arrogance* of it." The fist curled tighter, veins pulsing to the surface. "But now, I have that power. I am no longer a slave to the throne because I *own* it. And I have earnt it. And I shall do what that wretch never could…"

The response would not come – there was only silence.

"You hear me, creature?"

Silence.

"*Do you hear me—*"

He turned, his rage and extortion rampaging like a great beast, but the room beyond was empty. The curtains were drawn; the Mother was gone. Silence echoed faintly into the dark.

His cries of desperate glory, went unanswered.

†

Chapter 14

A Song of Greed and Glory

The last of their supply boats dislodged from the surf, oars pulling away through the white-waved swell off toward their anchored galleon – a hardly visible ship, swamped in a fresh coat of fog that had swept in from the sea. The tree-line, stretching off in both directions to the horizon's tip, fell away to little more than a black smudge of undulating air – the lap of waves at the shore, little more than a haze of broken blue.

Cavara let out a strained sigh, watching flecks of saltwater splash across her steel boots and the light flutter of rain tingle across her scalp. Further along the shore to her right, Broska was busy muscling the bindings of a smaller longboat that had been lashed up against one of the thicker-boughed birch trees. His meaty paws struggled with the more intricate parts, until he was reduced to shifting his weight back and forth to try and force the twine apart with sheer willpower alone. Part of her resonated sympathy and wanted to help, but the echoing dismissal of Revek not long ago seemed to keep her planted to her spot.

"If I'd wanted a fat, useless fool among our ranks," he had spat when she proposed Broska be her second-in-command, "I would've stuck a pig in armour and sent him waddling to the front line... not some bumbling waste-of-space who got his title on pity alone."

"Everyone deserves a chance," she'd replied.

117

And now that Revek's Supreme Commander, more so now than ever.

"You're fat friend there is having a spot of bother with that rope," came a call from her side. She turned to a crunching of sand and found General Ferreus approach. "Not gonna help him, *ma'am?*"

"He can manage fine by himself," she countered.

"I've seen dogs shit faster than he's *managing* to get that longboat out onto the waters."

"Why the rush? Scared, general? Or just a bit cold?" she goaded.

He didn't take the bait – only smiled. "Not at all. I just know we like things done with a certain amount of efficiency… something he doesn't seem capable of providing."

"Then by all means, *general*, give him some assistance."

"Oh no, I wouldn't want to patronise him – if I stay out of it, the hammer falls on him." He leaned closer to her ear. "*I'll just get a beggar's plea when he's going down…*"

"Do you have anything of use to say, general?" she said sharply. "Only there seems to be a lot of chatter with very little *substance*."

"I hate to be the bearer of bad news, ma'am… but as a matter of fact, *I do*." He scratched his thinning hair, splatters of water across a harsh wrinkled brow. "Think I've found something, set back from the shoreline amongst the trees. Wondered if you felt it important to investigate."

"Could it give us clues as to who killed the king?"

He shrugged. "Perhaps."

She took a moment to consider, then waved a hand. "Then lead on, general… let's see this little *discovery* of yours."

Within the thick wood of birch trees, the fog proved just as unrelenting, reducing the narrow dirt path they walked along to little more than a blind man's bluff. The skeletal trees, with tiny shoots of dying leaves at the tips of their branches, creaked and groaned overhead – the ferns, hacked away at either side, bristled in the low wind as they passed. Whatever used the path was large, possibly the size of a boar in width, but the methodical cuts of a cleaving blade across the widest stems was evidence enough that it had been cleared initially by a human hand. Where that human was now, whether from times of old or the night before, Cavara knew not. All she knew was, whatever had been left, General Ferreus had since found.

Her guide was always just out of sight, the heels of his boots disappearing into the white glean only to be rediscovered a step later. A few times Ferreus disappeared altogether, and it was only the linear meandering of the path that kept her on track. Often, she found herself wondering if she should have indulged upon the general's inkling – *the intention was to cast off with haste, after all.* But she knew, deep down, that had that been the case – had she rejected him and ordered their return immediately – then there was no stopping Ferreus bowing at the boots of the Supreme Governor and challenging her authority for the choice: that what he had found was of utmost importance; that had it been him leading, this wouldn't have happened. Any amount of lies could have followed, and she would've found herself without an answer.

So we play his games, and we investigate, she grumbled to herself. *So he doesn't get the satisfaction of the alternative…*

The path opened out ahead of her into a small clearing, where the fog seemed to recede slightly and the trees pulled away at the edges. Ferreus was already there crouched at the centre – studying the cold, ashen remains of a fire nestled in a small pit, littered with fallen leaves.

"Any significance?" she asked, crouching next to him. "Or just a fire?"

"I'm unsure: I'd say the fire itself was less than two day's old, by how the firewood is still holding together," he clarified, pointing to the thick wedges still held up in a tepee across the middle. "Could mean our killer passed through this way after they dealt with the king…"

"Or just a local doing a spot of fishing…"

119

He smirked. "I would hold your scepticism, ma'am..." Ferreus reached into the centre and plucked a tuft of grey matted hair from within, waving it in front of her. "This is the king's hair... and from what I know, it's common practice to burn the hair of those marked as traitors to appease the All-Mother."

"Common practice of who?"

"Of the High Priests of Tarraz." He smiled sadistically. "The head savages, if you would..."

"So this was a ritual killing?"

"No, they wouldn't have taken the body if it was a ritual killing." He stood sharply, flicking the hair away. "Our killer may have been the High Priest... but he didn't do this to appease the All-Mother."

"Then who were they seeking to appease?"

"A woman they've come to revere higher than even the All-Mother." Ferreus's smile broadened. "But... I have been ordered not to discuss such matters with *you*."

"You *what?*" She turned and glared at him. "As your commanding officer, I *demand* to know."

He shook his head, still smiling. "This comes from higher than you, sweetheart."

Revek... the bastard. "And why did they feel so inclined to withhold this information from me?"

"I was the first officer assigned to this task that they came across, so they parted the information to me with the strictest confidence." A pause. "That, and they don't trust you much for anything."

"I think Revek will find I'm just as qualified as everyone else of equal rank, so I would politely *ask* that you cut the *shit* and tell me what the hell is going on here."

"It's not merit he's concerned with, it's *conduct*." The face waxed into a snarl. "Your long history of insubordination and never toeing the line has become an eminent concern for him."

"The king encouraged discourse on issues."

"Revek does not," he said bluntly. "As a matter of fact, he loathes it. And as far as he's concerned... *loose ends* need to be dealt with, and dealt with quickly."

"What '*loose ends*'?"

"Who do you *think*..."

She swivelled on her heels, rising to her full height, anger burning in her throat, longing to shout him down. "If he expects me to hand in my resignation over this, I want to make *very clear* that——"

She felt the knife slide up under her breastplate before she saw it. Felt the pointed end rip against the tiny holes of her chainmail. A solitary nerve ending, so minute yet so singularly expressive, flicker at the base of her ribcage. Then the overwhelming warmth, like an open fire, as the blade tore through flesh and fibre into her chest.

Cavara stared at him, through him, dumbfounded. Ferreus gazed back, a sheen over his eyes, cold and expressionless, as if caught in the act and not of his own volition.

Then the knife withdrew, a shock of cold stabbing through her body, and Cavara felt the blood begin to pour out of her like river rapids.

She shoved him away, adrenaline pumping through her skull. Eyes blurring, the taste of copper on her tongue, red through her teeth. She stumbled, nearly fell. Regained balance, flung about like a wild animal, numb at the limbs.

Charging, suddenly, into the trees, a wicked laugh curdling at her back through the haze of a deep fog...

She didn't know how far she ran. Trees rose up beside her like shafts of light through heavy clouds, a haze of greys and greens and broken blue sky spiralling high above. She stumbled, rebounding off buckled birches to keep on her feet, ferns grabbing at her legs in the twisted groves – all the while clutching to the wound at her side desperately, the stinging pain sweeping up and down her chest in great waves. The swelling blood about her fingertips – her life slipping away.

The trees suddenly thinned, dirt underfoot replaced with

crunching sand. A pale blue expanse shrouded in mist forming ahead. Back to shore, back to Broska, back to the ship, perhaps her saving grace. She broke through the tree-line, stumbling across the sand—

—something hooking across her ankle, swiping a leg out, collapsing forward. Hitting the sand with a shudder, wrist buckling awkwardly beneath – the salt-kissed wound seething across her stomach. She screamed, tried clawing forward, felt pressure against the square of her back – foot, weighted steel, planting her to the spot. She began coughing uncontrollably, blood-spittle spewing across the sand, staining its untouched surface in pink and ugly grey.

Footsteps to her right: a voice. Something familiar, warming. A cry of help, or of anguish. A blade sheathed; a bigger blade unsheathed. A threat from above.

"Don't come any closer, you pig," Ferreus growled, pressing down harder, whatever air left in Cavara's blood-curdled lungs rasping through her nose in painful torrents.

"What the fuck is going on?" Broska growled, skidding to a halt. "Answer me! What is this? What are you doing?" He tried moving forward again, but Ferreus barked angrily.

"None of your concern! Now *turn away* and get ready to return to the *ship*. That's an *order*."

Another blade slide from its sheath to her left. "I take orders from *her*... *not* from *you*. What is this?"

"If you wanna disrespect a *direct order*... then you can answer to Revek for this. Your choice. You may have reservations, and you may have qualms... but I have *reasons*, and this is the result. And I will not fear mincing you down to the *bone* if you take one step closer, you hear me!"

A silence ebbed out, slowly. She longed to scream—

"*Do you hear me!*"

Broska said nothing, sword still in hand. She wanted to cry—

The weight lifted from her back; Ferreus stormed towards the challenger in a fit of rage.

A clatter of metal in her ear: Broska's sword slapping the sand.

A shallow thud, hardly distinguishable through the dull ache of her ears: Broska wheezed viciously.

"That's what I fucking thought," Ferreus spat.

She longed to screech out, to crawl up and strike him down and escape and *survive* — but whatever strength had carried her there, would carry her no longer. Only the desperate whisper of death remained in her, as crunching boots slowly falling away to the left, off toward the longboat in the surf.

"Get back to the ship," Ferreus growled, swinging an arm like a claw, "we're *leaving…*"

Staring out into the paleness beyond, she fell away from reality. Her skin grew cold, shivers shooting through her spine. A shallow, dispossessed pulse, still tapping in her ear. The sand around her a murky purple, as if she'd given her life away for the sea to swallow. A sea that stretched before her in hazy lights and dim brushstrokes, swirling fog caught in the wind, lanced by shadow and sun, slowly falling away.

She felt nothing, in the end. No anger, no betrayal. Her screams dried up; her lungs all but flooded red. Each blink became longer, slower — no time to comprehend that delicate passage to death. Just cold tiredness, as normal as the waves that still lapped the shore before her.

As she slipped away, a brightness formed on the horizon — the longer she looked, the more intense it became. A radiance, shapes swirling in its mass of light. Forming, breaking, forming again.

Until she blinked, and a face appeared, of the most beautiful woman she'd ever seen, singing to her sweet songs of nothingness, beckoning her further in. She followed the song, out into the light, and found the darkness rise to meet her.

The shoreline lay silent, once again.

PART II

A Dance of Fallen Gods

†

Chapter 15

No One Needs to Know

*A*ll is well... all is going as expected. The words scrawled across the papers at his desk seemed to weave in and out of each other like a serpent's coils. *That the expedition is expected back imminently... that the army is amassed across the western plains, moving off north toward the fire-stricken woodlands... that an enemy is at our border, guarded away by watchtowers and great metal walls, ready to be pierced like a swollen cyst to rid the rot of this world for good.* Sunlight gleaned in from the high windows above.

That our reckoning has finally come.

Within the confines of his palace office, quill to-hand, Alvarez was alerted to the chime of the metal latch just beyond his door. With a crank of hinges, it swung open suddenly, and a figure strode through to the clatter of metal boots. Before he had an opportunity to look upon the newcomer who had breached his calm silence, they were stood before his desk, and as he gazed up toward them Alvarez watched as they placed something down on the desk before him.

The mishappen shape of a rotting skull, speared through the neck with a lance.

Alvarez grimaced, placing his quill back in its pot, the stench of decay carrying through and lingering at his nostrils like spoilt milk.

"You could've brought it in a bag," he muttered, studying the hollowed sockets of its eyes and the purple-veined skin stretched over the old bone – an attempt to conceal his disgust, as he spied maggots eating at the flesh within.

"I didn't take you for someone who liked gift wrap, sir," General Ferreus replied facetiously, hands clasped behind his back like a vulture with a broad, curling smile.

"Perhaps this might've been an exception." He paused. "That being said, it would appear the expedition was a success."

"Momentously, sir... we found this one here speared on the shoreline amongst the trees, and the robe was buried in the sand at its base. That was all that remained, as far as we could find."

"It was staked at the shoreline, general?"

"Yes, sir, jutting out from tree-line."

Alvarez ran a finger through the knots of his beard. "So they wanted us to find it."

"If I may, sir, I would say that the intention was less so that we would find him... and more so to let us know what they *did* to him. Almost giving the signal: *'this is what's to come'*."

"That would be a fair assessment... as they spared nothing for the faint-hearted." A maggot curled out from one of the ears and landed on his desk, as if to prove the point.

"Expect nothing less from savages, sir."

"Exactly so." He shifted the papers to one side and clasped his hands together. "We'll have to arrange a ceremony for him... show the people we mean well by giving the old man a proper send-off. See to it that a casket is arranged – inform the militias that a funeral procession shall take place in four days' time. Find a suit of his old armour that we can attach the head to." The sickness in his stomach lurched again. "And for god's sake clean him up before you do... we want them to see him, not fucking *smell* him."

Ferreus produced a quiet bow. "It will be done, sir."

"Excellent."

A moments' pause; the general looked to say more. "There is something else, sir, that we discovered while we were out there that may be of some importance to you..."

"Go on," Alvarez replied.

"We discovered an old fire set back from the shoreline… something that we would have dismissed off-hand under normal circumstances I know. However, there was some evidence leading us to believe it was a fire used by the king's killer… and that they were no ordinary killer, at that."

"What did you find?"

"A lock of hair, sir… amongst the ashen remains. Now, I claim to be no expert, but the burning of hair is usually performed by a Tarrazi High Priest, as a way to—"

"Appease the *gods*." He spat the word venomously, Mother Katastro's words echoing through his mind. "I know the stories… I know the old rituals, sacrificing traitors of the world to bring good fortune on the weak. It means nothing. The Mothers may prophesise and the priests may cast their incantations… but we guide our own destiny in the end. This was little more than an act of revenge, intending to ignite war… there's nothing else to it."

But even as he said it, the words echoed hollowly from his mouth: dull, monotonous; a lack of conviction or certainty. The chimes of a bell growing fainter; the same truths he'd reminded himself of time and time again, now as only tired assertions. A reality he was trying to stitch together, that destiny was wrong and prophecy was wrong and he was a free man not bound by any supernatural fate. That no matter the signs – no matter the nature of the war that came, or the call of the dying Mother – he was still in control of fate, in the end. But the words continued to echo through him, and with each dismissal, they grew only louder: that there was destiny, and there was fate, and it would prevail.

Whether you like it… or not.

Alvarez reeled back from his mind, and was alerted to a shifting form at the back of his office.

General Broska slipped through the door at the far end, pushing it closed with a grunt of the hinges and standing just adjacent, the light of the high windows cutting across his form in long panels.

"Ah, yes sir... I was meaning to say that our General Broska here was quite a prodigious asset while we were out there," Ferreus exclaimed suddenly, turning to provide an awkward, wide-eyed grin toward the newcomer. "He helped load and unload the longboats, moored them on the shoreline... even did the excellent job of finding and removing this little trophy for you sir." He waved a hand at the rotting skull. "A skilled strategist, right down to the execution of a saw-blade, is our General Broska, sir."

Is that so? "Always knew he had it in him," the Supreme Governor said with false pleasure, clapping his hands together. "A good spirit in the army, aren't you, Broska? A man of many talents."

But for some moments passing, there came no response – no reply, no acknowledgement of the praise. All that changed on the large man's face was the delicate twitch of a fake smile, before his face submerged again into a glum sag. Eyes to his feet, hands clasped before him as if in attendance of a funeral, he offered only silence as his solace.

How odd. "What's wrong, general?" Alvarez pressed. "Can't find the time to address your Supreme Governor?"

Broska looked up to meet his eye – *red-rimmed,* Alvarez acknowledged. "My apologies, sir," he muttered despondently. "I was just doing my job out there, was all."

"A humble man makes a good leader... I admire that."

"As does an honest one." As he said it, Broska made a cautious glance to his fellow general, who had moved off to one side as if attempting to fade from existence – falling short, as both pairs of eyes suddenly locked to him and he seemed to squirm awkwardly on the spot.

"Absolutely, all noble qualities," Ferreus said definitively. "Exactly what this army needs."

"Of course," Broska replied coldly, taking a weighted breath. "And with that being said, sir" – turning to Alvarez suddenly – "I'm under the assumption you've been informed about the loss of one of our top generals during this expedition?"

Alvarez's eyes bulged, and his teeth ground against each other like chiselling stone. Eyes shot over to Ferreus, burrowing into him. In return came a look of disbelief, a twinge of anger. The fearful reprimand of a guilty man.

"No," the Supreme Governor growled, "can't say I *have*."

Ferreus screwed his nose up and glared at Broska. "We had a... quite serious incident while searching for the fire." A long pause, lost for a moment – then suddenly a smile, twisting further into a wide grin. "General Cavara was... speaking to me about her feelings towards our new administration... about you, and Revek... how she wanted to challenge it all, before we could consolidate our power. I was outraged upon hearing it – defended you vehemently, of course... but she just became enraged, started shouting. I was worried we'd be discovered by enemy patrols, so I ordered her to withdraw to the shoreline. But..." His face fell to one of glum acceptance. "She drew her weapon on me, and I was forced to engage. After a brief skirmish... I was given no choice as she refused to see sense... so I stabbed her through the chest, and she fled to the shoreline where she collapsed and bled out. We wanted to recover her body and bring it with us, but all the supply boats had already left, and we started hearing shouting from the trees ... we had no choice. We left immediately." He gave a slow nod. "My apologies, sir... I should have done more."

"You did what was required," Alvarez replied, inhaling slowly. "I question why you didn't mention this before, however."

"I felt it was news best left to a private discussion between yourself and I, sir... I meant no disrespect by it."

"Very well." Then, to Broska. "Is that how it happened, general?"

Broska waved a hand slowly, any emotion he held within on the matter refusing to show. "I only saw Cavara stumble onto the beach and Ferreus plant a boot through her back... didn't see anything else before that," he replied softly. "Beyond that, I was just told not to tell anyone about it."

Alvarez frowned. "By whom?"

A swing of the head toward Ferreus.

Is that so? "Is that true, general?"

The silver-haired officer, shadowed by the mid-morning sun streaming across his back, screwed his eyes closed and sighed through his teeth. "What I *meant* by it, sir... is that what happened should not become common knowledge among the army, for fear of *further insubordination* among potential sympathisers. That was my point... *not* the dismissal of such knowledge as a *coverup*."

"It was never an *accusation*, general," Alvarez grumbled, holding his gaze sharply. "Watch your tone."

"My apologies... sir."

Good. "Besides, I'm sure Broska – possessing the *noble qualities* you stressed earlier – would never dare make such an accusation. Am I right, general?"

The rotund figure stood at the back of the room gave a whimper of a smile. "Wouldn't dream of it, sir."

"As I expected." The Supreme Governor nodded once, once only. "Now, is there anything else to report?"

"No," Ferreus grumbled bluntly.

"Good."

"What are our orders, sir?" Broska inquired, crossing the chamber to stand alongside his fellow general – a fellow general who, despite being mired in shadow, seemed to burn with an anguished flame where he stood.

"I received word earlier," Alvarez explained, "that Revek has rendezvoused with the new Imperial Army in the field, and they're approaching the border wall as we speak. Now, with these other generals engaged, it's important to have capable hands at the capital to keep the peace as well... and I believe you two are up to the task." From the stack of papers at his side, he handed two briefs over to them. "Ferreus will be in charge of the militias stationed around the capital, including the barracks and the lower keep. You'll respond to reports of violence, rioting, and have the power to investigate suspects *liberally*. If you need to break doors... you need to break doors."

A smile returned to the older man's face. "Understood, sir."

"And Broska will be the face of our social relations in the capital, handling the press and trade unions. We need a good image of the new regime if we're gonna succeed at this... so that means being among the masses, keeping in touch with the upper-class circles, and striking deals with the unions to keep them toeing the line. We want passive control... that's your job."

Broska nodded, folding the brief within his belt. "Understood."

"That will also mean that I need some... *symbiosis* between you both, you understand? If one of you is enforcing control, the other needs to control how it looks. If someone starts a fire, make it a festival – don't start burning shit to the ground." He looked between them. "Do I make myself clear?"

"Yes sir," they echoed.

"Good... you're both dismissed." A twinge of his nostrils and the Governor scowled. "And get this fucking thing out of my sight... I've got enough maggots in this place to deal with as it is."

†

The doors to Alvarez's chamber fell gently to a close, and with a face like breaking thunder, General Ferreus watched the rotund mass of Broska waddle down the corridor and scowled fiercely.

The audacity, he grumbled. *The arrogance of such a fat, incongruous fool... to challenge me before the Governor himself.* Ferreus was a man of the army, a man of respect and good-graces – *I have no time for insubordination... especially from the likes of him.* There was no place for it; every action had to be calculated. In the grand scheme of it all, that was the army's job – a job for Revek, and Ferreus in turn. Duty-bound men, who wanted stability in the new regime. To bring balance – to hold every string in place, and break any counterweights to their plans as they emerged.

Counterweights like Cavara – he ground his teeth. It was just a coverup, for the security of a legitimate aim: that all they longed to do was keep the peace. That some people had to disappear – had to be 'made accidents' of – didn't matter in the end. Such was the way of the duty-bound, in maintaining that fragile balance in the world. *That's just how it has to be.*

He traced Broska's slow progress down the corridor.

Sometimes, people just have to be made to disappear…

"General!" he bellowed, thrusting the king's severed head into the hands of one of the guards at his side, who appeared entirely disgusted at the slimy pale orb now hanging in her palms. Ferreus made no acknowledgement to her, instead striding off down the corridor after his fellow general with fire burning at his heels. "A word, please, general!"

Broska turned, aware of the frightening pace by which Ferreus was closing in on him, and took a few cautious steps back—

The silver-haired officer was on him in moments, grappling the leather neck-guard of his uniform and shoving him against the wall. Broska spluttered, tried to wrestle the hand clear, but received only a solid gut-punch for his efforts.

"You've got a lot of *fucking* nerve, I'll give you that," Ferreus growled. "What were you exactly trying to do in there, hm?"

"Testing… the water…" he mumbled defiantly.

"On what?"

"How much he knows… how much you're *keeping* from him…"

The guards at the door began to approach at the commotion, and Ferreus speared a finger in their direction menacingly. "Stay where you are… this is no concern of yours."

"It could all slip away, Ferreus…" Broska continued. "It'd only take a few words… a slip of the tongue…"

"You will speak *nothing* of what happened."

"Your threats mean little… I rank as your equal."

"I've made Cavara disappear… I can make you do the same."

"But you didn't want to, did you? Never did… you were afraid of falling out of favour, losing your place in Revek's little circle… you never wanted to kill her, for all the shit it'd bring you... you just didn't have the guts to say no..."

"Shut your *mouth*."

"And now you've done it, and people know it... and you're so deep in shit you'll do anything to keep it under wraps. All for what? A petty favour from a dishonest man? You really are weak, you know that..."

Another punch, this time harder, slammed into Broska's stomach. Ferreus watched his eyes balloon, the swirl of sickness congeal in his throat, and snarled like a beast.

"You listen very closely, you disgusting fuck... you will speak *nothing* of what you know. You will not usher a *word of it*. No one needs to know... or I promise you, I will make your life, and the lives of everyone and everything you love, a torturous *fucking* anarchy until the end of time." He leaned in close to his ear. "*Mark my words...*"

Ferreus threw him to the floor, watching him buckle awkwardly under his own weight and roll onto his back in pain. Looking back to the guards, he saw their eyes flicker cautiously down the corridor and back again, refusing to get a closer look for fear of the same fate. Instead, they remained transfixed to their station, like two sentinels on the river of the gods, and Ferreus smiled delightfully at their obedience.

No one needs to know.

Chapter 16

Into the Breach

There is an ancient tale told by the elders of the mountains, about the day the gods will walk among us. That they will come down from the high towers of the heavens to meet us, and they will be disgraced by the nature of our ways. Our violence, our callousness, our envy, our desire... our greed and maleficence. They will find us foul creatures, and they will want to rid us of this world, for fear of how we may break its balance. So, in all their might and splendour, they shall pen us in like cattle with walls high enough to pierce the sun... and they shall scorch the earth around us, the grasses and the trees, until nothing grows and we cannot feed. We shall be brought to our knees, the savages that we are, until we do what they had expected us to in the beginning: slaughter each other until the last of our number, who shall starve alone in the desolation of his own making, wondering where it all went wrong." Revek shifted in his saddle and inhaled deeply. "We may be no gods... but we know the look of savages when we see them."

They had burned everything. From the border wall stretching unbroken along the horizon, right to the hooves of the horse he sat upon, the world had been purged by flame. Green grassland had been stripped away to a dust-bowl of yellow tufts and exposed rocks. Settlements of dense trees were now blackened and charred skeletons, never to grow again. And at the near horizon, a black smear across the landscape, strung the wall of the enemy, dotted with pinnacles of watchtowers and the squat metal blocks of artillery platforms. As far as the eye could see, it was impervious, stretching into the beyond. Had there been an eclipse that day, Revek may have mistaken it for a vision staring into the gates of hell.

One of his subordinates approached, his horse scratching at the charred ground with its hoof. "This is unexpected."

"That it is."

"Some reckoning of the gods, we suppose?"

"This is an assertion of *power*," Revek grumbled. "That which they've burned, they now covet."

"Is that not a formal declaration of war, sir?"

"What, and the execution of our king was just tempting fate?" The commander scoffed. "Come now, they knew exactly what they were doing all along. What you see before you just proves the point: they aren't here to play petty games... they're here for land and they're here for blood..."

"An invasion," the grey-haired officer exclaimed.

"Not yet." Revek studied the length of black wall and frowned. "This is something different..."

"Sir!" A voice from behind; the blonde, angular-faced general pulled up alongside him on her mount, a scout scuttling across the ground behind like a lost beetle.

"Report."

"The scout has some news, said it was for your counsel alone."

Revek glanced over to the doe-eyed man panting next to her. "Speak then, let's hear it."

"We were observing the length of the border, sir, checking for any irregularities or any enemy parties on our side of the wall," the scout mumbled. "Found that the burnt area you see 'ere stretches from end to end, as far as we know. We were navigating across it sir, trying to judge what kinda firepower they had on the wall..."

"Spit it out!"

"... when a lancing bolt speared one of our horses through the side and impaled the rider to the ground." The messenger gulped. "We tried getting the body out, but then another bolt came and knocked one of the others clean from his saddle. We came to you as soon as we could sir... we weren't sure what to... it'd come from the wall, sir, the lancing bolts... the burnt land is—"

"A demarcation line," Revek interjected, his head snapping suspiciously to the border. "This isn't the land they own... this is the range of their artillery."

"But that's over a thousand feet sir... near double what our catapults can manage," the grey face said warily.

"He has a point, sir," the blonde general added. "The beachhead bolt can fire from that range, should we find a weak point... but there's no way we can get our catapults close enough to breach the wall without getting ripped to pieces. It'd be suicide. All we can manage is a forward assault..."

"But surely that'd be even worse? We'd be peppered with enemy fire. Gods only know how much more they've got stockpiled out of sight. If you ask me, we..."

Revek held up a fist, and the squabbling subordinates fell to a deathly silence. He glared at them individually – *why have I been stuck with people like you* – before spearing a finger off towards the border.

"We might not need them."

Following his guide, a collection of thick-bodied towers extended out from the main length of wall off to one side, tiny white flags rippling in the wind at their peaks. Around its base, tiny campfires and tents formed a preliminary frontier post for the blackcoat scouts, who milled in and out the towers like a hive of bees. It was an imposing congregation of metal and weapons, and near impervious to the untrained eye. But it wasn't any of this that drew Revek's gaze: through the narrow crevasses between the towers, he spied the distinctive iron bars of a military gatehouse, and produced a wide grin.

Our way in.

"Round up the men, keep the bulk of our forces behind the line when we attack," Revek ordered. "I want the beachhead within range of the gatehouse and three divisions of our best mounted infantry flanking it. When the beachhead soars, we ride hard towards the gatehouse. Keep spread out, and watch the skies for lancing bolts – as we approach, slow and raise shields to avoid archer fire from the towers. When we reach the gatehouse those enemy camps will engage, so be prepared with your weapons. The sooner we get inside those towers and out of firing range, the better. I want no bullshit and no heroics: we charge as one unit, infiltrate as one unit, no exceptions. Am I understood?"

A few puzzled faces watched him, dumbfounded.

"Am I *understood*!"

A splutter of '*yes sirs*' and suddenly the world around him kicked into motion. Marching orders were volleyed over helmeted ranks; the oiled crank of wheels signalled artillery in motion. The thrum and dictation of progress sang peacefully to him, and he smiled off to the border wall pertinently.

Soon there'd be nothing left but broken metal, and soiled dignity abound.

"When the gods come down to us, they shall do so with torrents of fire, and the strike of great blades, to make us victims of our grievous wrongdoings. When they come, we shall flee the fields of our homes... and we shall cower behind great walls and peer from high towers, in the hopes we'll survive. We know it as a fruitless endeavour, but we do it nonetheless. For no matter how thick our walls are, or how tall our towers may be... the inevitability of fate shall come for us all, in the end." He took in a deep heave of air and sighed profoundly. "And it all begins, with a single crank of steel..."

He rammed the lever forward, and after several strains of gears, the beachhead ballista – little more than a massive crossbow in reality – snapped into motion and released its colossal cargo. The entire frame jolted backwards; the blunt-nosed spear of metal surged through the air. A glance to one side, and the engineer gave Revek a salute of approval that the weapon would hit its mark.

"Cavalry!" the commander roared, ranks upon ranks of mounted armour jostling beside him, steel caps donned and shields coiled in their arms. Revek puffed his chest, speared his sword at the gatehouse, and roared with glee.

"*Charge!*"

The horses spurred into motion suddenly; the ranks advanced in one seething wave several dozen men wide. They tore up the parched ground stretched before them. The drumbeat of hooves was deafening. The clanking shifts of armour braced across the horses' flanks echoed in the high winds. Revek led them forward, eyes fixed on the course of their beachhead as it sailed far ahead towards the gate.

Like a crack of lightning, the beachhead whistled between the first two watchtowers at a frightening speed, the camps of scouts studying it overhead, as it connected with the mass of the iron gate seconds later. The desperate sound of crashing metal pierced their ears, even with the thunder of the charge all around. A rip of dust exploded skyward; the gate was torn from its hinges, left floundering in the earth beyond. Their access point had been made.

And into the breach we go.

A cry from his left, and Revek noticed some of the soldiers transfixed by the skies above. Looking there, he saw the sleek black forms of lancing bolts arcing through the harsh glare of midday sun, before turning down towards them with expert malice. The commander kicked his heels in, spurred the horse harder. The beast thundered beneath him, as the rest of the cavalry accelerated too. A few poorly-angled bolts thudded into the ground behind them, but others began to fall into their path, and then amongst their ranks moments later.

The screams of the dead rippled through their charge. One figure fell away to Revek's left, the bolt snapping through the soldier's chest and breaking through the horse's back below them, sending both tumbling to a quick death. Another to his right, bursting through a woman's shoulder, throwing her into the maw of charging hooves beneath with the horse surging on unphased.

Suddenly a bolt fell directly at his side, and several soldiers went down in a mangle of broken limbs and twisted bodies. His own horse leaned sharply to the right, nearly throwing him off, before he readjusted again and glanced behind to find the bodies had piled up into a crush of dying beasts and broken faces.

And still they charged, on and on, with the bolts falling around like the meteors of angry gods.

Ahead, the enemy blackcoats had formed up and archers lined the walls overhead, crossbows and arrows poised on the incoming tide. Those camped at its base had formed a defensive wall, shields planted into the ground to create a barricade. The cavalry was approaching fast, a huge cloud of dust rising behind them, and when they passed beyond the range of the artillery, Revek knew the arrows would start to fall.

When the faint whisper sounded that the first bowstring had loosed, the rain of knives began.

"*Scatter!*" he roared over the din, and although he barely heard himself, evidently those around him did. Their spaced formations broke off into disassembled groups interweaving with each other at high speed. The arrows fell among them, the sudden shift in formation sending many arrowheads to the dirt, or glancing disobediently off metal guards. The swirling mass of mounted soldiers shifted and closed in towards the gatehouse where the enemy had formed up. Arrows continued to rain down. A few short, sharp cries pierced the dull rumbling of the charge. Scatterings of screeching horses. The thuds of fallen bodies, then trampled by others in the fray. The broken fearful screams of dying men, with Revek at the centre, revelling in the glory of the attack. There was no time to mourn, nor to regroup. The horses barrelled on towards the breach; in a matter of moments, the battle would shift from horseback to sword work. Reins would be dropped and blades unsheathed. The roar of battle chambered by the clatter of steel. The indefatigable terror they would inflict on the Tarrazi forces.

The moment we've been waiting for.

Revek closed in on the barricade of blackcoats, eying up the outliers who stood with swords raised; the commander broke from the ranks of his men into the arms of the enemy.

The blackcoats registered the change and formed up to brace against his attack, a few figures stood alone to lead their defence. Wondering what the arrogant fool would do next. The commander smiled.

What indeed...

Revek flung himself from the horse's saddle into a diving roll, feeling the strain of muscle against his tightly-buckled armour. A moment later, he was on his feet, sword swiping across his front in a single motion. The enemy blackcoat he found himself before had no time to adjust, as the blade snapped across his exposed throat, a torrent of blood spewing from the great wound.

Collapsed instantly.

On to the next one.

This one came charging, a warrior's axe swinging in one hand like a sling. Revek ducked, and kicked the attacker in the shin with such force that he heard a bone in the figure's ankle snap viciously. A howl of pain and the charging blackcoat was grounded in a heap – Revek seized the moment and pounced. Grappling the figure's flailing head like a toy, he speared the sword between the attacker's back-plate, a crunch of cartilage as the vertebrae were torn to pieces.

Died instantly.

On to the next one.

Turning, the next aggressor was already there with sword raised. Revek knocked two strikes aside, exchanging blows in a flurry of clean cuts, before stepping into the blackcoat's circle and landing a punch in their jaw.

The enemy spat; they grappled each other by the shoulders,

heaving to-and-fro. The world centralised. The caco-phony of horses swelled closer. He only just noticed arrows falling amongst them from above. Revek growled, spittle flying from his mouth. Outsizing his opponent. Jostling left and right, adrenaline seizing at his muscles. The commander prevailed and headbutted his opponent, grip released from his shoulders. He landed a punch across the blackcoat's cheek, another across the jaw. Stumbling, falling, the enemy collapsed to his knees, eyes wandering, spinning wildly. The game was up, it seemed.

In a single motion, Revek kicked the sword from the man's quaking hand, caught it from the air by the handle, and swiped the blade clean through the man's neck.

The head rolled from its broken stump and clattered to the floor.

And onto... the next one...

He broke into a run, gaining acceleration across the dust-covered terrain, towards the shield barricade straddling the gatehouse. Thundering hooves grew louder, and suddenly he was surrounded by his own soldiers, forming a streamlined barrier around him against encroaching archer fire. They led the charge, barrelling forward, and made the first connection with the shield wall a few dozen feet in ahead.

"Sir!" came a cry from behind.

Turning, Revek found one of his other generals by the name of Darius slowing at his side, red-and-green sash billowing prestigiously in the wind. An outstretched hand unravelled, which the commander accepted gladly, and moments later he was in the horse's saddle re-entering the charge of the battle.

"Some heroic work there, sir!" Darius boomed through his great ginger beard. "Something for the ages, I'd say!"

"The day isn't won yet, general, let's keep at it!" Revek replied, watching the battle unfold before him. The enemy ranks had broken, a disintegrated swarm of black armour trying to prize their way from the crush of horses. The archers above had slowed their attacks, struggling to pick targets in the fray. Some of the Provenci soldiers had found shelter under the gatehouse, but were then attacked by archer slits in the walls to either side.

Suddenly, the horses had formed a crush of thrashing bodies. A few reared up and dispossessed their riders; others became wedged and made easy pickings for arrows above. The fear suddenly capitulated within; what was once a clear earth was now devolving rapidly into a slaughter pen. Scanning the towers, blinded by the blazing eye of the sky, Revek needed a way out. Needed something, somewhere—

There!

The nearest guard tower, connected to the wall by a narrow gangway. At its base, he spied what appeared to be the dull shape of a hidden door.

"Get some of the men to lead the horses back to the artillery line!" Revek commanded. "The rest stay here on foot."

"But sir, we'll have no way of retreating if—"

"There is no retreat!" the commander roared. "We storm the gatehouse, leave no survivors. Now get the order to the others!" Revek speared a finger off to his left. "And get me to that watchtower!"

"It will be a time of great reckoning, when the gods storm the walls and breach the gates of humanity's last stronghold. Street by street, alley by alley, they will bring their wrath and flame upon us for our treachery. We will feel the burning sickness we have ourselves inflicted on so many. It will come as retribution; it will come as final sin. It will be the defining moment of all men... when the savages are slain and the gods walk free once more." The commander drew the sword across the bloodied woman's throat, and sent her tumbling down through the watchtower until she splattered in the dust far below. *"And today will be yours, savage..."*

Revek turned, wiping his blade with a stretch of cloth, approaching the doorway opposite which beamed with the intense glare of the midday sun. Several of his men stood to either side, swords ready, surveying the gangway beyond already sprinkled with the dead.

As he approached, a few soldiers hurled themselves from the gangway back into the safety of the watchtower, an arrow glancing across the last one's pauldron for his efforts. Behind them, another formidable figure with a rectangular shield strapped across his back sauntered into the room with a coy smile on his face. He was a burly man with a horseshoe moustache, who Revek recognised as another of the generals among his rank.

"Ah, commander," he acknowledged with a clasp of the forearm. "Was hoping you'd show up for the main event."

"I'd never miss a chance to split heads, general, mark you me," Revek mused, nodding his head.

"The men and I have just breached the second door onto the main wall, sir — it's clear for your units to advance. I warn you though, there's a hell of a lot of activity over there."

"Don't you worry about us general: we got it covered." Revek gave him a wink and slid the shield from his shoulder, bashing it with his fist. "Ready men!"

He stooped low, feeling the press of his soldiers to either side, sliding metal all around as their shields slid into place around him like the shifting scales of a great serpent.

"Steady!"

The cocoon locked tighter, the soldiers hunkering down like crabs in one hulking mass of metal. Revek locked his own shield at the tip, forming the front of their arrow primed on the gaping doorway opposite — that, and the gangway stretched imposingly between. The commander exhaled slowly, gritting his teeth into a wide grin, and gave the signal.

"*CHARGE!*"

A jolt of motion, and the interlocking shields drove forward.

They covered ground fast, the scuttling legs of a great centipede traversing the iron plates, shielded from the harshness of the world around. Kicking aside the fallen weapons left scattered across the gangway floor; treading cautiously over the corpses of good men riddled with arrow-shafts like some cursed ornament. A quiet prayer to the fallen souls as they pressed on down the narrow stretch towards the prize at its far end.

"Hold formation!"

Arrows pinged all around, snapping off the shield exteriors, seeking out the delicate innards of the great scaly beast as it charged onward. Most of the fire was concentrated along the back, where the soldiers continued to form up like a conveyor belt onto the end of the moving cover. The howls of dying declared the fate of an unhappy few, but the iron cocoon continued to battle on across the bridge unhindered.

"Hold formation!"

It had grown dense and humid in the cocoon, perspiration kissing the commander's cheeks and neck. He felt his arm grow numb, wavering slowly. Their progress slowed, the anarchic churning of legs finally facing the strain of their venture. The whole column began to sway awkwardly, the scrape of metal pinging in his ears as the shields skated the edges of the embrasure. Revek growled, straining his arms, heaving the cocoon back to centre, barrelling at the top of his lungs to—

"*Hold formation!*"

Suddenly the ground at their feet became darker, and the shimmering definitions of the world fell to shadow. Through a tiny hole to his right, he spied the imposing bastion of the gatehouse rise formidably ahead. Their masterplan was almost complete; only a few dozen feet and they'd reach the main wall. The luck of it, the swelling joy of success. A gush of air across his face, a remarkable blessing of the gods. Finally, his triumph would come.

And then the arrow hit.

A shriek of horror in his left ear. An arrow-shaft, rammed through the soldier's eye from the sudden opening in the shields. A spray of blood coating every surface within, splattering across the commander's cheek. A wail, sickening and merciless.

The shield slipped away.

Four arrows lambasted the soldiers behind, striking two more of his men in the jugular. Lurching, Revek was dragged sideways as the interlocking cocoon collapsed inward. Shields fell away, bodies screeching to a halt. Those behind bunched up like a harpsichord, now front and centre to the steel-tipped onslaught of the archers beyond.

The commander disconnected from the primary crush, sliding his arm from the shield, dragged up by two of his men towards the safety of the watchtower. He stumbled towards the breached door, risking a look back to find the exposed front of the cocoon torn apart by volley after volley of arrows. Disappearing into the watchtower, his desperate cries for them to rally up and charge came to nothing. What had been a perfect tactical manoeuvre moments ago, fell apart before his very eyes.

"Fuck!" he bellowed, landing a punch against the wooden frame.

"What should we do, sir!" a frightened figure beside him cried. "They won't make it alone!"

The commander ground his teeth, fists clenching.

"We need to help them!" another screamed, all heroism and no sense, as he bundled forward with his shield raised.

Revek grappled him by the shoulder and swung him back under the cover of the watchtower. "If you want a sure way to hell, be my guest... but not on my watch," the commander growled, the fear-stricken face he was presented with as much a reflection of his own as anything. He drew the soldier back and turned to address the other half-dozen men and women before him. "Now listen 'ere and listen well: if we wanna help the others, we have to follow through with the plan, understood?"

A few scattered replies, duty-bound and nothing more.

"They are out there dying, and will continue to die, unless we do something about those archers on the west wall." From a satchel strapped to his side, he removed a small metallic sphere and waved it around. "See these? These are weapons. You will take these and lead the attack on the west wall. Strike them against your armour and wait for a hissing sound… throw them into the nearest group of those fucking blackcoats and brace for what comes next." He removed the satchel and handed it to another of his men. "It ain't only me who's relying on you with this… it's everyone up here, and everyone still down below. Am I understood?"

A few worried nods.

"Good… now, make haste with it. We rendezvous here when the gatehouse has been cleared and a perimeter's been secured." He stabbed a finger out. "Do *not* fuck this up."

Dumbstruck faces, fearful eyes—

"So *go, move!*"

Revek was suddenly shunting a half-dozen frozen figures towards the sealed door to their left, barking orders as they passed like lambs to slaughter. The air was taut with fear, vapours in his nostrils, the squeals of the dying on the bridge before him sharp in his ears. Looking right, he found the door onto the central gangway above the gatehouse was unlocked – shadows of blackcoat soldiers shifting behind. The opportunist in him rose to prominence, and a taut grin caught across his face.

Perhaps there is time for heroism after all…

"Where are you going sir?" one frightful voice called to him from the opposite side.

Revek unsheathed his blade. "To entertain some heroics," he exclaimed.

He turned, raised a leg, and kicked the door open with a blast of air and light, hollering at the top of his lungs and charging forward.

The commander found himself immediately amongst the enemy, his sword raised and lethal. Several figures turned to the sudden commotion, and before they had a chance to react, Revek plunged his sword into the nearest blackcoat's throat, wrenching it through bone, watching gleefully as the man's eyes bulged and the blood began to spill.

Whipping the sword away, he found another attacker to his left, reaching for a sheathed weapon. Revek swiped across his body, felt his sword connect with the pale woman's exposed shoulder, and roared with satisfaction as the blade slipped through and sliced the arm from its socket. She screamed viciously, grappling at the gushing stump at her side, aimlessly crying for the redemption of some long-forgotten god.

A swift strike across the neck, and her screaming head soared skyward off the walkway and down onto the charred earth below.

"Have at it, you bastards!"

Two came for him at once, right and left, snarling with swords raised. Kicking out, he caught Left across the shin, dismantling his attack as Revek's outstretched blade knocked aside Right's sweeping blow. Fist clenched, the commander cuffed Right across the jaw, throwing him against the embrasures, before curving the sword back across to deflect Left's attack. Slinging it aside, he stabbed out, piercing the ailing blackcoat in the shoulder, a small cry of pain escaping pursed lips. Left fell back, as Revek knocked aside another of Right's attacks. The commander grappled Right by the helmet with his free hand and smashed his head against the iron wall, face splintering like old wood. A shriek went up, as Left lunged for Revek with his good arm. The commander elbowed him across the chin, before throwing Right to one side and slicing his blade across.

Throat slit, spewing blood like a waterfall, Left collapsed to his knees and died before he hit the floor.

Revek spat. "Good riddance."

Looking down, Right edged away along the floor, one hand clasped across the helmet and the broken bone structure within. Revek stood over him, seething, sweat dripping from his deep brow. His skull was pounding. He lurched about like a wild beast, searching for his next victim to maim. The bloodlust within him. That unhinged part, contained by the duty-bounds of the army regiment, let loose in the din of battle. None of the grovelling, the toeing of the line. That mattered nought when soaked in blood and dancing with life on one's hand. That was the beauty of it, Revek found. To be the god of life and death, for once.

"I'm going to enjoy this."

He raised his weapon—

His heart stopped.

There was another there with him.

Towering a full head and shoulders above Revek, the figure was a daunting shadow in the harsh sunlight. It wore nothing but black robes, a bastion of the dark, other than the sheath of a reticent blade at its side that a pale ringed hand lingered over delicately. Across the pale, earless face were concentric black circles widening around the left eye, ritual marks of some savage tribe or people. It remained unmoving, unblinking, faultlessly still. Revek found his eyes drawn to its pupil-less moons, trying to imagine the figure drawing some emotion from there, some sense of self or being. Instead, he found nothing – nothing but a hollow reflection of himself, staring back, and the frightful cold clutching at his heart. Only the blooded-steel blade in his hand offered him any solitude or remorse.

"Who are you?" he asked, trying to stress confidence when he knew sincerely he had none.

"*I am... a protégé,*" it boomed, an echo chamber in his mind.

"A protégé to whom?"

The figure's hand grasped the hilt of its blade. "*To the one who waits in shadows... a protégé of the Iron Queen.*"

Revek took the words like a bolt to the chest, and felt his stomach curl like a fist. "Lies..."

"*It is... no lie. They would not like it if I lied.*"

He scowled. "Who's *they?*"

"*The Forgotten Ones... those who serve her Highness... those who wait to strike out into the light once more.*"

"There is no such person left alive with that name, that title... whatever you wanna call it. The Iron Queen is *dead*" – his hand tightened around the sword-hilt – "and I will not accept otherwise."

The figure seemed to smile. "*A man may live a lie a hundred times, all with the conviction that it's the truth...*" It drew the blade suddenly, a long thin weapon of dark steel that shimmered like ice in the sun. "*... but when the lie is revealed, and the truth faces them once more, the end is all the more bitter...*" Whatever was watching the commander then, he felt eyes fall upon him. "*... and the reality, all the more sweet.*"

"I'll be sorry to disappoint," Revek mused, raising his own weapon.

"*You already have,*" it rumbled slowly. "*The Iron Queen lives... and by her hand, you shall die...*"

The commander felt a cold strike at his stomach, a lurch of anger suddenly erupt in his soul, and with a screech of anguish enough to shake the wall from its foundation, he charged forward with sword raised and the rotten paranoia of the unknown spiralling across his mind.

He swung, blade arcing towards the figure's collarbone – a figure that remained unmoving, even in the face of attack. The blade fell, like the axe of an executioner's block—

A hand snapped up and grappled it mid-strike.

With a delicate nudge of its index finger, the dark figure broke the end of the blade off like a toothpick, watching it fall to the ground and chime against the metal panels underfoot.

Revek recoiled, dumbstruck, staring at the broken sword as if his limb had been cut off. The anger boiled over; again he was cold. The world grew dim, and he was staring at a monster that he knew nothing about.

"How..."

"*Because you are a dishonest man fighting a dirty war...*"

Suddenly the pale figure raised its blade and struck across its body. Revek raised his hapless weapon in a miserable defence. He felt sickness; the world spun. A moment passed, and he heard the tinker of metal hit the floor.

The blade had sliced straight through his own like butter.

"*And no blade may save you from the path you have chosen,*" the figure boomed, stepping back, the blade retracting into the sheath at its side. "*Your fate lies beyond…* and *you will fear their name…*"

Revek blinked, and was about to ask who, but when he opened his eyes again, the figure was gone. Only an empty walkway lay before him, the din of battle drawn silent all around. As if what was, had never been.

The wind dashed his face, a cool breeze weaving between the rivets of his armour. A warm blanche of sun caught his back, an embrace of the gods, drawing sensation back into his numb limbs. He took in great lengths of air, exhaling in low ripples, the abrupt serenity of the world stilling the pulses of his heart.

As if nothing had even happened.

Boots approached from behind, triumphant soldiers calling his name in celebration. He turned to their broad faces and opened his arms wide with a smile. The victory of the day was painted bright across their faces, mirrored across his own, while the painful unknowing rippled through his mind. He tried to hear their voices, to make out the words they spoke, but only the words of the shadow called out to him.

You will fear their name…
The Iron Queen lives.

†

Chapter 17

The Undeserving

When they got there, all they found was a bitter, pervading silence. Charred earth crunching at their feet; a cold wind lancing at their backs. The smouldering remains of broken artillery dotting the squat towers around the gatehouse, itself little more than a mottled corpse of buckled iron and broken bodies. All that remained among the living were a few scattered horses, their master's long bled dry, grazing at what vegetation they could find, whinnying softly.

Redemption begins, Savanta whistled. At her feet, the tracks of Provenci artillery trailed through the chaos toward the broken gate, and out onto the deadlands beyond. Bodies had been cleared to make way for their progress - along the edge of the tall border walls, blackcoat skulls had been ceremoniously hung to dry at the ends of spears. Testament to what was to come, no doubt – a warning to their savage gods that war was their only volition.

Chaos all around, Markus sighed. Passing the bodies cast aside to make way for the machines of war, a sickening twist of his gut formed at the sight of familiar faces. Men and women of Provenci, rank and file, martyrs of the nation, cast at the side of the road with the same indifference offered to their enemy. No burial, no acknowledgement of passing. Just broken, bloodied corpses left to rot in the midday sun. As the day wore on, and the sun broke across the backs of the mountains, flies and beetles had begun to desecrate them, dispersing in huge swarms as they passed. He looked to the broken gate and smoking battlements, and wondered what the cost of life really equated to in the advent of war. Testament to what was to come, no doubt – to whatever hell-scape they were about to walk into, driven by the singular vengeance of one against the might of an entire nation. *It's a death wish, nothing more.*

"They made short work of this," Savanta muttered, knocking the head of a blackcoat soldier with her foot and watching some eight-legged beast scuttle within, snapping its pincers. "Makes our lives easier."

"Providing they keep the momentum," Markus replied. "If the enemy regroup and push back the Imperial Army, well… we could be trapped behind these walls someday soon." It was a dismal revelation, but the truth often was.

And it was a truth Savanta seemed to dismiss entirely.

"That plays to our advantage: they'll think they've flushed out any trace of us and seal the dam again. We can go largely unnoticed."

"Or they'll double their efforts on ensuring any imposters are found and executed. If this access point is left open for several days… why would they not?"

"Because savages don't think twice when they attack – just look at what happened to us a few days back."

"No, but people do," Markus remarked. "And once upon a time not too long ago, that's exactly what we thought them as."

"Don't humanise them," Savanta muttered.

"Why? Because it makes it more difficult to seek revenge on things you consider not so far from yourself?"

Savanta stalled and glared at him. "Tell that to this." Her finger tapped the metal plate across her cheek, producing a hollow sound devoid of any human quality. The black paste along its edges had settled to a blemished grey, supposedly now tough as stone and impossible to break. It did little for the rest of her face, however: skin still puckered with burn marks, stretches of broken skin and weeping gashes, her right eye sagging limply. It was an effective method, but never with the intention of making the survivor look any closer to normal. And Savanta knew it: her clenched jaw and inelegant composition betrayed any knock to her confidence. She was to all outward expression unphased by the wounds she'd sustained.

Markus knew better than to second-guess that.

"Let's keep moving," Savanta ordered, before her eyes fell to the ground beside her and she stopped.

Staring back were the eyes of a blackcoat, hand clutching at a wound at its side, breathing little more than a broken, alienated rasp. Realising it'd been discovered, the blackcoat coughed viciously and tried to shuffle away with what little dexterity it had left in its legs.

Poor bastard, thought one.

Get what you deserve, thought the other.

Savanta turned to walk away, not offering the dying creature another second of her thoughts, but stopped abruptly when she heard the unsheathing of a blade. When she turned, a small knife sat in the palm of Markus's hand. He looked up guiltily at her disgusted face.

"And what do you intend to do with that?" she said pointedly.

He waved the knife at the spluttering form on the floor. "Put the soul out of his misery."

"It doesn't deserve any of that."

"He doesn't deserve what?"

"Remorse."

Markus squared his shoulders. "Any man with a soul to his name deserves at least the decency of a quiet death."

"This *creature* deserves to feel the pain of his actions. Do you think in battle they'd go through our dead and offer *mercy* to those still dying? You think they'd care?" She scoffed. "They'd move on, leave 'em to the dust. Or they'd string 'em up and watch every ounce of blood drip from their bodies. I ain't about to offer this thing any mercy. It can die with the rest of its hell-kind."

Markus frowned. "What separates their people from our people?"

155

"They are *savages*."

"And by acting how they would... does that make us better?"

Savanta found no means to respond. Markus took a step towards the body and knelt next to it, shifting the helmet a fraction to reveal the man's forehead. The eyes beneath were composed and unwavering, the hands led limply to either side. Acceptance, at the pivotal moment of death. Markus watched him blink slowly – a glimmer of thanks, for the mercy it brought – before he raised the knife slowly above his head.

And heard a blade slide from its scabbard next to him.

"So, this is where we are," Markus said matter-of-factly, looking up to the blood-stoked stare of Savanta, blade quivering in one hand. "You will kill me, for this? For sparing the life of one man, doing what he can for his country?"

She remained silent, unperturbed.

"You think you're so different from them?"

Silence.

"You're not... none of us are, but especially not you."

Silence.

"These are a people driven by revenge against those who have wronged them. So you look this man dead in the fucking eyes, and you tell me, what's so different about *you* and *him?*"

The world spun with the whistle of the wind, but in those fragile moments, it came and went all the same. A knife-edge – seconds ticking by.

Savanta, hollow-eyed, returned her sword to its scabbard and flicked a hand dismissively.

"Do what you feel you must," she said slowly. "But if you have some belief in you, that when you come face to face with them one day they'll remember this little act of mercy you'll perform... you are mistaken, and will pay the price a thousand times over for it."

She turned and passed through the gate, crossing onto the vast stretch of open ground beyond, into a world that wanted nothing but her own destruction.

Markus found his mind wandering over what would come next for him. Looking down into the cold eyes of the dying blackcoat below, knowing that whatever remorse flickered behind there was only stipulated by the hand of death closing in. Beyond that, he envisioned the anger raging in the heat of battle, the battle-cries and the clashing blades and the wanton murder of the enemy without hesitation or thought. That this blackcoat, this soldier, this *enemy*... had he not been lying on the floor then, wishing death upon himself, then he would've been charging with sword raised, every intent on killing Markus just because he was on the wrong side of the wall. After all, they were only human, and were driven by the same pride and dreams of power that all types dream of.

Should he suffer as the enemy, if he has the same inner conflicts as I or anyone else has? Am I to make that choice?

He studied the knife hovering overhead, its delicate blade shimmering in the high sun. Perhaps he was just a better man, for wanting to end another's suffering. Or perhaps he was a naïve hypocrite, as Savanta said, demanding decency from those who had none, and mercy from those who knew nothing of it.

Would they offer me as much, should I die by their hand?

As he grit his teeth, and the blade fell, he wondered if fate had other plans for him. Whether mercy would repay him someday, one way or another, or if death were as cruel as it was inevitable.

He withdrew the knife.

Perhaps we'll never know.

†

Chapter 18

Fate Has Other Plans

L imbo: *a place between worlds. The delicate rift between an unfortunate life and a painful death, and whatever lay beyond that thin line she now found herself walking. It was vacuous, for a long time deathly silent. No beating of her heart, rattling through her eardrums. No rasping breaths coiling through her lungs. Her eyes pressed shut, refusing to open, refusing to see or blink or correlate the world around her. There was only her presence, her sheer being there. A mind, detached from body, half-abandoned of its soul, only just convincing itself that it was still anything at all. With no breath and no heart and no body to connect the two, what was really left of her, after all? Was she a slave to the silence; was this what life was beyond the grave? She sought some morsel of reality from the void that consumed her, some figment of what awaited her. But all she found was more of the same: that dense nothingness, bold and absolute. Perhaps that was all there was, and she almost convinced herself that it was so.*

Then, not too far away, a woman's voice began to sing. It was slow, melodic, containing no words or sounds. Drifting around, rising and falling with each passing moment, indicating no stress, or impatience, or concern — only the most beautiful monotony she had known, a small glimmer of reality in a shapeless world.

As it swayed closer, she found the abandoned vestiges of life return to her: her skin prickled at nerve ends, defining hands and feet and a body between. Her eyes rolled in her skull, tracking the motion of the voice as it gravitated the unknown. The slow rhythms of a heartbeat, deep within her chest. All the while the voice continued to sing its sweet melody, and the tension around her loosened and tightened like the benevolent strings of a harp. She almost welcomed it, was warmed by it, but even as the thought came, the woman's voice had gone again, falling to a whisper, then to nothing at all. The abruptness rocked her system, as she strained to rekindle that melody once more. The void settled again like a great beast brought to slumber — it was almost deafening. Her tongue twisted, larynx seizing up as she longed to scream into it, into the nothingness, and break from whatever confounded torture held her there. Time seemed to elapse, the void buckling around her with unenviable freedom——

A voice came.

"Wake up."

Eyes snapped open, throwing herself to her feet in an instant, the sudden confluence of sensation rattling through her. A body and a mind, and moving limbs and vertebrae. There was air, and a heartbeat, and she was sweating, and... and the world around her was nothing but white. A paleness, as if she'd looked at the sun for too long and found herself enveloped in it, with nothing of the world she knew left.

Nothing, that was, except for a tiny breach in the void before her. A grey opening, like a tear through paper. As if the light she was surrounded by was a façade, and reality lay only in what was beyond.

And beyond, in that timeless grey expanse before her, the black figure of a woman knelt as if in prayer, humming softly to herself.

The voice came again.

"Go, now."

Her legs carried her forward, into the grey breach of the void, but as she moved so too did the black shadow, who got to their feet and began to run away. Suddenly it was cat and mouse, predator and prey, but all she longed for was answers, a sign of life, and all the figure did was run faster. All around, the pale light she had awoken into leeched into the grey like blood vessels, meandering and pulsing around her, quickening as she ran. The figure ahead pressed on, stumbling about in fear, a formless mouth screaming but no sound coming out. As if all it could do was sing, or else face the silence like the rest.

They ran on, guided by the void, twisting and turning through tunnels of white and grey, merging through each other. Her head span, her heart trembling. As if being carried in a haze – as if her legs were not her own. In pursuit of a shadow, a half-being, a demi-urge that she prayed had answers to her questions, that could tell her why she was there, and what had happened to the world she knew. Where she was, what it meant, what she would become. Whether the sky would be blue and the grass green again, or whether they would run the marble nothingness forever with no end in sight. Just one pursuing the other, until the silence consumed them again.

All the while, eyes watched from afar, and the voice lay upon them once more.

"There must be an end to all things."

The figure stopped. She stopped too.

Before them, a hole had opened in the ground, light seeping into it like the roots of some great tree. She gazed around, confused, afraid. Along the other side opposite them, five totems stood watching, like the dark fingers of a giant's hand. They watched, lifeless and quizzical, as the two figures studied each other with twitching silent mouths, not a word passing between. Watching and waiting, waiting for the voice to speak again. For what seemed inevitable to happen: every step she took to get closer, the figure inched closer to the drop behind. It was fear, unrelenting – a fear she didn't understand nor comprehend why. All she wanted was answers. All she wanted was to tell them that. But nothing came. No words were found.

Then the voice came again, with its final command.

"There can only be one."

Reality came like a dagger.

A heartbeat, and she lunged forward, screeching silence, pleading for the figure not to go. Grappling, hand clasping just out of reach. The shadow turning away, throwing itself into the abyss, falling slowly down into the expanse beneath. A final soundless cry of defeat, the void shattering between them, coiling whites and greys erupting from all around. The figure falling, falling, further down below, the pale rounds of its eyes broken, defeated.

No songs left to sing.

As they fell, a darkness came, surging up to engulf them, until all the world became night, and the silence rang out once more.

†

"Wake up!"

Cavara threw herself awake to the taste of sea salt and the scent of damp cloth. She spluttered, trying to breathe, the surge of bile burning her throat. Eyes stung, lips split and bleeding. A deep-knotted pain emanating from her abdomen. She curled a blueish hand across it, saw the sand and dark blood plastered across her front, and found a wave of shock rush through her.

Ferreus.

"Are you okay?"

She lurched back in horror, glaring up at someone looming above her. Hit her back on something hard; her hand dipped over the edge and graced the surface of water. Cavara found the ground rock beneath her. Heaving air through her mouth, she twisted and saw the stretch of pale blue all around them. The dense cavalcade of cloud and fog smothering all things. The ripple of waves as the boat shifted with the wind through the waters. The faint whisper of a sail billowing overhead, carrying them into a grand unknown. The coldness licking at her fingertips – the cry of the Icebreaker Sea. In a boat of foreign company, in a world that no longer felt like home.

A hand touched her knee, and she kicked back like a startled horse, again aware of the unfamiliar shadow looming above. She heard more noise behind, felt the waves crash and the air grow thin and the sail above ripple closer as if ready to engulf her—

"It's okay," the shadow said softly. "Whatever happened, you're far away from it now."

The figure crouched, and Cavara found herself gazing into the eyes of an older woman, with a gossamer smile and soft curling hair growing grey at the roots. She had harsh, pronounced features, the signs of a life at sea, but wore them with a merciful, contented grace.

161

Her hands were broad and spindly, red swirls across the nails and wrist, disappearing under the sleeve of a rust-coloured coat. Every ounce of her spoke of calm concern, and it was into those eyes Cavara found her heart settle, and her hands unclench, and the delicate wash of the waves lap soundly in her ear.

The woman looked off behind her. "Evelyn, hand her the water pouch would you?"

There was a small boy in company as well, little more than twelve winters old. With the same curly hair as his mother, Cavara watched him move skittishly as he reached into a sack and handed a small pouch over, trembling nervously as he did. She took it graciously, trying to offer a smile in response, but found the small boy retreat back to one side and look off to the open sea again, as if pretending she wasn't there.

"You'll have to mind him, he's frightful sometimes," the woman said, smiling warmly. "Now please, drink."

Cavara was already unscrewing the cap, and with a long slow gulp of the water, she slowly found rejuvenation take hold. It was cool, soft to the tongue. She swilled the salt from her gums and spat into the vast waters around them. Several more gulps, bleeding the water-pouch dry. Handing it back to the woman, who gave a single nod of the head and fastened it onto her belt.

"By some luck we found you, out there on the shoreline," she explained quietly. "We rarely come so far west, with the open waters being so unpredictable. That being said, we came to shore to find wood for repairs... and there we found you, face down in the sand, nothing but a hollow rasp of breath keeping you alive." She sighed. "It's some miracle you *were* alive, really... whoever stitched up that knife wound of yours did a good job of it."

Cavara blinked slowly. *I don't remember being stitched up...*

"Either way, when we worked out you were stable and breathing, we hauled you into the boat and left as soon as we could. Was the safest thing we could've done. I mean, whoever did *that* to you... well, we didn't want to see what happened if they came back." She paused in thought. "What *did* happen to you, anyway?"

The general opened her mouth and stopped.

What did happen to you...

Cavara blinked, old memories suddenly resurfacing. Memories of the shoreline, guiding the longboats through the surf up onto the sandbank. Scouting the beach with the others, searching for... searching for the king.

The king. Finding his robe, his head speared amongst the trees. No sign of his crown or his clothes. Ordering Broska to remove the head from the spike for extraction. Calling the expedition a success – fearing the enemy may still be near, demanding a quick departure. Disagreement between officers...

Ferreus. Leading her into the woods because he'd 'found something'. The winding path to the campfire. A tuft of hair – evidence of a High Priest performing ritual. The general's remarks: loose ends to be tied. Those who disrespected command, facing punishment.

The knife...

Stumbling through the woods clutching her side, falling, Ferreus pressing into her back, bleeding, bleeding fiercely, life ebbing away. Broska's cries; Ferreus's silence. The ship leaving, the soldiers spun a lie. The pale waves and pale sands stretching far beyond.

The woman in the light, forming from the grey of the sea.

The one who called to me.

"*I need to find her*," Cavara said, not entirely of her own accord. As the words left her mouth, she was already attempting to stand, rocking the tiny vessel as her feet scraped across the shallow hull below. She found no purchase, the moment of motivation fading, slumping back onto the makeshift bed with tears in her eyes. Strength leeching away, with only her life to spare.

"Who do you need to find?" the old woman asked, voice awash with concern. "Is there someone we've left behind?"

Someone left behind. The thought stung her: Cavara wondered how much of herself was still led on that beach, bleeding out, inhaling sand and sea salt as life slowly drifted away. What had been left there on that shoreline, as she was bundled onto a boat and taken far out to sea. What remained of her now – and whether it was even recognised as her own, anymore.

"There was just me… no one else," she muttered, head slumped low like an old dog.

"That's good." The greying woman stood slowly, wrapping an arm around the thin mast. "I imagine you're quite tired from the blood loss… you should sleep. We have a long journey ahead."

Cavara gazed up to her slowly, eyes sullen and forlorn. "Where are we going?"

"To the City of the Sun, on the eastern coast… to my home."

The City of the Sun. She knew it from stories, told in training at the military academy. A city on a plateau, at the end of a great mountain overlooking the sea. Sprawling effortlessly down the cliffs, down the mountain's back, filtering out into small townships in the valley at its base. A sprawling metropolis of culture and secrecy, commanded by the Alderbane and his Council of Seven, who had ruled over the entire country with an iron grasp for near three decades. It was a place that held as many tales of hope as it did ones of horror and covert atrocity. Fear walked the streets and sharpened the blades; fear was the great redeemer.

And it's a long way from home. A bubble formed in her throat. *How can I abandon my people like that?* There she was, in quiet company far from danger, crossing the great sea to new lands and a new beginning. All the while her homeland was amok with fear, doused in flame as the enemy levelled their attack, and the crashing drums of war rattled on. A war she wanted no part of; a war that could've been avoided.

A war I'm bound to, by my honour above all else. She was a general, after all, and Broska's words hummed softly in her mind: *'we need people like you now, more than ever.'*

"I can't," Cavara muttered softly, voice cracking. "I can't go… my people are at war. People will die if I don't… if I can't be there…"

"I admire your stoicism, my dear… but it's not safe, not for you or for us to get you there," the woman replied simply, sitting next to her. "You suffered heavy blood loss, and are probably in shock. That's at least four days in a medical chamber, if you're lucky. A return to active service could take weeks, especially if you intend to lead any soldiers in the field."

"I can work something out," she said, albeit naively.

A smile. "I wish we could. But… if you're people are at war, then… well, there'll be no safe passage to the city, no way to get you in."

"Drop me off down the coast… I, I can sneak in…."

"There's no guarantee we won't encounter your enemy, and…" The old woman looked solemnly to the child behind her, gazing out to sea, and closed her eyes. "I can't risk it."

"Then what can I *do*?" she spluttered desperately. "What can I even do here?"

"Come with us, to Sevica, to the City of the Sun. Take a few days to recuperate with us – we have a bed and food to spare. Lie low, and see how you feel, and… and if you still want to return to your people, and fight in this war, then I can find a traveller to take you there." She lay a hand on Cavara's. "Just, please… come with us, at least for a few days. After that, the choice is yours."

The choice is yours. Cavara sighed heavily and felt her eyelids flicker, the sea around her growing hazy and dull. She didn't know what drew her back to the city, to the war, or to the people who sought to kill her and betray her so carelessly. For all she knew, that should've been the end of it: never to see her homeland again, either in death or new beginnings. Abandon those who sought to destroy her, and be done with it. But something drew her back there, beyond it all: some drive of duty, or honour; pity, or revenge. Calling to her, in those quiet moments, that there was still work to be done.

Her eyes fell shut, and her head lay still, and she slipped from the world again, dreaming of bitter truths, and even more bitter ends.

†

Chapter 19

Jinx

*M*y Dearest Eli,
> A coup has taken place within the army, the likes of which I've
> never seen before. A general was murdered by another on the banks
of the sea, some fifty leagues north-west, on orders from above — precisely who
ordered such an attack, be it the Supreme Governor or otherwise, I am not
sure. Only I know of this information, and only I can explain the horror I
witnessed.

With that, I write to you because I fear my life may be in danger. I can
sense it. There will be martial law within the capital come morning, searching
for spies and plots against the Governor. I fear I may be placed under watch
too. And with that, the treachery that has happened will not leave the walls
of this prison city, and will die with the tide of war. I write to you, hoping
that this may not be the case, and that at least someone, somewhere, knows
of the terrible tragedy that has occurred. It is desperate, I know — these are
desperate times. I will do what I can from here, but I make no promises of
success or my safety.

If this is my last letter, please send my love to Camilla and Davo. Tell
them the great bear is watching over them every night. And that you, my dear
Eli, are the greatest part of my life.

With all my love to you,
Arrenso

*

General Broska wiped a solitary tear from his cheek, and folded the letter in two. Slipping it into an unmarked envelope with shaking hands, he lay it on his desk and rolled back in his chair slowly, gazing at his low ceiling. An enormous pain clenched at his heart, enough to stifle his breath and punctuate his sullen face with tears. Whatever shock-induced reality he had been walking through since the day before, he found slowly recede, and what was left was the raw, unadulterated feeling that the world as he knew it, was gone. Days earlier, he had been stationed in the nearby town of Silestia, overseeing the local festival of harvest as the cold months set in. Now he was hunched over his desk crudely in the cold dark of his office, writing a final castaway to the man he loved, knowing that in any of the coming days he could be dragged off to some underground warren and have his life abruptly shortened.

Now I must live like a convict and fear those in high-command I used to call colleagues... all because I know and saw more than they wanted me to. Murder, betrayal of the highest order. *All for what? Controlling the ranks, keeping people on side?* No one who questioned the authority of the Supreme Governor would be safe; anyone who dared tip the balance away from the war effort would become an enemy of the state. *The invisible coup against the army, where nothing but yes-men remain.* Then martial law would fall, the gates would close, and the military state would reign unabetted. *This has never happened before in our history... never has the state seized such absolute control. And all because of war.*

No: all because of power.

There was a sharp knock at his door, and Broska's mind returned to the chamber around him with painful clarity. "Enter," he grumbled.

A skittering of metal boots, and a courier appeared at his right shoulder. "You summoned me, sir?"

Broska slid the envelope across the table, which the courier promptly swiped up and inspected. "There's... no name, sir..."

A small bag of imperial coin landed on the desk, and Broska turned menacingly to the small man. "For your silence: twenty crowns. Now listen to me very carefully." The courier's face seemed to swim with discomfort. "You will take this letter to Rendevir, the small township in the southwest. You will deliver it to Governor Kraskow, unopened, and say it is an urgent correspondence with me. You will then depart... and never speak of this again. Am I understood?"

A meek smile. "Of course, sir... as instructed." The courier then pocketed the gold purse as if it'd be taken from him at any moment, and withdrew from the desk without a word – only offering the customary bow of the head given to generals and officers. "Hail Casantri, sir."

Hail Casantri, Broska sighed.

Disappearing behind, the door fell closed and the courier's footsteps retreated. Broska was left to mull in the silence again, with an ache in his heart and trepidation invading his every thought.

"Hope you don't talk to everyone like that. So... *imperative.*"

"Only when I have to," Broska mused, turning to face her.

Hidden away in a darker corner of the chamber where the torchlight didn't reach, the silhouette of a figure emerged clad in black leather. Her motions were silent, composed, like a dancer at the king's court, the thin leather bindings across her feet gliding softly over the stone-slab floors. Two large knives sat at her hips, strapped in their sheaths with wool lining to reduce clatter. The leather seemed to curl across her body in one great seething measure, no buckles or fastens to speak of. Perhaps the only striking element of her presence was the shock of ginger hair that curled across her head in a great bloom, and the piercing red-grey pupils of her shallow, commanding eyes. Deception seemed to radiate off her, like the glow of the moon, an elegance overwhelmed by the temptation of lethality. She could break necks and break locks in equal measure – the only difference was how much you paid.

Unless you're me, of course.

"It's been too long, big brother…"

Family is family, after all.

"… how've things been in my absence?"

"Boring, passing to chaotic, passing to undignified, and now…" He scoffed. "I don't even think there is a word for it. I'm a man with a target on his head, for all the wrong reasons…"

"Welcome to the club," she muttered peevishly. "There isn't a street corner in the whole of Casantri without my name and price on it."

"Would that be your real name, or that pet-name you wear around like a medal of honour?"

She grinned. "Well '*Jinx*', of course. It'd be unprofessional otherwise."

Unprofessional. Broska rolled his eyes. She'd adopted the name Jinx from the papers, as some kind of amusing ploy that she revelled in. As much as he didn't want to admit, it was a fitting deception: when the city guilds had refused to buy insurance from theft because they saw it as 'low risk', they began to find things of value go missing in the night. They were left none the wiser, as the thief left no trace, and were sometimes revisited two or three times under the cover of darkness without being noticed. It'd earned her a wealth of reputation, and paid a high price in the bulging underbelly of Casantri. She left empty hands and bruised egos, everywhere she went.

And the only other thing it left in its wake, as Broska had found several times, was the headache it caused him not to have her strung up for it.

"You know you're the reason I like being stationed out of the capital, don't you?" Broska grumbled.

"My business doesn't cause you any irrefutable harm, does it? Doesn't haunt you in dreams, or anything like that," she teased.

"No, but it leaves me with a bastard headache and a lot on my plate. We don't exactly live similar lives, you know?"

"I steal from the rich for those who've been wronged… you keep

169

my trail cold and keep me out of prison."

"I don't raise a *finger* about you, Alva, and you know it." The use of her real name seemed to nullify her. "It's not my job to... if you choose this life, so be it, I won't rat you out and I won't stop you. But don't expect me to mislead my own people to save your skin. It's not my fault that you neglect the law constantly."

"Sometimes it needs that neglection, 'cause good people are given rotten deals in life."

"And that's the job of the courts... *not you.*"

"Then why have you called me here?"

Broska stopped himself, exhaling slowly and slumping in his chair. "Because these are desperate times... and I need your help."

A concerned look crossed her. "What's happened?"

"I..." He drew himself up – *here we go.* "Yesterday, we set out along the Tarrazi coast... hoping to recover the king's body after his untimely demise: myself, General Cavara and General Ferreus, along with two detachments of the army. We went to shore, searched awhile, and found the king's head and robe... one speared on a spike, the other buried in sand. I was told to remove the head and box it up for our return journey..." His pulse shifted. "When... I'd finished, and turned back, I saw General Cavara emerging from the woodland holding her side. She'd... she'd been stabbed by General Ferreus, who then proceeded to stand on her back until..." – bubble in his throat – "... until she bled out entirely." Jinx's eyes were watchful, conciliatory. "I was told not to speak of it, to anyone – that it came from orders from the top. But I knew it hadn't – it couldn't have. The Supreme Governor wouldn't have ordered it. And Ferreus *knows* that I know that, and he *knows* that I cared about Cavara..." He looked to his sister then, a glaze across his eyes. "I'm *scared,* Jinx. I'm scared for my *life.* For Eli, for my kids... I just, I don't know what to do. I don't know if my life is in danger, if I'm being watched. I just don't know." His breathing crackled like an open fire. "I don't *know...*"

Jinx crossed the space and embraced her brother tightly, his vast arms bundling around her like a thick blanket. They remained together some moments, Broska's tears reducing to a gentle drip, before she moved back and knelt at eye level.

"You always were a big bag of feathers, Arrenso," she said, smiling.

Broska spluttered a laugh. "It ain't always good in my line of work."

"Cavara would be proud." Broska's wandering eyes locked into place. "I've never met her, only seen her about the city... but she's got guile, and more'n that, she's got heart. Just like you. And against everything – even, perhaps, your better judgement to keep you alive – you just want the truth to be known. Not because you're a traitor to the cause... but because you know it's what Cavara deserves."

"She deserves it alright, more than anything. The truth and nothing else."

"Exactly." She grasped his hand. "So tell me... what do you need me to do to get that truth out there."

The truth. A calming thought, one that emboldened him suddenly, like the sun breaching the clouds of a storm. *We need to act, before this all gets swept away with the war.*

"Whatever we do, has to be kept between us at all costs. With martial law coming into force in the coming days, we can't take any chances."

"What does that limit?"

"Limits our one main avenue of getting the story out."

"The papers?"

"They'll all be censored, no stone unturned. If they see so much as an inkling of conspiracy in there, they'll shut the papers down altogether, and start torturing people for names. I don't want that on my conscience, nor my desk."

"So what does that leave us with?"

"There's only one option really... and it's a serious risk to everything if we do."

"I thrive off risk," she mused, "so, go ahead."

He pinched the bridge of his nose. "There'll be a note somewhere, with Ferreus. I doubt he's thrown it out, he's far too headstrong for that. He's probably keeping it on his person until all this blows over. In it, will detail the exact orders he was given to kill Cavara. It may be signed or blank – if it's blank, I have hand-written orders from several high-ranking generals in my personal files. Once we have the note, we can cross-reference the two and find a match of the handwriting – that'll give us the one who devised all this."

"And I'll be the one to retrieve said letter?"

He sighed at length, battling a great pain in his chest. "I don't want to put you in unnecessary danger... but I don't have any other choice..."

"Arrenso," she interjected with a smile. "A yes or no will do."

"Please," he muttered quietly. "I have no other choice."

"Then I'll see it done tomorrow night, and report back with what I find... you have my word."

He nodded once, slowly. "Thank you."

"And what will you do in the meantime?"

Broska exhaled noisily. "Keep my head down, carry on as normal – watch my back, most of all. Don't know who's listening in."

"A good idea." Jinx replied, standing. "And from my line of work, I can tell you one thing." Her voice drew to a whisper. "*Someone will always be listening, and someone will always be one step ahead...*"

†

Chapter 20

When the Storm Shall Come

Under the pale shadow of the moon, the vast floodplains of Tarraz stretched out endlessly before them, meandered by old riverbeds and the swelling depressions of marshland as far as the eye could see. Hills rose elegantly in the horizon, and far off to the west, but from where they had made camp down to the very edge of the Icebreaker Sea, the world was entirely flat, like the tabletop of the gods gathering for banquet. Revek inhaled deeply, absorbing the cold night air, and unscrewed the cap from the bottle in his satchel.

Our triumphs have just begun. Sat at the outskirts of the camp looking north, he glanced behind to see the faint glow of torches along the near-horizon at his back, steep plumes of smoke rising from the gatehouse and its surrounding battlements. The secondary ranks of the army had moved in not long after they'd broken through, sealing the border wall with their own defences and sweeping slowly outwards to attack more outposts east and west. Reports had trickled in throughout the day, and the overall result seemed promising: beyond the main gate, Tarrazi forces had been thread-bare, with long stretches of wall unoccupied and quickly overrun. The secondary ranks had made several inroads north from there, setting up staging posts deeper into the enemy terrain, preparing for another forward assault once the commander's own contingent had gained a foothold past the marshlands.

The machinery of war cranks on. The battle that day had been decisive. Losses on the main assault had been eye-watering, but Revek paid no pittance as the blackcoat bodies continued to rise. He'd said it before: the soldiers knew what they were getting into from the start. Victory came at a significant cost, a cost accounted for by the willing service of honourable men and women of rank and file. So long as victory came, and the enemy dead outweighed their own, each battle was marked by success and nothing more. Good people died every day – *may as well die putting yourself to good use.* Charging with the cavalry, marching the gang-ways, breaching the wall; all heroics for the good of the nation. As he had been there, securing watchtowers, destroying artillery, storming the gatehouse...

The pale man.

Abruptly, the world stopped. His stomach knotted at the thought: the marble eyes and the cold grin and the dark-steel sword slicing through his own. Some conjuring of the dark, that with a blink of the eye then disappeared before him as if it'd never been there at all. Leaving him with nothing but the memory, and the warning it spoke of, and the name tainted with the ghost of an enemy from stories of old.

The Iron Queen lives...

Footsteps trailing up behind drew him away from his musings, as Revek swilled the small bottle of rum in his hand and took another swig. A figure thumped to the ground beside him, and the commander looked across to see General Darius perched on the spot, quizzically silent and unphased.

"You don't mind if I sit here, sir?" he asked politely. "I mean no disrespect, if you were wanting to be alone..."

"I won't have you marshalled for it, general," Revek mocked.

"You have my thanks, then." Darius raised a hand out to the skyline ahead. "Although I will say... that's a mighty big cloud coming our way sir. Reckon we'll be in the throes of a storm sometime tomorrow."

The commander spied the rumbling black mass stretching off to the north and nodded in agreement. "Reckon you're right there, general."

"Apparently it's nothing like the storms we get in Provenci..."

"How so?"

"According to stories, they get storms here that put everything but the road underwater at the worst of times. Drags on for hours, they say, sometimes dawn 'til dusk. Anything not on stable ground or rooted deep gets swept out to sea when it's over, lost to the waves, never to be seen again." He scoffed. "Then there are the things that *come out* when the storm begins..."

Revek lowered his drink. "What kind of *things?*"

Darius seemed to seize up. "Well they're only stories, sir... nothing to take serious, really..."

"All the same, speak your mind, general. You've got my attention now." *And a touch of concern with it.*

"Stories say there are things out there, sir, lying in wait in the marshes. Big things with teeth and claws – big as galleons, they say. Can swallow a horse whole, in the blink of an eye. When we were in charge around here, messengers used to say about 'em, these creatures of the march. Used to frighten the shit outta them, every time they came out into the lowlands like this... where some never returned." He chuckled, taking another swig. "I think it's all just spinning a lie myself, so that they could get better pay for their efforts. They're bastards for it, the messengers... always have been."

Revek just nodded, eyes crossing the fire-lit threshold of the camp's edge out onto the floodplains beyond, and imagined huge serpent-like shapes waiting out there in the dark. Lunging onto the roads, gaping jaws ripping through horse and rider alike, before retracting silently back into its watery lair, awaiting the next hapless fool to come along. Hearing the merry-makings of his army, sprawled across the grass behind – wondering, in that absent part of his mind, whether any of them would be next.

"But that's frightful talk, sir – hardly the stuff of campfire stories,"

175

Darius blustered on. "Tell you what is though: our heroics today. How about it!"

The commander couldn't help but smile. "You're right there, general – we certainly earned our keep."

"Charging the cavalry, scooping you up onto the horse after cutting down enemy after enemy, breaching that gatehouse and taking the lot by force." He nodded whimsically. "Reminds me of the old days." Then a laugh. "Guess that kinda shows just how old I am."

"How far back are we talking?"

"With all due respect, sir... you probably weren't even born."

"And I look a damn-sight better for it."

Darius erupted with laughter. "I must say you are right there..."

Revek waved his small bottle and took another swig. "So, tell me... were you around during The Collapse?"

"Oh aye, sir, I was... just a fresh junior officer back then, though, I will say. I'm not quite that old."

The Collapse. Two and a half decades prior, when Tarraz and Provenci had gone to war as the two great kingdoms of the Icebreaker Sea, settling bitter old disputes in a vast conflict of tainted blood and sharpened steel. Ten months of bitter struggle and profound losses, pushing the Tarrazi back all the way to their capital in the far north, within the valley of the great peaks known as the Mountains of Sorrow. A final battle, marked by a ten-day siege and the slow ascent to the palace summit, where the now-dead king finally faced the Tarrazi leader, and cast her into the abyss to meet her doom. A pale woman with a crown of thorns, marked in legend by only her name.

"The Iron Queen," Revek muttered aloud.

"Now that's a name from a cursed time sir," Darius said, overhearing. "One I certainly remember all too well."

"Did you ever see her?"

"Not with my own eyes, no... but I was on the same battlefield as her once." His words drew cold. "The stories I heard, sir... the Night of Bleeding Skulls, the Fall of the Sixth... those were enough to make me sick to my stomach, even from afar. Never once laid eyes on her, probably never even came close... but you could feel her, feel that terrifying presence everywhere she went. Even from the outskirts of the battle, doing recon as I was... every shadow made you second guess. There was no escaping it... not even sleep let us be free of the stories we heard, or the cold we felt each night waiting for her to come." His face became sober, reflective, conjuring that which had been long buried back to the surface – perhaps wishing it could stay buried, for fear of what else could return. "There are few things I believe for definite in this world, sir... but the idea that some people are just plain evil, was from that day forward one of them."

Revek swallowed at length, the rum swirling violently in his stomach.

"But we don't need to worry about that, sir," Darius exclaimed. "She's been dead for near twenty-five years, and the Tarrazi have been in a state of chaos ever since. We'll reassert control of the country, wipe the dissidents aside, and it'll all go back to normal, I'd say. We don't need to worry about her anymore."

The general stood, toasted to the clear night air, and gave his blessings as he disappeared back into the throng of the main camp, a thoughtful and dutiful pace to each stride.

Revek remained seated, bottle hanging loosely in one hand, gazing off into the dark of the floodplains beyond. That he had nothing to worry about, he knew – that the Iron Queen was dead, of course. Yet wondering, above all that, whether the shadows that awaited him in the night were the beasts of the marsh as Darius had said, or whether they were shadows of his own mind, lost in the void of a frightening reality, waiting for the day he saw the pale man again.

Knowing what he said was true.

†

Chapter 21

The Dripping Tap

The rain had come around midnight, lashing at the windows of the palace chamber like a hail of arrows on the battlefield. The moon vanished in the sky above, the last watchful eye of the night, while the denizens of the dark wormed their way down through the narrow city streets below. It was a time of great conjecture, as shadows danced about where the light could not reach, and the endless silent corridors of the palace hid away all manner of betrayal and villainy. Most of the world lay silent and resting, in some unconscious fantasy or other, oblivious to the treachery the night could bring.

But Alvarez knew. Alvarez had known from the beginning.

Things are going on that I know nothing about. He took a long gulp of his drink. *There are enemies, enemies of the new order… they are among us, against us always.* Another gulp. *And they think I don't know.* Another. *They think I'll never know, until it's too late.* Another—

"Traitors!"

He threw the cup of dark wine across the bed-chamber and stumbled over to his grand posted bed, collapsing onto his back and wheezing slowly. Air swelled into his chest; the ceiling spun. The sleeves of his loose cotton shirt seemed to rotate around his wrists like the wheels of an old cart. He found himself smiling at that, flickering through a false reality of numbness and intrigue. That jaunting, ruinous fear of an enemy within, slowly slipping away as the ethanol took hold.

The world spun all about him, and all Alvarez could do, was laugh.

They can't betray me. He raised a huge hand, smirking at the gold rings stacked on each appendage, and tapped each finger against his thumb with muddling slowness. As if his hand was detached, the sensation never received. He was just moving digits he felt nothing of.

That made him laugh even more.

I'm Supreme Governor, after all. He tried wiggling his toes, and found the same dislocated numbness as his hands were. One of his night-shoes slid off and pattered against the stone beneath, a rush of cold air suddenly revitalising one foot.

That made him laugh too.

Not even the Mother can dare forsake me! His cheeks began to ache, as the laugh reached its crescendo. His head rolled back, in a haze of bliss, and gazed skyward at the shadowy ceiling high above——

That's when the laughter stopped.

There was a face, or what he thought was a face, directly above his own. A woman's face, all angles and broken stone, but the features were distorted, the smile too broad, the eyes too narrow, with a nose like a beak. It stared down, unmoving, the only central point in an otherwise swirling mass of stone.

Alvarez clutched the bedsheets beneath him. "What... who... what are you... why..."

As he spoke, the face cracked slowly, the smile forming with pointed teeth and a covetous grin splitting the edges of the stone. It remained unmoved otherwise, exquisite as it was terrifying, with singular interest held on the drunkard in his bed – the fool who thought he was god.

"No... no, I don't want this..."

His gaze shifted, and Alvarez studied the room before him, bathed in a cold light like that in the Mother's Chamber. Wherever he found shadows, he found the same faces watching him, over and over, glinting across the walls, that maniacal grin holding him in its grip. Hundreds of them, watching silently over this god-pretender.

"No, no," he blustered, stumbling to his feet again, swaying as he stood there accusing the dark. His heart thundered in his chest, lungs straining for air. The spinning chaos broke loose all around him. "This is all a ruse, a *lie*. Some twisted dream. You cannot make a fool of *me*. You cannot make a fool of *me!*" His voice had risen to a gravelly bellow, shaking the walls at their seams. "This is a fool's game – this is all *lies*. I fear nothing, nothing of any of *you*. *I* am in charge here... *not you*." Wild-eyed, shouting at the walls, the ethanol contorting in his stomach. "You're all traitors! Beggars, wanting my *head*." Spittle flew from his mouth as he shuffled forward, finger speared in the air. "I'll show *you*. I'll rip every fucking head off, you hear me! No one shall defy me!"

The words echoed into the beyond; the faces submerged with the gloom. They rang out for a long time, ricocheting off walls and back to his own ears, and sobriety returned to him then, one of distrust and brokenness. That the faces had gone, and the silence reigned free – and perhaps it had all been just a bad dream.

A droplet of water splashed across the back of his hand, the first sensation that had breached the wall of numbness around him. It was sudden, shocking. A sign of life, beyond the lie. He gazed up to the ceiling, as if following the path of the droplet, and found the world close in as he did.

There were faces there, hundreds of them, in one massive vortex of pulsing veins morphing across the ceiling above. His eyes drifted, his heart sinking deeper and deeper into the floor. Longing to escape, intoxicating, waiting... until his gaze singled out the face at the very middle, its near-perfect definitions taken from memory. The face of a woman, wide-eyed and grinning sharply. A woman from the time of once-forgotten.

A heartbeat passed, and the sky fell, and he was eclipsed by the faces of the devil – a woman whom he had long thought was dead.

†

Chapter 22

A Dance of Thieves

Theres's nothin' here," she mused, although she didn't really know where *here* was. Beyond the thin trails of smoke still rising from the border wall at their backs, and the plumes of dust channelling into the skies to their right as the Imperial Army marched deeper inland, the world was a barren nothingness. For miles upon miles in every direction, from the distant coast of the Icebreaker Sea in the east, right across to the rolling hills and barren peaks of the west, the landscape was still and absolved, as if painted into place and left to dry. The ground was parched and broken, dirt tracks meandering through the yellow grass where rivers once were. Tiny clusters of skeletal trees occasionally broke the unending expanse, some dismal purgatory of life addled with the smell of decay. The rolling hills to their left, woven with rocky cracks and the delicate trickle of freshwater springs, painted much the same picture. Only the rustle of grasses at their feet, the tiny fractious movements they made, animated the world. Beyond that, it was not unreasonable to think they were on the long road to hell.

"A wasteland," Markus added at her side. "The only thing this place knows is rot and decay."

And they'd felt it, too. That aura of suffering the place seemed to carry with it like a disease. Laying to sleep several hours before in an alcove of dead trees, hearing whispers deep within the cracks of the

181

earth. Waking suddenly with a surge of adrenaline, flinching shadows moving nonsensically all around. The pitter-patter of footsteps scurrying past like rats, only to find no one there – no company, but each other, and the indeterminate sleeplessness that haunted them in the dark. Even then, in the early sunrise hours, she could feel the shadows at the edges of her vision, skipping across the landscape around her like a spirit. Watching, waiting for night to descend again, plaguing her like an ancient curse, one the land around her carried as its burden.

The savage land and all its cruelties.

"Where do we go from here?" Markus inquired, the shadows under his eyes trying not to show. "It's all so barren."

"North-west, into the Kazbak Hills," she affirmed, pointing a weary hand off to her left. "Spoke to a couple of travellers back in the village, they said there's a route in the far west along the mountain ridge known as the Nomad's Path. Used to be frequented by ancient tribes a few centuries back, but now it's mostly abandoned. I doubt the savages will bother patrolling that stretch as much."

"Are we certain the path is still accessible? I mean, it could've been abandoned for a reason—"

"We'll take our chances," Savanta growled, all bitterness and resentment. *If only you'd shut up for once.* What had initially been admiration and comradeship – that he had demanded to come with her through the rungs of hell and beyond – now seemed to descend into a disdain at how much he *interfered* with things. Asking too many questions, debating her decisions, enforcing morality in a world that neither had it nor wanted it. Purposeless, lacklustre. A waste of her time and determination. Several times she'd toyed with the idea of just telling him to go home, back to a life now devoid of everything it'd once been. Out of her hair, out of her business. So she was free to walk the path of revenge as she pleased. No questions, only motion.

Several times, she'd toyed with going even further than that...

"What's that on the hill over there?"

Savanta drew herself back to reality, and followed Markus's extended finger up onto the Kazbaks to their left. Rising from over the brow of one slope, she spied a thin wisp of smoke curling its way skyward.

Signs of the enemy, no doubt.

"A camp, perhaps," she exclaimed, "or some small settlement. Best we stay well clear of it – don't want any of the locals raising alarms." She started moving off towards the next cluster of dead trees, but looked behind to find Markus fastened to his spot like a ship's anchor. A rustle of anger rolled through her mind. "You comin'?"

"What about supplies?" he muttered slowly. "You said it yourself: we'll be out of food and fresh water in the next few days. Maybe we should investigate what's up there… see if we can *borrow* anything."

"And risk being caught?" she grumbled. "We haven't gone far enough to risk an intervention with those savages yet… if they throw up the alarm, we're fucked." She sighed through her teeth. "I won't risk it. That ain't what we're here for."

"It may be the best chance we've got. If those hills are as barren as they seem, we won't be able to resupply for days. We'll starve before we get halfway…"

"We'll be dead in the next few hours if we get anywhere near whatever's over that hill," she interjected. Heat rose in her face. "Don't go chasin' this, it ain't worth it…"

"Please, Sav, think about this." The desperation in mentioning her name caught her off-guard. "Look we… we don't even have to go in and snoop around. If you don't think it's safe, that's fine, that's your judgement… but we should at least have a look, see what's going on over there, just to be sure."

A rattle of dialogue syphoned through her mind, anger and frustration and not a lot else besides. It almost overwhelmed her, swelling within like a balloon. In her throat, in her eyes: a gentle rush of adrenaline breaking through, breaching… until she caught

183

Markus's gaze – that caring, concerned expression he always gave in desperate times – and the chatter grew cold again.

And she knew, right there: *he only wants what's best.*

"You're right," she admitted. "We should... at least go and have a look. As you said, maybe it will prove useful to us."

"Thank you." Markus smiled gratefully with a slight nod of the head. "Now please... lead the way."

"It's called a Kan'vaz," Savanta explained, studying the sprawling settlement before them through the lens of a spyglass. "A semi-permanent village formed at the base of several hills, designed to remain hidden from an incoming enemy. All the tents are formed in circular rows, with the lowest ranks of the tribe at the edge, and the elders living in the largest canopy at the centre." She gestured to the features slowly, Markus nodding at her side. "They use coloured dyes to indicate their unique 'gift' to the tribe... so, the wisp of smoke from that green-marked tent there, y'see, would belong to the tribal cook." A long pause; some adjustments of the lens. "From what I can see from here... there's a small market front along the western bank, just in front of that longer storage tent. A lot of activity there..."

"Reckon that's our target?" Markus inquired.

She retracted the spyglass and gave a nod. "I would reckon so."

"Impressive, that." He adjusted his chest plate. "Although... how come you know so much about all this? You don't strike me as someone who'd know a lot about Tarrazi culture."

Savanta blinked; her answer came strenuously. "My father... was a regional governor in the north for a while, acting on behalf of the king. He used to be in charge of several of these little villages... used to come home for the winter months and tell me these wild stories about rituals and meetings, or he'd bring me home some trinket they made him as an honoured guest." Savanta felt herself mellow at the thought. "It was a long time ago... near two decades in fact... but I still remember the days he'd come home with tall tales of far-off lands. It'd be the thing I looked forward to most in life." *And part of me misses it... every day since.*

"He sounds like an admirable man," Markus concluded.

"He was."

"Must've retired with some healthy pockets, with that kind of service to king and country... got what he rightfully deserved."

"Yeah," she said, although the words came like a knife to the heart, a coldness rising within. "He got... what he *deserved.*"

Markus sensed the change in her, and diverted back to the task at hand. "Anyway, how um... how do you think we should go about this? I mean, you know this more than me, so you should lead."

"Only one of us goes in," she said flatly, "and it'll be me."

"Sav, I don't know that that's——"

"You're wearing too much armour; it will make too much noise. It'll be easier if I go in and take what I can, and you watch from afar in case the camp is alerted." *And if the worst comes to worst, I know you won't have the guts to draw knives* – but she left that unsaid. Instead, she detached the scabbard from her side and handed it to him. "Keep it close."

"Yes ma'am."

And if you lose it, it won't be the savages you'll have to worry about.

But she left that unsaid too.

Skating the outer western edge of the hill, she navigated down a small crag where a river trickled delicately at her feet and into the bowl of the Kan'vaz. Picking her moment, she slid down the tufted grass towards the sprawling tent at its base, and stopped just short with a skid of her thin overshoes. Wielding a small knife, Savanta cut a narrow slit in the storage-tent's cloth exterior, and passed into the smoke-scented expanse therein without a whisper.

Perfect.

Inside, she looked up to a high-rung ceiling adorned with dyed rings of cloth, producing a ferocious smell of ash and burning that stung her eyes. Around her were dozens of sacks nearly as large as she was, forming their own corridors with their enormity, all bound tightly with rope and heavily laden with unknown contents. The room seemed to spiral slowly, the air viscous with aromas of spice and fire, crackling in her lungs like a hearth's ember. Passing from the dismal essence of decay outside, to the overwhelming dysphoria of where she was now, Savanta struggled to decide which she hated more. She stifled a cough, spitting into the dry earth at her feet.

Rotten people, she cooed with chagrin. *Rotten nation.*

Keeping low to the ground, she peered around the stacked bags on her right to assess the space beyond. The central entranceway hung loosely open, a spirited cacophony of voices emanating from the market-front outside. Further along the tent, she pulled back suddenly at the sight of two young boys, no older than thirteen winters, as they sat and fiddled with small charms on their wrists. Storage handlers, she assumed, called upon by the vendors out front when they needed a resupply. *Another problem I need to avoid,* came the apparent concern.

Turning her attention back to the bags at her side and the task at hand, she rounded her knife to slit one open and reached deep within. At first repulsed, what she grabbed was round and covered in small depressions, and as she pulled it through the opening it was revealed to be a small potato dusted with mud. An ugly thing, far from appetising in its current state, but she knew well enough that it would last them the journey ahead.

Savanta stuffed ten in her bag, and promptly moved on to the next.

Hoping for more results, she found only dull irritation as the subsequent few sacks produced little more than a minor spillage of grain. Had she a mill and several days of labour, there was enough grain there to run a small bakery. *As it is, however... utterly useless.* She twitched the blade in her hand.

Need to find something better.

Peering around the edge of the bags, cautiously watching the two handlers at the far end – still distracted by the odd charms dangling from their wrists – she peeled a stone from the ground underfoot and pelted it into the boxes just behind them. The pang produced across the wood rattled in their ears – their heads twisted sharply.

Savanta crossed to the next row and slipped out of sight.

We need more. Knife clasped like a sadist, she cut down through the next sack and grinned devilishly. *And my prayers are heard.* Dipping a hand inside, she smelt the salty-succulent scent of dried meat before it emerged, thin strips of it bundled in her hand like a wheatsheaf. With incessant greed she started bundling handfuls of it into her shoulder bag, piling more and more in, only stopping when the stack of sacks overhead teetered slowly, their foundation significantly lessened.

Markus'll be overjoyed with this.

She passed to the next one, and the next after that, and found more of the same therein, delighting at the sweet smell they produced. She shifted to the next one, knife primed, and cut another opening in the old cloth—

And the salty scent of dried meat was mutinied, by the sudden and acutely foul stench of rotting flesh.

What the hell?

Tilting her head away, she slit the base of the bag open, gagging at the perverse aroma consuming her senses. Eyes watering, she wiped them with the back of her hand, and looked down at whatever contents had spilt from the bag like an open wound.

And what she found there, were human ears.

Savanta reeled backwards, studying the bloodied lobes of hundreds of ears spilling from the sack-like offal. Suddenly the heavy intoxication around her became suffocating, the air thick and leathery in her throat, bubbling and rupturing. Her eyes glazed, skull pounding, the volatile rise of sickness surging in her stomach. It was all too much, all of a sudden, like passing the drop off into a deep water abyss. Sinking, the weight of everything bearing down all around, skin sticking, a coldness welling inside. Welling up slowly, like...

Eyes blinking heavily, swaying through consciousness, she found an envelope in the crook of her hand – the same one she had found at her doorway, just eleven winters old. The crumpled edges and stained sides, and the peculiar shade of red soaking one corner. She remembered being curious as to what it was – she regretted that now...

Peeling it open, she removed a letter inside meant for the governor, but bearing the seal of some savage land with an address to her home. Turning the envelope, so young and bitterly naïve, she tapped whatever else remained inside into the palm of the other hand...

And out fell a single ear, matted and pale, with two gold rings pierced along the lobe. It was a quiet moment, studying that cold thing there in her palm. All numbness, the world silent and motionless around her. Her mind prying away for answers. *An ear with gold rings, an ear with gold rings...*

Father used to wear gold rings too.

The vision collapsed around her. Savanta hurled herself back to reality, clenching her fists so tightly that blood seeped from the ends of her nails. She lurched about, grappling with the world as if it were an attacker, the bag heavy and purposeful across her shoulder. Looking to the sacks before her, the slits in their sides—

The small boy staring bewildered at her, just before the end.

Fragile eternities passed as they locked eyes, a swell of emotions holding them in place with a tension that could cut steel. Savanta watched with fear and anger as the boy's gaze drifted slowly to the tent beyond, preparing his escape.

What followed came in slow motion.

Leg twisted, arms spun. The boy's mouth began to open, words manifesting on the tongue. Savanta was on her feet already, lunging forward. Grappling the child across the mouth, stifling his cries. Curling the blade up, lancing forward like a spring. Plunging it deep into the boy's back, through the spine, piercing the fragile pieces therein. Legs crumbling, arms breaking the fall. Retracting the knife.

The body collapsed before her.

She dragged the boy back behind the sacks, never locking eyes, blood gurgling at his throat as his insides bled themselves dry. She looked down on him, at the red that splashed across his body and lined his teeth like syrup — pitiless, vengeful, malevolent. Tears welled across her face, seizing at the debauchery of it all.

This is the enemy, the voice of her mind explained. *Whether the enemy now or not, this will become your enemy. It knows nothing but hate for you, and wants nothing but your destruction. It is a savage, and an enemy, and that is what you have killed.* Air rasped heavily through her nostrils. *One day it will grow to be a man; one day it may rule a tribe. One day it may come into contact with a man from another land, offering his services for the people's good. One day it may accept these terms... the other, it may not.* Funnelling anger rose within her, the knife decisively balanced in one hand. *They don't care who this man from another land is, nor what he holds dearest to him back home. They do not care, because they are savages... they will make a ritual of him, just as anyone else. There are no exceptions.*

She raised the knife again.

Not even your father.

She drove it through the boy's skull.

The voice stopped. The lights faded to white and beige. The warm aromas of the world around her phased back into being. The cool blood bubbled over her fingertips, from the wound she'd punctured in the now-dead child's skull. A thousand sins weighed heavy over her back — realisation came, agonised and bloody.

She left with only silence to show for it.

†

Chapter 23

The City of the Sun

Mumma used to tell me stories about people like you: people who came back from the dead. She says you've been kissed by the All-Mother. You've seen the light of the other side. I want to be kissed by the All-Mother, but mumma says not everyone is so lucky. Mumma says: the All-Mother only kisses those she loves. She does not like me, I know. She is picky. But she has seen you, and she has kissed you, and now you are alive again, even when you have died." Evelyn stopped rolling the tiny hook in his hands and gazed up to her. "Have you ever seen the All-Mother?"

Cavara smiled delicately. "I don't know that anyone has ever seen her. I don't think they're allowed to."

"Why not?"

"Because the Mothers are here to guide us, but they can't guide everyone: only the important ones. Only they can speak to them, and see them sometimes too."

"What do they talk about?"

She breathed deeply. "I don't really know... destiny, maybe, or the future. How to keep peace and make people happy." She paused. "They want to guide the good people to do the right thing – that much I know for certain."

"Does that make you a good person... because the All-Mother

kissed you?"

She laughed. "You know what? Just maybe... maybe you're right."

"But you aren't a leader."

"That is true."

Evelyn considered. "Or... maybe you aren't one yet."

The little boy turned away and began searching through the bags for more hooks to play with, leaving Cavara with his final words, staring out into the vastness of the Icebreaker Sea. Somewhere out there, in the distant expanse of unbroken clouds, the All-Mother was said to take refuge on an island of marble stone, where emeralds bled from the rocks and stars fell from the sky when they left this world for the next. A solitary point striking from the deep waters below, unseen by any traveller of the known world. A legend, a tale of hope told to children at night: that their world was protected by a deity of such immense power and benevolence, that she could sprout new life from the ground just with a touch of her hand, and could kiss the cheek of a dying saint so that they may live again. A being that communicated through her Mothers, guiding great leaders in peace and war, in the hope of sustaining the world for generations to come.

So the story goes, that is. Of course, nothing had ever been proven – the stories were bold and fantastical, but evidenced by nothing. Cavara had lived her entire life doubtless that the All-Mother was anything other than a dream of the travellers of old. A legend, nothing more.

And yet...

"You'll have to excuse him," the elder woman called from her side, coming to sit next to her. "He hasn't worked out yet that not everything his ma told him is an undisputed fact. He likes to... *indulge* in the *extraordinary* sometimes."

"He's a bright spark."

She nodded. "Don't get too caught up with his nonsense, mind."

"Yeah..." Cavara replied, disheartened. *Nonsense.*

"He's a delightful boy, all the same, is Evelyn... an excellent first-mate out at sea. He can cast lines, repair holes, tie ropes – all the skills of a reputable trade."

"He seems fascinated by the hooks."

"He loves to fish... something his father taught him to do when he was very young, I assume. Makes a fine marksman with the line, I tell you."

"What happened, to his father?" she inquired suddenly, but after exchanging a dishonest glance, Cavara swallowed her words. "Oh, I um... I didn't mean... I'm sorry if that's not—"

"My dear, don't fret," she replied, smiling so the wrinkled lines of her face creased like tilled soil. "It's fine to ask these questions, I don't take offence. In fairness, I don't know what happened to his father, or his mother. You rarely deal with that stuff in these kind of arrangements."

Cavara frowned. "So, you're not..."

"He is like a son to me, but no." She sighed shallowly. "I adopted him a couple of years ago, after my... after my own boys died. They were miners, hardworking boys to the end. Iron miners, burying deep into the mountains. One day, they went down and the cave collapsed... and they never came back. I grieved, marked by a black dog for months... everything I'd worked so hard for stripped away." Her face hardened. "But in my country, it's considered most honourable to adopt a child without a family of their own. Many parents are conscripted among my people, and die out in the field... the children are told the news, and sent to Education Districts, living in barracks like soldiers. So to adopt, well... it's to show you're giving something back to your people, after they have lost so much in life." A quiet smile. "And it was there I found Evelyn, the single greatest joy of my life... and I've never parted ways with him since."

Cavara nodded slowly, smiling, placing a hand on the woman's own. "You have my respect... you're a remarkable woman."

The elder woman squeezed her hand. "Thank you, miss...?"

"Cavara," came the muted reply. "Formerly *general* Cavara, of the 9th Legion of the Provenci Imperial Army."

"Well, former-general Cavara... it's a pleasure to meet you

properly." The woman stood, grappling the central mast of their small vessel. "As for me, my name is Azura... former teacher, now tradeswoman at sea."

Azura stood and crossed to the ship's bow, saltwater glazing her face as the boat skimmed smoothly across the waves. Watching, Cavara saw a woman totally in her element, at one with the natural balance — *or lack thereof* — in the world around her. A woman who had lived and breathed the breadth of the great sea beyond, as if she had been borne from its deepest trenches and grown on its wildest shores. A woman and a boy, not entirely her own, but with that same delicate bond that all mothers bear to their children. Unbreaking and resolute; defiant and studious — everything Cavara had always found herself aspiring to be.

And here it is before me... a woman of my own image.

"I'm surprised," Azura turned to speak to her, "you haven't asked any more questions about our destination. Do you know much about Sevica?"

"Only from stories," she replied, voice powering over the wind. "And I don't tend to take those as gospel."

"Then you're wiser than most." She laughed. "Everyone hears about Sevica and its "military rule" and screams tyrant... but that doesn't quite paint a fair picture."

"You're saying it's *not* like that?"

"You assume it is?"

Cavara screwed her nose up. "Call me ignorant, but I assumed there's only one way military rule goes."

"That isn't ignorance, dear general... it's *commonality*. Every great nation that falls at the hands of armed forces, faces the same descent into chaos. Soldiers line the streets, people are made to disappear... the world comes apart. We were there once, too, when the Alderbane and his officers seized power from the king... although I expect they told you he was murdered?"

She gave a slow nod of the head.

"Hm... of course they did." A long sigh. "Guess it's no wonder, really: had you all known the truth – that the king was overthrown and then sent to live in a quiet estate in the mountains for the remainder of his days – then you may have got... *ideas* about your own leadership. And your king couldn't have that, of course..."

Cavara considered. "It doesn't surprise me."

"What doesn't?"

"That we were lied to."

"It's the last dice roll of kings, my dear – they all lie, just in their own ways."

"Then what else is a lie?" she pressed. "What other falsehoods have been spun to keep people out of *ideas*?"

Azura clicked her tongue. "Probably a multitude of things: that we're run by a close circle of tyrants, all ceded power by the Alderbane in exchange for money and favours. That we live in squalor, servitude, a military state with soldiers at every street corner. A ban on press, public gatherings... a curfew to keep us in check. Paints quite an ugly picture, doesn't it?"

"It does."

"Almost *too* ugly."

Cavara thought back to the state Casantri was in when she departed – how she thought *that* was too ugly – but decided that was best left for another time. "And you're telling me it's all lies?"

"Of the highest order," Azura mused. "Once upon a time perhaps, but not now – once there may have been these... well, *draconian* ways of doing things. But that was a mere purge, when royalists used to rove the streets and governors tried to bargain their way back into power. It was chaos, a time with little other choice beyond the bloodshed that came... but, in the same breath, it was also a time that has since *passed*." A touch of pride crossed her eyes. "And now look at us. We have a local paper, and we have unions. We have a bustling nightlife and a thriving education programme. And when the 'old guard' of generals had been in power for a decade, they were asked to step aside by the Alderbane... and were replaced by elections, free and fair." A pause. "It's the beauty of history, really...

how the most unlikely things form reality before your very eyes."

"That's quite the story," Cavara admitted, the fate of her own people never straying far from her mind. "And what of the Alderbane?"

"He remains in power, and has the final say on many things... but there are lines he drew once before, and he sticks to them. All he asks is to remain in power, and that the people continue to prosper before him, and when he dies... that's it."

Cavara looked puzzled. "So, no succession?"

"When he dies, he will be the first and last of his kind, a revered figure of our great nation, for the sacrifice he gave. Any successor, he fears, may not be as sure-willed or responsible as he has been – he doesn't want to undo everything he's built." A pause. "So the leadership shall pass over to the Council of Seven, elected by us, until the time for change comes again. And until that day... *Long May He Reign.*"

No new leader. She felt almost sick. *No succession, no ceremony, no ruler, no tributes.* A place where the citizen became the statesman by a vote of their own people. A new way of life for the commoner – some great experiment of power beyond her better understanding.

A wanton abandonment of all things civil, Savanta cooed. *A sure way to a bitter end, if you ask me.*

"And this is agreed?" the general exclaimed. "This... *lack* of leadership? I don't understand. Surely there's dissent, or distrust, or... *something?*"

Azura smiled. "There are a few, naturally, as with all things. But we're a people that know that our lives are in a constant state of flux... why should the laws that govern us all, be any different?"

What? Cavara scratched at her knotted hair and tried to make sense. To organise life on a whim, anticipating that a new order may rise one day that you know nothing about. For better, for worse, for hate or grandeur... *the great unknown of it all.* She recoiled, her mind clouded with doubt, trying to see sense in it and finding the barrel empty. Looking up to the eyes of Azura, that soft joy she possessed at the wonders of the world – Cavara pondering how much of that was the truth, and what was just a muddled vision of a proud people set on a course of destruction.

"We're getting close," Azura said suddenly, raising her hand to grace the billowing winds. "Shouldn't be long now."

"How will we know?"

The old woman grinned. "Trust me, my dear… you'll know."

As the fog parted before them, and the sun illuminated a new world stretching effortlessly beyond, Cavara watched as the horizon manifested into a grandiosity the likes of which she had never seen before.

A flux of shimmering aquamarine danced across the waves all around their boat, stretching ahead across the great length of sea where the fog could not reach, up to the distant shoreline of pale stone and white sand. A massive woodland lined its edges, sprawling across the horizon with infinite beauty, pocketed with tiny houses and fishing huts nestled amongst the trees. Shifting left, the land grew rockier and denser, the trees growing sporadically wherever there was purchase, riveting the land until the whole earth seemed to tilt skyward, as if some fallen god had left their blade buried there, spearing from the ground out across the vast waters below.

And at its peak, spilling down the mountain's edge like a rolling stretch of tapestry, was the place they called the City of the Sun.

It was vast, a massive conglomeration of wide-stacked houses and domed towers, speared with cenotaphs and monuments, scattered with wide-walled bathhouses and the great smoking columns of factory wood burners. There were causeways too, she saw, navigating down the edge of the cliffside, into more elaborate wooden structures pinned to the walls like an eagle's nest, likely entranceways to underground passages within the huge mountain itself. The same image continued for the entire length of the grand metropolis, from the vast palace complex at its peak right down to the double-layered walls at the valley base below. She could only see a very small section of it from their tiny vessel, but with every roll of the waves it seemed to grow exponentially before her – the all-encompassing majesty of Sevica's great capital.

"It's incredible..." she muttered, receiving a smile from Azura at the helm. "I imagined nothing like this."

"It's a sight that never gets old, I assure you," the elder woman replied.

"It certainly bears its name well..." Cavara squinted at the reflections of light glancing from the domed towers.

"Naturally... that's the thing when you have an abundant supply of bronze right beneath your feet. You treat it like flour: the building block of all things made."

And she was right: bronze was the apparent force at work within the bustling cityscape, blending with the beige stone of the buildings and the dull grey cliff-faces below. As the city descended, the stone became darker, the bronze more pronounced, the beige falling away to colours of cream and mottled yellow, bleeding into the sudden flush of green at its base as the trees conquered the landscape, backed by white-capped mountains and sun-glazed peaks. There was a romanticism to it, order and beauty harmonising the natural world. It was almost beyond belief. *To think man built this.*

"And that isn't even the masterpiece of it all," Azura sang. Cavara followed her direction, off towards the base of the spearing mountain where land met sea, and there on a great stone pedestal marching out into the waters, a colossal bronze statue stood pronouncing itself to the world.

Several thousand feet high, it depicted a huge man in flowing robes gazing out onto the Icebreaker Sea, hand outstretched as if to summon the wind and tide. Its other hand curved about a giant sphere carried across its shoulder, its surface depicting huge landmasses and swathes of ocean shimmering like the moon. It was a defiant edifice, glistening majestically in the waning sun, a treasure of an ancient time and the gatekeeper of the known world. Cavara found herself gazing at it in awe, with the little boy Evelyn at her side, smiling gleefully.

"That's the Globe-Walker," the boy said, almost vibrating on the spot with excitement. "Mumma said it was built in the ancient times when the city was born…"

"And it's stood there ever since," Azura added, bundling the boy in her arms. "Incredible, isn't it?"

"I've never seen anything like it," Cavara conceded.

"There isn't such a thing anywhere else in the known world – and here it is, at our doorstep."

"Who built it?"

Azura sighed through her smile. "Like many things in this great city… we have no record of its designer. It was marked in the palace archive by its materials, not the mastermind who put them to work. All we know was that it was a massive endeavour of remarkable skill… and that whoever constructed it, knew far more of the world beyond the Icebreaker Sea than we do now."

At the thought, Cavara looked off to the blanketed fog to her left, smothering the skyline and any opportunity to see the coastline beyond, and knew the intrigue that lay there. Somewhere in those undetermined stretches of water lay another world, beyond the swamplands of the northeast, that had piqued the resolution and chauvinism of travellers for decades gone. Not since ancient times had anyone gone beyond the known world's edge and survived – many believed the world simply ceased to exist beyond the fog, fell away into an abyss of shadow as a sacrifice to the gods. Whatever was out there, had remained a mystery for near a millennia.

And will likely remain that way, forever.

"But that's not for us to concern ourselves with… not yet at least," Azura continued, ruffling Evelyn's hair. "Our priority is to get to shore, and into the city before nightfall – dusk comes thick and fast out here." She paused. "Now, Cavara, this may come as a strange question… but have you ever been smuggled before?"

"Not personally," she replied, "but I know a thing or two. Why do you ask?"

"Because... because the Alderbane isn't entirely welcoming to newcomers... and his border officers at the capital would sniff you out from miles away if you walked up to the gates with us as normal. We wouldn't be able to talk our way around it if we tried."

"So how do I get in?"

"We... have an old cart in the dock, and enough goods to make a sale in the city. If you hide amongst our goods and we cover them with cloth blankets..."

"It won't work," Cavara interrupted. "If they're in any way good at their jobs, they'll make routine checks of any goods coming into the city. There's no way I'll just pass through without being searched."

Azura nodded slowly. "I see..."

"What about the hatch?" Evelyn spoke up between them.

"What hatch?"

"The loose board... on the bottom of the cart. If you remove it, you can slip into a little comp...*compartment*, below the cart. She could hide there."

"Would it be big enough?" Cavara asked.

"Just about," Azura replied. "It's where Evelyn here keeps his toys... I'm sure he wouldn't mind hiding them someplace else, just this once?"

The little boy looked up to Cavara and nodded his head enthusiastically, pleased that he'd saved the day.

"Then I'll do that," the general pronounced.

Azura ruffled Evelyn's hair. "Excellent."

"What do I do once we're in the city?"

"Stay quiet and stay low," the old woman warned, concern leeching into her voice. She gazed back for a moment to her homeland, the vast city reaching over the mountain, and sighed. "There will be eyes *everywhere*, my dear... just waiting for people like you to come by..."

They moored in the dock of a large stone house, and fixed the boat to an old pillar jutting from beneath the surface. Azura told them to wait, navigating up to the shoreline and entering the pale structure to inquire with whoever lived inside. All the while, the stretches of white sand around them remained still, the dull whimper of waves and the rustling of the great forest ahead animating a delicately serene world.

Azura appeared at the door again sometime later, followed by a man with a broad, uncompromising stature that more closely resembled a great bear than any human Cavara had ever met. He was huge and oddly terrifying, yet Evelyn seemed to ignite with joy at the sight of him, and rushed along the crooked dock to embrace the man's leg. The ox leaned down and patted the boy softly on the head – Azura gave Cavara the all-clear to follow them inside.

The man's name was Brutus, she learned: formerly a cleric of the Church of the Sun, since forced into exile after being wrongly charged for the murder of a senior bishop. Since then, he had lived in the old ruins of that house as a fisherman, selling to village markets when he made a decent haul. He was also a close aide of Azura – *whatever that means in this strange land* – and in exchange for his rights to fish in the waters, Brutus had offered to house her cart and horses while she was away. Apparently he was an honest man, a good man, trying to turn his life around, making amends and that – and Cavara knew as much, because it was all Evelyn seemed now to talk about.

"You're a good man now, aren't you, Brutus?" he chimed.

Brutus offered little more than a grunt in reply.

The horses were stored in a barn outside, the mangled roots of a massive oak tree acting as a new foundation across one side. Peering in, the horses were already at the front entrance, snorting and rapping their front hooves joyfully at the scent of their master's return. They were beautiful beasts, tall piebald mares with long manes and strong backs, in prime condition for pulling draught up and down steep mountains. Cavara had only ever seen the thin, spry horses used by the mounted cavalry in training exercises back home – these beasts, she found, were an entirely different affair.

"Quite remarkable, aren't they?" Azura acknowledged, running her fingers through one of their manes. "Raised them since they were foals... seems like a lifetime ago. Must say they are quite special to me, without a doubt."

"They're lovely," the general agreed, then paused to consider. "They were your boys' horses, weren't they?"

She put on a brave face. "Nothing gets past you, does it?"

"I just know the look of a grieving mother when I see one."

Azura bowed her head and sighed at length. "They were gifts, for the boys' rites of passage. It's customary, among our people, that boys receive on their eighteenth winter gifts of passage from their mother, to take them forward in their new lives. What better to give two strong-willed and strong-headed young men... than two equally formidable horses?" She stifled a laugh. "Seems silly now, to hold such sentimentality for them... but it just reminds me of time passing. That when the horses finally go on to another land, that'll be the last hold my boys have on this world, before they're gone forever. And that what was, then becomes just a memory."

Cavara bowed her head, a solemn acknowledgement, and caught the gaze of the old woman, eyelids streaked with a shiny glaze of tears. Within that moment, Cavara found a deep well inside her, as she longed to sympathise with something therein. It was not a look she held for anyone, not a weakness she knew how to show: she had no children, no closeness to anyone or anything. It was a foreign exchange, a message lost in translation. She didn't know of it, couldn't grasp it from memory. Not even her own mother...

No. She caught herself, caught the sensation before it broke. *Now is not the time.* Not that she believed there ever was a time. *It's in the past... it's gone.* The only closeness she'd ever had for another person... *the pain it'd caused.* Looking into Azura's gaze – into the eyes of a mother mourning her two boys – she felt the harsh realities of her own life simmer under the surface. Pain, guilt, grief, anger, sadness, despair. How that look had been for her once before.

The ruinous memory of a terrible woman.

"Have you ever had an animal in your care, like these ones?" Azura asked. "I'm not sure if it's as customary among your people as it is with mine."

"We had a hunting dog... used to let it roam the woods near my house killing deer," Cavara muttered. "Name was Muscov."

"A good dog?"

"For a time. He was loyal to a fault, and incredibly tame... although we had to have him put down after a few years."

"Oh that's terrible... how come?"

"He ripped my mother's hand off," she said coldly.

The old woman seemed astonished. "Goodness... was it bad?"

"Three fingers gone, another mangled to a stub. Knuckle was fractured to dust. She screamed a lot, my mother... wanted the whole thing to be cut off and done away with. In the end all she was left with was a club fist of shrapnel bones and the papers demanding Muscov was shot."

"Terrible thing to have happened... especially to a dog so good. I can't imagine the hound usually acted that way."

"No. As I said, he was loyal to a fault, but he was also trained as a scout dog. He knew how to comply with orders." A cruel smile appeared on the general's face. "We can only imagine someone must've ordered him to do it, for whatever reason."

"Your mother had many enemies?"

You could say that.

A knock from behind: Cavara turned and saw the ox-man Brutus pass into the room with them, to the snorting delight of the two horses.

"We are ready, ma'am," he thundered to the old woman.

"Thank you Brutus, we'll be with you shortly."

He bowed courteously to both of them, keeping his eyes low when addressing the newcomer, before disappearing back out the door.

"He doesn't speak much," Cavara acknowledged.

"Brutus is a quiet soul by nature," Azura explained warmly. "He only speaks when spoken to, or when necessary. I know very little about him beyond that – most of my knowledge comes through Evelyn."

"He speaks with the boy?"

"More often than anyone else alive, I'd wager."

"And what does Evelyn say?"

Azura rolled her tongue across her teeth. "That Brutus... *sees* things. *Knows* things, that other people don't. He's haunted by his past, but also by his future. That there's this... *voice,* this *thing,* in his head that speaks with him, tells him about the future, about his life. Again, neither Evelyn nor myself know very much about it – and the boy is more susceptible to these things than I am. I have my doubts, after all. I think he's just a troubled soul trying to do good in life." She paused mid-thought, and Cavara was about to prompt her again before she carried on. "Although... he told me something earlier, which was very out of character. When you arrived, and he saw you from the door."

"What did he say?"

"He said you had an aura about you, something that made the voice in his head speak more directly. It told him that you were important. He said that you saw *'her'*."

Heat rose in Cavara's face, heart fumbling to stay level. "Saw *who,* exactly?"

Azura caught her gaze again.

"The shadow woman."

†

Chapter 24

Screaming Thunder

Whatever gods the Imperial Army of Provenci had angered entering the rotten desolation of Tarraz, made their presence known when the skies grew suddenly steely overhead, and their path forward was drowned in the surging rains of a thunderstorm. For miles ahead, the skyline pulsed with light where it broke from the suffocation of the storm. The winding path they walked down crossed from the greys and yellows of dry earth into shades of mottled brown and glistening black – a path that had been a dustbowl moments ago, now suddenly overcome with the heavenly deluge that swelled puddles into lakes and rivers into landslides. It had all happened so fast; what had been borne a day of triumph now died the death of a convict. Revek gazed out to the ruminating, rain-sheened landscape before him, water spilling across his body as if passing under a waterfall, and wondered what kind of hell they had walked into.

"You were right, Darius," Revek muttered. "A storm is upon us."

"And certainly one to be reckoned with, at that, sir," the general exclaimed at his flank. "Never seen anything quite like this."

The commander spat into the wind. "Everything about this fucking place speaks of misery… even the weather cries murder."

"Savage people, savage land sir… is a truly morbid place."

Morbid doesn't even come close. He'd envisaged glory to come on sun-baked battlefields in pitched battle, howling into the wind on horseback with his sword singing, marching from city to city like the conquerors of old. The din of battle, the roar of the cavalry – he'd hoped the triumph at the border would press on into the beating heart of Tarraz, where he could drive his blade through it and proclaim the greatest victory his people had seen in a generation.

But what he got instead, was rain.

And with that, comes the logistical nightmare. Already, three of their artillery platforms had slid from the roadside and landed in deep mud, wrenched out by horses not designed for heavy labour, soldiers stood about impishly watching the beasts struggle. They'd already had to abandon one of the supply carts, capsized on a grass verge, the provisions therein finding a new home in the belly of a swamp. How he'd screamed at them for their incompetence; how they'd soldiered on dimwittedly into the next catastrophe not even a mile later. How his skin crawled, not only from the water droplets weeping down his back, but from the sheer *idiocy* of it all. The slow progress, the biting winds. The hurricane of water slicing across them every waking moment. The unforgiving nature of such a barbaric place, epitomised in the long line of disconsolate faces stretching along the road ahead.

"Barbaric," was all he could manage in reply.

"Aye sir," Darius said warmly. "It's no great thing to see men brought low by the evils of the enemy."

"Or the bastard weather their homeland brings."

"That is the truth of it. I do pity the soldiers for their sacrifice… it's hard work out here."

"I don't." The commander soured. "They signed up for this – they're doing their job, as are we. It's shit, and it's vicious, but there's nothing else to expect from it. As you said, we're in a savage land." He paused, sighing. "Least they could do is keep those damned supply carts on the road…"

"I suppose… although we have gone several miles without incident, sir, so perhaps things are looking up for us."

"Don't tempt fate, general. That's the sure-fire way to our

demise."

"Or maybe… the men have finally learned their lessons."

Revek scoffed. *That'll be the day.*

Turning to the front again, his horse suddenly dug its hooves in and drew to a halt. Revek lurched as if vomiting, and looked up to find the line had drawn to a halt again, with a messenger skirting along the edges towards him with some motley excuse to say. He was half a mind to strangle the runner when they arrived, just to get some redemption for all the chaos that was going on.

"Seems we have… a spot of bother," Darius admitted.

"You'll eat your words, general," he grumbled to the man at his flank. "You'll eat your *fucking* words—"

"Sir!" The messenger stalled at his side, catching her breath. "We've had an incident at the front. The soldiers won't continue."

Well someone give them a shove. "And why's that?"

There's a problem, sir – it requires your attention. Someone's… died."

"*Died?*" Revek scowled, turning to find Darius expressing equal confusion. "What do you mean, *died?*"

"It'd be better if you came to see yourself, sir." The lady stepped back, recoiling from his rage. "It's one of our scouts, sir. The forward division found him by the roadside. We would've left him, but… well…"

"Speak, woman!"

She gulped. "He's had his intestines torn open."

Revek had thought it some sort of exaggeration, when the messenger had explained it to him. That a man was found at the roadside dead with his entire chest ripped to pieces. It seemed too surreal for his liking, too much like lousy storytelling. Yet he recalled the words of Darius, describing just what kind of place they were in, and what type of enemy sat waiting in the dark. By its very state of being,

Tarraz was a place where nature knew no bounds – and where the despair it wrought, had no end. So when he finally saw the body, stretched across the grass bank to his left, Revek found that judgement was entirely true.

"What the *fuck* happened here..."

The body lay crooked along the verge, head partially submerged in a quagmire that had formed at the base. The arms were broken and the legs were mangled into awkward shapes, but it was the chest area that sent a vicious twinge of nausea up into his throat. It'd been flayed, the skin almost peeled off like a canvas, revealing a spluttering mass of organs inside that had been all but mutilated by whatever had done the killing. A few stray intestines hung loosely out the wound, still oozing a foul liquid into the dirt below, but beyond that, all that remained was an empty cavity of snapped ribs and pooling blood.

The commander's head snapped round to glare at the small gathering of soldiers at his side. "What *happened?*" he spat.

"We dunno, sir," one of their number replied mutely. "The scouts were patrolling the path ahead, and we were just marching and... came across the body."

"Any sign of trouble ahead?"

"Wind is too loud for us to make out any noise, sir... and this storm makes it hard to see ahead. This is the first sign we've had that there's somethin' wrong."

Right. "How many scouts are out there?"

"At least seven others," another said.

"Any way of recalling them?"

"Not in this weather, sir... they're ordered to only come back to the main contingent if there's danger."

"Well as you can *fucking well see* there is something out there that is causing us some *slight concern*, wouldn't you agree?" Revek thundered, rising to his full height. "So I don't care what it takes, or how you do it – I will order you to march out there after them if I have to – but you are finding a way to get those scouts back here, do you understand? Or so help me *gods,* I will—"

A scream rang out, somewhere in the darkness ahead, agonising wilts of pain echoing out through the storm. The commander swung himself round, taking a few steps forward, heart thumping in his chest suddenly.

The screaming fell short; a body fell to ground.

What the hell——

Another scream, further down the ranks behind him. Several other cries following. An unadulterated sound of fear. Revek turned to see lights swinging wildly, soldiers crashing between each other, one torch disappearing into the swampland over the bank.

A splash of water; another scream fell to silence.

"Wait here," Revek ordered, as if an alternative were available, and marched back down the road with fire at his heels.

"What's happened?" he roared as he approached, swinging his hand around in frustration. "Why aren't you in line——"

"There's something out there, sir," one of them quivered, clutching the torch as if it were a shield. "There's something in the water…"

"What's in the water?"

"Some *thing,* I… don't know, I didn't really see sir. We heard a noise, and then it took him…"

"Took who?"

"That thing, it reached out and grabbed one of us in its jaws, and then it dragged them away again. I don't know, I didn't see it really but it was big and… it was in the swamp and… and they're gone now…"

"What's in the swamp? What happened to them?" the commander bellowed sporadically.

The reply was mute. All he found were terrified faces, clutching torches, bundled together like children afraid of the dark. Everywhere he looked, the same was all he could see. A fear of the gloom that surrounded them – and a fear of whatever thing called it home.

"What happened to them? Anyone?" Revek swayed about, arms raised, every organ in his body swelling with unease. "Can anyone tell me what the *hell* is going on here!"

Then he heard it, somewhere behind him. A clicking sound, deep and reverberating, coming from the swamp.

He turned sharply, eyes trying to pierce the black veil, rain lashing down all around. The grass verge, illuminated, stretching to the edge of the swamp at its base. The space beyond fading to black. The flicker of torchlight; the dull twitches of the grass.

And somewhere beyond, that clicking sound, matching the rhythms of his breath.

There are things that come out, when the storm begins...

"Form up, now," Revek whispered, then louder: "*Everyone form up!*"

Around him, grating metal and coiling blades saw the soldiers raise their shields and form tight circles along the path. Each one shifted into the next, interlocking sections like the pellets of a loaded crossbow, awaiting attack at any moment. Only the commander remained separate from the throng of soldiers, eyes transfixed on the gloomy expanse before him, waiting for the clicks to change again. Lights illuminated the world around them, the narrow road they walked along, and tried to seek out whatever lay in the shadows.

"It's moving," Revek sensed, the edge of the swamp rippling slightly as the clicks shifted right. Sidestepping, he stayed parallel to the sound, watching shadows and illuminations dance across his vision.

When the ripples stopped, so did he, but the commander felt the unsettling weight dawn on him when he realised the clicking had stopped too. Suddenly he was without reference to his enemy of the dark, out in the open, rain blasting across his face in a feeble act of bravery. *This is a bad idea...*

The next click he heard came several metres further down.

What came next, was a monster.

It lunged up the grass bank along the roadside, a huge blunt skull of undulating frills and teeth and eyes, shifting like a phantom on eight thin clawed legs, barrelling into the nearest cluster of soldiers.

It smashed its way into the mass of metal, jaws crushing the first man it found in a nest of fangs, while great talons speared everything else in its path, armour and flesh in equal measure. It howled ominously, throat bulging as it consumed the lone soldier, its great length surging past into the deeper water on the other side, an oar-like tail slithering behind into the murky depths beyond. Those fighters that remained reformed slowly, half-heartedly into their closed circles, the groans and screeches of the dying rising up over the thundering rattle of the storm that still raged on all around.

What the fuck was that thing. Revek twisted, frightful of where it was, of *what else* could've been out there. *That thing is massive.*

He studied the darkness around them, eyes twitching, heart in his throat, lungs heaving air that felt so deprived of all that was good.

But if it's that big… then what killed the first man?

His eyes flicked to the waters below, out beyond the simple void the torchlight could reach, and found dozens of eyes were watching him. Glowing points, speckled like a constellation. Slowly shifting closer, just out of sight.

In a flash of panic, the commander ripped a torch from a nearby soldier's hand and cast it end-over-end out into the swamp beyond.

As it spun, illuminating a world of death and shadow in its path, the eyes manifested across tiny pale faces with shimmering teeth, just above the surface. Tiny iterations of the same beast that had attacked moments ago – hundreds upon hundreds of them, a mere ten feet away.

As the torch hit the water and fizzled out against the dark, the eyes began to move towards them.

And all he could do, was run.

Barking orders as he turned heel and ran, the enclosed ranks of his soldiers broke apart at the edges, and started streaming down the road like a split artery. Suddenly the crackle of the skies above was overrun by the thundering clatter of running metal. A world of flux, where the ill-defined road ahead was illuminated only by the swaying beacons they bore, exposing a landscape bludgeoned by surging rivers and ruptured by swellings of mud. A world of pain and misery, as savage as it was godforsaken. A world in the throes of a thunderstorm.

And that was when the screams began.

Scattered at first, but within moments a staccato of the dead and dying cried out behind them. Bodies fell, the tiny creatures of the swamp lurching up onto fleeing faces and gouging eyes from their sockets. Tearing away at armour and burrowing into chests. Snapping ankles, seething all over the writhing corpse-to-be. Some soldiers found their way into the swamplands, thrashing arms trying to be anywhere but there – the blunted cry as tiny claws carved out their throats, and sent them to a sleepless grave.

At his feet, Revek sensed the rumbling intensity of movement. There was no sound, beyond the rattle of armoured ranks and the screams of their dying outcasts. Nothing more, nothing less. Only the shifting of the earth beneath his feet, as if the very land they walked upon was preparing to swallow them whole.

A rush of water off to his right, and the commander's heart bulged in his chest. Risking a glance back, he spied the great beast swarming up the bank like a serpent. Charging, howling, screeching, clicks chiming all around.

The beast impacted the charge like a cannon. Bodies fell. Bodies were impaled. Bodies were flung about in its enormous jaws, cast off to feed its children tearing up the embankments. Revek watched as it locked eyes with him, thundering across the road, jaws arcing down, sweeping across the fleeing figures towards him, tearing through everything in its path. Attached to those piercing eyes, shimmering with fire and blind ferocity. The anarchy of it all.

Revek leapt forward, clattering to the ground in a spray of mud and debris. The beast scuttled past on eight spindly arms, a pale blur breezing past him. His head hit the ground; a coldness edged the corners of his vision. The jaws snapped overhead, some savage spluttering of noise gargling from its throat. Crashing into the swampland to his left, disappearing again in moments. Leaving carnage in its path.

The clicks echoed on into the distance, awaiting the next attack.

Revek clambered to his feet, a tug of pain down his left leg. Ambling forward, surrounded by the screams of the dying, he watched fearfully as wave after wave of soldiers surged along his right flank, their horror-eclipsed eyes darting frantically about for the enemy.

Bastard, he mused, clutching at his leg, the awkward fall rebounding up his hipbone like a steel drum. Movement became numb agony; the sky blinkered ahead with titanic shifts of cloud. Snapping jaws echoed to his left – every glance down the grass verge saw scurrying legs approach. Strangled sounds and wounded cries all around; the swiftness of the end when it came. Limping forward, falling behind, as the might of Imperial Army was slowly reduced by the monsters of the swamp, and the great mother who lurked silently in the gloom, awaiting the next stir of chaos to arise.

We're all going to die.

The guttural screech at his side, and Revek peered over to find the edges of the swamp sweeping up against the bank as something approached. Eyes lifting, the haze of dark shifted, shadows pulling away to reveal the paleness of the great beast making another pass. A few sharp clicks and it was upon them.

We're all going to die.

He threw himself to ground, landing across the grass bank as the beast lunged. Crashing through the metallic tide, its claws heaved great bowls of earth from the path, tearing apart anything else in its wake. Clawing, driving forward—

Ripping the grass verge out from under him. Revek skittering down the slope towards the death-swamp at its base. Hands grappling at slick tufts of grass, kicking against the squelching mud, legs dangling at the water's edge—

The beast above disappearing; the clicks at his heels spiking terror to his heart. Turning suddenly, kicking out, a tiny form that had been jumping for his leg now spinning off into the dark. Other eyes, other shapes and comprehensive sets of teeth swarming forwards in a frenzy—

Hands buried in thick mud, tugging at old roots lacing beneath the road, heaving away from the hell of the beyond. Clicking, shrieking behind, all around. The slow spectre of inevitability, approaching like an old friend—

Hand slipping, head twisting back to find another beast at his side, tail coiling behind, teeth chattering incessantly. Watching with its dull black eyes, leaping with tiny claws. Crossing the air before him, poised to rip his head to pieces—

A shimmer of silver; the creature carved in two, spilling across the mud before him in translucent pale lumps. Sudden silence, only the clatter of metal remaining.

Revek blinked heavily.

What the fuck is this place.

Rolling absently onto his back, cast in shadow before him stood the striking blond general from before, a blood-streaked sword in her hand, the patient accompaniment of two horses at her side. A hand was outstretched to him, which he took almost instinctively, and was hoisted back onto his legs without even a whisper of strain.

"If there were anyone I'd find on his ass in a time like this," she mused, "you would not be my first guess."

"I slipped," he blustered, "and... we need to move."

"Yes sir – lead the way."

Revek found his footing, leg still throbbing quietly, and mounted the nearest horse, spurring it on alongside the tide of soldiers with the other general keeping pace at his back. Ahead, the road was swamped by orange light, horses charging at the flanks, deafening thunder in his ears. Screams still echoed all around, with tiny pale phantoms leaping from the grass and tearing into his soldiers left and right. A constant thrum of activity, pinging through his mind like snapping twigs – the sudden all-encompassing boom of the great beast tearing through the crowds at their back.

"We need to protect the main ranks," Revek commanded, his

voice hoarse and quivering with pain.

"We are," the blonde general hailed. "We've organised the cavalry to run to either side of the road in rotations to fight off the little ones. The generals are leading from the rear and middle – Darius ordered me to come to the front and lead the charge... assuming you'd be there, of course."

"It was my intention, I assure you."

"Of course, sir."

"Any idea what these... *things,* are?"

"Nothing at all sir. All we know is the little ones die fast, the big one has torn through at least four ranks already, and I want fuck-all to do with any of this."

"Agreed."

A howl erupted from behind, followed by the screams and clattering metal of fallen men. As they turned, the leviathan made another crossing, tearing through entire divisions of his army in one fell swoop, casting broken bodies in all directions, disappearing again moments later.

Revek ground his teeth and snarled. "Need to do something about that one."

"Can't say anyone disagrees."

"How far are we from the nearest vantage point?"

"We spotted a small hill about a mile or two ahead, buried in dead trees. Could be of use to us."

"Then we make for there, regroup at the summit. If the trees are dense enough they'll keep the big one at bay... hopefully the rest will follow suit." Looking behind, the howling bellow of the beast raged again.

We just have to hope we hold out long enough to get there...

†

Chapter 25

The Trojan Horse

They had left as dusk approached, bundling goods and provisions into the cart in neat arrangements, providing sufficient cover for the general locked cautiously in the lower compartment. Goodbyes had been moot, cautionary smiles and nods of the head as Brutus had seen them off. Evelyn had taken the reins, whipping the two piebald beasts into motion, and the cart had edged slowly forward, the beginning of its long passage onward to the City of the Sun.

Surrounded by the fortuitous barricade of trees, Cavara observed a world of colours and shadows, creeping through the cracks in the lower beams, the jolts and rattles of the cart's frame channelling around her. The scent of pine needles and fresh rainwater stirred whimsically with the smell of dye, stained into the fabric carpets draped across the floor of the cart. The twitter of birds and rustle of trees were just audible, beyond the therapeutic clatter of horse hooves and the slow winching of the wheels. It was amicable, composed. Nothing like the distant shores she came from, where the world seemed to seize and rupture with every breath of the wind, and the very ground sprouted chaos with the coming tide of war. There was none of that there, on that distant shore, none of the anger that bled her homeland dry. There was only a deep serenity, echoing from the very earth they travelled on. There was only peace, in the

Land of the Sun.

I wish that same peace were in me.

Looking within herself, Cavara found the peace that surrounded her admonished, longing for something more. Since the conversation in the barn, she had been tensely aware of the words Azura had spoken, and of what Brutus had said to her when the general arrived. How that ox-man *knew* something, knew something that she too experienced but something that, unlike him, she hardly understood. She had tried to find him, before they departed, tried to understand what he had meant, what he knew. But then they were leaving, and she was being bundled into that wooden coffin, and Brutus had said his quiet goodbyes and never spoke a word to her. As the cart trundled on and his footsteps faded away, the exact three words ricocheted through her mind, unanswered and untethered.

Those three words: *the shadow woman.*

She had thought it just a dream, at first, her mind spinning some illusionary tale as she waved through a slow concussion, sat in the rocking boughs of that boat. It had been as if her thoughts were fragmented, navigating plain colours and shapes with no real sense or structure. And that voice, echoing and vacuous, her own but not quite her own, some paradigm of her thoughts. Only that had seemed significant; only the voice had given the sense that what she was experiencing was anything *more* than a fever-dream. It had been almost invasive, telling her to pursue the shadow, as colours died around them, watching the void form ahead … watching the shadow fall to its demise and the darkness that came to swallow it all.

There can only be one, it had said.

Only one of who?

Then: *Brutus knows.* The huge man had seen her on that pier, seen the vision she had had as if it were scarred across her face, and he *knew.* Somehow, by no means that she understood, he *knew* she'd seen this shadow woman. And he'd seen it too. It was not a dream, but a vision.

And then her thoughts had started running.

Brutus, did you chase her too?
She did not know.
Did the voice speak to you too?
She did not know.
Does anyone else know?
She did not know.
What do you know?
She sighed.
I just don't know.

She reran the questions with unenviable tenacity, spinning them round and round and round, but coming to the same uncertainty as before, and likely as the next would bring. There were no answers; there was no end. Her mind grew tired, inconsolable, still. She found tears at the corners of her eyes, desperation seeping through. The world of shadows and colours continued to pass her by, but she felt none of its beauty. Only the curse of those three words, dancing about her soul.

Those three words: *the shadow woman.*

The first thing she registered, was the sudden absence of shadow, as the trees that had marked their woodland passage fell away to open land. Crossing into an unfamiliar world, she began to hear voices, dotted all around her, waddling shadows passing left and right about their business. From there, a general ruckus manifested: the periodic wrenching sound of cart wheels passing along the roads beside them; horses stamping and snorting as they greeted each other; pigs, goats and other livestock wandering aimlessly about producing all manner of noises and smells, extrapolated by how close she was to the road beneath; the chime of a blacksmith's anvil, forging tools and supplies for the locals; the calls of a market selling fresh bread and bags of wheat from harvest, setting her stomach off at the thought of a good meal. It was loud, all-encompassing, the thrum and perverseness of human settlement reeling in her ears. After the serenity of the forest whispering in her ears for miles past, the sudden obnoxious cacophony of civilisation was as unwelcome as it was obscene.

The City of the Sun, she thought. *Loud and proud, even from here.*

"These are the settlements along the outer wall, Evelyn," Azura said from above, more so for the benefit of their hidden cargo. "Not part of the city proper, of course... but almost like their own little cities, under the watchful eye of the capital. They receive money in exchange for goods, and get to remain here so long as they keep the peace. Quite a sight to see."

I'm sure it is, Cavara mused, shifting her numbed limbs trapped in that tiny space and grunting dismissively. *And wouldn't I like to know it?*

"Lots of militia work in these quasi-cities too... *lots of them.*"

As she spoke, the general noted the distinctive rattling of marching soldiers passing by on her left, and her stomach froze. She counted at least three – no, five – no, seven rows of feet go past, steel boots crunching the loose gravel below. She held her breath, stifled her racing pulse, as if anything would betray her position. Onerous moments passed, fearing the worst, before the feet dispersed and merged slowly back into the general clatter of the world around them.

They really are everywhere.

"But no worry; they don't bother doing routine checks unless they have a lead," Azura added.

Cavara exhaled. *Would've been nice to know.*

"It's only goods entering the capital that need assessment... that's the job of the gatekeepers." A long pause; a flick of the reins. "Speaking of which, we're approaching them now..."

As they trundled forward, whatever bustle and provocation they had passed through suddenly came to pass, little more than a quietening thrum of activity behind them. An unsettling stillness set in, only kept alive by the cart wheels gliding over cobbled roads. Passing under the gaze of the outer wall, where once there was an orange haze of the setting sun, there was now only a slate-grey perpetuation of shadow. Darkness became her only solace – *once again.*

"Keep quiet and leave it to me, *Evelyn*," Azura said broadly. "There are eyes everywhere wanting to ask too many questions. Let's not give them any reason to..."

Cavara waited hesitantly, encompassed by the silence of the unknown for some time. The shadows grew heavier beneath her; the bustle of the outer settlements grew fainter still. The world simply passed by.

It was only when an order from the gate called out to them, and the cart drew abruptly to a halt, that the general grew still, and felt her heart stutter gently at the approach of heavy boots.

"Evening, officer," Azura cooed overhead. "Requesting entry to the capital, to sell our goods at the market."

"Evening." A thunderous woman's voice, heavyset, echoing from deep in their chest. "What goods are you to declare?"

"Only some small wares and specialities: we have fine strung carpets, cloth garments for pantry workers, a wide array of...."

Her voice trailed off – Cavara's occupational thoughts drifted away – to hear another set of footsteps crunch beside her, heels twisting sharply near her head. Stifling her shock, she listened to the sacks and bundles dislodge as the guardsman sifted through them. Light flickered overhead through the layers of carpet bundled atop her, the distinct bulb of the man's head swaying left and right. A few drawstrings slid open, hands prying inside, searching for hidden weapons – drawing closed, a nod to the gate, confirming they were clear. Moving to the next, and the next, and the next. Coming ever closer to her—

"*Cavara.*"

The general lurched, the noises prickling the air around her drawing to a numb, foreboding silence.

"*Cavara.*"

The voice. That *voice*. Whispering through her head as if directly in her ear. Speaking *to* her. Separate to her, yet so distinctly *her*.

"*Cavara.*"

What? her mind replied, the conscious mind she had control of, as opposed to the cold eminence of whatever else spoke to her then.

A long silence drew out, awaiting some sort of reply.

"*I am inside your head.*"

Heat rose; the thin air she drew clouded her mind in a dull rash of pain.

Why are you here?

"*I feel your pain.*"

The voice was deceptive, meandering, present in her mind but never quite engaging in her thoughts. Exploring, wandering the recesses of her thoughts. Places she had no active control of. An invasive conduit of some other power, whom she knew nothing of, and feared she never would.

What do you want from me?

"*I want nothing from you.*"

A direct response; Cavara found sweat plucking her eyes. *Then why are you here?*

"*Destiny guides you; you are guided by it. I must stop you, but I do not know how to.*" Then, more acutely: "*I must win.*"

Why must you win?

By some perceptive turn, she felt the voice smile to her.

"*Because there can only be one.*"

A pain in her skull, as if being stabbed. She lifted her hands to cover a scream, brought back to reality by a hand spreading across the carpet above her. The general's heart reeled for a good gasp of air, as she lay silent and asphyxiating in the compartment below. Sweating, toes curling in broken boots, hands clawing into her palms. Wanting to be anywhere but there. *Anywhere* but there with that thing in her mind...

The guard above began to draw away the thin stretch of carpet slowly, wondering whether the other bundled sheets were of the same quality as the first. A cold realisation crossed Cavara's face, as her cover was slowly drawn aside...

"Are we clear, officer?" the strong woman's voice called. "We're forming a queue as it is."

The hand withdrew from the carpets. "Yes, ma'am... all clear."

"Well then, miss, you're free to pass."

"Thank you," Azura replied warmly from above.

Moments from the end, moments passed, and the cart slowly shifted forward again, onward to the City of the Sun.

Masked by the creaking wheels of their cart, Cavara drew in great stretches of air in a frenzied panic, eyes blinkering like clouds passing over the sun. She led there, twitching, longing to stretch, to cry, to run, to fly – longing to be free of the hell she felt in that small coffin strapped to the cart. Longing to drag herself away from the memory of the voice now echoing through her mind.

Somewhere nearby, a great set of gears ground to motion, and the breaching of a great door slid open ahead revealing the pulsing heart of the capital, in all the glory she could not see. The bustle and rancour of civilisation surged again like an orchestra striking a fresh chord. The City of the Sun opened its arms to greet her.

But all she found the strength to do, was scream.

†

Chapter 26

Eye of the Storm

With agonising miles at their backs, and the stretch of thundering dark landscape before them, the marching ranks of the bruised Imperial Army were overridden with relief as the land slowly clutched away from the floodplains onto higher ground. The incline gained momentum, striking out from the mud-addled death-trap they had fled, until a strike of perfect lightning illuminated a great hillock before them, and the narrow pathway leading to its peak. All around, a once indeterminate stretch of rain-lashed grass suddenly sprouted the skeletal fragments of dead trees, growing dense and comforting as they ascended. The road ahead gained some solidity, narrow channels of rainwater skimming down its edges like tiny rivers – no longer the mud-curdled sediment they had trekked through thus far. At the higher reaches of the hill, a few scattered horses stood with torches raised, beacons guiding the dispossessed masses to the light.

The end of the nightmare grew ever closer.

At its base, Revek watched the soldiers slowly navigate the incline, rank after rank disappearing into the mass of trees, and looked out to the floodplains beyond with a face of bitter despair. Even then, with the end of the line snaking its way to higher ground, the howls of the dying continued to beckon out into the storm. Through the faint haze of the sky, where the splits of orange and crimson red stained the blackened clouds, he could see the pale shimmering beasts swarm through the grass towards his men like tiny knives. The ghost-like flash as they leapt up into the rushing masses and ripped a soldier to the ground, tearing through metal, flesh and bone with unreserved savagery. Dragging men off into the grass to feast on; snapping ankles and burying the dying in the mud. The mounted cavalry circled, defending the stragglers with their very lives, as the squirming monsters of the dark continued their assault on those left making their desperate escape.

Revek shook his head. *But they have another problem.*

Off to the right, a number of the cavalry were engaged with the huge, lumbering terror that was the mother, that twisted and coiled about in the grass like a python, and lunged at any soldier who strayed too close. As he turned his head, Revek spied one of the riders being consumed, torn from his saddle, the beast's serrated teeth ripping through the horse's flank as it too stumbled and collapsed into the mud. That same howl ripping through the air, the click of the beast's gills chiming through his eardrums like a scuttling insect. The chaos breaking all around.

An anger rose within him, a raw heat coursing through his very fibre. *My men are dead,* he scolded. *My supplies are ruined. My artillery is left abandoned on the road.* Fists clenched, the cold winds nipping at his fingertips. *All for nothing, in this ruinous fucking country.* His horse snorted, lifting its head, sensing the anger of its master. *All because of that fucking thing out there, tearing my glory to pieces.* A tempestuous moment, stood on the edge of a precipice – Revek puffed out his chest and inhaled slowly.

I won't stand for it.

Amongst his fellow officers, Revek dismounted his horse, unhooking a shield from the saddle and swinging it across his back.

"Sir, what's going on? What are you doing?" the blonde woman asked, hand already lingering at her sword expecting trouble.

"Get the soldiers up to safety," he deflected. "Get camps set up around the hill, headquarters at the top by the old tree. Watch for the little ones." He paused, donning his steel helmet. "Whatever happens, don't follow me."

They appeared bemused. "Why? Sir… what are you doing?"

Revek drew his sword. "I'm gonna teach that fucking thing a lesson or two…"

He marched out into the dark, feet trudging through mud and clotted stumps of grass, clattering sword against shield to announce his agenda to all those concerned. To his left, the final stretches of the army passed him, watching with an awe-stricken gaze as their commander strode decisively towards the beast. The cavalry ahead – those who remained – broke off from their attack, the beast convulsing about trying to centre a target. Suddenly the world was a roar of thundering hooves, with Revek hailing them onward to the safety of the hill as they passed him by.

And from there, he was alone.

The beast ahead locked its six eyes on him, and stooped low like a predatory cat. Approaching, Revek found the beast was a foul thing to behold, some great tumour of translucent flesh with rippling frills across its neck. Its head was massive, a great disk of tiny, jagged teeth pursed in a permanent grin, with only the small taloned legs visible below. Occasionally, the tail would twist through the grass behind: that grotesque paddle of skin writhing about. Revek could think of nothing more appalling to the senses, than what stood before him then – it was only the pungent aroma of stagnant water and rotten flesh that suddenly assaulted his nostrils, that told him that that assessment was by far a gross under-exaggeration.

"You really are a foul fucking thing, aren't you?"

A sporadic fluster of clicks resonated from the beast's throat, rising to a crescendo and then ceasing entirely. Its head tilted, assessing this new-found prey with intrigue.

"It's gonna be fun when I carve you to pieces."

A low, rumbling howl escaped its throat, head stooping even lower to grace the ends of the grass beneath, back arched like a striking serpent.

The commander grinned.

"Just you watch."

The beast lunged forward, jaws stretched wide, expanding across Revek's vision at a frightening speed. Revek dived to the left, rolled across the underside of his shield to dodge the worst of the mud, a barrage of broken earth splattering at his side as the mother crashed gracelessly to the ground. He righted in moments, sword bearing, cutting a long streak across the beast's exposed flank, splitting one of its many pulsating frills. A howl, something close to disappointment, rang through his ears. The beast rounded slowly, their eyes locked—

Forgetting the curling tail snaking across the grass to his left, the painful groan of his spine as it whipped him across the back. The falling sensation, hands burrowing into thick mud to stop the rest of his body following. The beast twisting, bulging up like a maggot, head tilting to clamp down on its prey again—

Revek rolled forward, gritting his teeth at the foul column of cemented mud now down his back, and twisted sharply toward the beast's tail. Three small, beady eyes watched in horror as the end of the tail became severed from the rest, writhing on the ground like a dislodged parasite.

The beast rolled away howling, wriggling across the ground as if it were a worm lay bare for the birds, overcome by the excruciating pain lancing up its tailbone. Revek sidled around, lungs heaving, watching the huge deformity tear across the earth. The pleasant weight of the sword in his hand; the even more pleasant sight of blue-green blood dripping from its pointed tip.

Told you, you grimy piece of—

The thought broke with the rain, as another lash of thunder struck the sky and the beast was suddenly on the move again. The commander saw the anger prickling its eyes, dancing in phosphorescent hues of red and grey across its frills. The tiny legs half-dragging it forward, ground rocking underfoot, Revek's legs numb and saturated by the rain, the sky swelling and breaking overhead—

The mother drove to the side and brought a taloned hand across his front just short of his chest. Revek brought his shield across to redirect the attack, the impact snapping at his elbow sharply. Deflecting, falling away. One of the claws slipped past, wrenching a huge opening across his chest plate, scoring the chainmail beneath as it pinged away like upended shrapnel.

Twisting away, the beast already turning for a second run, rising into the air, howling into the bleeding storm, driving its weight down towards him—

Revek struck out, sword clasped in both hands. Caught the beast across its mouth, a deep gouge tearing through soft tissue and the mangled flesh beneath, dislodging several of its small, perfectly-aligned teeth, a spear of blood striking the ground—

The beast reeled, its great length suddenly turning into him, crashing into the mud at his feet, barrelling into his chest. Revek falling backwards, hitting the mud hard, legs half-churned into the broken ground beneath the mother's flank. Shield cast aside, half-buried and broken. Sword flailing limply in his other hand – sword suddenly the only singular thought in his mind.

He was suddenly grappling, twisting towards the beast's back. Lunging, striking out, driving forward. Impaling its back, the chisel of a bone cracking ripe in his ears, the howl it produced surging adrenaline back into the commander's system—

The sudden spur of weightlessness. The realisation that he was now out of the mud, off his feet, twisting his legs desperately onto the back of the huge beast. Hand braced to the impaled sword with every ounce of his strength. Rising skyward, at the mercy of the monster. In the throttle of the storm, atop hell's own creation.

Fuck.

As the beast began to buck, Revek swam with terror as he tried to grab at the beast's hide for purchase. His mind, a protrusion of spinning shapes and colours; sweat leaking across him like an open tap. Strapped to the sword, the body all around him a pale, shapeless mass of undulating organs beneath a sheet of organic ice.

The insanity of it all.

His free hand at his belt, he navigated the strap to prize open his knife, skimming dangerously along the mother's flank as it bucked about. Feeling the knife slip away, curve in his hand, lifting—

Jolting his wrist, dislodging the small blade, watching its metallic edge spin into the mud below.

Fuck.

The beast slowed, legs teetering, weight shifting left from right.

Fuck.

One side lifting, twisting, Revek watching the ground abruptly rise to meet him.

Fuck!

As if by another hand, he tore the weapon from the beast's side, sliding against its mud-slick stomach, the hilt of his sword dancing through his fingers.

Twisting, back landing against hard ground. A brief glimpse of fate; the beast rolling in front of him, completely exposed.

His sword plunged deep, feet digging as he tore down, splitting the stomach open with one lethal curve of the blade. Organs spilling, opening. Blue-black blood, shimmering across the mud, across the grass. The sword retracting as the beast continued to roll—

The talons of the beast's foot striking up from beneath its body, arching across his chest plate. Tearing the chainmail beneath apart, the wilt of blood flowering across his shirt. A screech like a banshee erupting from his lungs. Teetering backwards, legs failing. Legs falling. Hitting the ground in a spasm of metal.

The sky spinning, all around.

The beast scrabbled its way back onto its front, a low whimpering howl catching the wind, a slew of its innards splashing delicately against the mud. It studied the rain battering on overhead, the puddles below tainted with the blue mark of its wounds. The acrid taste on its tongue; the dislodged teeth burrowed under its gums.

The motionless metal carcass at the corner of its vision, half-buried in the mud.

The flush of anger bristling across its neck. Limping over to the prey, the sickening churn of its half-emptied chest cavity insignificant in that shallow moment of redemption. Gazing down at the helmeted face, the red blossom of blood where the talons had sliced.

The mother lunged down, savouring the feast of its meal—

Missing the twitch of the dead man's hand, curled about its sword—

Revek spearing his blade up... into the roof of the beast's mouth.

At that pristine moment, everything stopped. There was no rain, no thunder, no blood or twisted metal. No anger, no fear, no chaos of any kind. There was only the beast and its conqueror, the vanquished foe, the dying enmity of the beast's black soul breaking across its eyes. Revek gazed into the mouth of the great mother, at the leviathan he had banished from that world, and saw a tiny glimmer of the red sun break through the clouds above.

In that pristine moment, the gods had witnessed him again.

Triumph returns.

Another moment, and the beast was collapsing to its side, the last reckoning of its being finally giving way, fading to silence. The blade slid free from its jaw, landing at Revek's side like an old friend.

Then the huge carcass bludgeoned the ground with a tremor beside him, claimed by the mud and the elements, and the commander sighed heavily at the stillness of the world, and the faint trickles of rain against his face.

Rolling to his front, held aloft on shaky arms, he grasped the short-sword in his hand and used it to rise slowly to his feet. Looking off to the hillside ahead, spotted with the tiny fires of his army, he heard the quiet thunder of horse hooves approach from within the mass of dead trees.

With the rain dropping to a cool mist, and the sky blemished with the red-gold of dusk, Revek sighed, and began the slow walk back to sanctuary.

†

Chapter 27

A Kiss of Fate

They found shelter for the night in a cluster of dead willow trees, their fibre-thin branches hanging limply over a dry riverbank speckled with the droplets of fresh rain. Hills rolled quietly around them, atrophies of rock forming ridges and small gorges between, spotted with bushels of gorse and pine. A tranquillity, stemmed from the natural rise and fall of the Kazbaks around them, tempered by the bleeding skies of the mountains to the west. It was only the rumbling grey clouds overhead that threatened to break the serenity, stretching off across the skyline to the east, gaining momentum until the valley below was overcome by a black maw of thunder, surges of rain blurring the thin horizon everywhere one looked. Somewhere out there, she knew, the Imperial Army was marching on like a great metal serpent, as the indignation of the gods rumbled viciously in the skies above, lashing them with hell for the sin of their being.

"That's a hell of a storm front," Markus exclaimed. Sat atop a rock he'd dragged from the dry earth of the riverbed, he sat fiddling with the leather bindings of his sword handle, which had begun to unravel at the base. "Nice to know Tarraz offers such warm welcomes."

"Savage country, savage people," Savanta said bluntly.

"So long as it stays down there, it's no concern of mine."

She drew her whetstone across the edge of her knife, the blade still tainted by the redness of blood. "It never strays this far into the hills… we're safe."

"Is that a guarantee?"

"It never rains in the Kazbaks. It's why the Tarrazi build their homes here, in the natural bowls of the hills. Good cover from enemies, and no threat of flooding… all they have to contend with is run-off from the mountains." She waved a hand across the deep, mud-cracked trench running alongside their camp. "These riverbeds are near the only source of water this place gets."

"That so…" Markus said distractedly, driving a small blade into the end of his sword handle, in a feigned attempt at wedging the leather back into its slot. "It's certainly hard living…" A few more plies of the knife, growing slowly restless, and it slipped away, nicking a small cut in his index finger. "Ah, bastard!" he groaned, whipping his hand away, shaking it to stem the pain.

Markus watched as Savanta struck a hand out, palm facing skyward. He flinched, anticipating attack, watching her stern gaze flick from him to the knife at his side.

"What're you gonna do with that?"

The gaze remained unchanged; she said nothing.

Reluctantly, Markus handed over the knife and lay it in her open palm, which she grasped and pulled away slowly, as if negotiating a truce. Turning, she gazed up at the thin trunk of the willow tree beside her, its bark mottled and bruised, and with a sudden twist of the elbow speared the knife into it. Savanta dug it in slowly, meticulously, prizing it free again to reveal a thin stream of sap seeping from the wound – a lot of which also coated the tip of the dagger in her hand.

Wiping a length of the sap around the knife's base, smearing it like fresh honey, she bound the leather back across and tucking it neatly into the studded hilt at the end. As she peeled her finger away, the binding remained fastened in place.

"The sap of the Tarrazi Willow, when the tree has gone so long without water… becomes incredibly malleable and sticky." Savanta studied her handiwork, before passing the blade back across to a dumbfounded Markus. "So long as it does not come into contact with fire, its binding is as strong as forged steel."

Her looked down the length of the weapon like a spyglass. "Thank you... it's impressive that you—"

"It's not a problem."

Markus bit his tongue. "Of course."

For some time after that, not a word was spoken. An aching, uncomposed silence ebbed between them, like the whispers of a shallow wind. Watching, Savanta seemed to disorientate herself, staring off across the vast landscape stretching all around but never quite finding anything there to hold her gaze. Just wandering, plagued by thoughts, detached from that small cluster of trees by the old riverbed, as if nothing really existed. As if the world had abandoned her, and beyond the physical body she walked in, there was nothing left. The glistening plate of metal embedded in her cheek, that caught his gaze suddenly as it shimmered like the moon, told the same story a hundred times over: what there had been; what had been taken from her.

That the scars she bore now, were all she had left.

"Sav, I... I need to tell you something," he muttered faintly, a tickling anxiety pulsing in his chest. "We need to talk about this, all of... all of this..."

She tilted her head, registering his words, but not quite enough to draw her eye, which remained fixated on the riverbank nearby and never quite lingered his way.

"I'm not really sure what's going on, with our journey, our direction. I mean, you say we're gonna go through these hills... to somewhere, to something, to the next place... I feel like a blind man in this, being led at the arm on this revenge story that I know nothing about..."

His words were pleading, heartfelt, but even they failed to grant him any more of Savanta's attention, as her eyes rose slowly up the length of the willow tree, and back to the ground again.

"I just want to speak to you, because we are in this together, and I... I just want to know what's going on... so please listen to me. Please." She offered nothing; wouldn't even meet his eye when he peered round to catch sight of her. "Please... just some idea of what we're doing."

Still nothing.

"Sav, c'mon, I'm not asking for much..."

Nothing.

"Sav," His voice was pointed, angrier this time.

Still nothing.

"*Listen* to me."

Only silence.

"*Savanta fucking listen to me!*"

Her head snapped around, some flair of emotion shimmering behind her eyes as if she'd been sleeping. She stared at him, long and hard, trying to make out what he was, what he was *saying*. As if she'd never heard him at all...

"Sorry," she said flatly. "I..."

His face contorted with horror. "Can I even trust you?"

Her frown deepened, confused and concerned. "*What?*"

"Can *I* trust *you?*"

"Why shouldn't you?"

He said nothing, only gazed down at her hand – where his sap-streaked knife was curled in her fist.

As if bitten by a serpent, Savanta cast the blade to the floor, kicking a flurry of dust over it so it no longer caught the fading sun's glow, looking to her hand with disgust.

"I..." The words tasted sour, like they weren't her own. "It's not..." She met his eyes and saw the tears there. Saw pain, longing, a loss that was not as simple as mourning death. It was different, she saw that – it was electric and alive and yet so broken within him. She saw pain, only pain, and beyond that, the overriding drive of fear. The fear of what would come next; the fear of the unknown. Fearing when the next conflict would start, what the next turn of the road would bring.

Fearing where the knife would next strike out from; fearing his world coming abruptly to an end.

"I didn't mean for that... I didn't, I'm..." A void opened in her stomach; sickness boiled over in her throat. "I'm sorry... I... *fuck*..."

"What's going on?" he mumbled softly, holding himself within.

"I don't know, I..." *I feel like I'm going insane.* "I think I'm... just really tired... or something." *I feel like there's someone inside my head.* "I keep having these weird moments..."

"You seemed quite vacant, a moment ago, as if you weren't really here... is that what you mean?"

She felt a shudder. *A voice, it was talking to me.* "Yeah... something like that..."

"Maybe your mind was just wandering... I mean, we've walked a lot today, and this place makes me jumpy sometimes too."

It wanted me to get the knife. "Something like that..."

He laughed half-heartedly, receding into a deep, despairing sigh. "We all get like it, it's perfectly natural."

Her breathing stuttered.

It wanted me to hurt you...

"But, let's not worry about that now." Markus stood, dusting himself off, trying to remain animate to hold her wavering attention. "We have a long day ahead as well tomorrow, and as you're navigator, well... I wanna make sure you have a keen eye on the road ahead, yes?"

"Yeah..."

"Exactly so." He clapped his hands together, a false bravado of joy. "Well, then I recommend we get some rest as soon as possible... and I hope you feel better tomorrow, Sav." Markus smiled quietly, the tears finally closing off. "I need you... we need each other, in this, more than I think either of us care to let on."

A nod of the head, and Markus turned his back to remove the rolled blankets from his bag, peering about to assess the best place to lay a makeshift bed.

Meanwhile, Savanta found her mind wandering again to a dark and distant place she did not know. As it manifested, the world around her grew numb and undefined, and her skin smoothed over with coldness like the icy embrace of winter. For what felt like an eternity she waited there, in that sleepless, soundless place, waiting for some recollection of what she once knew.

And in the haze of oblivion she found herself in, her mind wandering further and further away, only one beacon of light fastened itself to her. A cold touch of reality; the delicate kiss of fate.

The knife in the dirt at her feet.

The voice ticking by in her head.

It wanted me to hurt you.

†

Chapter 28

The Underestimation

It had been easy enough to break-in. Easier than most, in fact. She had to admit, she'd stolen from brothels with more efficient security. At least in a brothel, there was a bit more creativity needed. With the brutes guarding every entranceway, the bell chimes strapped to every door – the pimps who had no wives, but slept with their money like they were wed to it all the same. Versatility was required; an expert's touch. The kind of venture that really paid for her talents. She'd expected much the same when gazing up at the towering pinnacles and high walls of the palace keep, illuminated by the moon. At the circling shafts of light from patrols scouting the grounds, or those that passed the windows one after the next high above. All manner of cadaverous protocol could go on behind those ancient walls: staggered guard rotations, barred windows, triple-lock mechanisms. Not to mention an entire military arsenal locked away in the basement. It was almost impregnable, the untrained eye would assume. A death wish, they could say.

So when Jinx had crossed the courtyard, mounted the outer wall, scaled two storeys of the palace keep, and slipped inside a shallow stretch of window into the military quarters, she'd almost laughed at how ridiculous it all was.

It's a testament, she mused, *to how the city is so oblivious. What a shame for them.* A smile pursed her lips.

And how wonderful for me.

Landing softly on the thick stone floor, she found herself in a narrow stretch of corridor that stank of roasted goods and the rustic sweetness of tobacco. A dim aura of torchlight trickled through the edges of the doors, the whisper of snoring twitching in her ears. Marching boots echoed from the courtyard outside as the guards made another – *half-hearted, far too spaced out* – pass. As for boots in her immediate proximity, there were no signs – only the eerie silence, dull and exquisite.

Excellent.

Adjusting the mask across her nose and mouth, Jinx skulked along the corridor to her right and shifted the latch on the door at its end. Prizing it open slowly, her eyes trailed the stone steps spiralling up within the stone pinnacle of a palace tower, rising several stories, until it reached a single wooden door, behind which resided her target – the man she was there to steal from.

A man not to be underestimated, so Broska had made clear. He'd been succinct, describing General Ferreus as a conniving, ostensible man capable of a great many nothings covered by a thin web of lies. A man who could have you disappear with a few simple words, and with a few more could guarantee no-one asked questions. A man as capable with a pen as a blade; an elder of the army with enough tenacity to split stone. A man, as Broska had made firmly and unmistakably clear, *not* to be underestimated.

Ascending the staircase, Jinx found her thoughts trace back to how serious he'd been, describing what had happened the day before. *A fellow officer, murdered by another in broad daylight.* It almost sounded like a poor theatre pitch, had she not met Broska's glazed, wandering eyes and seen the reality of it there. *And he'd gotten away with it, too.* She saw that that had bruised him most – more perhaps even than losing a close friend had. The fact justice had not been served. The fact his hands were tied, and his mouth was sealed shut. *The fact it could've been him.*

And it could still be.

She came to the wooden door at the top of the staircase, and stopped. *Your brother's life is in danger.* She unhooked a small metal implement from her belt. *This is your chance to redeem him.*

She knelt and inserted the metal rod into the keyhole, slowly twisting left and right until she felt the mechanism within lift away. Trying the handle, turning it smoothly to the left, she pocketed the lockpick silently and slipped through the gap into the room beyond.

Immediately fastened to the delicate scent of earthy spice, Jinx found the room beyond speckled with dying candles and the wisps of fresh smoke. Within the dancing gaze of the light, oak cabinets rose across one wall, occupied by a miscellany of half-finished spirits and torn hardback books. To the other side, an ornamental bed half-draped in fine silks moulded with the slanting ceiling, the bulges in the quilt identifying the shape of a man deep in slumber. His snoring echoed about the room, reverberating across the thick walls and dangling tapestries, crossing the space between with——

With a desk at the far end, a collection of papers scattered across the top. Papers, she found, with one haphazardly folded into a tattered square on top, *as if it's been stuffed into one's pocket...*

On the ends of her feet, her target in sight, Jinx shifted silently across the room towards the desk opposite, hidden in the shadows that the candles couldn't reach. Glancing left, she caught sight of the austere, dishevelled face of General Ferreus between the draping silk, eyes still and silent like a phantom. He was inanimate, straight as a bowstring, head arched directly at the ceiling as if consulting the gods. Jinx watched the rise of fall of his chest, the expulsion of air creaking through his lungs. In those few moments, she wondered whether putting a knife through the tired man's heart as he slept would be justice enough for Broska, and whether the tumult he had felt over the death of his fellow officer would finally be put to rest. It would be so easy, she knew. So easy just to slip the knife between the ribs, and cover his mouth while he screamed——

No – that's not what we're here for. Broska would want justice... that's what we're here to deliver.

Eyes shifting back towards the desk, she gazed up at the tapestry hanging alongside it, and felt a stir of shock in her heart at the sight of it. There was an embroidery, stretching across its centre, of a goblin-like creature gnawing through a soldier's throat. Beneath it, written in gold, were several words written in the ancient tongue of Provenci, typically reserved for the books of law. It took only a few moments for Jinx – *practised thief, and avid reader of old legal code* – to work out what they said.

'*Non düna prosta anti vïstala*'... '*none are free when the rats are running*'.

What does he mean by that?

A loud snore from behind, causing her to swing sharply behind the nearest cabinet, told her such trivial pursuits were far from important.

If that were my wager of death, I'd be as much a bastard fool as any.

Turning back to the desk, she skittered over to it like a mouse and snatched away the note on top. Unravelling it like a child on their birth-day, Jinx scanned the contents within with sweeping glances of disgust.

'*A job needs doing... utmost secrecy required... during your assignment to retrieve the king's body... General Cavara leading... find a time when the soldiers are out the way... keep a few informed to offer reassurance to the rest*'. As she continued, a villainous resentment burned within her. '*You have my full authority to execute General Cavara by any means necessary... keep that bumbling fool Broska at bay... threaten him with extradition or arrest if he does not comply... do what you must to keep this under wraps.*'

Then, signed at the bottom: '*from his Excellence, Supreme Governor Alvarez of Provenci.*'

She frowned.

Alvarez?

The words on the page, reading them over again, remained unsettled in her stomach, churning through the back of her mind. *This doesn't sound like he described.* For all she knew – and from what

Broska had made clear – the Supreme Governor had known nothing about the betrayal. Ferreus had failed to report it until prompted by Broska, at which point Alvarez became angered and demanded answers. Alvarez hadn't known a thing about the plot to kill this General Cavara. Broska had said it was someone else, some man called Revek. That he and Ferreus had orchestrated the whole affair, right under the Supreme Governor's nose.

But it doesn't make sense... why would this be signed in Alvarez's name if he never authorised it, and knew nothing about it? She plied for answers, trying to see it from Broska's perspective, filtering through what little knowledge she had.

Then her heart stalled.

Because it's been forged, she thought. *Because someone else signed in his name to cover up the real perpetrator.*

The heat left her body.

Because they wanted to frame it on someone else, and Alvarez would believe them. They wanted to frame it on Broska: that he would steal the letter to cover this all up... and that all they needed was an alibi.

She turned, eyes seeking out the dark.

And I've given it to them.

"I was hoping he'd send you," Ferreus grinned, sword hanging loosely in his hand. "That way I could make it *personal.*"

Jinx whipped her knife out before Ferreus struck, their blades chiming together suddenly in the echoing void of the night. She dodged left, trying to strike up into Ferreus's nightshirt, only to find her blade skitter away as his own rose to meet it. They exchanged several blows, Ferreus growing insatiable, restless, his blade coiling about like a serpent. Jinx shuffled backwards, on the defence, knife barely managing against the barrage of attacks channelling her way.

Switching sides, Jinx closest to the door on open ground, Ferreus lifted his hands as if feigning surrender.

"Y'know, if you lay your weapons down now, this can all be over easily enough," he mused. "We can offer you immunity, knock some of the bounty off of your head... we can make agreements."

"And kill my brother?" she spat. "That's no honour I can live with."

Ferreus's grin disappeared, like the broken promises of a dishonest man. "Then you will die, like all the rest."

The general struck; Jinx brought her blade up to meet it, skimming the edge as she stepped in closer, knife twisting menacingly in one hand.

Within his circle, she landed a solid punch into his stomach. He grunted, the sensation receding faster than she had hoped, as he brought a hand up to grapple her hair. Yanking it suddenly, sword rising over her body, ready to strike down—

Her own blade swiping up, a streak of blood sprouting across his arm before he could get ends in. Hand releasing her hair; Jinx tumbling to the ground—

Sword striking down, barely enough time to knock it away. Lunging up, leg coiling about his neck, bracing between her kneecaps. Tearing him down, felled like a tree, Ferreus plummeting, crashing across the floor. Her blade striking out, driving towards his chest—

His own blade spearing towards her head. Jinx forced to disengage, spiralling to her feet, blade curved across her back. The general swaying stubbornly to his feet, movements jagged and stiff, bruising up his leg and right side.

"You're a shifty little bitch, I'll give you that," he muttered, sword slicing overhead, coming at her again.

Jinx slipped to her left, driving her elbow across into his cheekbone, the knife following close behind. Ferreus turned towards her, her blade biting across his cheek, hissing at the pain suddenly emanating there. He recoiled, striking out, watching the blade glance across her side, its edge slicing through her leather codpiece, nicking the exposed flesh therein. She was already cutting across again, wielding the knife like a broadsword, his own weapon only just glancing it away before striking out with a fist, connecting with her nose, watching her stumble back and fall—

Jinx clattered against the bedpost, spinning, watching the despot swing towards her, sword raised, face full of menace and anger. She struck out, stabbing like a frightened animal, realising she was backing into a corner, suddenly very small and alone and still.

"This will be short work I promise you," the general grumbled seditiously. "Just stay right there..."

Nose almost broken, the bitter sweetness of blood fresh on her lips, she felt the world close in about her. The inevitable seemed painless, staring into the covetous eyes of the general, looming over her like a titan. Everything seemed to grow silent again, hollow and resolute. A calmness, in the end, the likes of which she hadn't seen in a long, long time.

Against her better judgement, and against all manner of morals posited to her, Jinx flicked the blade onto the bed to her left, and watched the dull smile curl about the general's face.

"Good," Ferreus exclaimed. "We can make a good girl of you—"

Not on your life.

As he reached out to grab her, she grappled him around the wrist, spinning him on his heels, using his own weight against him as he pirouetted across the bedpost and cracked like an egg over his bed frame. Knees buckled, collapsing to the ground, the crunch of his spine echoing about the chamber. A few moments of incapacitation, sprawled across the floor like a dismembered corpse—

Jinx seized the moment, springing towards the doorway—

Ankle caught by Ferreus's outstretched hand, suddenly falling to the ground again—

Kicking out like a startled horse, her leather overshoes crashing into the general's disorientated face—

Ferreus watching as she reached the door, snapped the latch open, disappearing into the beyond with the letter stuffed in her pocket and...

And letting her go.

Climbing to his feet, hearing her shallow footsteps dissipate in the space beyond, Ferreus ran a finger along the slice across his cheek, and found a crooked smile curl across his face. Sure, it wasn't the outcome they had discussed — Revek had been meticulous on the details — but it was what they had wanted all the same. Someone had broken into his office, attempted to plant incriminating evidence on his desk, bearing the Supreme Governor's name and the crisis he had supposedly 'authorised'. The criminal had escaped; Ferreus had fought valiantly, despite having only just woken up. Not lying awake for hours, awaiting the inevitable. Not having his sword tucked away under his bedsheets. Not leaving the note on the top of the pile, so inexplicably easy to steal away. She had been an imposter, after all: how could he predict that?

He stumbled over to his bedside, his jaw aching where the thief had kicked him, and wrapped his night-gown across his waist. Reaching the door, he prized it open. Descended down the steps. Rehearsed his plea to Alvarez, every sinew of the lie falling into place. The overwhelming evidence, that they were not safe. The simple fact, that there had been an attempt to usurp his power. The indefatigable truth, that Broska was the one pulling strings.

That none are free… while the rats are running.

†

Chapter 29

The Hollow Crown

W hat have I done to deserve this? Have I wronged you, in
some way? I fear I know nothing of it, if I have. Have I
disgraced your rulers? Do the gods... do they laugh at
me? I fear what they think of me. I fear their *wrath*, you understand.
Because I am a mortal, down here, walking these lands and breathing
this air... and they are high above, in the alcoves of a heavenly realm,
watching in all their reverence the world ticking by down below.
That they live in splendour... and I, in destitution. That they possess
all things, and at times, I feel like I have nothing. That I'm sick, or
insane, lying awake at night in my sickness, festering. It hurts me, to
suffer this way... rots me to my core. And I think about those gods
high above, I think about what separates me from them. And that is
what I fear... that is the wrath I fear I will invoke. The fact that I am,
really, so close to them in so many ways, yet they hold over me the
one thing I can never have... the *truth*."

Sat at his bed facing the wall, the demonic faces painted across the
stone there continued to spin slowly, their blackened smiles rigid and
broken, staring out from the abyss. Alvarez sat watching, his eyes
bloodshot and sore from sleeplessness. The ethanol-induced
headache thundered across his temples, skin lined with a thin
plastering of sweat. His gaze lingered blurrily on the face at the
centre of the consternation: a motionless mask with sealed lips and

hollow eyes, gazing blankly out into the wider room.

"Why do you do this to me?" Alvarez muttered despairingly. "What have I done to deserve any of this? I am Supreme Governor, ruler of a great people, as declared by the laws of the land at the king's passing. I am no monster. I should not be blamed for what happened to him. I never knew a thing. We knew about the corruption... about the taxes on the Tarrazi tribes... we knew the danger it risked if things got out. But it was the king's decision... he *knew* the danger it upheld. I've been nothing but supportive of him, as a man of the imperial army, and a man of decency and respect. My place in this arrangement... the new *power* that grants me... is as law decrees." He curled his toes, sighing across the floor. "It's *not* my *fault.*"

Anticipating some remorse, he found the faces remained un-changing, unconvinced by his reproach.

"You plague my mind, assault my dreams. Sleepless nights have passed and you've given me *nothing.* All you've done is torment me, and ruin me, and I have *nothing* to show for it." His desperation bled into anger. "Is this you, Mother Katastro? Is this your bidding? For calling out your lies about destiny, and the fate of all things. I'm now to be punished like this, like an animal, because I would not bow to you and all your *wonder.*"

The mass of faces continued to spin.

"I *know* it's you... I know you're behind all of *this,*" he spat, hands clenching. "You think you can mock me with this insubordination? I am in charge here!" The room rocked as he spoke. "I am god here! There is no other but *me.* My will is not yours to devise. *My* fate is in *my* hands, you hear me?" His expression swelled, as the face at the centre remained unchanged. "You *hear me?* I am god here, not *you!*"

The blank gaze of the mask in the middle snapped into a smile, as if Alvarez had conjured some spell to awaken it. The Governor jolted back, a surge of fear funnelling through him. It hadn't happened before. He did not think it could. He didn't know—

"*Destiny prevails,*" the face suddenly rasped.

Alvarez felt his heart bleed at its words, his terror-stricken soul melding with the blemishing anger cranking through his bones. He stood abruptly, drunkenly, hand coiled about the neck of a wine bottle, swinging loosely in one hand.

The face spoke again.

"And you, shall die."

Alvarez cast the bottle like a hatchet, spinning end-over-end towards the stone wall before him. The faces dissipated slowly as it approached, their smiles peeling away at the edges, row after row towards the centre, where the face continued to smile.

The bottle shattered against the wall, spraying a cloud of red liquid across the stone.

The vision fell away to shadow.

The door creaked open at the other end of the room.

"Sir...?"

Ferreus peered around the door's edge to see the Governor looming like some savage, the shattered contents of a wine bottle sprayed thinly across the wall opposite.

Alvarez swung around to face him, his expression one of fury and grievance muddled into one. Swaying like a troll across the bed-chamber, the Governor stopped short of the door, hands still curled into tight fists. "Yes, general?" he spat.

"Is now a good time...?"

"Yes, now is fine, so stop fucking about like a child and come and speak to *your ruler*."

The last word produced a concerted frown from the general, who nevertheless stepped into the room and delicately closed the door behind him. "Apologies to come to you at such a late hour, sir... we've had a problem."

"What's happened to your face?" Alvarez slurred, spying a thin cut across his left cheek.

"We had a break-in, sir. *Someone* attempted to enter my room and plant a letter on my desk, which would've likely put me in a... rather difficult situation, concerning its contents."

"How did you get hold of the letter?"

Ferreus puffed his chest. "I woke in the night to the sounds of movement – assumed it was the night watchman checking my door was locked and sealed – and rose to get a glass of wine, when I found it on my desk. Assuming that whoever had put it there was long gone, I opened it and read the contents." He exhaled slowly. "It was an order, forged in your name, to have me execute General Cavara during the expedition. It would incriminate me as a murderer... and you giving the order to kill one of your own."

Alvarez seemed to chuckle slightly. "Would never... would never order such a thing..."

"My thoughts exactly, sir," Ferreus reassured, smiling. "Now, unless I am mistaken – and forgive me if I am –what happened to General Cavara on that shoreline was an act of *self-defence*, as I explained before. She drew her sword against me, and I was forced to engage. We then reached the shoreline, where I took the blade from her and she bled out there and then. Broska was present, demanding answers as to what had happened – *visibly* angry and aggressive about her death – before we began to hear noises in the woods behind. Fearing patrols, we didn't have time to recover the body... and when we left, I had little thought about it..." A small smirk, quickly extinguished. "After tonight's incident, however... I am forced to reconsider what happened on that shoreline from another perspective, and have come across a... *quite alarming* set of presumptions."

"Spit it out, general... I don't have all night."

"There were only two people on that beach who saw the events unfold, and one of them only witnessed the final stages, whereby I disarmed General Cavara and she died—"

"General Broska."

"Which puts him in a unique position."

Alvarez considered, then his face beamed to life with the sudden realisation. "You think..."

"I make no guarantees, sir... but for the story in the letter I read to be fabricated in the way it had been... before the imposter emerged and attempted to kill me, stealing the same letter away in their escape... it requires particular knowledge of what happened. Something no one had, except either Broska or myself." He opened his palms out. "As I was the one who was targeted by this rogue... we can reasonably assume the letter was forged by General Broska in an attempt to overrule *me*... and in turn, incriminate *you*..."

The Governor pinched the bridge of his nose. "You think Broska was behind all this... that he plans to challenge me?"

"I'm simply going off the information I have, sir, I'm not—"

"He thinks he can challenge *me?*" Alvarez blustered, hysteria seizing the moment. "He thinks he can arrest officers left and right on his own authority... and then usurp others, climb the ranks... in an attempt to get to the throne? To *my* throne." He waved a hand about like an orator, mumbling incoherently. "They warned me about this... that's what the faces wanted. What they *wanted from me.* They wanted me to see the light, to see the truth... the gods know it, and why shouldn't I? They knew, they *always knew...*"

Ferreus shuffled, scratching his thinning hair. "Sir... who warned you of this?"

"Find him," the Governor exclaimed. "Find him, arrest him, lock him up, torture him. Make him bleed every last droplet... find out everything. Maybe there are others... maybe they plan to destroy me, like the faces said. The faces know... maybe I can speak to them. They *know...*" He grappled Ferreus by the shoulders. "I give you full command. Rat them out. Find them... bring them to *me.*"

Ferreus nodded blankly. "Yes... yes sir. Will do sir."

Alvarez released him, grinning, staring out from the abyss. He turned sharply, pacing back towards his bed, mumbling quietly in fits and starts about faces, about gods, about a true reality...

Ferreus studied the pacing drunk, the haunted fixation he seemed to carry, and found the room grow cold around him. Turning to the door, he twisted the handle and descended into the light beyond.

Hearing the door close at his back, the mad tyrant began to sing.

†

Chapter 30

Duty-Bound

From the attic of Azura's two-storey house, Cavara peered from the alcove window out past the other houses below, out across the stretch of wall lined with the tiny lights, and finally to the great iridescent expanse of the Icebreaker Sea beyond, glittering with the spots of stars. There was beauty in its stillness, in its sheer being – a mellow sensation at the base of her heart. Somehow, it reminded her of home – she found everything reminded her of home in some rudimentary way. A home that was so far away – a home that sat under the same stars as she did then, only rather than the tranquil safety Cavara felt in the quiet space of the attic room, she knew that on those distant shores blood was being spilt, and lives were being lost.

And there's nothing I can do. A stab of pain in her soul, deep within, almost enough to make her keel over. *They suffer and I'm not there.* She knew their fearfulness, found it within herself too – of the world as it was, and what it would become. Fear of the war, of the enemy on their doorstep. Fear of the new regime, its intentions, its seemingly ravenous desire for land and blood. Fear of the gods, and the breaking of the world.

Fear that this will be the end, and that there is nothing more to come.

Stood there, looking off to the open sky, she found it called to her, that desperate shore in a faraway world. Called to her like a lost soul, foregone its true path. And she would return, one day, so she believed: not for the army – and by all reasoning not for those leading it – and not for the war; not for swords or steel or battlefields or blood. Never for the duty-bounds of the dishonourable few who had cast her away – not for them ever again.

I would return for my country and its people, she declared.

It is the only way.

Drawn back to the real world, she was alerted to the sound of footsteps behind her, and saw the grey wisps of Azura's hair climb the stairs beyond.

"Oh, I hope I'm not disturbing?" she said, realising that Cavara was up and awake.

"Not at all," the general replied, offering a smile.

Azura crossed the room to the window at her side, and looked off to the Icebreaker Sea. "It's beautiful, isn't it?"

"Very."

"Not another place like it in the world."

"I've come to agree."

Azura turned to her, face sloping slightly at Cavara's despondent gaze. "Is everything okay, my dear? You seem... lost."

"It's nothing, really... I'm okay."

"You're about as bad a liar as Evelyn when he's stolen biscuits from the tin," she mused, smiling delicately. "But... if there is nothing wrong, or you aren't wanting to talk about it, I understand. It's not the place of a stranger to intrude."

Cavara sighed, the words prickling at the end of her tongue. "It's not that, it's... it's just that I don't really know what to do. Or how to say that, or what that's even supposed to mean."

The old woman considered. "You feel like you're drifting, when you've spent so much of your life anchored down."

"That's about as close to the mark as you can get."

"I can understand that."

"And now that I am... drifting, as you called it... I don't know what I'm supposed to do with anything anymore. None of it seems feasible anymore."

"Because it's not as easy as just going back home and picking up life where you left it?"

"Yea..." Her heart seemed to weep slightly, her gaze dropping to her feet. *There is nothing left*

"You never told me how you got that scar," Azura prompted, tapping the base of her ribs. "It's quite the wound."

Instinctively, Cavara reached for her chest, and felt the ridges of skin there knotted over the wound. A deep aching suddenly swamped her senses, as if she'd been punched – realisation bubbled to the surface, reopening dormant spaces of her mind that she'd fought to suppress. Something stirred viciously inside – only her forearm resting against the windowsill stopped her from toppling over with the weight of it all.

She pushed it down, more anger than anything, forcing it to kneel. *You're stronger than this,* her mind cried. *Don't let it claim you.* A deep exhale from her mouth, tongue rolling across her teeth. *Don't let it claim you.*

"I was attacked," Cavara said simply, defiance punctuating every word. "One of my fellow officers... stabbed me with a knife, while out on an expedition. I tried to escape, but he caught my leg and I fell, thrown to the floor at the shoreline where you found me. They left me there to die, y'know. They weighed anchor, caught the tide, and returned home... threatened for their silence. It was probably hardly mentioned back in the capital. Probably painted over as some 'terrible accident', a martyr of the cause." She scoffed. "Everything coated in *lies*... and they don't even know the difference."

Azura remained quiet for some time, hands clasped before her as if in prayer. "It's testament to your valour, I would say... from the simple fact you're still alive," the old woman said softly. "Testament to who you are... how you deserve this life you've been given, more so than most." A bitter sadness plucked at her face. "Who could've done such a thing? Who could've ordered another to be treated in such a way?"

"Could've been anyone... I know several names who could have made the order." *Although one in particular sticks in my mind.* "Part of me felt like it was a long time coming. They said I was too merciful, as a superior officer goes. Too opinionated in times of crisis... that I didn't lead with honour like they did. They'd discussed getting rid of me several times over the years... but I didn't quite think that what happened was what they were intending."

"Certainly not... enough to make you turn your back on the place, and never set foot there again."

Cavara blinked slowly.

"Do you not agree?"

She looked forlornly to the floor below. *Don't let it claim you.* "I can't..."

"Can't what?"

"Abandon them..." She sighed at length. "I can't abandon everything I've ever lived for... abandon my duty to the nation, to its people. It's what I've wanted my whole life: to serve, to protect, to pursue the betterment of the country. I can't abandon that... no matter what's happened. If I can't rely on the army's loyalty, that's one thing... but the people still remain. They need my help."

Azura smiled warmly. "The honour you bring to this world is beyond compare, my dear... but some fights are not yours to win. A noble cause and a good idea don't always align so well."

"I must, Azura," Cavara persisted. "It's not a case of it being a good idea or not — I *know* it's not a good idea to go back there, to put my life on the line at the hands of enemies I once called my comrades. That's not what this is, it's not as simple as that."

"But it's your *life* on the *line*—"

"And what's the alternative? That I sit here, knowing that my people will suffer, and doing nothing? Knowing that we are at war, and I don't take up that fight with them?" Her fist clenched and unravelled. "The rights and wrongs of it, the grey areas, the nuances in every decision... it's all just hindsight, revelling in the obvious errors after they've happened. If it were a time of peace, perhaps it wouldn't matter... but they are *at war*. Soldiers are fighting; people are dying. What kind of a person does it make me, if I just let that happen and do nothing? Regardless of my feelings, regardless of bad people doing bad things, regardless of the risk to my life... I have a *duty* to protect my people, to defend my country, because there are people out there without safety, people who need leadership." She paused. "I don't expect you to understand, but it's not about *me*. It's not about *my* life or *my* wellbeing. None of that matters. What matters, is that I can do what I can for my people and my country, and work on the rights and wrongs when the storm passes." Cavara looked up to the old woman, caught in the pale glow of the moon, and met her eyes longingly. "It's not a choice... it never has been."

Azura clasped her hand in her own. "My dear, everything is a choice. What you've made is a choice: you just don't see it. Because although you feel like you're drifting, you've actually never been more certain in your life. In reality, I wager you don't really fear that you've become detached from everything that once was... you fear how certain it's made everything that will be."

The old woman squeezed the general's hand, a moment of newfound serenity stretching out between them, before turning and moving back towards the stairway. Cavara seemed lost in the moment, the dislodged pieces of her mind slowly slotting back together as the words echoed around in their wisdom.

It's my choice. The certainty of it was refreshing, like the warm burn of ethanol blossoming in her chest. That what she experienced within, in those dark intervals of pain, was not conflict, but certainty – resolution of all things. That here was her path, and that her path was a choice. And that for her, that choice was the only way.

It's my choice, she repeated, a glow in her soul. *And that's the way it's always been.*

"Azura," she called out.

"Yes, my dear?"

"I... thank you, for everything."

The old woman's face seemed to lift, the wrinkles of her ageing face easing into a youthful smile. "That's okay, my dear." She made to turn back for the stairs again, but stopped herself and nodded. "You know, Brutus was right about you."

"Why's that?"

"That there is something special about you... in more ways than one."

Azura descended the stairway into the lower chambers of the house, and the general turned once again to gaze out onto the coruscating expanse of the Icebreaker Sea.

Which now, for whatever reason, seemed a touch more at peace than it had been before.

†

Chapter 31

Redemption

*F*uck!"

The needle speared through his flayed skin, pulling tight across his chest, an officer rushing over with cotton flowers to stifle the jet of blood. The wound was massive, carving a jagged line from his collar to his waist, ripping the skin open like a peeled fruit. Every inch of it had been sealed off with resin and stuffed with cotton flowers – looking now, the flowers had become bulbous red blots snaking through the wound, like an inflorescence of roses, weeping a yellow ooze at the edges as the wound began to seal itself. As more pressure was applied and the blood slowly stifled, the medical officers stood back with sweat-stricken faces in the dull candlelit glow of the tent, watching as Revek bit back waves of nausea and the foul texture of the sedative with intermittent exclamations of one simple word.

"*Fuck!*"

"More sedative, sir," one of the officers cooed, dangling the vial of bruise-purple liquid at his nose. "It'll dampen the pain."

"Nothing is dampening the fucking pain, you bastard!" Revek growled, threatening to raise his hand and swipe the bottle aside. "I need someone to close this thing off!"

"We're trying, sir, but you've lost a lot of blood... we need to seal internal bleeding before we carry on."

"Then why the fuck are you talking to me about it? Get on with it!"

Sudden pressure struck across his stomach, and Revek curled like a foetus, saliva spewing from his mouth through gritted teeth. He swore violently, screaming for someone to seal the wound. Watching the needle thread through, coil back, pull tight, thread through, loop around, pull tight, thread through, coil back, over and over again. Lights flickered at the corners of his vision, blurring into hexagons of colour as bodies loomed above him, muted mouths and thrusting hands weaving across his chest like knitting clothes. Above, the ceiling was low and suffocating, marked with shadows of the night beyond. Everything else was dim, becoming slowly darker...

"The wound's closed, cut the stitch!" a voice chirped at his side. "seal it with the emplastrum."

Clattering glass rung out in his ears, and moments later an exquisite pulse of freezing pain shot through his abdomen. Revek lurched like a striking snake, bubbles curdling in his throat, officers grappling at his arms trying to pin him down. More serum was splashed across the wound, snapping nerve ends across the exposed flesh, a glossy shine forming like frost over the stitching. The commander winced and bucked, head turning to vomit across the tent floor, his medical staff scattering like deer. His chest ballooned with red inflammation, body trying to fight off the emplastrum now dripping across his skin. Rushes of pain accompanied those of nausea; it seemed to never end.

"Let it set, let it set!"

The officers released his arms; Revek grappled the edges of the woven cloth bed and bit his tongue. Agony seemed to stretch on for centuries, rifling up his spine into the base of his skull. Despite the cold, sweat enveloped his entire body, droplets pooling in his eyes as he blinked furiously to stay conscious. The moments ticked by, unwavering, until the pain slowly ebbed away, a fraction at a time. Little by little, trickling away, until what remained was no more than a dull, frozen ache, and the nauseating sensation of a cavity struck through his chest.

He sighed, heavily, weightlessly, and slowly unclenched his white knuckles from the bed frame. "*Fuck...*"

"You've done well, sir," the chief officer said warmly. "We report no issues with the surgery. The wound has sealed over with the emplastrum, and the cotton flower will stop the bleeding until the wound has sealed."

"How long will that take?"

"At least until high-sun tomorrow, sir. We recommend you remain stationary until the emplastrum has hardened."

"Bedridden, then?"

"Although I understand the displeasure, it is necessary for your recovery, sir. We would not suggest it otherwise."

Revek acknowledged his displeasure with a single grunt.

"We also recommend, sir, that with your recovery it would benefit if you had regular intervals of—"

"*Sir!*"

A cry from the mouth of the tent.

Revek and the other officers turned sharply, to find a young woman in leather armour brush her way through the throng of black gowns, searching out her leader. The chief medic was about to call for an intervention, before the woman reached the bedside and blurted out her message.

"We found something, sir," she mumbled, eyes averting from the grotesque wound across his stomach. "In the valley to the north... we need you to come and see."

The chief medic intercepted, waving his hand. "The commander is bedridden, he should not be disturbed until—"

"What have you found?" Revek interrupted.

"We're not sure, sir... our scouts haven't returned yet. But there's smoke, and livestock roaming the edge of the forest, maybe a few houses amongst the trees..."

Revek's eyes came alive with activity. "Show me."

The officer placed a weary hand on his shoulder. "Sir, I wouldn't recommend doing anything too strenuous——"

The commander grappled him by the throat and rose to meet him. "I don't care what you fucking *think,* officer. I've saved this army from all manner of hell and nearly died doing it. This could be my *redemption...* and you are *not* taking that away from me." He released his grasp. "Now get me to my feet, and get this ridiculous overall off me!"

They had discovered it while on night patrol, scouting the lower edges of the small hill for signs of activity, looking out onto the northern landscape beyond with a keen, wandering eye. For what seemed an age, a vast skeletal forest stretched across the horizon, from the rolling hills of the west to the rippling shorelines of the east, grey shadows lunging from the dark as far as the eye could see. At first unassuming, the scouts' gaze had been drawn to the dull but distinct glow of torchlight nestled among the trees at the base of the hill, illuminating the colourless expanse like a mirage. Investigating, they had found boar and pigs roaming the forest floor, sticking close to ill-defined stretches of fencing carved among the trees. Some were attached to wooden stockades and small stone houses buried deeper among the trees – exactly how many, they were unsure. As they retreated back to camp, ready to report to their superiors at the summit about what they'd found, one thing seemed quite clear.

"We've found a village," Revek exclaimed, lowering his spyglass and grinning sharply. "How about that..."

"A healthy population too, sir," one of the scouts addressed. "Although we couldn't get too close, we estimate around two-hundred people living down here."

"Any signs of supplies?"

"Food and animal barns, storage houses, a water well..." She speared a finger out to a grey line of smoke curling from one of the squat rooves just visible through the branches. "We believe the building with the smoke is a blacksmith... so there could be weapons down there, too."

"Any soldiers patrolling?"

"None that we found, sir, no."

"Hm." Revek curled a finger across the pommel of his sword. "Can we assume they're undefended?"

"Ain't uncommon for militias to leave and join the front lines... if there's no one patrolling, we could assume that's the case here..."

"Undefended..." Revek's grin broadened across his face; it was almost too good to be true. His first great conquest of the war, without a blackcoat sword in sight. A single sweeping blow; the death of the savages and another medal to his honour.

"Any idea what we should do, sir?"

Oh, I have a few ideas. "Organise the men, tell them to be ready with swords sharp tomorrow morning."

"Yes sir."

"We'll march at midday..." – a fiery glow flickered across his gaze – "...and shall spare *nothing* that crosses our path."

†

Chapter 32

Bitter Consequence

They had been two years old, he recalled, when he'd found them trapped in that cellar. Two tiny infants, coated in dust, grazed up the elbows and knees, holding each other in one corner of the room with tears streaking their eyes. Above them, beyond the splitting stone ceiling that protected them, a landslide had torn through the house and surrounding village, burying nearly a hundred dwellings beneath huge torrents of broken rock. Those who could sought shelter in the valley below, or hid away in the deeper ruins of their homes – but as the death toll climbed and the bodies continued to appear, the reality became that those who hid away, rarely saw the light of day again.

He had been sent there with a relief detachment of the army, some two hundred men carrying wagons of food and aid up the steep valley slopes, the path ahead meandering like a ruptured vein. Their arrival had been quick; camps were set up for the injured survivors, who lined the outskirts of the town in quivering rows. Beyond them, looking upon the devastation – an entire walled settlement, gone in a few short minutes – he felt a cold despair rock inside his chest. Even from there, the bodies half-buried in the rock were evident in their dozens.

He had led a number of his detachment up onto the rocks, shifting delicately over its loose surface, calling out into the dust-smothered skies to see if anyone would reply. Occasionally a voice would cry out, muffled within the confines of the landslide, and a delicate operation slowly prized them from the rubble. Some made it out in one piece, and were sent back down to their families again. But he found more often than not that the cries that emerged came from the dying and dead, a final plea to the gods as men scurried to set them free, only to uncover a corpse moments later, the life since departed within.

They'd searched, and cried, and waited, and when the bodies began to dry up, he knew they were drawing to the end. Hours passed, without a single sign of life – only the echoing destruction breaking all around. For all he knew, whatever remained, would remain there forever. Bodies buried in the dust, and not a word spoken in their prayer.

And then, as they began the slow descent back to camp, he'd heard the muted sounds of weeping beneath his feet. Faint, almost indescribable, but undoubtedly there. A team was summoned; rock after precious rock was removed. Beneath it all, an old iron hatch revealed itself, half shattered by the weight of the landslide, yet with the handle still very much intact. Plying it open with the pointed edge of a hammer, he had descended into the dismembered abyss below.

And it was there, he found Camilla and Davo.

It was there, he had fostered the children who he now called his own.

I miss you dearly. Looking down at his hand, Broska studied the tiny card there that his children had drawn for him. A collection of people, two older men with beards and big stomachs, and two smaller figures, one boy and one girl. The big men were led down, bellies protruding like two hills, and the small children were sat atop them, scrawled drawn across their faces. The caption beneath read, *'you saved us – we love you'* in winding letters that barely fitted the tiny page. It was the first thing they had made for him, several months after they had been adopted. The first time they'd said, *'I love you'*.

The first time, too, that they'd referred to him as their father.

Even five years on, Broska looked upon that same small card with as much joy and fulfilment as he had then. A warm tear curled across his cheek at the thought of it, at the joy those two faces brought him. How he longed to see them and Eli again. How he longed to have them in his arms.

"I will see you again," he whispered sweetly, rubbing his thumb across the page. "I promise."

He pocketed the card, attention shifting to the latch on his door, which rattled intently as someone peeled it open.

Jinx slipped through the narrow gap, watching the corridor outside as the door gently closed again and she locked it tight.

She turned to him, her face blanched with sweat, a nasty purple bruise exploding across one cheek. Her eyes wandered, carrying her forward to his open window, which she promptly snapped closed and drew the curtains down. With only a thin streak of orange illuminating the space between them, Broska looked upon his little sister with a weight of concern in his chest, and a blooming sense of dread at the fear in her eyes.

Something had gone seriously wrong.

"What's happened?" he exclaimed.

"It's... I don't know how, but they... they knew..." Inhaling lengthily, Jinx calmed the stuttering in her voice.

"*What?*"

"Arrenso, they knew what was gonna happen. They knew we'd try and steal the orders. They knew you'd send me... they *knew everything.*"

Broska felt his heart tense up. "I don't understand... how could've they known? How could've they... it doesn't make any sense..."

"Because the letter Ferreus was given, was a forgery. It was signed in Alvarez's name. They *knew* we'd break in expecting to find that General Revek's name on it instead, so they signed it from the Supreme Governor, to make it look—"

"Like we've planted it to incriminate Ferreus..."

Broska lurched back, sickness mounting like a vortex in his stomach. His legs were numb; his head rattled like a thunderstorm. *How has this happened? How could they know?* His eyes searched about; his hand landed on the edge of his desk, steadying his swaying mass. *That bastard... that fucking slimy bastard. He wanted my head from the very beginning... that* fucking *bastard!*

"Arrenso?" Jinx muttered quietly, laying a hand on his shoulder. "Are you okay?"

"What can I do..." Broska spluttered, fresh tears peppering his face.

"I'm sorry..."

"What can I *do*..."

"They'll be coming after you... I imagine Alvarez has already been told about the break-in. They'll be coming for you soon... I'm so sorry."

"My family... Eli... what's gonna happen to them?"

"Nothing, Arrenso." She squeezed his shoulder. "Eli is more than capable, and will keep your young ones safe. He would have it no other way."

Broska bit his tongue. *Why must this happen...*

"If anything, it's my fault. I should've been more cautious, expected there to be some kind of ruse. As you said, he shouldn't have been underestimated..."

"It's not your fault," Broska declared firmly, biting back the coming tide in his heart. "All I know... is that I need to leave this place and save my skin... as soon as possible."

"Then let's go," Jinx said resolutely. "Grab your things, grab your sword, we'll... we'll find a horse, we'll get out. It'll be fine—"

"And you're not coming with me."

She physically recoiled. "What?"

"I can't risk having you trapped here as well – they may imprison me, but if they get to you... they'll have you killed. I can't have that."

"But how will you escape?"

"I'll find a way... I'll buy my way out, or escape through the southern gate..."

"Arrenso... I can't just step aside like that. I'm the one who got you into this mess... whether it was my fault or not doesn't matter. I have some responsibility in all this."

"Doesn't mean you need to risk your life for me."

She knocked his chin up, locking eyes with equal parts honour and defiance. "Arrenso, you don't have a choice. I'm coming, whether you like it or not. You're my brother... and this is family." She let him go and tapped a finger against his collar. "And I know you'd do the same for me."

She smiled then, perhaps the first time he'd seen that smile for almost a decade. Reminding him of his childhood, of the times they used to play out in dense forests to the south. Throwing sticks like axes; climbing trees and scouting deer. The warmth in her eyes, full of life and compassion. The delicate elucidation of their blood-bond; Broska found himself smiling too.

Perhaps she's right, he thought through it all. *Perhaps I need her after all.*

"You can get me to the southern gate, no further," he decided. "This is not your burden to bare... so when I pass through those gates, you will disappear again, understood?"

"You have my word," she replied, standing purposefully and reaching for the door. "Now grab your shit... let's move."

†

Chapter 33

Hounds of the Kazbaks

As first light broke, and streaks of gold and grey sun blanketed the Kazbaks for miles across, Savanta and Markus departed their overnight camp and followed the rise and fall of the world around them, seeking the Nomad's Path. The land quickly became treacherous and cryptic, broken apart by shattered rocks and trenches of uneven ground, sudden bursts of tufted grass twitching sporadically in the low winds. In the narrow grooves between each swelling of the earth, the land became even more dislocated, splinters of stone forming a loose bank for the tiny rivers rippling between them. The rivers themselves were fast-moving, creating small pools where the ground levelled, populated by tiny fish and aquatic worms that burrowed into the wet mud for food. Occasionally little rodents navigating the waterways would dart off into the grass, or disappear into their burrows at the water's edge. Beyond that, and the sudden shriek of small raptors hovering above looking for their next meal, the Kazbaks were desolate, skipping across the earth for as far as the eye could see.

There's nothing here, Markus found himself thinking. There were no great beasts of the open plains, no lizards hunting rodents through the rocks. No thin-legged deer leaping the rivers in search of fresh pasture. No predators or prey, bigger than perhaps a rabbit. *It doesn't make any sense.* Where there should have been nature and splendour, there was instead the unnerving silence of a sparse world, devoid of the colours of life that he knew from back home.

But this is not home. It was a place denounced for its destitution, its savagery. A place subsumed by the bloody wars of its cannibal natives, upending any balance in the wake of anarchy and decay. A place of pagan gods and coveted sin, crippled with disease and rotted to its core. *A place we could never call our home.*

And it seems all other life has been found to agree.

As they pressed on into the hinterland, the sun began its long journey overhead, mellow orange and dappled grey fading out into streaks of white clouds and hazy blue skies. The landscape around them also shifted, the hills breaking apart into mountainous crags as they neared the base of the great peaks. Sudden explosions of cracked rock carved open the earth, the hills' rolling composure now jagged and deformed. The tufts of strong grass fell away, replaced by bushels of spiky gorse nestled in the rocks, and huge plumes of yellow algae splashing across stone slabs. Their progress slowed, trying to pick a path across the uneven ground – sometimes a single footfall triggering a small landslide, carving up whatever route they had made out. The rivers they had followed disappeared into the recesses beneath their feet, only to reappear as surging rapids moments later.

This is a lesson in madness.

From there, it only seemed to get worse, as dislocated stretches of uneven rock gave way to huge crevasses several dozen feet across. The only feasible way through was to skim along their diagonal walls – and even that presented an ungodly task. Markus often found his feet slip away, sliding several feet down into the ridge, his hands eviscerated with tiny cuts trying to scrabble to safety. Navigating one huge trench, and finding another much the same directly after, and again after that, until the stinging slices across his hands left red raw handprints across the rocks, and the mountains to the west seemed like they were another world away. It was a fool's gambit, he found, trying to navigate such a place. A fool's gambit to go anywhere near the mountains at all. Yet Markus still found himself pressing on, hands bleeding, ankles burning, straddling the rocks of the Kazbaks, for reasons that had long since abandoned his mind. Maybe it was because they had come so far; maybe it was the reassurances that they were nearly there.

Maybe it's because, for whatever reason... I can't just let this bastard fool of a woman go through this hell alone.

She had said little since they'd left camp, beyond entertaining the occasional joke or warning him about precarious spots ahead. Her gaze had been steadfastly locked to the path, meandering across the broken backs of the mountain valley with little consideration for anything else besides.

Something's wrong with her. There was a coldness to her, something spinning deep within her mind that kept her locked away in her thoughts. To all accounts, had it not been for his presence, he guessed she would have just wandered off into the ether, a dwindling sanity as her only guiding light – the slow descent to madness. As much as he was ignored, Markus truly believed he was the only figment of the real world she had left. The only fixed point, beyond the embattled trepidations of her thoughts. The only way that the real Savanta could be reminded of herself – a real Savanta he knew deep down was still there.

And perhaps that's why I still follow her into hell, he found himself think. *Because, in the end... I'm the only thing that's gonna get her out the other side.*

They continued across the disjointed valley for some time after, the sun rising steadily overhead with them. It continued to grow, shifting shadows across the rocks at their feet, onward and onward relentlessly until Markus finally looked up to find Savanta had stopped at the peak of the nearest ridge, surveying the landscape beyond inquisitively. Clambering to meet her, tired arms dragging his near-lifeless corpse up the ridge, he reached its peak and took in great lengths of air.

"What is it?" he asked, head pounding under his cowl.

Savanta pointed off towards the mountains. "Your prayers have been answered."

Tracing her finger, Markus drew his gaze to the base of the mountain stretching broadly to the west – and there, much to his relief as to his surprise, was the narrow, barely-definable stretch of paved road weaving its way through the jagged earth. Slightly discoloured, it diced across the valley for miles along, an ancient artery spanning the length of the Kazbaks like a river.

"The Nomad's Path," he exclaimed. "By the gods... we made it."

"You doubted it?"

"Part of me did, perhaps... but I can't say, after all that, that there's a more beautiful sight in this world than flat paved ground."

"And the good news is – for this part at least – that the worst is over. If the path is as accessible as it seems... this should take us the length of the Kazbaks, and on into the Heartlands beyond."

"Song to my ears, that is... song to my *bloody* ears."

She laughed slightly, a dim flicker of emotion bubbling to the surface, and smiled. "I've been meaning to say thank you, Markus."

He frowned. "For?"

"For sticking with me. I know it's no easy ask – I mean, the road ahead is mighty long – and that I've often been distant... but I am at least grateful to travel in honest company." The words seemed uneasy to her, straining through her gums. "So... I thank you."

"It's no problem to me." He gave a nod. "A long time ago I was posted to your company as second-in-command... and it seems that even here, in the deepest recesses of fuck-knows where... that some things never change."

"I can admire that... even though the company's gone."

"The company never left, Sav," Markus replied. "The company ain't just the number involved. Never was. People came and went as the seasons changed. That wasn't what made it what it is. What marked the company, what *defined* it... was a belief in you." A glow seemed to resonate from her as he spoke. "The company was ideological... a belief in you, and in the service of our country, in

267

our own little niche of the world. And I still believe in that, even after everything that's happened… I still believe, deep down, that you're not guided by revenge or anger or betrayal. None of that. Deep down, you're still guided by that same belief in the good of the nation… in your own stubborn, unique way."

The smile widened, curling at the edges. "My thanks, Markus. You are a humbler man than I could ever be."

"And you have enough tenacity for about six o' me, so that about calls it even."

Markus laughed, and Savanta laughed too, and he found himself laugh even more. He saw the warmth in her face, the flicker like a candle dancing behind her eyes. The toothy smile, plucking at her cheeks, and the sweet sound of her joy reverberating from within. He found himself laughing more, laughing long, watching her smile, until he'd forgotten even what he was laughing about. Just holding onto that moment, fragile and fleeting, where the world came away and it was just two old friends again, as it always had been.

"I guess this is just my way of giving something back that I can call my own," she explained. "I've always been *given* orders, by command posts and whoever else was in charge, but I've never done anything… *of my own volition*, shall we say. Perhaps this could be my opportunity to do that, for once – to make a mark and call it my own."

Markus was reminded of their conversation in the medical chamber back home, and felt his elation cool – the laughter stopped entirely. "And where does that take you, Sav?" he inquired cautiously. "Where does that take *us*?"

A long, wavering silence struck out between them, the ruminations of reality and ambition coiling across Savanta's face. The turmoil of whatever had been plaguing her mind, slowly falling away to resolution. In part, Markus already knew the answer that would come – as Savanta thought it over, it could almost be painted across her face. *Part of me hopes,* he thought, *that she might've reconsidered.*

And part of him knew as well, that he'd be left wanting.

"To the heart of it all," came her answer, in the end. "To the Iron Queen herself. Someone needs to die, for what they have done to us... to *me*... and the buck stops with her. I'd sooner die than accept anything less." She paused. "But that's a long way from where we are now, and not entirely important. We need to make good headway through the Kazbaks before nightfall... there's no time to worry about beyond that yet."

And with that, she marched off, that blustering defiance catching flame with every step, as Markus stood there languishing with worry at the path that lay ahead. At her words, blunt like hammering stone, and that utter conviction that there was no other way. *The sentence to death, rather than accept anything less,* he mused, almost in disbelief.

A wish that may come with greater ease than any of us care to admit.

†

"They've crossed the Balzul Crags, heading north onto the Nomad's Path... they'll reach one of our outposts in the coming hours."

"Good."

"An ideal place to mount an ambush, wouldn't you agree?"

A pause. "No: the outpost is too open, the road too wide at that point. There are too many places for them to escape."

"But we would have the advantage."

"The advantage would be lost, if we were to be discovered beforehand."

"Then what do you propose?"

A smile. "We let the beasts do their bidding."

Beside them, a low, thundering growl sent shivers across the ground at their stomachs. Turning slowly, the huge skeletal jaw and four wide eyes of the Kazbak Hound rose slowly over the crest of the hill, sensing the vast landscape beyond with the twitching antennae across the frills of its neck. It snarled, catching wind of the invaders, clawing at the ground in great trenches to ease the temptation of the hunt. A hand was raised, pressed against the tufted fur along its shoulder, and the beast recoiled slowly, turning back to the river at their feet, where the other hounds lay sleeping, awaiting their summons to rove the lands and kill any that they found.

The blackcoat raised his finger, tracing the mountains to the north. "They'll reach the Lake of Souls by midday, and probably set up camp in the ruins of the old viceroy's house." The finger stopped at the base of a great peak, shrouded in the black shadows of a storm. "In the fading light, we'll make our move... there, we'll let the hounds have their play."

†

Chapter 34

Playing Games

*Y*ou *will learn, soon, what we want from you. You will feel it, shifting like the tide washing over you. Nothing but brightness, then nothing but darkness, then an absolution will overcome. And it will be beautiful, to watch you suffer. Truly, there is nothing greater in the world. There is no other way...*

"Cavara?"

She looked up suddenly with a sharp exhale of breath. She was in their kitchen, at a wide, low stone table with a bowl of churned oats sat untouched in front of her. In one hand, she clenched a spoon in a white-knuckled grasp, its frail handle slightly buckled from the pressure. The other lay flat against the tabletop, tapping furiously, drawing the attention of Evelyn and Azura sat opposite, who now frowned towards her wondering what she found so fascinating about the wet slop in the bowl beneath her nose.

"Sorry, I..." Cavara dropped the spoon, hands retracting from sight onto her lap, eyes wandering awkwardly about the room. "I'm just..."

"Didn't sleep well?" Evelyn asked politely.

She smiled. "Yeah, exactly."

"That's okay. When we first moved into this house... mumma always worried because I didn't sleep very well. I slept with her quite a lot. I missed my old house; I missed the smell of things there. It

271

was nice." A pause. "Do you miss your house?"

"I do," she admitted, her eyes meeting Azura's gaze. "More than I care to accept myself sometimes."

"Will you go back, one day?"

"I reckon so... one day." Her thoughts seemed to drift. "But not yet, don't worry. You're stuck with me for a little while yet."

Evelyn beamed at her words, then looked expectantly to his mother with a fresh thought at the tip of his tongue.

"What's that look for?" Azura teased.

"I was just wondering..."

"About?"

"Well, the market is today, and I was wondering if Cavara could come too. It'd be really fun. I'd like that a lot..."

"You already know the answer," she replied, an unusual firmness tainting her voice.

"But why?"

"Because it's not safe for her. You know how the officers treat anyone from outside the borders... she'll be locked up. We can't run the risk, for our sake as much as for hers." Azura looked up to the general, tucking away the hand she was waving in her direction. "Sorry, I'm speaking for you..."

"It's okay," Cavara replied, turning to the young boy. "Look, Evelyn, I would love to come to the market and see what's there, but listen to your mother... she's right after all. It's not safe for me out there. I need to be kept a secret, so long as I'm here."

Evelyn seemed to look at her as if by betrayal, and slumped in his seat with his arms folded.

"You'll have to excuse him," the older woman exclaimed. "He's used to *getting what he wants* all the time. Doesn't quite understand what '*no*' means."

"I know what no means," he said. "I just think it's not fair."

"And you're allowed your opinion, my dear. But I'm your mother, and ultimately, you'll listen to me."

He grumbled under his breath, legs swinging beneath his chair.

"May I go upstairs now please…"

"Yes, you may."

The young boy swung away from the table and skulked up the narrow wooden staircase to his room just above, giving a final optimistic glance back before he disappeared beyond. As his footsteps receded, Azura sighed and rubbed her face vigorously with her hands.

"I'm sorry, I know it's not the best situation…"

"You don't need to apologise," Cavara reassured. "I'm grateful for your hospitality, and for a safe place to stay. I couldn't ask for more than that."

"I appreciate your understanding." She nodded, smiling softly. "And on that note… I was wondering if I could ask of you a favour."

"Of course."

"I need to go out to meet with my contacts, get prices for the goods we brought in yesterday. I won't be gone long… but I was wondering if you could watch Evelyn for me, make sure he doesn't get into trouble or do anything stupid."

"I'm sure I can manage that."

"Thank you immensely." She stood, depositing her bowl at the kitchen dresser, grabbing a wool coat hung across the back of the chair. "Although I will warn you, he does like to play games, and should he want to mess about, well… he has quite a few tricks up his sleeve."

You think this is a gift, don't you? You think this makes you special. Because you, and that other brutish murderer, can see things and hear things. You think this is all some great game. You think you can make sense of it, make sense of the shadows. You cannot. You never will. We are in control here; we know the ways of the shadows. You have nothing left here but pain. And you will learn of that pain and suffering — I promise you that…

She wrenched the faucet closed, the water receding down the pipe at the base of her shallow sink. Reaching for the towel, she dashed her face of water and lay it to hang in the attic windowsill, gently warmed by the morning sun. Looking out on the beautiful turquoise waves of the great sea beyond the walls, she sighed despairingly and turned away to the staircase.

What does it want from me? It was anarchical, appearing in moments of quiet as this foreboding weight across her shoulders. *What purpose does it serve?* It was incoherent, stressing hatred that she didn't understand, or that she found had no source. The vicious ramblings of some malignant force, clinging to her mind like a parasite. *Will I ever know what it really wants?* She didn't know, and with all reasonable expectations she had a feeling she never would.

What does it mean?

Descending the staircase, she turned at the first floor and crossed the narrow corridor to the end. The pale door there stood ajar, with no noise from within. Only a dull silence rung out through the house, the occasional creak of wooden boards as the wind crept through the cracks. Beyond that, she heard no other life nearby.

How strange.

"Evelyn, may I come in?" Cavara knocked three times, awaiting a response that never came. She frowned. "Evelyn... are you in there...?"

The door peeled open, revealing a lime-walled room of basic wooden furniture and a metal bed frame propped against one wall. Small wooden blocks lay scattered across the ground; a stack of books sat in the window-sill, and in a pile in the corner that seemed long abandoned to the dust. Clothes were bundled on the pillow at the head of the bed, but there was no sign of the small occupant of the room.

Cavara's frown deepened. *Downstairs, maybe?* She called out his name again, but found no response. *Unless this is what Azura meant with 'tricks up his sleeve'...*

She left the room and descended the staircase to the spacious kitchen and living room, untouched since earlier that morning. A few broken biscuits were scattered across the tabletop, half-eaten by Evelyn before his mother left.

Where the hell is he?

"Evelyn?" she cried. "This isn't some joke! I need to know where you are!"

The world replied with silence.

She scanned the small living room, peering behind the wide pillowed seats, finding no sign of the child, or anything of great interest besides. *Where...*

"Your mum will be very upset if she found out. Don't think I won't tell her!"

Silence again.

She crossed back into the kitchen, leaning against the low slate dresser, tuning her ears to a house that had all but abandoned her.

"Come on Evelyn, I know you're around here somewhere——"

Her heart dropped, stomach clenching, looking to the mat at the front door.

At the pair of shoes missing, and the key still hanging loosely in the old lock above.

Shit! She lurched about, panicking, sickness swimming in her throat. *Where the fuck has he gone!* She thought for a moment, the glaringly obvious presenting itself like a cocksure prince. *The market... he's gone to that fucking market!* She stared blankly at the door, Azura's words spinning in her mind. *What do I do? I can't go...*

Hanging on a hook beside the door, a brown shawl and stained black overcoat caught her eye suddenly, and something desperately rebellious crackled to life inside her.

You can't... you can't go out. She said... it's not safe for you to... what else can you do? Cavara sighed longingly, gritting her teeth. She knew authority, knew respect, knew with every bone in her body that it was in her best interest to stay put and stay quiet and do nothing. But Evelyn was out there, somewhere, alone in the vastness of the capital, and he was her responsibility ultimately, whether she liked it or not. Time skipped past, hesitant and unchanging. *What else can you do?*

"Shit!"

She grabbed the coat and cowl and crossed the threshold, disappearing into the vastness of the City of the Sun, the eyes of the enemy everywhere and never straying far.

Off to find the boy with a trick up his sleeve.

And will it be worth it, in the end? When the shadows come, and the darkness with it, and you're left wanting, wandering aimlessly trying to make sense of a world you were never destined to understand. The pain that must cause for you… knowing the end times are coming, that your people will die and your nation will fall, and that you can do nothing about it. The sheer ignorance of it all, is priceless. I shall await that day with bated breath, I assure you. I shall await the day the world ends, and the day you go with it…

Stretching across the city's central plaza like the roots of a great oak, the marketplace was a massive conglomeration of beige tents and sprawling stalls criss-crossing the paved floors like some enterprising worm. Lengths of blue and white flags hung between them, the insignia of Sevica emblazoned across each one in swirling streaks of silver. At the centre, harshly contrasted with the lustrous mid-morning sun stretching across the sky behind, a carved monolith of pure black stone speared skyward, with a sphere that she assumed to be a globe wedged neatly at its peak. At its base, an enormity of people swarmed across the plaza, robed in fine silk garments of pale blues and striking reds. The bombast of merchants crying from their stalls, mixed strikingly with the general clatter and thrum of city life, animated the world around her with an obnoxious yet charming extravagance.

Not that she found much time to acknowledge any of the city's grandeur, that was. Beyond the dull ramblings of passers-by, her mind was wholly somewhere else. Looking at waist-height, following the higher-pitches of children's voices weaving through the crowds. Seeking some sign of the boy – the boy with a trick up his sleeve.

Evelyn... where are you?

Pulling the brown shall down over her face, she passed into the crowds of artisans and patrons with her gaze held low. Tall figures loomed all around, adorned in their beautiful robes lashed together with patterned bindings of silver, spilling across the pale tiles underfoot as they swept past and disappeared again. Looking up occasionally, she spied the youthful chestnut-coloured faces of the citizenry, their twinkling orange pupils and straight-haired beards woven into neat braids. There was an enchanting sophistication about them, she found, in their warm eyes and in the mellowness of their voices, speaking a local language she far from understood. Some wonder of the unknown, perhaps – to be part of a world she felt entirely separate from, where the only fear she had was the fear of being discovered as an outsider, a sheep in wolf's clothing.

Just need to find Evelyn and go.

Moving out into a small opening between two stalls, she spied a small cluster of children playing together just ahead. Her heart skipped a beat, frantically scanning faces as she skated towards them, jostling with a few robed figures who snaked slowly in her way.

Breaking free of the crowds, she found the children dispersing, several of them running off past the central monolith towards the huge bathhouse to the west. Unable to register any of their faces before they disappeared, she broke out into a short jog across the opening, diving back into the crowds under the shadow of the bathhouse, heart pounding through her chest like a drum.

I'm gonna get caught if I have to keep this up.

The crowds tightened, shoulder-to-shoulder, vibrating their way past each other in ill-defined conveyor belts. Shapes rose and fell from every angle; the children's voices amplified and wavered with each step she took. In the baking sun, the overcoat across her shoulders was overwhelming, sweat leeching from her body, streaking across her brow. With the stress clamping across her back, and the unrelenting wave of people blocking her way forward, Cavara attempted to supress the urge to scream it all away.

Where the fuck are you!

She began pressing forward doggedly, receiving the occasional disdaining look from one robed figure or other as she elbowed her way to the front. Row after row she crossed, against the tide, battling her way slowly to the bathhouse that loomed mercilessly overhead. Charging through, breaking free, spilling out onto the forecourt of the huge building, surrounded by white robes and expressionless faces that paid her no notice, much to her relief.

Must be somewhere here.

A few lowly faces lined the alcoves of the bathhouse, their gloves cupped to receive the residual coin of charitable passers-by; staff of the building stood at the grand entranceway addressing patrons nearby; a few street performers stood on neat squares of grass spinning knives and pirouetting with lengths of black cloth. Cavara moved between them, eyes flitting cautiously about. Too many faces, too much movement. Her head spun trying to pick anything out. She reached the alcoves of the bathhouse, waving away any intrigue from the homeless crouched there. Scanned faces behind her, finding nothing. Looking left to the crowded street-side, finding nothing. Looking to her right...

A small boy with brown hair crouching at the street corner, a small spinning toy cupped in his palms.

The boy with a trick up his sleeve.

"*Evelyn!*"

The boy looked up to see her and smiled broadly as she rushed over to him, grappling his shoulders tight.

"I knew you'd come!"

"What are you doing out here!" Cavara blustered, not caring who heard or what for. "You know you shouldn't be out by yourself!"

"I just wanted to come to the market..."

"Your mother said no, *I* said no. That means no, Evelyn... you can't just disobey us and run off!" She leaned closer. "*You know being out here is dangerous for me..."*

"But why is it!" he exclaimed suddenly. "Why can't you come to the market with me!"

"Because your *mother* asked me to look *after* you while she's *away*, now please... let's go back *home*..."

"But what about—"

She pulled him closer, grasping his shoulders tighter than perhaps necessary. "Look, Evelyn, I'm not gonna tell you again. We need to go back *home* now, that is an *order*. We are not going to the market today, we are going back home, because it is not safe out here for us. And let me tell you, when your mother finds... finds out..."

A dubious sensation caught her like the wind. Air thinning, lights blinkering like stars. Almost toppling over. Trying to fight it, planting on two feet. Mind swimming, a dislocation of sound and colour, nearly lost to—

Cavara.

She froze, locked to Evelyn's gaze.

You think you're in control, don't you? You think you can say when we do and don't talk.

Evelyn's face conjured a tight mixture of fear and guilt, as her gaze tilted absently off to one side.

You think this is a game, don't you? Like the one this little shit is playing with you. You think this is all a game.

"Miss Cavara, is everything okay?" Evelyn whimpered, nudging her shoulder. "What's wrong?"

You are wrong... you will always be wrong.

She tried mouthing words, but found nothing break free.

You will live with that consequence until the end times come.

"I'm scared... what's going on?" Evelyn pleaded, trying to shake her off as her grip tightened, her eyes spinning like a rabid dog.

This is the way it will always be.

She began shaking, arms seizing at the elbow.

You will suffer; you will die.

Evelyn screeched.

The shadow woman shall come for you all.

"Carto denoma qa tendis?"

Reality surged back to the surface. Cavara looked up – the distinct shape of two silver helmets loomed above her, studying her hands strapped aggressively to Evelyn's shoulders.

Remembering Azura's words: *there are eyes everywhere.*

She peeled her hands away slowly, wrists twitching and shaking, a pleading fearfulness translucent in her gaze. The officers looked down on her with disgust, one of their hands lingering delicately next to the pommel of their sword.

"Exo teré cor tanda demonicadas?"

Cavara got to her feet, coated in sweat, hair plastered across her face, blinking stupidly without a word of acknowledgement for what was going on. At their mercy, she watched as the smaller figure began to draw his blade, the big one ahead staring into her with hostile intent.

"*Carto denoma qa tendis?*"

"Oyada je medesco!" Evelyn spluttered from her side, holding her hand. "Oyada je medesco…"

"Demonicadas."

"Jo na fenturi-ma. Jo na fenturi-ma. Je'o sadanti."

The big man seemed to relax slightly; the smaller one drew his hand away from the blade.

"Ayudo so tero grappella?" the big one spat.

"Jo no gratizanti… jo, jo'ada rendisenitas co fenturi-ma popeno. Je'o sadanti."

The big man turned back to her, pupils like pinpoints. "To demi *asanó?*"

By instinct alone, Cavara began to nod daintily. She didn't know why, or how, or by what gravitation of her mind decided that was a good idea, but she nodded at length to the large man stood before her and prayed it was the right answer.

Evelyn squeezed her hand and smiled. "Fedo… jendoza gi mantas homedi." He looked to Cavara and squeezed her hand again. "Po demenis, Cavara?"

She continued nodding, seeing the boy's eyes glow. She then offered a small smile to the officers for their time, running away with the apparent ruse Evelyn had devised.

The big man grunted, staring her down for any flicker of doubt, before conceding and waving his arm to let them pass. "Malto garzel, malto garzel..."

Evelyn drew her away by the hand, away from the officers, back into the shifting mass of people still feeding through the marketplace in their droves. She was just whisked away blindly, following the boy with a trick up his sleeve into the city streets beyond, her mind wandering delicately between her subconscious and the beyond. All manner of emotion rising and falling in the numb alcoves of her heart, lost in a world that was not her own.

And a world that now knew her name.

†

Chapter 35

Hallowed Be Thy Name

They had travelled for most of the morning, navigating the bending roads and steep ridges of the Nomad's Path as it snaked its way along the base of the mountains, parallel to the great Kazbaks that continued to roll onward on their right. As the sun rose and the day warmed, Savanta had shed several layers of clothing and bundled them into her pack, cursing at the sheen of sweat that seemed to coat every square inch of her body. Looking back, Markus was much the same, although he maintained a steadier pace than she did as his knees began to give way. She couldn't say she shared such hardship: he was many years her senior, and the harsh wrinkles across his cheeks almost doubled that in appearance. Even now, as his eyes strained against the glaring sun and his legs buckled their way up the steep incline of the road, he looked almost ancient to her, like the youth of before had been bled away from him on their journey into the heart of Tarraz.

Looking up, he noted she was watching him and sighed. "I don't mean to slow you down, Sav, I'm sorry if I'm not keeping pace…"

"It's no problem, Markus, really," she said, a noticeable weight off his shoulders as she spoke. "There's no great rush."

"I know… but I also know you like good progress."

"I also know that you're here because you want to keep an eye on me, so I can't work you too hard." She scoffed. "Otherwise, who's gonna save my frail, delicate self when danger comes?"

"Fuck yourself," he replied, laughing too. "That being said... any chance we could have a break soon? Knees are killin' me..."

"We'll cross this ridge we're on now and look for a spot to rest up in the next valley."

"Thank you... my joints are most gracious."

The path curved off into the throat of the mountain, splintered spears of rock rising several hundred feet to either side. Beneath their feet, the road had collapsed in some places, dislocated pale bricks shattered across the cliff-face below. A few stray crows circled overhead, occasionally landing on nearby rocks to observe the travellers with keen, hungry eyes. The incline continued, levelling off slowly as the road stretched on, the landscape unravelling before them as they crossed the ridge's peak.

Savanta looked out across the mountainside, following the path as it curved left across the cliff, a pale snake of stone that connected to a wide plateau on the far side, a natural shelf in the mountain, and there she saw...

What the hell?

"Markus..."

"What?" he wheezed, several steps behind.

She smiled. "I think we've found something..."

Projecting from the cliff-side in grand pillars of pale rock, Savanta found herself at the base of an elegant structure of stone blocks and ornate carved entranceways. Lost in time, the half-dozen steps at her feet were worn and cracked by disuse. The doorways had been unhinged and stolen away, revealing a hollow chamber within illuminated only by the fractious lights that the broken pediment overhead allowed through. At its coronation, Savanta imagined it had been a grand spectacle to behold – to cross the Kazbak Hills and gaze up at the great structure embedded in the mountain, overlooking the world beyond like an omnipresent god. How beautiful it must've been – how ruinous it was now. A shadow of its former glory, etched into the cliff-side, now little more than a memory. The last vestige of a once glorious past.

Left to rot like the rest of it.

"It's quite the structure," Markus remarked, sitting on the highest step sipping water from a flask. "Any idea what it was in its glory days?"

"Could've been anything," Savanta admitted. "The architecture is very simplistic... smooth lines, fine engravings on the walls... whatever it is, it wasn't built by Tarrazi hands, that's for sure."

"So it was built by *Provenci* workers?"

"Quite possibly... judging by its age, I'd say it was at least forty years old."

"That would've been around the time of The Collapse." As he said it, a low howl caught the wind and brushed gently by, like the recast shadow of ancient times drawn up once more into the world. "Back when Provenci governors moved in at the end of annexation, starting their programs and building projects... reckon this could be one of them?"

"Perhaps." She ran her hand against the nearest column. "Although I'm not sure what purpose this one served."

Markus got to his feet and screwed the bottle shut. "Well... whatever it is, a look inside can't hurt."

She waved a hand. "Lead the way."

They passed through the entrance into a wide square room, with a low ceiling riddled with swellings of moss. Sconces lined the walls, the wood within them long burnt to ash. Bushels of gorse burst from cracks in the tiled floor, stretching at awkward contortions to reach the few coils of light that entered from above. The trickle of a small mountain spring was apparent at the back, feeding through a crack in the roof and spilling across the floor below. There was a musty, forgotten smell hanging thickly in the air like dust, a sign that nature was slowly reclaiming the ancient structure for its own.

"Look there." Markus pointed to a few torn rags sprawled across the floor to their left, and a haphazard pile of sticks beneath one of the torches on the wall. "Seems like someone's been here fairly recently... and left rather quickly."

"Probably just local travellers," she replied coolly. "They use these routes to access better hunting grounds to the south."

"And you're sure on that?"

She cocked him an eye. "If you think we're gonna get attacked by a legion of blackcoats, Markus, I assure you we aren't. They wouldn't bother going this far west, what with an entire army marching through the lowlands. It'd be a waste of resources."

He gave a shallow nod. "S'pose you have a point there." His eyes drew away for a moment, towards the centre of the room. "Although, I'm not too sure what those are..."

She'd spotted them too when they'd first walked in: three stone blocks, a half-dozen feet in length, partitioned in neat rows. One of them sat partially collapsed, spilling lengths of brown stained cloth across the floor amongst its rubble, but beyond that as unassuming as the rest.

Symbolic, Savanta thought, *although quite underwhelming, for the size of the room they occupy.*

"Must be quite important," Markus mumbled. "I mean... I'm under the assumption this whole place was built for them."

Savanta took several steps forward, stopping between them, running a hand across the flat top and shifting a great length of dust onto the floor.

"There's writing," she exclaimed. Brushing more of the dust away, she found three rows of engraved text buried beneath. *"Here lies Master Porfirio Devesky... First Governor of the Kazbak Regional Government... served with honour and dignity."* She paused in solemn realisation. "These are *tombs*..."

Turning to the one opposite, she cleared the dust again to find a similar description. *"Here lies Officer Calista Orderlenz... First Marshal of the Kazbak Regional Army... served with honour and dignity."* She withdrew her hand and stood back. "They're tombs for Provenci leaders... people who must've worked here during the annexation. For whatever reason, they requested burial here too. All servants to the crown, dying in the duty of their country—"

"Not *all* of them," Markus interrupted, standing by the third tomb. "See for yourself."

Savanta crossed over to him and hunched over the inscription, finding some difficulty in making out what was written there. "*Here lies... The Verlunz of the Kazbak Tribes, Az-al Kar'malla... who served with honour and dignity to the crown of Provenci...*" She frowned sharply. "The chief of the Kazbak Tribes... buried and commemorated by the Crown of Provenci, among its own servicemen..."

"Quite something, isn't it?" Markus added, with a tinge of pleasant surprise that made Savanta's blood boil. "To think they'd honour their people as well is quite—"

"*No*," she growled, hand withdrawing as if it'd been doused in acid. "No, that can't be right... why would they honour a *savage* among our people?" A fist clenched. "*Hundreds* of officials died at their hands, across Tarraz, hundreds of the innocent slaughtered by their tribes... and yet here they've honoured one of their chiefs with a tomb among the men whom they sought to *destroy*..."

"Maybe things were different here."

"A savage is a savage, Markus," she dismissed. "It's the same everywhere."

"They were once our people, you know—"

"They were *never* our people."

"And why is that, Savanta?" Markus grumbled, taking a step closer. "What makes them so different to you?"

"*What?*" she snapped.

"Because it's only you, Sav... it's only you who revolts at their being here. It's only you who ever questions their place in this world. It's *obsessive,* and it is *rotting you*..." He paused. "Why do you hate them so much?"

Savanta felt her blood rise, the urge to scream uncompromising, the pulsing sound of the voice in her head reeling back to life.

But as the question came again, the agitation in her soul seemed to simmer – whatever anger had surged to the surface, now dipped its head again and descended into the gloom. As it receded, a vacuum opened up, cold and unforgiving, like a great cavity in her chest.

With a shaky hand, she leaned against the tomb's heavy surface and sighed weightily. *There's no escaping reality... not anymore.*

"My father... was one of the governors here, in Tarraz," she struggled, eyes wandering lamely. "Worked in a mining city to the north of here called Var Xoshna. My Father was sent out just after my seventh birthday... rarely saw anything of him after that. Got letters, the occasional trinket or medal he sent home... I saw him perhaps twice in the years that passed. It was cruel... I wanted him back bitterly, selfishly almost, but I knew he was working. He told me not to worry, that his posting was only five years." She paused. "Five years is a *long* time when you're a kid... and gods did it feel it. I waited by the post-master office every week, waiting for another letter to come through. Sometimes I'd get several... other times not for weeks on end. It was a weird limbo, y'know, when he didn't write for a long time... believing he was alive and well, but also knowing quite reasonably that he could be butchered to death and we'd know no different. And he was alive, of course, alive and well and doing his job for king and crown and country..." – she stifled a tear, reality biting through – "...until one day he wasn't."

The memory of the envelope returned, exquisite and painful, part of some broken buried place in the back of her mind she had long rescinded from use. "One day... we received a letter addressed to our house, but written in different writing. Eleven winters old, I took it upstairs to read, and... and when I opened it, I found a letter scrawled in blood, and a token gift from the chief who wrote it." Her breath crackled in her throat. "They'd cut my father's ear off, and sent it to us... with a letter telling us that their pagan *fucking* gods had told them to, and that they were watching us." Anger surged. "That was how it ended. My father's four long years of service, his

287

help to the city and its people... and the only thing I see of him, after *two years* without being in his arms... is his *dismembered ear* sent by some *fucking savage* in this godforsaken *fucking country!*"

She crashed her fist against the tomb, a flurry of dust scattering as she did. Boiling over, the rage within her fell away, and her legs buckled beneath her. She tried stepping forward, but found no sensation in her feet, in her arms, in anything, beyond the knotting pain eating at her chest.

She collapsed against the opposite tomb, sliding down its edge, streaked in broken light, salt burning her cheeks. Markus rushed over, bundling her in his arms, locking tight as she began to cry violently, convulsing with the force of it, reams of tears spilling down her face as her heart wrenched and every fibre of her being succumbed to the agony of the world.

Time seemed to stop altogether.

†

Chapter 36

Playing God

Today, my friends... we stand on the shoulders of giants," Revek pronounced, raising his hands to the sky, overlooking the lowland forests stretching off below him. "Today, we march against our greatest enemy... strike the first blow against Tarraz and its people, and finally rise to the commandments of our great nation's struggle against evil in this world."

He spun on his heel, facing the vast congregation of soldiers sprawled across every corner of the hilltop before him, their faces glowing and expectant. From the makeshift podium he stood upon, the commander gazed across the masses, from those mere inches from his person to those barely visible over the crest of the hillside some distance away.

"This is the moment we've been waiting for!" he cried, to the cheers of several hundred. "Half a century of tolerance, watching these people disobey and manipulate at every turn... being made fools of, as a once-great people, soiled by our pride and our wanton benevolence. Sending good souls out here to govern, left to die at the hands of pagan cannibals, hell-bent on our destruction. The *arrogance* and *insubordination* of their way of life... shall not be tolerated *anymore!*"

Another cheer erupted, fists pummelling the air, a bubble of elation swelling in the commander's chest. "This is *our* time... this is our time to prosper, to put our foot down and assert our rightful place in the world, as gods among men…"

"This is the only way…"

Alvarez drew his eyes away from the palace window and blinked heavily. Looking down to the small silver cup clenched in one hand, and the mudded-orange liquid sloshing delicately within. The warmth he felt, thick in his stomach and veins – the pulses of pain quivering through his skull, throbbing in his liver. A quaking, vacuous numbness punctuating every word and thought, and the stillness that brought to his rotting soul. Where there had been pain there was indifference; panic became dullness; the fear of the unknown blurred into dull shades of grey. As if there were nothing wrong in the world.

As if the shadows weren't watching, from the corner of the room behind.

"Are we not deserving, of all this?" he remarked to his own company. "Our fruitless years of trying to make those *savages* see any sense… the countless humanitarian missions under the Crown, trying to teach these animals about duty and morality and good government. Failures, all of them." He paused, taking another swig. "But not us, oh no… the failure was not on us. We gave them *everything* they needed, everything that could've brought them forward into a modern world and they *butchered it*… like they butcher everything else." He raised his glass, watching the pale shine of the mid-day sun glance across its rim. "They called it corruption, fraud, mismanagement… we called it *repayment*. And you see… that's what makes them savages… that's, that's why they're these simple pagan animals with their false gods and their rituals… because even right to the very end, they could never be *civilised* about it."

Alvarez turned suddenly, eyes gravitating to the shadowy corner of his bed-chamber – and within those dark recesses he saw the foreboding shape of the grinning face watching him acutely. His heart stuttered at the shock, subdued by another swig from the silver chalice, as his eyes wandered lazily across the dark, picking out other unblinking faces watching from within.

"And to think, for all those years, they championed me a fool... for wanting to seek my vengeance against those bitter *savages*. They called me all manner of foul things, entirely unfounded, obnoxiously untrue. A tyrant, a warmonger, a devil, a snake..." He giggled inanely. "And they called me mad, would you believe? A madman... seeking revenge against these poor nobodies, whom they hoped to *civilise*." A sharp grin coiled across his face. "Well, I say to them..."

†

"Who's laughing now!"

Another cheer launched skyward, the soldiers jostling with adrenaline, swords swaying attentively in their hands. Awaiting the call to arms – awaiting the fight to commence. Palpable, tense across the air that Revek breathed. That exaltation, that feeling of being on the right side of history, in the greatness of the world. There, on the podium, in the radiance of the midday sun – the moment of triumph had finally come.

"The day is upon us, my friends! The day we show these wretches the true might of the Provenci Imperial Army, in all its grandiosity!" He drew his sword, swinging it wildly in one hand. "We shall march upon their villages, raze their homes, slaughter their people like the hapless animals they are, and they will *know*, then, their place in this world. They shall know the suffering we have endured at their hands, for *far* too long. They shall not defy us any *longer!*"

Another cheer; the clattering of swords and shields. Revek stepped down from his podium and thrust his sword out to the valley below. "We march! We shall hail the might of Provenci; we shall hail the might of our people! We shall march to them, and they shall know..."

"*I AM GOD HERE!*" Alvarez growled, stabbing a finger at the shadows. "You have no *control* over *me*... I am the god of this land, of all that I survey. You cannot *take that away from me*. You, or that she-witch Mother of yours. She talks of destiny, of fate, of this predestination as though the world is beyond our control." His fists clenched, teeth grated together, eyes bleeding with tears. "She is *wrong*... she will *always* be *wrong*. There is no fate beyond the one I dictate. You cannot *stop* that."

The face remained unchanged, staring calmly into the eyes of the crooked tyrant as if wishing the world away.

Alvarez sneered, spat at it, hand curling wildly for the knife at his belt as if intending to slice it from existence, hating its silence, its sheer indifference to the world, to his pleas, to everything and nothing all at once. Hatred, cold and raw in every part of his soul, coiling about his face, a primal energy longing to be free, demanding and pervasive, battling on and on until the pulse in his head grew unbearable, and the ceiling felt about to collapse.

A grin struck out across his face then, wild-eyed and unforgiving. "You will never say a *word* to me, because you *fear* reality. You are just a figment, a hollow shadow in my mind – there's nothing to *you,* really. You just linger there, watching... amounting to *nothing!*" He reeled against his bedpost. "It's that bitch's doing, isn't it? That she-witch of the dark. This is her *nightmare*." His face became gaunt. "She wants to do away with me? All that about fate and destiny... and *she* is the one controlling it, the one willing it to life." The anger flared back, its intensity growing. "She wants to *use me*, like she used that old bastard king! She wants to *betray* me, to betray my people... to betray what *I love*..." His face sunk away, tears pinching at his eyes, before turning suddenly defiant.

"*Traitor!*" he roared, swinging round to the exit at the other end of the room. "She thinks she can control me... thinks she can betray *me*... I'll show her." He threw his hands up. "I'm god here, you hear me! *I am god here!*"

As the door swung shut, lightning struck outside.

Moments later, the rain began to fall.

†

Chapter 37

A Matter of Time

Within minutes of their departure from his office, armed troops had rallied along the street outside and raided the building in broad daylight, ransacking the general's belongings in search of treachery and betrayal. Upon finding nothing – Broska had made clinically sure of it – the soldiers had widened their search, spanning entire streets, housing blocks, stretching to whole districts, until the city seemed to swarm with a hive of militant activity in search of the general and his accomplice. Searching every corner, every alley and every door, but finding no trace of either person. No sign of their quarrel.

As if they had vanished in plain sight.

Broska tipped his wide-brimmed hat down, catching the dull shimmer of silver boots marching along the street beside him. He stood deathly still, the crunching of polished heels rising and falling like the tide, before he glided from the street corner onto the main thoroughfare, blending silently into the crowds. Keeping pace with the robes around him, he spied another figure cross his path ahead. Another step, and a gloved finger snaked around his thumb.

A striking flash of red, and they drew up alongside him, shrouded in a crimson cowl.

"We're about seven blocks from the nearest gatehouse, due southwest through the Merchant Quarter," Jinx muttered, eyes flickering cautiously. "Central plaza is three blocks ahead... expecting heavy militia activity around the marketplace."

"We should divert left, stick to the side-streets," Broska whispered.

"Depends on if we want to risk a stop-and-search by patrols... could get messy if we're caught in the open."

"Any more than a bloodbath in the marketplace if they decide to take a peek under the hat?"

A pause. "Point taken."

"Then by all means... left at your next convenience, ma'am."

Jinx sighed with a grin. "I'll give you a swing at my next convenience if you keep that '*ma'am*' shit up..."

A rap across the knuckles, and Broska lifted his hat slowly, guiding his stride away from the thoroughfare, following the red cowl across the street, disappearing amongst the shadows of a narrow alleyway, silent as a fox on the hunt.

"Of all the things I thought I'd be doin' today," Broska mused, adjusting the collar of his coat, "this was certainly not it."

"Being chased out of your hometown as a wanted criminal for crimes you didn't commit... ain't exactly the top of everyone's to-do list, no," Jinx teased. " That being said, just as good I got to you when I did. They made short work of your office ..."

"Wouldn't expect less from traitors and thieves..."

"Goodbye, lovers and friends..."

Taking a turn, they passed into the warrens of the Merchant Quarter: narrow crisscrossing alleys under canopies of draped cloth, pastel tones of red and green and gold flourishing gently in the low wind. Street after street, they skittered down narrow paved paths with shoulders skimming the sides, edging ever closer to the dull-grey edifice of the city's outer wall, slowly manifesting across the horizon. An echo chamber of voices, Jinx found her head spin trying to locate friend from foe, her periphery assaulted by broken conversations and roughly distinguished orders. With Broska as her ever-present but severely overdressed shadow, the chime and clatter of metal was never far away, as rogue patrols navigated the side-streets like rats in a sewer, awaiting the glimmer of their next prey, so close yet so far.

"There's another thoroughfare up ahead," Broska acknowledged, the glow of midday sun striking across the street ahead. "Do we stick to the alleys or make a break along the main road?"

"Main roads this close to the wall will be a hotbed of activity – if you wanna hand yourself to your old pals on a silver platter, then be my guest." Jinx stopped sharply, looking left-right across the next intersection before crossing straight ahead. "By my estimation, if we can make it through the side-streets unscathed, and carry on west from there, we'll land ourselves opposite the stables, only a few streets from the south gatehouse. That'll be your easiest way out of the city – archers on the walls won't have time to respond to any commands before you're out the gate and away, so all you gotta do is dodge the guards at ground level and you're clear."

"What about you?"

"Once you reach the stables and make your escape, I can slip away easy enough… I have contacts who can lend a hand."

"I guess they're just as resilient to law and order as you are?"

She turned and grinned sweetly. "Wouldn't have it any other way."

"Could've guessed as much…"

They reached the main road, embracing the confluence of activity that bustled there, the threading interwoven lines of people stretching left to right as far as the eye could see. Near impossible to follow, their eyes were drawn opposite, where another thin alleyway stretched off into the cloth-draped shadows.

"No sign of patrols," Jinx exclaimed.

"So we go now?"

She stalled, a moment's hesitation, ticking by, ticking by—

"Yes. *Go.*"

They drove into the bulk of the crowd, Broska leading, his immense size breaching the mass like a meteorite. Jinx trailed behind, pushing through, their progress stalling halfway across, suddenly drifting with the crowds, the opposite side-street falling from sight, lost in the surge—

Broska continued to push ahead, sweltering in the heavy heat of the sun and the enormity of his disguise, forcing his way through, muttered apologies all around—

Finally breaking free, the outliers of the crowd slipping away, crossing under the thin shadow of the nearest house, and—

Three soldiers, camped at the street corner, surveying the crowds ahead. Observing, watching intently... turning to see a huge figure and their small follower emerge from the throng beside them. Watching them dip away, eyes adrift, streamlining down the alleyway with hurried, determined steps, disappearing out of sight without a word...

And something didn't seem quite right about that.

"*Keep moving,*" Jinx whispered, heart stuttering, the heavy footfalls of the enemy suddenly approaching at their backs. "*Left at the next intersection, then run.*"

"*Run—*"

"*Do as I say, or we're both fucked.*"

The steps drew closer; the alleyway shortened. Broska burdened the cold surge of dread within him, knowing the game was up – that they'd come so close, yet so far. He blinked rapidly, head pulsing.

Am I going to die?

"Oi!"

A cry from behind. Broska ground to a halt, gritting his teeth and turning slowly. "Yes?"

"What are you two doin' down 'ere? Off on business is it?" They took several swinging steps forward. "Care to show some identification?"

From the corner of his eye, Broska saw Jinx slip down to the knife at her belt and unbuckle its sheath. Behind her back, Broska waved her hand away from it and leaned in close to her ear.

"*No blood here,*" he whispered. "*We negotiate.*"

Shifting his great mass past her, he strode with some confidence over to the soldiers and slowly eased a wallet from his breast pocket. "Officers... I don't feel that this whole business is entirely necessary. We're just passing by, hoping to find a way through the city without getting caught up in the midday rush." Tipping the wallet upside-down, a scattering of coin fell into his broad palm. "Now, I'm sure you understand what I mean... and won't have any problem letting us past."

At the sight of coin the two men stood behind began to waver, their eyes wandering, shoulders slouching and docile. Broska buttered them with a smile, but found his face harden when laying eyes on the third and foremost soldier, whose expression remained as contentious as ever.

"I believe bribing an imperial officer is a rather pernicious crime," they said with little amusement. "That being said, we can let *that* slide on the understanding that you *show us your identification, sir.*"

Broska bit his tongue.

"Or might that be because you shouldn't be here..."

The general sighed, scraping his foot across the cobbles. "I didn't want to have to do this."

The officer frowned. "Do what?"

"This."

Clasping the man's head in both hands, Broska bucked his neck forward and broke the man's nose open in one hit. Reeling back, the general stepped in and grappled the second man's head, throwing it against the stone wall to his left, the chime of the helmet hitting solid rock sending numb reverberations down his arm. The soldier collapsed; Broska rounded once more on the first man and cut his legs out with a kick, the broken face crashing to ground like a felled tree.

Ahead the third man turned, running back towards the main street in a disjointed sprint. Instinctively, Broska slid the baton from the man's belt at his feet, wielding it like a tomahawk, and threw it at full force down the alleyway, spiralling end-over-end until it connected sharply with the back of the man's head. The knees buckled; the arms went limp.

A jolting crash of metal, and the man hit the dirt like the rest.

The general exhaled deeply, watching the officer with the broken face wriggle helplessly across the floor at his feet, clutching what remained of his nose as it seethed with warm blood.

A scoff from Jinx behind. "You call that negotiation?"

"I call that... being shit outta luck with not a lot of options," he muttered, stretching out his back and turning to her, wheezing under his breath. "Now let's get moving, fast... before someone——"

A scream erupted from behind them.

Turning, they found a woman stood at the end of the alleyway, a small crowd gathered in horror, studying the three incapacitated men sprawled across the cobbles below. Suddenly fingers were pointing, looking up at the perpetrators, looming over the bodies, caught in the act. The rising bloom of shouting and condemnations, scattered but resolute, echoing down the passage towards them.

The sound of metal boots, approaching from all angles.

Broska turned tail, and began to run.

†

Chapter 38

There Can Only Be One

What happens now?

Cavara stared out blankly across the Icebreaker Sea, a cold chill whispering through the narrow slits in the window, twinging down her spine. Her mind wandered, agitated, reminiscing the day like an obituary, pervading all sense and thought. How the voice had come to her, and held her, and couldn't be drawn away. Its demands, its threats, hollow nothings yet with all the potency of a knife-blade. The scene she'd caused – the terror worn heavy in Evelyn's eyes, his cries for help. The officers approaching, studying her: this dull, mute woman reprimanding this child. This woman they'd never seen before.

And now they know my name.

When Azura had returned, Cavara hadn't had the heart to tell her about any of it. For whatever reason, her lips were sealed, only passing off awkward smiles and blunted acknowledgements, the wary gaze of the small boy burning holes in her skull. They had eaten, and joked, and Azura had spoken of her business, and the clients, and the profits on offer. Cavara had done nothing but nod, picking limply at the food before her, a hyper-flux of activity raging behind her eyes. Still she said nothing.

What happens now?

As her blind gaze studied the waves stretching out along the

300

horizon, the general's hand drew across the deep trench along her abdomen and she hissed with unease. Along its central ridge, the skin caverned inwards like a ravine – deep enough to puncture organs, deep enough to never stop bleeding until the blood ran dry. The knife had driven in up to the handle, several agonising inches of metal rifling through her liver. For all she knew, and for all that was natural to the world, that should've been the end of it. Death should've greeted her, in its slow and unconquerable procession, on the distant shores of Tarraz. And for all she knew, she had died there: face down in the sand, the boot-print of General Ferreus stained across her back, bleeding the ground purple as the life slowly ebbed from her soul. That should've been the end of it, of everything she ever knew.

And yet here I am, a dead woman walking, living my life like a shadow at the other end of the world, she mused, drawing her hand away. *With a voice in my head, telling me there is only pain yet to come.* She scoffed. *If there is pain greater than the life leaving your body from a stab wound… I'd sure like to see it.*

Footsteps echoed behind her; she turned to find Azura ascending the stairs like a phantom. The old woman smiled, stopping at the end of her bed, perching at its edge. "Are you free to speak?" she asked.

The general nodded once, and once only, studying her fingers splayed across the windowsill.

"Only, I have some information for you."

Cavara hesitated. "Go on…"

"While discussing business with my colleagues today… one of them said that he'd recently visited Casantri." The general's chest swelled. "And was… taken aback, by the developments there."

"What's going on?"

The old woman clasped her hands. "Well… for one thing, there's been a declaration of martial law, so he was forced back offshore once the authorities realised a foreign merchant had docked. Apparently everything's locked-down – I mean curfews, militias roaming the streets, stop searches on every street corner… sounds like your people are undergoing quite the ordeal."

"I had a feeling something like that would happen," the general acknowledged, sighing with disappointment. "Did they have any news of the war effort?"

"There was something about a border wall… apparently the bulk of the army have breached it and are now pushing through Tarraz, with detachments leading off north to raid villages. As far as he could see it, things seemed to be in your favour."

Association with the war made Cavara wince internally. "I suppose that much is good," she managed. "But if things are going so well… then I don't understand why they're under martial law."

"Fear, perhaps… can do vicious things to people, in times of trouble."

The general exhaled slowly. *Or things at home aren't quite as sweet as success in the field makes them out to be* – but she left that unsaid.

"That being said," the old woman continued, "being cooped up here isn't far off it."

Cavara nodded slowly.

"All the same, you seem to have made quite the mark on Evelyn. He can't stop talking about how great you are…"

The urge to pull the rug out from under him tempted her for a moment, receding like the autumn tide. "He's just being nice," she lied.

"Always a good kid, he is… always a good kid." Azura paused in thought. "I owe you my thanks, really."

"It's no problem to look after him while you're away on business…"

"Not that," she corrected. "It's more that… Evelyn's always struggled with disconnecting from his past. He's always been very attached to his birth parents, always speaks of them, and what they'd do and say if they were in his position. Sometimes it's led to some… very difficult conversations." She sighed. "It's not every day you have to tell your fostered child that his parents are gone and will never come back. And he never understands, no matter how many times I tell him – he's still too attached for his own good. So I just carry on doing what I can and hope that people come about in his life, who will finally give him someone else to look to. Someone to show him that he can think for himself, and that the memory of his birth-parents should be just that: a memory. Brutus has done it, over time – he's been a father like the boy has never had. And I try, of course, to do my best." Azura levelled her eyes, a deep sadness glowing behind them. "And even though you've been with us for only a few short days... I have never seen him so happy. Now you may brush it aside as nothing, I get that... but what you've done, or at least started to do for him, is drag him out from the shadow of his past. And I... I can't thank you enough for it."

Cavara smiled warmly, a contentedness singing through her words. "It's a pleasure and an honour, Azura, trust me on that. I just want what's best for him."

"And for the world over, I am grateful."

The general crossed the small attic and embraced the old woman, her thin arms holding tight across her back, a low sob bubbling in her throat. Cavara closed her eyes, squeezing tight, before parting and holding her arms tenderly.

"Bless you, my dear," Azura said softly.

"Is no worry," she replied.

The elder released her grip and fussed delicately with her hair, exhaling at length to qualm the watershed tide. "I'll leave you in peace. Let me know if you need anything——"

The sentiment was abruptly muted by three sharp knocks at the front door.

Azura whipped around to the stairs, then back to Cavara with a grave, porcelain face and an alarming lack of composure. "We aren't expecting guests... and they don't——"

Three more knocks, followed by a growling voice demanding entry.

The floor seemed to fall out beneath them.

"Get under the bed, *now!*" the old woman hissed.

Cavara was on her stomach in moments, shuffling slowly under the metal frame suspending the mattress, Azura pulling the covers down haphazardly to conceal her from wandering eyes.

"Do *not* move under *any* circumstances, *do you understand?*"

The general muttered the affirmative, and the cold rush of dread rose in her as another barrage of knocking cracked against the door, and Azura's heavy footfalls descended the stairs swiftly to greet them.

Dammit Evelyn, she found herself wanting to cry out. *If he'd just stayed at home, listened to his mother, been a good boy and done as he was fucking told...*

The door slid open downstairs.

"Hello, officers," Azura cooed. *"What seems to be the problem?"*

Cavara bit through a scream. *Fuck!*

"We've had reports of an unknown individual entering this property – do you know anything about this?" a gravelly, disdaining voice inquired, the dull clank of metal rocking through the house.

"A strange person entering this house? No... I can't say I do know. When was this reported?"

"A few hours ago." The steps shifted deeper into the house.

"Oh I see... well, I've been out on business most of the morning, so any comings and goings in the house are beyond me."

"And what is your business, miss?"

"Tradeswoman. I deal in fine cloth garments and rugs."

"And do you know of anyone who would wish to have access to anything concerning your business? Any safes, legal documents, permits..."

"Not to my knowledge, no." A daunting pause. *"I'm sorry... if someone has entered my house in the past few hours, then they would've broken in. I locked the door when I left."*

"Is there anyone else living here with you?"

"My boy, Evelyn... he's in his room at the moment."

"Was he home while you were out?"

"He was."

"Then we'll need to speak to him."

"He's upstairs."

"Lead the way."

Cavara jumped at the sudden creaks of heavy boots winding their way up the staircase, stretching through the house as if they were directly below her. She counted three sets of boots, potentially one or two others keeping check at the door. Four or five total — *too many to make an escape.* Time seemed to waddle by with agonising certainty, as the officers navigated the corridor below and the door to Evelyn's room creaked slowly open.

From there, the conversations were diluted into tones of voice: the chirp of the little boy and the low hum of his mother, blending disjointedly with the baritone musing of the officer in charge, pressing questions on Evelyn like an interrogation. Cavara tried to hone in on any particular words, any string of sentences that could allude to what they were saying... but found the sounds grow numb and distant as time passed. Everything seemed isolated, until she was left with only the sounds of the attic room in her ears — before long, even that felt distant and out of reach. It was cold and soundless, the tapping rhythms of her heart echoing through her head. Panic set in; she found herself growing faint and dishevelled. Beyond the shadow of the bed frame above her, the world was pale and unhinged.

Trying to reach out, grasping helplessly to keep hold of reality, Cavara found her throat open, trying to scream, but with only the terrified whimper of a child escaping, puny and obsolete.

Then a darkness came to engulf her, and all the world became night, and into an unknown world, she found herself submerge again.

†

"Wake up."

She snapped to life, throwing herself to her feet in an instant, the sudden confluence of sensation rattling through her. Finding a body and a mind, and moving limbs and vertebrae. There was air, and a heartbeat, and she was blinking, and...

305

She was back in the white void again.

She lurched around, suddenly very afraid, the cosmic disorientation of a world without definition spinning through her head. There was no up, no down, no fixed point on any plane beyond the simple knowledge that she was stood up. Stood up on something, on legs she didn't feel, on a body she could not see. A floating, morphing entity in the vast void of unblemished white, trapped in the spiralling of her mind. Still searching for some point of reference, her eyes wandered aimlessly about, drifting slowly...

Until the white began to grow grey ahead of her, and something manifested from the gloom therein.

Striking out from the pale horizon like the curled fingers of some giant's hand, five grey-black totems formed before her — the one's she'd seen from the first vision, just before the shadow cast itself into the pit. As their features became more striking — the markings and etchings on the left three, and the scars and deep trenches of the right two — she became aware of a low humming sound emanating from each one, microscopic noises only acknowledged by the sheer silence of everything else. Part of her longed to touch those humming totems, to find some reality in the otherworldly vacuum of white.

So she began walking towards them, but with every step she took, the totems drew no closer — even as she began to run, nothing of the world around her threatened to shift. Still, she continued to run all the same, charging forward weightlessly, no air heaving through her lungs, no sweat on her back or wind across her face.

Only the motions, the numb repetitions of one leg after another, told her she was actually doing anything at all.

An age seemed to tick past, and her drive began to wane. The totems gazed at her, humming contentedly, almost mockingly, knowing they would always be beyond her grasp, beyond her understanding, just as the voice had said. That this was a world beyond her control — a great unknown that she would always be apart from, a hollow chasm in the unending space, chasing shadows in the hopes they'd be merciful.

Always knowing that was a lie—

As she thought it, something blossomed at the corner of her vision. Before she had a chance to react, a shadowy figure stepped out from the right-most *totem—*

A hand suddenly morphed, and struck out at her neck.

A cosmic surge of cold swam across her throat, the shadow pulsing before her with the rhythms in her chest. Slate-grey blotches leeched across her eyelids, a vignette around her vision, seizing upwards slowly. Her invisible hands reached up to try and fight it away, gaining nothing from the swimming darkness massing all around her. Swamping the void, breaching the mechanisms of her very soul. Threatening to consume her entirely...

The shadow released its grip, throwing her to the ground, its rippling darkness suddenly far larger than before.

"Pathetic," it spat in a woman's voice, muffled as if from behind a pane of glass. "You shouldn't be here."

She tried to scrabble backwards, but the shadow remained fixed at her side, looming like a titan over her.

"You try to run... but you cannot run from me, from any of this."

A scream bulged in her throat; nothing beyond a whisper escaped her lips.

"It's pathetic, watching you squirm like an animal... you have nothing here."

She tried to stand, but found the coldness strike her down as the shadow stood on her chest. Whatever air perspired from the void, suddenly disappeared – a closing tenseness in her chest followed as she began to choke. Blacks and whites numbed to greys and shallow hues, wavering as she heaved viciously in a squandered attempt to scream. Fighting against herself, against the weight of the nothingness around her, throat collapsing, every muscle screaming for life, searching for a voice, for words and—

"Why?"

A croak, like stepping on fresh gravel, escaped Cavara's lips.

Like cloth caught in a gust of wind, the paleness of the world seemed to ripple around her. Weight shifted; the explosion in her chest fell away. Whatever was in her chest, inhaled again. She looked up, blinking slowly, the shadow still looming above, all angles and rippling greys, no longer pressed against her abdomen, seeking out a face...

Finding pale eyes blinking hollowly at her, like the spectre of a ghost.

"What did you say?" it spat in disbelief.

Cavara found her way to her feet slowly, painfully, as if the very fabric of the universe pulled against her. "Why... why am I here..."

"You speak... how can you speak?"

"I don't... I don't know..." The white around her seemed to hollow out, revealing a microcosm of grey lines. "What is this place..."

"You... don't know?"

"Why am I—"

"If you don't know, then how can you be here?" The shadow seemed to reel backwards violently, as if hit by a hammer. "Unless that means—"

With an abrupt, inexplicable certainty, a chime ran out through the pale vacuum, like the bell of an innkeeper's door. The shadow stumbled back, seemingly in pain, as Cavara searched for the source of the sound.

Looking off towards the totems again, she found the centre-right formation begin to shimmer, its surface swimming with grey-silver waves, following the rhythms of her breath...

"I'm breathing," she said aloud, shocked at the rise and fall of her chest. "So I'm alive." The words hummed delicately on her tongue. "And this is real... and..." She looked up to the shadow stood before her, who stared malevolently at her like a reaper of hell.

"...and you're alive."

The admittance hit the figure like a gut punch, as it swayed awkwardly in front of her. "No... this can't be," it stuttered, the stem of anger never straying far from its tone. "You weren't supposed to happen. You were never supposed to be here. This was supposed to be mine for the taking... she promised me it would be." A quick pause. Then, in the monotone mutters of hatred: "there can only ever be one..."

The shadow screeched suddenly, its face flaring with shape and colour and definition, a human form harshly contrasted within the dark void. It clawed outwards, reaching for her, grappling for her throat, the charge of death wrought in every stricken feature it possessed, a mass of ill-defined parts manifesting a conscious, terrifying whole.

Suddenly hands seethed all across her vision, grappling her arms and chest and face, trying to pry at her and tear her down, savaging whatever presence she held in that white world. Fighting them off, the unbroken swarm of fury *tearing at her, the shadow at the head of it all, the piercing white of the eyes burning through her skull like a brand mark, screeching its demands.*

"There can only be one!"

A blazing flash of light, and the shadow's gaze appeared suddenly across the face of a beautiful woman. A woman like her, with chestnut eyes and slim cheek bones, gritted teeth snarling like a dog. The exquisite features of the face before her, and the stone walls of room beyond, rising and falling and disappearing before her very eyes — finding a human in the shadow, screaming wildly into the void.

As the black mask returned, and the white nothingness around her thinned, Cavara felt the darkness rise beneath her. Fighting on, her strength was waning. Vision tunnelling, streaked with shadows; the blotches of purest sunlight dancing in the sky above. Swaying, breaking, unravelling before her.

Falling into the unknown again.

†

"Grab her!"

A metal pauldron swept the covers of the bed aside and another caught the cuff of her shirt, dragging her out from beneath the frame onto her back like a landed fish. Eyes swimming, she tried kicking out but found a metal boot planted firmly on her right shin, excruciating spikes of pain snapping up her leg. Hands flailing, realisation slowly swarming back to the forefront of her thoughts, she tried to right herself. A sharp kick to her side stopped that in an instant, her chest buckling and lurching like a worm. At the corner of her eye, Azura's expression of dread and shock echoed volumes, beyond the snarling faces of the officers rampaging above like wild beasts.

And then the brutish, inevitable end came to greet her, when the pommel of a sword lanced down into the square of her forehead, and the world became black and cold.

†

Chapter 39

The Lake of Souls

As a burgeoning storm crackled to life overhead, and the ancient Nomad's Path descended gently along the mountain's ridge to a plateaued valley below, Markus gazed through the sudden blossom of sickly, small-leaved trees to discover a great lake nestled therein, shimmering in long streaks of white and aquamarine. Drawing closer, he studied the flourishes of reed-beds at the water's edge, and the haze of waterborne flies skimming the surface, snatched from the air by the leaping shapes of small fry just below. For a few fractious moments, stood there on the mountain ridge gazing down at the graceful waters in the valley, he found himself surprised that in such a wretched place there could be such beauty.

Then a crack of thunder, loud as breaking glass, shattered the peaceful skyline high above. The beauty and serenity he saw in the world for those few moments, disintegrated before his very eyes, as the black cavalry of clouds swept down from the peaks of the west and cast the land in shadow.

"Savanta!" he called to her, several feet ahead. "That storm doesn't look too good! We need to find shelter!"

"We'll search the banks of the lake!" she cried back. "See if there's anywhere to hide out until it passes!"

Markus chewed his lip and spat. *So the fun begins.*

Their descent was swift, sensing the tautness in the air and the cold chill through their lungs. Reaching the base of the Nomad's Path, where the stone-tile road gently collapsed at their feet, the rain began to fall. Specks at first, tiny pincers against the skin, but as the great stretch of lake expanded before them, the pincers became bullets, and the sky became hell-fire.

"Any sign?" he half-squealed into the storm, a vicious typhoon of wind and water lancing across him.

"Bank north, think I see something!" Savanta responded, little more than a grey blur somewhere ahead, arm raised to shield her eyes from the worst of it. "Between the trees!"

Tilting left, more by the force of the gale than his own volition, Markus stumbled towards a great shadowy edifice buried between clusters of trees that hissed and snapped in the wind. There was no distinction to the massive object they ran towards — only that it was almost completely square, and almost certainly made by human hands. Drawing slowly closer, divisions of grey appeared, marking out windows and pillars, two-storeys tall, and the dull but inviting box of a door forming from the mist ahead. It seemed to be some grand building work; a lakeside house of an esteemed noble of old, most likely.

And, more importantly… shelter from the storm.

Reaching for the desperate sanctuary of the porch, he crashed into the door next to Savanta and coughed gracelessly. The landscape had taken on a defiant shade of granite, growing steadily darker the higher one gazed. Beyond that, sudden columns of blue lightning crackled through the grey, followed by the terrific boom of thunder striking off over the mountains high.

"Door's jammed shut!" Savanta cried, shunting against it with the round of her shoulder. "Can't break it loose!"

Markus grappled the handle, cranking at it with white knuckles, spasms lancing up his hand before he finally gave up and released.

"Okay, stand aside," he commanded.

"What are you gonna do?"

311

"Trust me."

Savanta backed into the corner, nestling between the doorframe and the pillar, as Markus waded slowly back out into the surging torrent of rain and violent winds.

Rounding, he lowered himself with his shoulder raised and charged at the huge door. As it snapped into view, he tucked his head away, his arm connecting sharply with the double-door's centre. Lock snapping, it cracked open brashly; Markus collapsed to the ground inside, a numb ebbing pain pulsing through his shoulder. He whistled a curse through his teeth, but remained grateful nonetheless that they were finally free of the storm raging outside.

Savanta braced the door closed again, sliding down its flat edge to sit at its base. "I admire your heroics, Markus," she exclaimed, "although I question whether that was a good idea."

"Discerning from the bastard fucking pain in my left shoulder…" he blustered through gritted teeth, "… I'd say no, it probably wasn't."

"Is it broken?"

"No, just bruised… although that comes as more luck than judgement."

"Guess I'll be doing the heavy lifting from now on then."

"You wouldn't have it any other way."

She scoffed. "You may have me there…"

"That I might," he teased, smiling. "What's this place we've found ourselves in, anyway?" He rolled onto his side, using his good arm and his awful knees to rise to full height. "Ain't exactly a fishing hut, is it?"

"No it certainly is not," she replied, also musing the question, standing and brushing herself off. "A huge building like this, in the middle of nowhere on a serene hillside by the lake… whatever it is, the owner either had a lot of money, or a lot of power."

"Provenci design?"

"Definitely, meaning it was likely owned by some high-ranking official during the occupation."

"Any idea who?"

She shook her head. "Although I expect a quick search around could tell us more."

Markus nodded and stood to one side. "Lead the way."

Drifting through another set of doors, where one side was drooping lazily on its hinges and the other had disappeared entirely, the house beyond opened out into a moulded-white expanse of snapped furniture and broken glass.

To the left, an open conference room with a central table cracked across its middle, the chairs in pieces or wedged awkwardly around windows. Cabinets along the walls had been desecrated: broken bottles and unbound books spilt from their innards like a slit stomach. Paperwork splashed chaotically across the tabletop and onto the floor beneath, as if the soul intention of the thieves who had ransacked the place was to manipulate as much destruction as humanly possible, leaving no stack of paper to waste.

Gazing right, several doors led away to deeper alcoves of the house: a pantry, barren as it was filthy, overrun by the putrid smell of rot; a living space where the floor had partially collapsed along its centre, stagnant water swelling with ooze and spreading sheets of mould across the tiles; a kitchen space, where the scuttling of rats navigating long-emptied cupboards sent chills up Markus's spine. Every inch of the space stank of depravity, every damp-infested beam and board marked by the abandonment of its master. His skin crawled, at the welts of black coiling across the ceiling above, and the yellow crowns of algae creeping up the balustrade of the stairs ahead.

"This place hasn't seen love nor life for some time now I'd wager," he exclaimed, running a hand across the wall and feeling the cold twinge of moisture at his fingertips. "What a waste."

Ascending the stairs, Savanta grimaced at the layer of pale slime that seemed to excrete from the algae on the railing. "Can't be worth much now." She waved a hand. "C'mon, let's see what there is upstairs."

Markus drew a breath and climbed the creaking stairway slowly, the aggravation in his joints never wavering for a moment. Crossing the landing, he looked up to find Savanta had stopped, clinically surveying the long corridor ahead, hands at her hips. Several doorways dotted both walls at even intervals, most of their frames torn to pieces as thieves had made off with the woodwork. At the end, an open balcony with a blown window revealed the grey void of the world beyond, still lashing with rain and throwing great hurricanes through the house towards them. Markus reached the last step and found his balance shift as one such gust nearly swept him back down the stairway, reeling suddenly before planting his feet again and rising to the second floor.

"Bastard wind that is," he muttered. "Any chance we could board that thing up?"

"We won't be here long enough to worry, I'd say," Savanta replied, pointing off to the room to her left. "This room here seems to be the master's office... could give us some idea as to what this place is... and what happened at that."

Entering the antechamber, Markus noted with some surprise that the office desk at the room's centre remained intact, along with several marble headpieces dotted across the wooden shelf on the back wall. A worn red rug stained by the damp stretched the length of the room, squelching unpleasantly underfoot. Tapestries hung loosely at the edges, their imprints long-worn to insignificance, the bottom ripped to delicate shreds by—

Claws.

Markus stooped next to them and drew a finger down one of the trenches in the stone with a composite look of horror. "What the hell did this..."

"The Tarrazi are known for their savagery," Savanta mused, "but it's nought compared to the savagery of their beasts."

He turned and looked up to her pointedly. "Should we be concerned?"

"Not in this weather... they're wild beasts, and rarely attack during storms." She paused. "Just... listen out for howls, in case."

Markus gave a single nod. *Noted.*

Savanta glided over to the desk and began rifling through the drawers, removing thick-bound ledgers of paper and depositing them on top. She then stood, a small clump of letters in her hand, frowning at the scrawls of writing. "There's a lot here... which is surprising."

"That they ransacked the rest of the house, but left the office and the most important contents in near-perfect condition?"

"Exactly... makes me wonder what they were actually looking for." She threw the letters on the desk and drew the topmost one open, her face curdling like old milk as she read it through.

"What is it?"

"This was an old viceroy's house... these are her correspondences with someone in high office back in the capital."

"What do they say?"

She puzzled over an answer. "I'm not sure... this is the last letter in this pile, meaning the most recent, and... I can't find any sign of anything going wrong. It just lists reports, officer numbers, a few small issues with bandits... nothing that would suggest any of *this* was gonna happen."

"Perhaps that was the point... perhaps the ransacking was part of a surprise attack by the local tribes."

"I would agree..."

Markus squinted. "But you *don't?*"

"Well, it also says here that those put on watch around the lake have reported... strange sounds and sightings in the night. The viceroy down-plays it, naturally, but does also report that they've had several of their horses go missing since the last letter was sent."

"Any suggestion of why?"

"Nothing written here." She folded the letter and cast it back onto the desk. "It doesn't make sense. They seemed oblivious to any threat at hand, and then suddenly..."

"Unless they knew, but didn't want the capital knowing, in case it turned out to be nothing. There are plenty of possibilities."

She nodded distantly. "I suppose."

"All the same, it doesn't completely matter what happened..." Markus got to his feet and brushed himself off, before raising his arms like a preacher. "Because, we are safe from the storm, safe from all manner of hell outside, with plenty of food and water, and can stay as long as we want." As he spoke, Savanta's eyes seemed to bulge wildly. "So, regardless of what's happened here in the past, we don't need to worry about that now, because really it hardly affects us in the—"

"Markus," she said sharply.

He frowned. "What?" Then, with a strike of fear: "Savanta, what is it?"

She seemed stunned, locked to the space just behind him. "On my mark... I need you to run, directly towards me, and get behind this desk... yes?"

His heart thundered through his chest. "Oh... okay..."

"On my mark..."

He felt a burning sensation along the back of his neck. The room seemed to blur and sway before him. Savanta held out an open palm just above the edge of the desk, her fingers twitching delicately. Everything seemed to tilt on its axis.

A low growl erupted from behind him.

The hand snapped shut.

Hell broke loose all at once.

Leaping to the corner, Markus twisted his body to catch sight of a huge six-eyed hound the size of a bear drive towards him with its mangled jaws wide and lethal. In moments, it crossed the space, Markus scrabbling into the corner fumbling for his sword, the beast lunging at his legs.

Savanta rounded on them, sword glaring, and swung it overhead like an executioner's axe. It drove into the beast's wrinkled neck, snapping bone and lodging itself there, the creature spitting and snarling wildly, saliva spewing from its mouth. It seemed confused, battling with the pain, before making to lunge at Markus's leg—

As he drove a knife up into its throat, the warm breach of blood coating his hands. The beast's eyes shimmered hollowly, the snapping of its jaws drawing still as it seemed to acknowledge the desperate finale of its own existence, gently tugging sideways and collapsing against the desk-side.

A blink and it was over.

Markus withdrew the knife, hands shaking, studying the huge animal sprawled at his feet. "What the *fuck* is that thing?"

Withdrawing her sword and clearing the blade, Savanta grabbed his arm and dragged him to his feet.

"*We're being hunted,*" she whispered.

"What?"

"*Keep your fucking voice down or we're both dead.*"

Markus swallowed deeply. "*Okay... what was that thing?*"

"*A Kazbak Hound... incredibly fast, and incredibly dangerous. Usually hunt in packs of six or more.*"

"*Six? So there are more of 'em?*"

"*Most likely — that one we killed was a scout, probably a young male. If there are others, they would've been alerted to the growls and the commotion.*"

"*And that's a big problem?*"

"*Yes.*" She paused, listening a moment, then turned back to him. "*We need to find a safe place to hide out, fast — they'll storm the house any moment.*"

Markus drew his blade slowly, stooping low and moving off towards the door. Savanta remained close to his back, her own sword coiling maliciously between her fingers. The storm raged outside still, battering the walls of the old viceroy's house — Markus wondered if they were safer out there than they ever could be inside, knowing their little sanctuary had become a hunting range, and they had become its prey.

He reached the doorway, a sealed door opposite, the stretch of the corridor between silent and unnerving. Waiting some moments as the silence ebbed out, he looked back to Savanta worriedly, finding in her broken face strength and judgement – she gave a nod to move on.

He shifted into the corridor, looking left to the porch, then back right to——

The hound pounced from the stairway, barrelling into him, shoving him backwards into a spinning contortion of wrinkled skin and sweating flesh. Twisting on his neck, Markus kicked out, jarring his knees, casting the beast down the corridor where it landed on its feet and rounded on him again. Markus carved his sword down, slicing its jaw; driving past, the beast shunted him with its muscular forearm, forcing him against the opposing wall, knocking the air from his lungs. He got to his feet and rolled forward, spinning tensely on his heel, eyes wandering, waiting for——

The hound charged, lunging for him. Markus gave into his fear; he glimpsed a flash of Savanta back down the corridor fighting another beast that had emerged nearby, before he turned——

Diving away into another room, landing on a thick saturated carpet, pushing towards the old table at its centre. The beast bounding through, propelling from the doorframe, locking eyes, pouncing forward with blood-streaked teeth——

Raising his sword, catching the bite before it struck, the beast clamping down on his blade with its mangled teeth, drawing blood as the cutting edge dug through. Claws scrabbling, swiping forward for his chest, pointed claws denting the thin armour across his thighs, desperately close to the skin——

With a sudden spur of force, Markus drove the small knife coiled in his other hand up into the roof of the beast's mouth. It whimpered suddenly, rising onto its hind-legs above him, bearing down with swiping claws——

Slicing across his cheek, a terrific strike of pain across his jaw. Markus withdrew the knife, eyes straining from the shock, swiping the weapon wildly in front of him. The beast dodged left and right, the blade dicing small cuts across its gums, finding the opportune moment to engage——

Driving past the knife's range, Markus's eyes bulged with horror as he watched the hound clamped down on his exposed forearm, the sudden explosion of pain from each puncture wound sending shockwaves through his chest. The ferocious might of the beast's jaws engaged with a firm grasp, forcing themselves closed around the arm...

Snapping his elbow backwards, shattering every bone therein.

Markus screamed, an unapologetic noise crackling with agony, and drove his knife into the beast's huge skull. The blade jabbed through its head over and over, spearing into its crown with clumpy strands of blood streaming out. The hound's wild eyes and slathering jaws snapped and wrenched at his arm, crazed by the sweet dislocation of blood, almost entirely unaware of the blade cutting through its brain cavity like butter.

Desperate moments passed, Markus hoarse with the wrenching agony of his broken limb, shivers wracking his system, the knife slicing down over and over as the beast became limp and confused. Its leg began to twitch violently – suddenly it all collapsed in a seizing mass, back legs kicking out across the carpet. Still he continued stabbing, screeching, the six pupils of his victim growing dull and absent, the tongue sagging lazily to one side.

Then the hound collapsed onto his lap, dead, and silence ensued.

Markus dropped the knife, shaking vigorously, studying the mass of bloodied flesh and bone that now formed his right arm. With numb appendages, he shoved the dead animal away, squealing again as the teeth slid slowly from the puncture wounds. His head spun; his heartbeat pounded ferociously in his ears. Every tiny motion of his arm drew a great sickness to his throat that not even the adrenaline could ward off. Dragging his arm onto his leg with a seismic twist of his stomach, he grappled the table-leg and vomited across the old carpet, the bones creaking through his neck at the force of it.

Wiping the residue away, heaving in great pits of air, he reached up against the table and dragged a length of old cloth from its top.

Through gritted teeth he began binding the wound with the tablecloth, the frequent stabs of pain enough to conjure the sickness all over again. Stringing it tight at the end, he found some momentary bliss in the fact that the makeshift bandage held firm, and the wounds had slowed their bleeding – even if the arm itself was now entirely without use.

Using the table as a support, he hauled himself onto numb legs and fought back the urge to wretch again. "Savanta!" he roared, stumbling forward, swinging himself from the table's edge to the door-frame, eyes blinkering slowly. "Savanta, where are you…"

Markus pushed himself out into the hallway, twisting right down the corridor to see where she was—

To find another hound charging towards him, its howls pummelling his ears, eyes drawn to its prey with all the savage joy the world could muster.

Markus raised his good arm, blade shimmering, awaiting the attack.

A down-swipe, aiming for a head that ducked suddenly downwards, the crown of its skull knocking the wind from his chest. Its taloned feet scraped against the white stone walls, trying to find purchase as Markus dug his heels in. They tilted backwards, spinning – the blade coiling inwards, skewering the beast's neck as it fell. Cold funnelling down his back, and Markus saw the sky above sink to meet him—

Reality, a cruel mistress, came to greet him.

A heavy thud across his spine and he cracked against the balcony, the beast flying overhead like a condor, missing the balustrade and tumbling down towards earth below.

With his loosening grip, Markus let go of the blade, recoiling his arm sharply before—

The hilt of his sword caught in the bindings of his wrist-guard, attached to the heavy animal now tumbling down two storeys. Trying to wrench away, but finding the force against him too great, his arm locked in place, sliding against the railing…

His legs slipped away underneath him, and he skimmed over the balcony's edge with the hound, tumbling through the wind and thrashing rain to the cold earth beneath.

To the moment he finally thought he would die....

It had been worthless, in retrospect: a terrible excursion into a god-forsaken country, plagued by savage peoples and marked at every turn by the coming spectre of his demise. As if the very land they walked on existed for the singular purpose of exacting death.

And the gods had laughed above, tearing the ground up at their feet, washing the skies with darkness and unending storms. Even they, from their omnipotent perches at the gates of another world, could see the futility of his efforts. How worthless it had all been, in the end, to follow the broken woman into the gates of hell, knowing the entire way that at some point, somewhere in the chaos and ruin beyond, he was simply destined to die.

And he knew that death was a cruel mistress, wherever she roamed – and, most of all, that she never revealed just when death would come, only that you were always on the cusp of it, never wandering far from that bitter, beautiful end—

The hound hit the ground with the full force of gravity, its legs and neck snapping on impact, only a shallow whimper of pain escaping before the light left its eyes.

Markus fell seconds later, the crunching thud of metal snapping in the wind. He bounced from the beast's stomach, landing heavily on his side, trapping his mutilated arm beneath and rolling to plant his face in the fresh mud. Despite the overwhelming pain tearing through his system, he let out little more than a wheeze, the cold numbness of the rain a soothing consolation across his beaten, battered body. He lay there for some moments, the delicate tightrope between the living and the dying playing out in his mind – that he wondered if he felt close enough to death to actually accept its grace, or whether life still held its hand out to him, and his time had not yet come. Moments ticked by – moments again, and nothing seemed to change.

In the end, death did not come.

On a shaken arm, he drew himself up out of the mud and swung upwards, his knees faltering but extending nonetheless as he rose slowly to his feet. Turning, planting a boot in the beast's huge skull, he withdrew the shimmering blade from its neck, its weighted certainty in the palm of his hand a welcome sign that he was still among the living. Lifting his head, he noted the crackling of conflict in the building above beyond the patter of rainwater. The simmering sounds of slicing steel and the vicious snarls of the attacker told him Savanta was still in the throes of her own battle and struggling to fight them off.

Hoisting his blade from the ground, Markus found the strength to shuffle slowly forward towards the building's porch, his feet buried deep in the thick mud, each step an exercise in his stamina which was already disconcertingly low…

And then a whistle chimed, off to his left, and the world seemed to falter once again.

Markus looked off into the grey gloom of the storm and saw three shadows standing there watching him, the left-most figure sided by two of the hounds on thick rope leashes. He could make out very little of them in the haze, beyond the pale skin of their faces.

That, and the black coats of armour strapped across their bodies, marked by red streaks of warpaint, and necklaces of talons bleeding their sin.

"You look a bit lost, sir," one of them called out through the gale. "Any chance we could be of assistance?"

Markus raised his sword, rounding on them slowly, a throb in his knee causing him to stumble slightly. "Stay the fuck away…" he warned. "Stay where you are…"

"Feisty one, ain't he?" another mocked.

"Got some kick for a guy who's taken a beating," the other mused.

The third one, supposedly their leader at the centre, took a step forward. "We mean no trouble…" he assured. "We see you're in a bad way – we were just wondering if you could do with some help."

"I need no fucking help from any of you," Markus snapped. "You's the ones who gave me this, anyway, so stay where you are."

"We do apologise, we assumed you were bandits this far north. *And* our offer of assistance is with the full understanding we're the ones who put you in this... rather unfortunate mess."

The other two stifled laughs; their leader took another step forward.

"Stay the fuck away!" Markus rasped, swaying his sword loosely.

"You really must give this up, we only mean to help..."

"I can help myself." He nodded towards the door. "Now my friend and I are gonna grab our shit, and we're gonna leave... am I *understood* in that?"

The leader shook his head slowly, the dimensions of his helmet more distinct now. "You are a poor, rotten fool, you know. You must understand that... considering the circumstances, we just can't accept that kind of an agreement. We need you and your friend up there for other things, you see... we can't just let you go."

"Then why send the dogs? Make us easier targets for you?"

"No, no, that'd be poor sport." The leader took another step closer, only a few feet from him now. "We needed to make sure we were getting... *the right quality* for our efforts."

Markus grasped the sword tighter. "I'd sooner die than submit to your *efforts,* you arrogant prick."

The leader seemed to darken, his shoulders pulling back. Raising a hand, he beckoned the right-hand figure out from the grey and pointed off to Markus, before returning to the other blackcoat and watching from afar.

The newcomer was a tall woman, pale-skinned, a short-sword swinging loosely in one hand. She was heavily armoured, her body streaked with white crescent moons and red talons, the coiling impressions of a serpent down one arm. She had the look of a killer and the stride to match it, sauntering up within a few feet of him and smiling barbarously.

"If you won't come nicely, we'll have to teach you to behave," she said with an undertone of mockery. "Which is a shame… you would've made a nice servant."

He raised his sword across his chest, stooping slightly, ushering the simple words of his displeasure.

"Get *fucked*."

She shrugged. "Have it your way."

A stride forward and a strike across the body – Markus chimed his own blade and knocked hers aside. Several attacks crossed the thin air between them, each deflected, until the final overhead, where Markus shifted right and speared out towards her.

Conceding, she took a step out of his circle and scoffed. "Not bad… for something that looks like the back end of a sewer."

She struck again, several times, the blades sweeping faster, striking with more venom. She lunged; Markus strode back, launching his own attack across her flank. The blackcoat leaned across in sudden defence, but in the opening Markus coiled his arm up and slit a sharp cut across her cheekbone.

She stumbled back slightly, hand rising to tap the slice across her face, studying the droplet of blood at the end of her finger. Looking back to Markus, her face swarmed with malice.

"Just leave us be," he pleaded suddenly, his knee trembling, using his sword as a walking stick. "We just want to pass through… we mean no harm, we want nothing of you… just leave us alone."

"I don't play those little games," the blackcoat grumbled. "I don't care for what you do or don't want… you will do as we say whether you like it or not." She raised her blade again. "Now, will you come nicely, or not?"

Markus sighed, finding his sword impossibly heavy as he lifted it back across his chest.

"Hm… then you will learn the cost of insubordination."

She surged forward, striking down. Markus raised his blade far too late, far too slow for his opponent, who carved down sharply towards him…

And cut his ruined arm clean from its socket.

For an instant, he felt nothing. There was nothing beyond the frozen droplets of rain across his face, the sweeping channels of wind crossing his vision. The hollow shape of the sun, a dull encompassing glow in the clouds overhead, and the magnitude of the thunderstorm shielding it from the land below. The trees, tiny bristles of leaves forming at the ends of their branches, stretching to his right. The viceroy's house, nestled between, a once beautiful structure detailing the intricate beauty of his people and his homeland, grown tired and lonely in its disrepair. The hounds, walking out the front door, dragging the disorientated, bloody body of a woman from within – the only person he'd ever called a friend.

And even as he collapsed, his knees buckling from the strain of keeping him upright, he found no pain in him anymore. Not at the gouges across his face, nor the claw marks across his legs – not even at the absence of a limb, now stricken and half-buried in the mud at his side. The world was warm, and strikingly colourful, as if on the verge of wanting to sing. As his back hit the mud, the sky reeled with tiny glimmers of sunlight, like twinkling stars breaking free of the shadow. Delicate, fleeting – like when he had first gazed down on the lake that day and found it to be so beautiful, even in a place so rotten with hate. It was enough to put his soul to rest, one last time.

That it had been worth it, in the end, to die in peace at last.

†

Chapter 40

End of the Line

I t's a statement, you see. When the military does anythin', they like to make a statement, don't they? Whenever they negotiate, there's always a crossbow on the rooftops keepin' an eye out... whenever there's a parade, there's always plenty of sharp steel to keep everyone in check... and this ain't no different. We're under martial law, because they wanna make a *statement*. They wanna show us, that they're here, and they're in charge, y'see?"

His counterpart shook her head. "I gotta disagree with you there... way I see it, this is done outta fear, plain and simple fear, y'know? The king is dead, there's a war goin' on somewhere up north for whatever reason I could care about, and they're *scared* about it, 'cause I bet there's plenty o' people who want a shot at that top spot, and plenty of people who don't like war, or don't like the soldiers, or shit like that. So, under those circumstances, they give us martial law: tell us all to watch our backs an' go to bed at dusk an' don't cause trouble. Would someone makin' a statement do somethin' like that?"

"Yea they would, 'cause that's *why* they're doin' it. Because they want us reminded of who we are and where we are. They're in charge, and we listen. It ain't outta fear, c'mon... that's the fear comin' out in *you*. What could they possibly be afraid of? They're the military for gods' sake, they got more forged steel than the city has stone. They ain't afraid of anythin'."

"Not even afraid o' rebellion, or terror, or protest?"

He scoffed. "As if someone'd be stupid enough to try that. There ain't no rebellion happenin' – hell, most people are as shit-scared as you are. They ain't planning to overthrow anyone anytime soon. We may be at war, but there's still plenty of steel round here to make a fair mess if people try anythin'."

"And what about among their own ranks? Rumour has it some types ain't too keen on the new high commander and his friends..."

"Come off it, they wouldn't dare," he laughed. "That's all gossip y'hear in the tavern on a cosy night, ain't got any weight behind it." He wagged a finger at her. "If y'ask me, the army and their lot in power have got shit locked down with steel nails... and lil' eyes on every wall, door and window in that palace up there. There ain't any ruse goin' on up there; everything's air-tight." He paused. "And even if there were any kinda funny business up there, they'd rat out the true culprits soon enough. Everyone gets their due one day, no matter how high up you may be—"

His counterpart waved a hand at him. "D'you hear that?"

He stopped, frowning. "Hear what?"

She pointed off to her right, down into the Merchant Quarter, and her ears prickled to the sounds of whistles and shouting drawing steadily closer. "That," she acknowledged.

"Sounds like a mighty fuss," he replied. "Wonder what's goin' on?"

He looked left down the alleyway, picking apart the beige shadows of the side streets, and found a broad-bellied figure charging towards them, the skittering form of a smaller woman close to his back. Following them, the chime of soldier whistles echoed through the district, the dense clattering of metal making a resolute effort to pursue.

"Seems like someone's on the run," he said. "Some coward or other trying to run from the law for their crimes." He shook his head. "It's all a statement, y'see... a statement of the mighty Imperial Army, showing everyone just how far they'll go to show who's in charge."

"And something tells me they've come up short," she replied.

"Oh aye... very short indeed."

†

Charging past a couple at the alleyway's end, Broska broke from the side-streets out onto a main thoroughfare of the city, and banked sharply south towards the outer wall. In the swelling heat of early autumn, his skin swam like liquid beneath his overcoat, a great sheen of sweat blanketing his forehead and stinging his eyes. And yet he continued to run on and on, the determination almost like his life depended on it.

Which in all respects, I guess it kinda does.

"There's a horse merchant ahead, right-hand side!" Jinx cried from behind him, her final words battling against the stinging breach of another patrol whistle somewhere off behind. The unrelenting fear of capture ate at Broska's thoughts.

Cursed be the bastards who put me through this shit...

Diving right through a cluster of blue-robed bystanders, he spied the small stable Jinx had seen a few streets ahead, a single brown mare hooked out in front with the young stablemaster at her side. It was a formidable horse, well above sixteen hands, with a cold certainty in its eye that gave him the subtle glimmer of hope that things may work out after all.

And the sharp whistle in his ear told him that hope was a poor determinate of success, especially in a place like Casantri.

"I'll get the horse and ride to the gate!" he boomed above the ruckus of the crowded street. "When we get there, you run and hide!"

The wooden shack drew closer with every stride, Broska shunting his way through groups of civilians going about their lives with few cares to name. All around, the panic of the chase drew soldiers from every street corner, filtering through the masses in narrow streams.

Glancing right down an alley, Broska found his heart jump at the sight of armed patrols only a few feet away, alerted to the cries, boggling at the huge general surging past and the tiny thief at his tail. Everything seemed to close in, sucking the air from the sky as he ran.

Won't be long now.

"They're getting close!" Jinx warned.

"So are we!"

Ahead, alerted to the commotion, the stablemaster stood in front of his brown mare and held a hand across its flank, registering the huge man barrelling towards him with wild eyes and a half-conjured smile, which made him appear more like an inpatient at the city asylum than any well-to-do officer of the law.

The general ground to a halt just before the young man and buckled over, swelling his lungs with air as if he'd been suffocated. "Hello, sir... we need... to use your horse..." Broska blustered, reaching for the reins and finding the man snap his hand away.

"And what business do you have?" the stablemaster spat.

"Important business." Broska pointed off behind him. "Hear those whistles? We're catching a crook, he's on the run for the gates. Gotta get after him. You know how it is..."

"Or are those whistles for you, and I'd be aiding your escape——"

Jinx barged forwards impatiently, grabbed the man's open palm and unloaded a bag of coin into it, sealing the fingers closed and patting it gently. "I'm sure it'll be no trouble whatever the circumstances... now *will it*, sir?"

The man gulped, and drew his eyes back to Broska. "Certainly not. You stole the horse and I'm not involved. Have a good day."

The general slapped him across the shoulder. "There's a good lad."

Planting his foot in the stirrup, he mounted the great beast swiftly and slowed its temper with a gentle brush of its hair. Readying the reins, he found a hand touching his leg, and looked down to Jinx at his side.

"Go easy, Arrenso," she said softly. "Please be safe."

"I will be, don't you worry," he replied, producing a wide smile.

"Now go. I'll see you on the other side."

With a flick of the reins and a twitch of the heel, the horse jolted into action and broke out into the crowd, tearing trenches through the swarms of people as they shifted fearfully to the side. Broska drew close to the beast, feeling the muscle tense and turn across its flanks, the snorting exhilaration it gave at finally being free to run. Crashing through the crowds, far faster than any of the soldiers could manage, their whistles growing fainter and fainter as he pressed on towards freedom. Not a cloud in the sky threatened the commanding midday sun overhead – it was a beauty that made his heart sing.

Ahead, the ominous shadow of the southern wall snaked across the horizon, the crowned watchtowers dotted along its top walkway surveying a vast world both within and beyond its border. Ahead, the watchtowers accumulated into a great citadel of flags and pointed spires jutting from the walls like fangs. At its centre, the claws of a gate hung open, a thin congregation of gatekeepers at its base managing the crowds who drew too close, letting couriers slip by to deliver their goods elsewhere. Broska knew the gates would be open around midday: couriers typically collected their letters and parcels in the mornings and made off before the afternoon bustle came out, choosing the southern exit to avoid the huge crowds to the north. It stayed open for several hours despite the imposition of martial law – and much to his delight, that made it an awful handy escape route.

Breaking out onto open ground, the crowds thinning suddenly as he drew closer, Broska found some pre-eminent joy in the barely-recognisable cries of whistles far behind, with not an officer in sight to challenge his progress. The southern gatehouse ahead remained entirely unaware of the situation, gatekeepers continuing to profile the few stray messengers who crossed their path and sending them on their way. In the beyond, the general saw green grass glossed with the early autumn rays. There, he saw hope again.

Tantalizingly close, it almost came as a shock to his system, what had occurred to get him there. The murder of his only true friend in the army; threats to stay quiet or fear his job going to the gutter; a ruse by the same villains who'd killed Cavara, sending patrols of his own men to raid his office, and now pursue him to the very gates for crimes he had no part in. The delirium of it all, the madness – the crooked generals at the heart of it all, longing to keep their boots shiny and their hands clean. His defiance of it all, in the end, and his choice to run and be free from the lies and deceit. Start over again somewhere far away – and when the time was right, come back to set it all straight.

It will be my crowning moment, he thought, the thundering of hooves in his ears. *All they've brought is shame and lies, none of the glory once promised. It is a disgrace, and it will be the ruin of this great city if something isn't done. Maybe one day... we can put it right again.*

Maybe one day, we can save it.

And then the bullet struck.

All he heard at first was a snapping sound, echoing above the general thrum of people's voices. Then a tiny metal rod entered through the horse's eye, exiting with a slew of brain matter and spinning off across the street to his right. The first reaction came when the horse screeched, and its front legs bent inwards, but by that point Broska had already left the flat of his saddle and was hurtling through the air.

He hit the ground several feet ahead, with the snap of metal plates ringing out from under his overcoat. His head smacked against solid rock, jarring his neck, spinning an otherwise pristine world into a vortex of yellow, blue and black. Pain bucked and writhed across his body, seizing through his skull like a drum. Everything beautiful about the sky seemed lost for a moment, fragmented in his gaze.

Nothing happened for some time, with only his barely-realised self as company, until a shadow loomed overhead like a circling crow, the distinctive shape of a crossbow sat in the crook of their arm. Nothing was distinguishing about the shadows of its face, nothing he could place for certain – it was only when the figure spoke, imagining the foul grin across his grey face, that Broska felt the weight of the world bear down on him and swallow his soul in its misery.

"You made quite the escape, I'll give you that," General Ferreus said. "I tried warning you, that this would happen, and you just couldn't keep your hands out of it. And now look at you, some fat old fool sprawled across the floor, with nothing to show for it but a poor man's dead horse and an arrest warrant around your neck for good measure." He paused. "They'll never believe you, Broska, you know that... they'll never believe whatever stories you have to tell. You'll be found guilty, and rot in prison, and remain there until you die." He bent to his knees, leaning in close enough to see his broken smile. "And don't worry... I'll take *good care of you* until you do..."

†

Chapter 41

The Abattoir

Revek drove the blade up through the man's chest, snarling like an animal, the whimper of the savage's dying breath humming in his ear. In another turn, he withdrew the blade and stood back to observe the man sway limply, clutching his torn cloth shirt where a bloom of red had appeared. Revek then stepped forward, blade cutting across, and struck the man's head from his shoulders – the skull cart-wheeled skywards and spun off into the distance; the body slumped meekly to the floor. The commander heaved in a great swell of air, eyes wild and unforgiving.

Studying a world of ash, and fire.

Running alongside him, one of the soldiers let out a cry and hurled a flaming torch at the nearest thatch-roof house, already ablaze along one side. It was the same image, replicated across every house they had found, until the village was nothing more than a crackling orange inferno, and the sun was blinded by the torrents of smoke smothering every inch of the sky.

To his left, the fire that had been cast roared to life in a matter of moments, swelling the interior with a viscous black smog, the frightful screams of other savages prickling his ears intently.

Revek turned, sword swinging in his hand like a hatchet as he approached the building's door. Tearing it open, he caught the frightened eyes of a mother bringing her child to the door, dressed in little more than a blouse and skirt. The commander grappled her across the shoulder, ripping her from the child left cowering in the doorway. As she collapsed to her knees, he dragged her upright again – she began pleading and begging and clawing at his arm like a savage, the child squealing for his mother at the door.

"Quenti mora di mes... quenti mora!"

"Shut up!" Revek cuffed her across the face, a vicious slap that nearly knocked her unconscious with its force.

The boy at the door reached out a hand. "Mumma!"

"Oh, this is your mumma, is it?" Revek mocked, pointing his sword at the child. "Then I'll make this quick, shall I?"

He caught the woman around the jaw, her hands scraping about trying to prize him away. As the child watched, Revek curled his blade across the woman's collar and slit her throat.

The child screamed.

The woman, inhaling her own blood as it spewed from the gouge across her neck, collapsed to the floor in a choking wreck. Revek studied the great pool of red at his feet and cackled like a dog.

How wonderful.

Looking up, he found the child had disappeared back into the vortex of smoke within the house, sooner choking to death than finding it at the end of a blade.

A soldier pulled up beside him, a small hatchet in his hand – Revek pointed his blade off towards the house.

"There's a child in there," he muttered. "Kill it and bring it to me."

The soldier found his face tighten. "A child, sir..."

"*Get on with it!*" He shoved the man off towards the open door. "Or I'll put you in his fuckin' place instead!"

The soldier disappeared into the house, and the commander walked away to the sounds of the child's screaming deeper within. It was a helpless scream, the child knowing he was about to die and could do nothing about it. At the hands of these invaders he did not know, speaking words he could not comprehend. With a roof burning to ash above him, his dead mother wallowing in the mud outside. The sheer pitilessness of it all; the torture Revek wrought on the savage kind. In a place that most found remorse, he found only satisfaction at their demise.

They get what they deserve.

Drawn suddenly to the sound of distress, Revek twisted to find a savage hurtling towards him with tears streaking his old face, a broken scythe in one hand, muttering some ancient curse or other in their foreign tongue. The commander shook his head, almost laughing at the miserable attempt at rebellion. He ducked the fumbling attack, the scythe wobbling cleanly overhead, before swiping across and snapping the blade toward the man's elbow. It cut cleanly through, the forearm attached to the weapon dropping to the dry mud underfoot, the man boggling at the crimson stump now in its place. Revek sliced again, tongue curling across his teeth, carving the man's face open down the middle. The savage's hand rose desperately to the gaping wound, trying to hold his shattered jaw together, stumbling forward and collapsing onto his front, screeching into the grass. The commander followed him for some moments, watching his blood streak across the earth as he tried to crawl away.

Several strides later, the entire act had become boring to him once again – he jammed his sword through the old man's skull.

They get what they deserve.

Withdrawing the blade, he found blankets of black smoke had caught the strong southern winds and suffocated the skyline overhead, the village around him shifting to resonant greys and reds as the ash fell to ground. Everything played out as silhouette around him, shadows dancing in the smog: soldiers off to the right, sparring with the pitchforks and farm-tools wielded by those savages stupid enough to fight; kicking and screaming to his left: a soldier dragging a woman by her ankle through the mud, off behind the burning houses to be silenced evermore; the crackling of cinder across every house that remained, the gates of a new era marked by steel and flame.

My era, he grinned, admiring the shine of his blade. *The era of blood, and the end of the savage kind.*

The sound of running at his back, and he turned to find a frail boy no older than sixteen stumbling past – at the sight of the commander, he lurched away fearfully, trying to regain speed as he scampered away like a deer.

Revek inhaled deeply, the immense pleasure of hunting prey soothing his muscles, as he slowly unhooked the knife from his belt. Slinging it back behind his head, he cast it forward like a bullet, the tiny shimmering point lancing through the ashen air and impaling itself squarely in the boy's spine.

A squeal, and his legs buckled underneath him, collapsing to the ground beneath almost in slow motion. The commander approached like a vulture; the boy whimpered softly, trying to drag his now-paralysed body to anywhere else but there.

Revek bent down and withdrew the blade from the boy's spine, watching him writhe like a worm, holding his head aloft by a scruff of hair. "You savages thought the world was yours," he spat, the boy squeaking in agony. "You inflicted a great pain on us for generations... and assumed we were too naïve to feel it. Well, we did, and we felt *all of it.*" He flicked the knife in his grip. "And now you will know that pain a hundred times over... and you will know *who is god here.*"

He drove the tiny blade into the boy's neck, just at the base of the skull, jamming it deep enough so the end-point pierced through the back of his mouth. The boy wailed, an almost inhuman noise from deep within the ruptured enterprise of his lungs. With his arms now in disuse, and blood from the artery in his neck spewing across his jaw, Revek watched the tiny glimmer of life whisper away from the boy's eyes, knowing from there he was only destined to die.

"You get what you *deserve.*"

He threw the body to ground, inhaling deeply as the boy began to cry, pleading in his foreign tongue for mercy from the great civilisers who had come to redeem them. Revek scoffed, lifting his arms out, gazing skyward, rolling his tongue across his teeth. Smiling, chuckling almost at the black spirals of smoke coiling above. At the roaring fires tearing the village apart from the top down, and the screaming savages reeling within. The wails of their pathetic children; the pitiful cries of their fathers raising farm tools against the soldiers' steel blades. The maddening beauty of it all.

And Revek, finding himself at its very centre, as if the world seemed to orbit around him for just a moment. That this was his world, his chaos and his beauty. That here was the triumph he had ordained, the great civilisation he would bring. That here, at the centre of all things, as the village of the savages and its people burned around him – here, he was finally in power.

"I am god here," he whispered.

"But you shall die a coward all the same."

His arms dropped, eyes lowering sharply—

Landing on the pupil-less moons of a pale man draped in black robes, concentric circles branded around his left eye.

Revek stumbled backwards and fell to the floor, the air suddenly thin and bubbling at his throat. The figure remained entirely still, looming over him, the piercing whites of its eyes burrowing into his skull, breaching his thoughts like a hammer.

It took a step forward. *"There is no god here."*

The commander found himself squeaking inanely, seeking out any support from his men – men who were nowhere to be seen. He shuffled back on his elbows but found the distance remained the same. Kicking out with his legs, scraping wet earth, the looming shadow of the pale man ever-present before him.

Another step. *"There is only the sin of tyrants."*

He began to cry for help, dismantling noises snapping on his tongue, hardly a whisper over the din of battle. With his elbows, he pressed harder against the earth, abandoning his sword to the mud. In the madness, his left arm slid away slightly, touching something hard. The shock broke through to him, twisting suddenly—

To gaze into the cold, dead stare of his own rotting corpse.

"You get what you deserve."

He screamed, reeling away. Clawing at the ground, grabbing at the moss-covered stones of the village well – pressing his back against it, crying into the ashen void beyond. Lungs burning; skull ablaze with fear.

Glancing over to the pale figure, gone once again, fading to nothingness like the last.

Revek inhaled again, watching the black plumes of smoke overhead. Their simple waves, their maddening beauty. Spiralling, spiralling around him. Reminding him of the world at the end of his fingers. Reminding himself of who he was, of what this triumph was to him. Reaching for it, reaching for that greatness again, and finding himself alone, broken and screaming, a god among men.

Getting what he deserved.

†

Chapter 42

A Dance of Fallen Gods

ome out then.

The throne room had not spoken a whisper since his arrival, the curtains behind the iron chair drawn across as if no one was home. Cobwebs lined the wooden covings high above, stretching across the walls like thick ivy. Around its outskirts, stacked chairs and tables sat miserly in their sleep. Beyond the shaded windows of the palace keep, a world bustled on down in the capital, full of life and colour and splendour. It should've been enough to draw some pride from his splintered heart, but Alvarez found the opposite was true. As the rhythms of a new age called up to him from Casantri below, it only emphasised the unperturbed silence that ate away at every inch of the room around him.

A silence he wanted desperately to fill.

"Come out then," he called off towards the curtains. "Let's see what you have to say for yourself, *she-witch.*"

Whatever command he thought he had over Mother Katastro, locked away in the shadows beyond the fabric veil, proved worthless. Nothing moved of the scene before him. All remained silent, and calm.

"I'm not interested in your games, Mother... I want *answers.*"

He paced forward, the clatter of his steel boots almost deafening, awaiting an answer that never came.

"You think you can defy *me*, witch!" he boomed, ascending the podium before the throne. "You think your magical veil can hide you away like a frightened child, afraid of the truth you've been so deceitfully *hiding from me*..."

With great exertion, Alvarez flung the curtain behind the throne aside with an outstretched arm, eyes seeking the hidden shape of the Mother lurking desperately behind, cowering away—

To find a solid stone wall in its place, with no cavern nor alcove in sight.

Alvarez curdled with anger, sweeping the other side across to reveal more of the same: nothing but stone, and silence.

What the hell is this?

He stumbled back, looking up and down the huge black veil with its silver-laced edges. Utterly lost, and increasingly angry, by the Mother's failure to comply.

"What have you done, she-witch!" he boomed nervously. "What trickery is this?"

Only the echo chamber answered his call.

"You think you can play games with me, can't you? You enjoy it, don't you?" Alvarez scoffed. "You torment me every day with your foul visions of faces and arms and unbroken smiles. You *think* you have this control over me because of it, and you have *nothing of the kind*. My sleepless nights are my rapture, Mother! There is no vestige of the whole world you could wield against me, for me to stoop to such lows as you have. So I dare you, *I dare you,* oh witch of the palace keep, Mother Katastro of the high realm... I dare you to challenge me, I dare you to *mock* me any longer!"

Silence rang out—

"*Speak!*"

Not a word—

"You will *answer me!*"

It was hopeless—

"I am your ruler and you answer to me *now!*"

Burning with anger, Alvarez stormed to the far corner and

grappled an old chair propped against the wall, stomping back to the centre of the room and levelling it with the curtained veil. Hauling it across, he swung it toward the black cloth with full force, watching it snap to pieces across the throne and disappear behind the podium.

"Speak to me!"

And yet silence was all that came, bitterly in denial of the demands he so wished.

And Alvarez just stood there, his shoulder stooped, knees buckled, dressed in full uniform with a contorting twitch across his left eye. Gazing at the curtain and its magical nothings. The irredeemable fact that there was nothing there, and that the Mother as he had known her, was all gone.

What has happened here?

He drew himself back, a cold touching his soul, peeling through the days that had haunted him of the past. The Mother's words, calculating and decisive – the lies she stole and the hollow threats she imposed. The sickening fallacy of it all, that made his skin boil. To think he was not master of his own destiny, that fate was predetermined and far beyond his power. That free will was a guise of ignorant humankind. The lies she told, all of them. The hate he had come to know.

The words replayed themselves over and over again, clearer with each recital. The Mother's talk of power, Tarraz, the Iron Queen and the Icebreaker Sea, and the end of all time. The prophecies and doubts and the coiling desire to be something more. The All-Mother, the silence, the fear of her passing...

He looked off to the curtained veil suddenly with wandering eyes, her words whispering to him.

I fear, with her strength gone, my days are also numbered.

Alvarez swayed backwards.

"She's *dead...*"

PART III

A Plague of Once-Forgotten

†

Chapter 43

The Alderbane

A day had passed, locked away in the damp recesses of the prison block. A day of silence and pain, eating whatever meagre pickings could be spared, staring at slate-grey walls carved from the rocks of an underground chasm. Beyond the fluorescent algae strung across one corner, no light passed through, and the warm but distant glow of a burning sconce somewhere along the corridor beyond. Down in the dark, an eternity could pass without so much as a whisper – even the other prisoners she had passed on the way through remained solemn and largely speechless, their only words being those of disdainful prayer to false prophets and broken lives, echoing through the deepest reaches as if the place had a voice of its own. And without the sun's redeeming eye, or its blind equal of the night, the dark seemed to ebb on where time did not. So when Cavara lay her head to rest, and the world gave way to the unconscious void, it was done so under false pretences, plagued by nightmares and the cold embrace of fatigue, when she awoke once again to find nothing had changed. That she was still locked away in the damp recesses of the prison block, without sun and without sound, accompanied only by the delicate pulses of her heartbeat and the rattle of her lungs, and the sheer abandonment of time that seemed to swell all around.

So when they finally came for her – guards approaching, a sharp barrage of knocks at her door that she almost expectantly rose to meet – their demands were not met with fear or consequence, but rather the quiet inflexion of relief that, wherever she was going in the vastness of the world outside, she would be glad it was anywhere other than the sunless, soundless nothing that she occupied in that cell.

Anywhere but nowhere, would do.

They dragged her from the cell by the chains binding her hands, up through the labyrinth of interchangeable corridors and sloping stairways that made up the dense underground of the capital. Climbing narrow steps, Cavara found the prison extended another three floors above her own, interlocking channels of cell blocks cutting left and right through the rock like a woven thread. At the last, they walked the length of the corridor to a stairway at the end, bathed in the warm light of torches, sided intermittently by wide, heavy iron doors with no bars or windows. For a moment, shuffling across the tiled floor with an awkward slowness, she almost believed they were uninhabited, and that the rooms beyond those great doors lay barren and obsolete.

That was until the prison guard thought it amusing to pound his baton against one of them, producing a sharp clang of metal that ricocheted down the stone walls. At that sound, whatever thing lay behind the door began to wail and cry, hammering its fists against the iron like a drum, rising to a crescendo of wild screaming and crashing metal as the other cells joined in, until Cavara found herself overwhelmed by the maw of primal anguish. It barrelled on, to the jeers and jaunts of the prison guards at her side, the corridor seemingly endless before her. She began to ascend the steps at the far end, rising to a summit of dazzling lights, and the hellscape of the prison slowly faded at her back, returning to an echoey nothingness she had long resented, but now welcomed with open arms.

At the summit of the stairway, a certain warmth crawled back into the room before them, with fine wood covings lacing the low ceiling above, and long blue-white tapestries draped stoically across both walls. Opposite, a wide metal door framed with marble greeted them, the coiling shape of a woman on one door spearing a snake on the other, emblazoned in purest gold. Cavara didn't know the significance of the image, or for the grandeur of the room she entered — only that within a few feet of the doorway she was told to wait, and one prison guard stepped forward to knock three times.

The door slid open a fraction, and a guard in a round-top helmet poked his head through. "Carto do'me?" he said.

"Prisona," the woman to her right acknowledged. "Noya tinamas redo sa bossa."

The guard frowned. "Certina?"

"Arjo." The woman at her side grinned. "Noya teré solda, carto coltzas uy quino de'desomas..." The prison guard imitated drawing a knife across her throat, drawing a sudden shrill of laughter from her colleague to the left.

The guard opposite swallowed, eyes wandering off to the descending stairwell behind them, a hundred minute fears plucking at the edges of his mouth. A moment's hesitation and he drew the door open fully, beckoning them in with a flick of his hand.

A flutter of thanks, and they passed into the room beyond — into a room that seemed, just in that brief glimpse, like an entirely different world altogether.

They entered a vast corridor of pigmented stone, light glossing in from the wide-windowed ceiling, detailing every surface with the warm hues of yellow and white. Guards in their glistening dome helmets were stationed across the handful of small doors on either side — drawn to the sound of the prison guards emerging, their incarcerated cargo dragging behind like an old mule. Each soldier gave a nod at their passing, a disdaining smile to the general shortly after, as they began the long walk of the corridor to the huge gold-wood doors at the far end, where a similar set of guards awaited their arrival.

Cavara crossed the space with swelling trepidation, the gleam of the corridor before her a mirage of colour slowly phasing into one.

She lowered her gaze, a sting of pain through her mind at the sudden brightness of the world, to watch her manacles swing low across the stone floor, sliding left-to-right like a pendulum. Inactivity had rendered her body tense, every step a lumbering swing – trying to maintain pace with her captors, the jarring fatigue in her joints caught her several times, and she was jostled back to a stand with a disgruntled shove.

Along the corridor's edges, she began to pick out small statues in tiny alcoves in the stone. From what she saw, there was a strange brusqueness to their features: one half of their face and torso coated in blue-white checked cloth, moulding into the face beneath like a death-mask; the other half marked by smooth marble features and hollow voids where the eyes would have been, producing an almost daunting expression of deprivation and despair. She found herself drawn, captivated by the unseeing stare of every man and woman she passed, until she looked forward once more and the door finally reared its ugly head before her, and Cavara realised her time had come.

"This is the entrance chamber to greet the Alderbane," one guard exclaimed – she was taken aback by the sudden use of the Provenci tongue. "Once inside, *shlaktum*, you will not speak unless spoken to, and you will look only to the floor at your feet." The words were crackly and broken in his accented voice. "Especially as you are *other*... and the Alderbane does not take pleasure in dealing with those of your kind..."

She gave a nod, and the guard hammered his fist against the great door, announcing entry – the heavy hinges groaned into animation and it swung slowly open.

Pushing her forward, Cavara was half-thrown into the room beyond, her eyes locked to the floor, never straying from the awkward cloth overshoes coating her feet. A clatter of metal from either side announced the guards exiting the room, and the door lurched to a close. Their trailing voices and bitter laughs faded with each step, quashed by the sharp crunch of the door sealing.

And so she found herself, once again, desperately alone.

For a while, nothing happened. There was no noise around her, no shadows crossing her low gaze revealing motions in the room beyond. There was only the rasp of air through her nostrils, the minute snaps of her chain bonds knocking the floor – that, and the rapidly accelerating thud of her heart knocking through her chest, unnerved by the silence, the lack of anything in the world out of reach. Cavara pleaded to herself, seeking out sound where there was none – wondering, maybe, if she just had a peek at the room ahead of her—

"*Outsider.*"

She nearly jumped at the voice, intimidating yet uncomfortably docile, rippling through the space between them.

"Your kind is rare among our people."

The voice ebbed and flowed, often slow, but always drawing the fullest attention from those who listened.

"We haven't had one of your kind for decades now."

Every word came almost as a monotony – no emotion on display, no slip of the tongue or pause for thought. Concise, and definite, and always meeting the mark.

"Part of me hoped we never would *again*…"

A screech of a chair; the figure before her made to stand.

"I expect you were told to lower your eyes in my presence," it boomed at length. "And for ordinary circumstance, I would expect nothing less. But these are not ordinary times… and you are no ordinary *visitor*." She felt her heart wrench, skin crawl as if infested with lice. "So, I charge you: look upon me, outsider, and let me see you for all the fear you have. Let us see what the tides have brought us, from the shores of desperate lands…"

Cavara held her gaze to the floor, but with each beat of her swelling heart she found her eyes slowly lift to the room before her. Crossing a broad marble table, oval in shape, melding with the odd concaves of the chamber walls that curled over as if she stood within a grain of rice. Lifting, rising across the two small candles ahead, drifting behind, onto a great throne of...

Dragon horns. Knotted twists of spiral bone, spearing outwards from the throne's hard backpiece, like the spearing branches of a dead tree.

And Cavara looked there, studied the shape of the throne in all of its shadowed wonder, and a frown curled across her lips. At the absence of a being – an absence of a figure with which to place the voice she had heard moments ago. Trying to pierce the sheer blackness of its shape, seeking out a face that wasn't there, but had to be there, because otherwise where would—

Something within the great shadow blinked, the tiny specks of white flinching therein, and suddenly the entire central mass began to rise, a towering figure a full head-and-shoulders taller than she was emerging from the gloom.

And she found herself gazing into the eyes of the Alderbane, and all thought seemed long-forgotten.

There was nothing warm or human about the figure before her. Bound head-to-foot in black robes snaking across the skin, there was little indication of a physical body beneath beyond the droop across its shoulders and the curved cloth appendages that she believed were hands. Like a sword's blade, her eyes were drawn to the spear of tiny animal skulls rising from its abdomen to its throat, their hollow sockets watching on with cold despair. Her gaze lifted, reaching the figure's face, where a malformed human skull was fixed across the folds of black robes, its jaw snapped clean off to reveal the bleach-white human skin of the figure's actual body beneath. At the circumference of its head, six huge teeth coiled forward across its shrouded scalp, that seemed to click and pulse like the tendrils of some insect.

Before her stood the ruler of one of the greatest imperial kingdoms of the known world, a figure of legend and distorted realities, and all Cavara found within her thoughts was a singular reckoning of horror, lost in the blind stare of the devil's forgotten child.

The Alderbane had come.

"And there you are," it rumbled, the thin strip of its mouth hardly moving despite the resonating power of the words it spoke. "A lost soul from desperate lands, seeking her redemption. Tell me... what is your name, outsider?"

"Cavara," she spluttered, bursting the bubble ballooning in her throat like a frog.

The Alderbane produced a deep, guttural grunt of acknowledgement, tilting its head to the side to study her more closely. "You are of strong blood... of the military, I may assume?"

How can you know... "Yes... formerly General Cavara, of the... of the 9th Legion of the Imperial Army."

"Nation?"

"Provenci."

"*Provenci...*" The black slit of its mouth curled at the edges. "It has been some time since I've had any business with a *Provencian...* not since your king sent a fleet to tear down these walls, some forty years ago. You are not here for *those* purposes, are you, outsider?"

She shook her head vigorously. "No... I am the only one of my people to come to your shores."

"And why might that *be...* outsider?"

Cavara suddenly found her words dry up, staring blankly at the black figure opposite her without an answer to hand – knowing there were many, but offering none. "I..." *What do I say? The truth? Will it be my end?* "I'm sorry, I..." *To lie would be death – the truth may be equally so.* "It's..." The words seemed foreign to her, separating on her tongue as they came. She bit back, caught in the maddening gaze of the Alderbane, cold shadows sweeping her mind, wondering what to do.

You act as your principle, she sighed. *You tell the truth.*

And she did: the truth of all things. She told it of the death of the king; the new imperial rule; Alvarez in power; war with Tarraz; their invasion of the lowlands as she spoke; the betrayal that had seen her stabbed, condemned to death, healed and shipped halfway across the known world to the shores of the Alderbane's mighty kingdom. She

351

reeled it off like a script – the facts she had known for days now and accepted as little more than the way things were. But reciting them then to the Alderbane, watching its head twitch and consider, the half-skull displaying glimmers of feeling and incite in tiny, half-imagined ways... Cavara realised just how insane the entire situation was, and how a scenario she had placated as normalcy, was indeed anything but. Even as she drew to the end of her monologue, she found her hands were shaking, and the nagging numbness of the gnarled wound across her chest had begun to quiver acutely. Drawing her eyes away to the bruised trench buried beneath her heavy cloth shirt, when she looked up again she found the Alderbane had followed her gaze, the corner of its mouth spasming coldly, making sense of it all. Some time passed before it spoke again.

"The outsider comes from a broken land," it muttered, "and longs to return... the outsider has seen good men fall and bad men rise, and seeks her redemption as *duty*." A single, slow nod. "How *poetic*."

"If I may... it was not my intention to come here," Cavara replied on instinct, forgetting procedure and finding her stomach churn.

"You intended to die." Whatever looked upon her then, stared closer than it had done before. "And by your estimation... and the wound across your chest... that should have been the end. And yet you live... and here you are, an outsider within my palace, within my walls... no doubt praying for sympathy."

"I just want to be out of your way—"

"And I want you out of *mine*," it boomed, laying two cloth-strangled hands across the table. "You should have never come here, with your rambling tales of distant lands... *they* should have never let you *in* here."

Her heart skipped a beat. "Who?"

"That merchant woman and her child – it's their doing that you are here in my capital."

"They meant no harm."

"They knew what they were doing—"

"They just meant to help—"

352

"*Do not interrupt me,*" the Alderbane growled, a strike of cold lancing at her as the room froze. Cavara lowered her eyes, exhaling quietly, before returning her gaze to the dark figure who seemed to pulse and swell with the shifting lights outside. "I do not take insubordination from people of my own kind," it continued, "let alone from outsiders like *yourself*... am I understood?"

"Yes," she mewed faintly.

The hands recoiled from the tabletop. "You should know that I don't intend to reprimand the merchant woman and her child for bringing you to my city. Punishment is a foul beast when left untamed." The claws atop its scalp twitched. "I don't care for your quarrels, or a foreign war by filthy hands... I care for none of it other than that which benefits me. Your kind has done enough in past generations to make that point... and I want rid of you as soon as can be arranged."

"You have my word, I shall leave as soon as I am ordered."

"That is not for you to *decide*." The claws drew still. "Who knows that you are here? Who have you spoken to, or been in contact with within this city?"

"I have only been here one night, and was told by the merchant to remain inside that entire time—"

"And yet you were reported wandering the plaza in broad daylight... I did not think it was in the ways of a general to *insubordinate?*"

"The child ran off," Cavara declared. "Having been placed under my care while the mother tended to business, I was obliged to search for him... and had every intention to bring him straight back—"

"You preach honour in your reasoning... yet you did not tell the mother what had happened, when she returned?"

She swallowed. "I was afraid for the child, and was hoping the incident would come to pass... because I understand your people do not like outsiders—"

"Do not lie to me, general," the Alderbane interrupted. "You hid the truth from that woman... to save your own skin, no one else's.

You knew the woman and her child were in trouble the moment you were discovered in that plaza – you knew exactly what you were doing. You hid your shame to last just that little while longer in her care, knowing she would have been killed had we found her hiding an outsider. So when we stormed her house, she hid behind her ignorance – and you hid behind your *lies*." It lifted its head skyward. "And it is only the knowledge you have from the desperate shores of your homeland… that means either of you live at all. That is your burden to bear, no one else's. You lied your way into this city, and you lied to those who cared for you… and now you lie to me, thinking I a fool who does not know what someone of your *skills* would do to save their skin."

Cavara ground her teeth, eyes stinging with fresh tears.

"You are betrayed, forsaken… you are a castaway from a world away, a world lost in war and the chaos of its own greed and lies. And I know that much is not a lie… I can see it in your eyes. The pain bleeds from you – your people dying, your leaders tearing the stone from the ground… it *eats at you* and you have nothing to show for it." And then a grin of black teeth coiled across its pin-stretched face, seditious and foul. "And from that chaos, thinking back to the past, maybe we have a use for you, after all."

"I will not betray my people for *you*…"

"You will do whatever I so wish," it thundered, the smile receding. "You are my prisoner, *outsider*… your life depends on your compliance." The Alderbane raised a buckled finger to her. "You will tell me everything you know about this war, about the army, about which players command the board. You will tell me everything I need to know… or so help me, I will *bleed* it from you. Mark my *words*." It lowered itself back onto the throne, morphing with the darkness as before. "We shall speak again, in time… and I am sure when that time comes, you will be most *forthcoming*."

A flick of the hand, soundless, and by some unseen indicator the doors peeled open behind her, and the guards shuffled into the room with their eyes lowered, hissing at Cavara to lower her own gaze.

But she refused. Every bone in her body screamed of challenge, of open defiance. Locked to the half-skull staring sightlessly from the throne — locked to the creature and its long shadow. Its unconstrued certainty, demanding fear from all and expecting nothing in return. Even as she was dragged from the room by her chains, her eyes did not sway from the half-skull of the gloom — not until the great doors themselves swung closed, and all thought seemed long-forgotten.

The Alderbane, had come.

†

Chapter 44

What the Dead May Sing

He awoke to the sound of rattling wheels and the creaking strain of wood against metal, and found it was definitely not what he expected the afterlife to sound like. It was oddly mystifying, the gentle sway and rocking of the world, as if he were on a boat in open waters, in search of distant shores. The slow rush of air across his face; the warm glow of some ethereal light dancing gracefully across his eyelids. The passage into the next life proved an unusual one, he found – but the dull, methodical drive forward seemed to calm him slowly, as he settled into the throes of the great unconscious unknown, waiting to wrap him soundly in its arms.

Death had come to greet him several times, he recalled, but never quite met its mark. Several times he had scraped its door: in the crosshair of a quivering arrow, or the driving course of a short-sword's blade; impaled through the shoulder; knocked across the head by falling rubble; his left kneecap trounced by the bluntness of a smithy's hammer, and another to the neck on the way down for good measure. There had been times, he knew, when he had seen that radiant light hollowed from the dark; times when the harbinger had whispered sweet nothings in his air, and had lain its lips softly on his cheek. Always drawing close; always falling apart moments later. Waiting, it seemed, for the opportune moment, the unenviable truce that was a shortened life, brought about by the most exacting death. He had longed for it often, waiting for the moment to strike – and in that rumbling, glowing void, he almost believed he had found it.

And then a voice grumbled at his side, and the snort of a draught-horse ahead followed the snap of reins, and Markus's eyes shot open to reveal a world that he had assumed was the afterlife moments before, only to find that afterlife to be a rather ugly, unfortunate place.

"He's alive," the voice at his side called out. "For a second there, we were's wondering if you were dead an' all."

Markus swung himself upright.

So did I...

He was in a wagon of some sort: a dull, wood-panelled block with metal frames and two locked doors to his right that betrayed any knowledge of the world beyond. Light glossed through from barred windows along the top edges, swamping the interior in mellow browns and yellow ochres. The ceiling swam with clouds of smoke, billowing from the pipe of a black-jacketed figure he spied at the opposite end, her complexion hidden beneath the wide brim of a hat.

She, whoever she was, seemed to possess a strong self-assurance and composure. She moved little, almost a fixed statue beyond the slow drag of the pipe in her hand, that fell away every so often to release a whisp of strangled air. There was nothing discernible about her, and from his assessment, she had been the focal interest of the six other thin, sparsely-clad men and women of the wagon sitting like him across the benches to either side.

They were a rotten half-dozen on first glance, shackles strung tight across the heels and wrists, laced with a miscellany of scars and brand marks detailing their capture and crime. Heads slung low like beggars in the burrow, he found therein eyes drawn heavy with wrinkles, caught by the sleeplessness of their capture. Such were the eyes of the condemned in all walks of life.

And he found himself numbered among them.

At the call of the man opposite, Markus sat up to find all eyes had rounded on him, studying this now-animate figure perplexed by the reality he now entered. All met his gaze, wherever he looked, their eyes revealing little of the machinations within – all meeting his gaze, that was, except the man opposite, whom Markus frowned at before realising he was almost entirely blind.

"Dead men do walk again," the blind prisoner mused. He was tall, robust of the chest and shoulders, the weathered scars across one side of his face evidence of a broken jaw once upon a time ago. The left eye sloped awkwardly, rolling in its socket dumbly, while the other remained dead-straight and alive with activity, the white-grey pupil piercing every point it landed on like a lunging blade. "Did you see the light, my boy? Did the old hag of the Icebreaker Sea come to sing you a tale?"

"The light ne'er saw him, ya blind fuck," the brusque woman at his side jested, her thin cloth shirt overlaying several great scars, tracing from beneath her belt up to the gouge that cleft her chin in two. "By the look of he, the one-armed man o' many nothin's… I'd say he ne'er was with the dead, but he's always longin' to be one of 'em…"

Markus looked down to the shackles across his lap suddenly and found only the one secured across his left hand, the other binding drooped lamely to one side. Twisting right, the woman's cold words resuscitating in his mind, he gazed levelly at the absence of his other limb, still buried in the mud of a distant land he had long lost hope for. All that remained in its place was a blackened, crusted stump, the white sheen of bone buried within the folds of his swollen skin. Even though it appeared to be a day old at best, a ferocious smell of burnt flesh snapped across his senses and made his eyes water, fixating on the orange-red ooze that continued to seep from every crack. It looked as if the earth had broken apart, and revealed the great red swamp within, crackling into black tar as it melded with the air and seized up. It looked, by all accounts, horrific.

The mark of a condemned man.

"By the sheer horror on his face," another man blustered, only the darting pupil visible behind the other curious prisoners, "I'd say he's seen a ghost... you'd say?"

"An ol' fool like he," the woman replied, "I reckon has seen many a-ghost in his time. Ay, ya old fuck?"

"He is a man haunted by his past," whispered the blind one. "You may be without an arm, but nay beyond redemption, my boy..."

"Shut it: he's dead meat in every kind."

Another: "dead men walkin', won't be walkin' much longer..."

Another: "won't be swingin' much more neither..."

"He'll be no use..."

"Nought wager cast for he with one arm..."

"By all accounts condemned; there be only redemption..."

"There is no redemption where you're going," the jacketed figure at the far end suddenly boomed, her voice carrying with far greater gravity than Markus had expected. With a tilt of the head, the hat lifted, and through the shadows was revealed a woman made entirely of angles, the cheeks unnaturally concaved, with a slight nose and eyes that sunk deep within the skull like an owl. As if life had been sucked from her – or if it had ever even existed within her at all.

She drew the smoke pipe away and tapped it with her index finger – little more than a stub of skin and bone, its ends sliced clean off much like his own arm.

"There is only blood, and there is only pain," she muttered soullessly. "And you, are the bastard-lot who bring it for the masses. That's the truth of Val Darbesh... nothing more."

At her words, Markus found eyes drop, a great quiet descending, eating at the world around him. Without recognition, the woman lowered the hat back down across her face, and blew another thin trail of smoke skyward, as if nothing had happened at all. Whatever power over the other prisoners the woman possessed, he found, it seemed to present itself with her words alone. A great fear, when she spoke of blood and pain. The cold acceptance of bringing such things to the masses. A mosaic of untold truths that he hardly knew.

And somewhere at the end, called Val Darbesh.

*

Wheels turning, time ticked by in the silent, smoke-smothered wagon with nothing to show for its passing. An unnatural heat seemed to consume every inch of the interior – the smoke hung thick over the barred windows above and indicated no sign of wind in whatever vastness lay beyond. As the colours shifted, and the browns and oranges gave in to yellows and whites, swirling shafts of light pierced the smoky veil. Hot breath and sweat-plastered skin wore heavy on the faces of those around him, their eyes hung limply to the floor like carcasses hung to dry. It was a disquiet worn by every prisoner donned in their rattling shackles, but as his eyes drifted left to the black coat and stooped hat of their handler, a great pain welted within at the sight of that same composure as before, unphased by the heat and untouched by the strain of their journey. Never watching, always patient and omnipresent, the thin spiral of smoke snaking the edge of the wide hat to join the clouds already bubbling across the ceiling. As if she did not care.

As if the world is nothing.

When his resolve began to fail, and Markus found the lingering dissent of fatigue take over, he was alerted to the sudden hum of voices ahead, and the sharp chime of a ringing bell that seemed to stall their progress. Eyes began to stir within the wagon at the sound of fellow humans, the blind man in front tapping his feet softly. The churn of the wheels like a bread mill began to slow, until the voices fell to a close again and the bell stopped its mellow cries.

The cart stopped; footsteps approached. A hammering fist thudded against the doors to his right.

The handler stood and extinguished her smoke pipe.

"We depart," she said.

To where, Markus did not know.

With a wrenching motion, the handler released the two chain-links from the benches they sat on, hoisting them in her curled fists, and ordered the prisoners to stand. Markus shuffled to his feet, swinging awkwardly at the absence of weight along his right side, suddenly very aware of the balance of his feet. The handler loomed beside him, the scent of her jacket musty and worn, a criss-cross of scars lacing the base of her neck like threaded cloth. Aware she was being inspected, she turned and glared at him maliciously — Markus averted his eyes, looking absently forward as the latches came undone and the door slid open.

He was more thrown outside than anything, skittering down the ramp and stopping at the presence of a great shadow placing a hand across his chest. Gawking up, Markus studied a pale, dirt-skimmed face mottled with red paint, adorning thin sheets of armour and a gilded chest-piece with a crown of spikes at its centre. The figure grunted with disgust, pushing him aside along with the others, following the trail of the handler into the great sun-scarred plain beyond.

Whatever land of green rolling hills and great mountain peaks he had travelled through before, had been manifestly abandoned to a world of sand and bleach-yellow grass. Risking a glance behind, the green lowlands were now little more than a colourful streak across the horizon, swamped by a sudden cataclysm of salt-white rocks and sudden tufts of brown bushel. Following its length, Markus saw the great peaks to the west, now little more than a blue-grey squint, and the final remnants of the Kazbak Hills starved of their former vibrancy splashing like waves to his left. Beyond that, the world seemed unreservedly flat, a great yellowing rash across the earth marked by the occasional rise of a black-rock hill: its thin, crumbling layers spilling across the otherwise-unblemished landscape like dried blood.

A desolation, he acknowledged, squinting at the light. *If I thought that the Tarraz I've seen so far was a cruel, rotting place... then this is the hell it will become, when judgement finally comes.*

Ahead, a small wooden shack stood dormant at the roadside, its metal frame rusted orange by the sun's incessant weathering.

Looking past the handler, Markus spied two blackcoats approaching from there – although rather than carrying the weight of traditional armour in the unrelenting heat, he found instead they wore robes of deep grey, the inscriptions of an ancient tongue woven along their sash and belts.

Their prisoner convoy stopped just short of the blackcoats, the handler stepping forward to bow and clasp the leader's forearm, the other two looking past to acknowledge the sweat-soaked congergation trailing slowly behind.

"*Az-kabza,* my friend," the leader boomed, black circles painted around the edges of his mouth to give a permanent impression of a grin. "How goes business?"

"It is strained in these times," the lander replied. "Many criminals an' fighters were conscripted for the war. Our intake is limited… and those left are *mixed* at best."

The blackcoat shifted his gaze to Markus, who flinched suddenly at the attention. "I see you have one without a limb… do you intend to watch it dance or something?" The other blackcoat stirred with laughter.

"I would share in your jests, friend… only that that one in particular is rather a prize."

"Then I must be missing something," the leader mused.

"He is of *Provenci* stock," the handler said, Markus straining to hear her hushed tones. "Gave some of our scouts in the Kazbaks a run for their money. Say he's a skilled fighter an' all."

"A Provencian?" The pale face considered. "How *interesting.*"

"Should fetch a bigger crowd when he fights, you see… in the current climate there's all the more taste for killin' the likes of him, both arms or not."

"Agreed. I'll have to send word to the citadel in Val Darbesh, see if they can find him a few good fighters to put on a show…"

Markus found his attention sway, the melodramatics of business falling short of his already-faltering conscience. He glanced behind absently, scanning the bruised faces of his fellow prisoners – catching the eye of the pale-faced Tarrazi who had first greeted him out of the wagon, the same burning disdain worn heavy in his expression. Markus decided to turn front again and look to his feet like the rest, *lest I find myself at the end of someone's sword.*

Not that I fear that much anymore.

"Deadman walking," the blind man beside him suddenly spoke, his eyes lodged absently at the sky above. "Come to see the arena..."

Markus swallowed, eyes lifting to watch the blackcoats cautiously. *"What do you mean, arena? Where are we going?"* he whispered.

"The dead shall sing a merry song, to the pits of Val Darbesh: *merry are we who come, condemned are we to die, sing the song of blood and sacrament, to blood and steel we fly...*"

"What the fuck are you on about?"

"Prisoners and slaves, ye rotten souls, broken bones do come — these are the songs of the fighting pits; to death a deed is done..."

"Are we condemned to die?"

"Such is never clear," he said suddenly, pointedly. "You are a dead man walking... you have seen ghosts; as have I. You may not have died yet, my one-armed friend" — raising the shackles, the blind man extended a gnarled finger off to the north — "but Val Darbesh shall claim all in the end..."

Markus traced the finger around the blackcoat cluster to the wide stretch of desert beyond. Tracing the horizon, the blocks of black-rock polka-dotting the landscape, each one rigid and slanting awkwardly—

Except one.

From afar, blanketed by the rising heat of bleached rock and sand, it appeared as little more than a grey-black silhouette not markedly different than any other at a glance. But as he squinted, guided by its sharp protrusions, he found that what he was looking at was not a black rock at all — it was a city, and a huge one at that. Curved at its outer walls, tall spires of metal rising several thousand feet in the air, arching over the city like a crown but never quite meeting at its middle. Stretching between them and lashed together with rope, haphazard lengths of cloth sprawled the skyline, shadowing the citizens within from the raw anger of high sun. It was like nothing he had ever seen before: nothing like the great palaces and cityscapes of Provenci, with stone blocks and wide towers and great palace spires of copper and iron. Nothing like the civilised world he had understood long before. What he found there, in the desolation of such an unfortunate place, was a transfixing abhorrence of metalwork and rope binding, visible from miles around by its sheer opposition to the natural landscape it inhabited. Some great artery of the enemy, out in the swamping heat of the desert. A place he knew nothing about, and wanted even less to do with. Somewhere called Val Darbesh.

A place he was destined to go.

The handler manifested into view suddenly before him, her business coming to a swift end. She crossed a few faces, scowling at the blind man who seemed yet so oblivious to the world, and gave a nod to the pale face at the rear of the column to load them back into the wagon.

Markus lurched sideways, a sickness growing in the base of his stomach with each half-realised step – shuffling back to the smoke-smothered box to be drenched in sweat once more, into the great unknown masked by its perpetual silence, this time with a destination at hand.

He thought himself going mad, in the beating hate of the sun, until he heard the song of the blind man in his ear, little more than a whisper over the coursing wind.

"*Prisoners and slaves, ye rotten souls, broken bones do come – these are the songs of the fighting pits...*"

To death, a deed is done.

†

Chapter 45

Truth's Shadow

A strike across the face, the full force of the knuckle cracking against his cheek, where a red-purple boom had already formed. Blood lined his gums; he spat across the stone floor. Two shadows circled like dogs of the night, hunting their wounded prey.

"*Traitor*," Alvarez scoffed, clutching Broska by the jaw and pressing a thumb against the rising bruise. The large general hissed, his sweat-coated face prickling with residual pain. Knees wedged underneath him as if in prayer, the sky seemed to spin overhead, blotches across his vision where several punches had already landed.

"A scoundrel in our midst," Ferreus cooed from his side, stood before the wide chamber window. "Who'd've thought?"

Broska scowled, turning to study the sneering figure. "You really are a soft little prick, aren't you..."

The general stepped forward and kicked Broska in the side, forcing a grunt of agony as it struck his ribs.

"A scoundrel indeed," Alvarez mumbled, standing back to observe the broken general in his chains. "A liar, too."

Broska gazed up to the stooped figure of the Supreme Governor — the black shadows of his eyes, the paleness of his skin and overbearing definition of his hollowed cheeks — and sighed. "And you believe every word he says, sir..."

"Why should I not?"

"Because what he tells you is *lies*, sir. Poison, dripping in your ears. It's cowardly—"

Another kick to the side, this time harder, angrier, forcing Broska to sway violently as his stomach rolled, almost toppling across the stone.

"He toys with you, sir," Ferreus interjected, wiping spittle from his mouth. "He thinks you stupid and of ill-mind... thinks you can be manipulated into his little schemes."

"The only scheme here is the one you're propositioning, *general*," Broska growled. "You and your cronies in high-office, pushing pens to have good people killed..."

"There was no murder... I acted in self-defence and you *know it*, you're just so lost in blind hatred for the new regime that you can't face the truth."

"Had I ever before seen someone lie so callously, I'd think they were the ones fearing truth, you *bastard*—"

A final kick, planting the base of his boot into Broska's shoulder. The general swung too far left and spilt across the floor, the opposing arm taking the brunt of the fall, hissing and wheezing against the cold tiles like a lame fish.

Another moment passed, and he was pulled back to his knees by the hair of his scalp, Ferreus slathering through his teeth, lining up another punch—

"No more," Alvarez commanded suddenly, raising a hand.

Unamused, Ferreus withdrew – Broska inhaled shallow lengths of air through lungs that felt entirely without function. Every muscle ached; every sinew in his neck felt knotted and malformed. A bubble of blood popped rhythmically in his throat with each breath, the bitter iron taste of his own life coating every inch of his mouth. There was no telling, in the abandoned state he found himself in, just how much damage had been done to him inside.

The weak ripple of his heart told him plenty.

The Supreme Governor crouched before him, a pair of cold,

twisted eyes gazing into his own, almost through him, conscious and recollecting but not entirely there. Broska studied his unshaven features, the welts in his skin where pockets of dirt had built up, the coarse texture of his hair. The glint of the pupils casting their long shadow, some haunting presence wavering behind, lost on him but clearly attached to Alvarez like a curse. The general couldn't help but think, *what the hell has happened to you?*

"He must provide some answers first," the Governor muttered, studying the signet ring on his right hand. "And you will answer them honestly, won't you, general?"

"With every bone in my body, *sir,*" Broska lamented.

He scowled. "Where were you the night before last?"

"In my office, writing up a report on theatre company contracts... as I was *assigned* to do."

"And you did this all night?"

"Evening 'til sunrise... sir."

"Why so late?"

"I found it difficult to sleep."

"And why was that?"

The collar of his cloth shirt tightened. "Restless, sir... been struggling to sleep these past few nights..."

"The guilty conscience does unsettle the mind," Ferreus cooed.

Alvarez waved a finger, silencing his unkept remarks. "Did you receive anyone overnight?"

"No one of note, sir."

"What does that mean?"

"The watchman likes to tuck me in at night, sing a sweet song and kiss me on the forehead..."

"Don't toy with me you fucking *fool,*" Alvarez gruelled, a flare of fire in his eyes. "Did *you* receive *anyone* that night?"

"No, sir."

"Do you have any knowledge of the break-in that occurred at the palace that same night?"

"Yes, sir."

"And what's that?"

"Well, it's the reason I'm here." Broska tilted his head toward the other person in the room. "And it's why *he* looks like *that*."

Alvarez shot a hand out instinctively, stalling Ferreus's broad stride towards their prisoner with a white-knuckled fist primed and ready. Boots skidded to a halt; the grey-haired officer grimaced towards their prisoner. "And why might that be?" Ferreus spat.

"Because you think I orchestrated it."

"We *know* you orchestrated it."

"And why is *that?*"

"Because it was your sister what gave me this." He stroked the thin slit of open skin across his cheek, covered in yellowing scabs. "And she'd have no interest in me if it weren't for your intervention."

"My sister is a character unto herself, you know this – I have no sway over her business in this city. I've hardly seen her since she went rogue."

"You've done little to have her arrested, either," Alvarez intervened. "Which seems at this moment entirely out of your favour."

It was Broska's turn to scoff. "You think I've kept her out of the cells, just so I could plot against one of you, in the inconceivable event that the king is murdered and the military orders a government takeover?" He blinked slowly. "Sounds a lot like playwright's bollocks to me."

Alvarez cuffed him across the face, stabbing a finger at his chest. "*Liar!*" he thundered viciously. "Don't toy with *me*. I *know* what you've done, I know *all of it*. You're a traitor and a conspirator with a known criminal in this city. You've had every intention to undermine me since my ascension, every intention to undermine our new order, and when the time came... *you took it*. You knew all along, what would happen... you and that whore-general, lying dead in the sand—"

Broska lunged forward and his forehead crashed through Alvarez's nose, sending him reeling back onto his arse in a daze of blundering cries. Ferreus stepped forward, the long-awaited punch finally seizing its moment, connecting sharply with his temple. A blinkered moment, and he was thrown back across the tiles, head snapping, a grey cataclysm skimming his gaze. The sky spun overhead, Alvarez and Ferreus lunging down.

The Supreme Governor dragged him by the leg across the tiles, rising to his feet and stamping down across Broska's thigh like a spooked horse.

Ferreus drew across his side like a phantom: the boot came thick and fast, snapping across the back of his head, a raw burning sensation blanketing his skull.

Rolling to his side, a kick to the stomach set his guts in motion. An opposing kick across the midriff of his spine speared him forward, a crackle of blood-spittle splashing over the stone.

Rolling onto his back, wheezing, Broska gazed up at the beasts looming over him, wild-eyed and baying for blood, dogs of the night and their insatiable lust of self-certainty. A cold discomfort therein, gazing into eyes of tyrants – ones he once called colleagues.

But never called friends.

"Any more wise remarks?" Alvarez blustered. "Or do we have to knock your teeth out for good measure?"

"I'd find great pleasure watching a fat pig squeal," Ferreus added, grinning. "The butcher'd make a fine piece of it."

"That he would." It was Alvarez's turn to grin. "And we'll see to it that he gets his *due,* when the time is right."

Broska wheezed, ribs bruised and very unquestionably broken, the ballooning sensation across his spine causing enough grief to sink ships. Whatever bruising graced his skin plucked tears at his eyes with its agony.

"I want... *nothing,* of this..." he begged. "Please... nothing more..."

"It's not what you *want*, general," Alvarez spat. "You are a traitor and a liar, and you will find nothing but hell awaits you."

"*Please,* no..."

Alvarez lashed out, kicking at his side again, forcing a splutter of tears from the prisoner sprawled across his chamber floor. "*Stop grovelling!* You deserve *nothing!*"

"What shall we do with him, sir?" Ferreus asked, twitchy with the draw of merciless hate. "Shall we bleed him?"

The Governor seemed to steady himself, swaying softly, looking off to the darker corners of his chamber – whatever swimming tide of hate had bulged within him now seemed to recede back into its glass bottle. Broska wondered, in a faint and feeble way, if perhaps mercy would follow – if perhaps the end would not come, and he could perhaps be spared.

But when the gaze returned, and the fire continued to burn brightest in the hollows of his eyes, he found those same prayers went to mud almost as soon as they'd been born.

"Lock him back in the cell," Alvarez said flatly. "Chain him to the wall opposite his bed and leave him with his wounds. We'll see to him later."

Ferreus was already approaching, dragging him towards the door in a mangled mess.

"Let's see if the pig sleeps or squeals tonight…"

†

Chapter 46

The Better Among Us

They had camped overnight among the burned-out hovels of the village square, where the muddy, ashen earth buried tent poles and boots alike as the night grew suddenly colder. The overwhelming smell of cinder that had suffocated them throughout the day slowly ebbed from their nostrils, replaced by the more abundant scent of rot and wet as moisture crept its way through the alcoves of lost homes. And alongside that, in its lingering moments, came the unmistakably aversive stench of flesh. A cold reminder of consequence, with bodies piled high in open graves off among the trees, and shrunken faces half-buried in the earth with no recollection left in their blue, bloated eyes. That an enemy had come and bled them dry and left them to decay beneath the stars, mattered nought anymore. Even tucked away in their candlelit tents, using their packs for pillows after the others had been lost to the swamp, every man and woman of the camp knew that insurmountable truth to be real: that the blood of their slaughter never strayed far, staining the puddles at their feet or dried like paint across worn faces. And that, given time, that blood would wash away and they would pass to another place, and nothing would be left but the memory. But even that, they knew, was not the same as a stain of blood in the end.

That, they knew, would always be a scar.

When the quiet dawn came at last, Commander Revek rose from

his tent and sat against the water-well at the centre of the square, surrounded by small scatterings of tents and cold campfires damp from the morning mist. There's was a world of blue and grey, the stone pillars and hollow interiors of ruined houses jutting from the gloom like a sea-serpent breaching the waves. Pillars of trees marked the outer boundary, with an icy-blue glow of the rising sun prickling across his back.

When they had arisen, the soldiers had been ordered to search the burnt remains for anything that had survived their purge: food, materials, clothing and medical supplies topped the list, with any valuables thrown into sacks to sell for a good margin when they came home. But as he watched the shadows of soldiers drift through the mist, or noted the muffled orders escaping the lips of his subordinates, everything was done reservedly, as if they were being watched. Every motion like a flickering candle; every demand hinting an unease and trepidation. To be there, among the husks of the former savage, among the blood of the dead and with their corpses left to rot just down the road. As if their ghosts remained, all-seeing and envious, and every sip of air they breathed was sacrilege, being in a place so foul for so long.

They want to run from consequence, the commander grumbled inside. *As if expecting when the savage die, they should leave no trace.* Thinking back to the harbourside when the attack had first occurred, and the bodies dotting the water like dead fish, the commander recalled the *sentiment* he had received from one such general of rank that seemed to share their reluctance just then. *That they're all people, all deserving that individual recognition – that these lives matter and no matter what, we should feel shame and guilt for our loss.*

He scowled, a sheen of heat rising at his neck.

How pathetic.

"The men seem restless, sir," Darius exclaimed, rolling his shoulder as he approached to snap the joint suddenly, a wheeze escaping his pursed lips as he eased down on the wall beside him. "There's an odd spirit among them from the night."

"They are restless because they fear this place," Revek muttered, shaking his head. "They fear the dead... and they fear consequences."

"Because it's bad luck lingering by battle like this, sir," Darius continued. "They say they keep seeing things in the gloom... something about a pale man in robes lurking amongst the trees."

Revek found the air thin at his lips, exhaling before it took a hold. "They're jumping at shadows... when they should be looking for supplies."

They'd mark it differently, sir, given the chance. They'd say that's the job of robbers and thieves, not good army men on the road."

"I apologise for our short supply of robbers and thieves, *general*," the commander growled. "I'll opt to bring them next time."

"I merely meant it as a reasoning behind their... *discomfort*, sir."

Revek found his temper rise and fall, and sighed. "I can understand that, general... it's no easy business scavenging from the dead. So long as it gets done, then I bear no ill-will to any of 'em."

"Of course, sir. They know it's meaningful work, what we do here... despite their unrest." He paused. "That being said, I'm sure the news from the scouts has lightened their spirits."

The commander produced a smile.

Lightened mine too.

Reports had come a few hours before from the small detachment he'd sent out overnight to survey the road ahead. Detailing the journey, they had found nothing but empty roads and a few disfigured settlements winding through a thick forest adjacent to the coast – with only a few patrols of blackcoats in the area, and no major cities until the mid-eastern plains, it was almost too good to be true. The terrain seemed promising, and all indications made that it'd be a smooth passage snaking along the shoreline. Revek had briefed the scouts as soon as they'd returned, expressing his sentiment with them over a hearty breakfast of pig meat slaughtered during the night. In a foray of satisfaction, the commander had given them healthy rations and ordered them to their tents where they could sleep out the day and drink merrily through the night, hoping to be on the road the following dawn with everything in place. With warm food in his stomach and the sound of work outside already, it was almost too good to be true.

And then it was.

He'd stepped outside to observe the skyline, and tracing it towards the western mountains, had found a thick knot of black clouds shuddering and rumbling there that not even the low mist could hide away. In a sudden fit of rage, storming out the tent to cuff the nearest man, it was explained to him that another storm-front had been sighted in the far north-west similar to the one before – black clouds sweeping off the hills, where it would reach the lowlands and catch against the wind pulling off the sea. There it would remain, an ironclad vessel of the sky raining down along the coast – and right across the road they were using to head north. The commander, apoplectic and seething, had confirmed the news from several other officers, and by the sixth he found it was not only the weather that appeared to be preparing a spell of thunder.

We shall suffer, yet again, from the rigid incompetence of simple men, Revek thought with a blustering sigh. *The rains will come as we march, the road will swell as it did before... and we will be bastard-fucking lost at every turn, straddled in the earth like children, wishing for the life of us that we could be anywhere other than this godforsaken fucking country.*

He spat into the mud.

Perhaps the gods do hate us after all.

"Shall I check on the barn progress, sir?" Darius inquired at his side.

"That would be a good idea," the commander expressed, drawing himself back to reality. "I need any supplies in there bagged up and in the carts before dusk, or they'll be struggling through the night under torches—"

"Sir!"

Footsteps approaching; Revek's head snapped sideways to find a soldier filing through the tents to the left.

"What is it?" he spat.

"We've found someone, sir."

As if my day couldn't have more foul weather. "Found who?"

"A child, sir... well, not a small child, but a young one. He has a knife."

The commander frowned, waving his hands. "A butter knife? A cleaver? Why are you bothering me with this..."

"He's... got it to a soldier's throat, sir."

Revek was on his feet in an instant.

Pathetic.

In a clearing of trees just beyond the loosely-defined boundary of the village fence, a small cluster of soldiers with their swords drawn stood in a taut line muttering soft words. Beyond, half-concealed behind a dead tree, a child of perhaps fourteen winters stood with a skinning knife quivering in one white fist, a soldier grappled across the chest on his knees in the other. The captive had been bound around the hands and feet, a cloth wedged into his mouth like a hog on banquet's day. His muffled pleas for peace were drowned out by the hissing of the savage child, who adjusted the blade whenever anyone took a step closer.

Revek approached from behind the soldiers, the messenger skittering like a fox at his back. There were some suggestions of caution from the amassed, but the commander pushed the line apart defiantly and stepped out ahead of them, only stalling his rage when the boy began to hiss again.

"Who the fuck let this happen then?"

The soldiers looked across to each other dumbfoundedly, before one managed to conjure a few helpless words. "We don't know, sir," they replied. "We were patrolling for any livestock we could requisition as food... and when we returned to camp we found one of our number was lost. So we went back out... and found this."

"And what does the little bastard hope to achieve here?"

"We don't know, sir. All we know is he won't stop... *hissing*."

Revek cocked his head. "Has he said *anything* of note?"

"Nothing, sir. We found him, attempted to negotiate, then summoned you."

Attempted to negotiate. The commander almost found it laughable. *What do you attempt to negotiate with a creature such as this?* "I see," he said simply, then turned to the boy. "Do you speak, creature?"

The boy was short and pale, as if cast of marble, his scrawny arms and features unassuming beyond the heavy white pupils of his eyes, and the volatile twitch he made every time someone spoke.

"Are you to let this man go?"

Revek took another step forward; suddenly the boy was reactivated, stamping his foot, hissing like a serpent, pressing the knife closer to the pleading man's neck.

"You will be hurt, *a lot*, if you don't."

The boy continued to hiss, unwavering, a thin ripple of blood sliding down the captive's neck. Watching it trickle away, the commander's patience drew thin. *First the weather, then the shadows... everything about this rots of idiocy.*

I won't stand for it.

He turned, waving his hand at the nearest soldier. "Give me your sword."

"What do you intend to—"

"*Give me* your *sword*, soldier, that is an *order*."

The soldier blinked once, once only, before handing his blade over obediently and skulking back to the line.

Revek rounded on the boy, the embers burning in his chest and igniting the flame in his eye. "I give you a single chance," he commanded, using the sword to dictate. "*He* comes to *us*, and *you* will *go*. If *he* stays with *you,* then *I* will come get him *myself*."

Gravity seemed to weigh in the boy's eyes, a realisation of what was to come. An inner conflict visibly assaulted him, and his face seemed to tilt slightly with wonder – but despite its reeling digressions, the knife did not release from the boy's hand, and the thin pulse of blood still meandered its way down the captive's neck.

Testing the water, Revek took a step forward — the boy snarled like a rabid dog again.

The commander ground his teeth.

Pathetic.

Suddenly Revek was moving, storming forward with the sword clasped firmly at his side. The squelch of deep mud underfoot, his stride unhindered by its force, burning through the thin veil of mist with fury wrought across every inch of his being.

The boy panicked, hand shaking violently, eyes boggling at the huge, armoured man pacing towards him. Closing the distance; the air growing taut around them. The boy hissing, spitting, defiance and insubordination — Revek scowling, raising his sword, bitter hatred biting at every bone in his body.

The boy screeched; the knife slipped across the soldier's throat. Blood gushed from the wound like a torrent. The body fell from the boy's arm, writhing blindly across the ground, the last ebbing of life drawing thin and cold—

Revek struck down like a brute, cleaving the small boy in the shoulder, driving through the chest with such impervious force that the small frame crumpled at the knee, a squealing blood-streaked corpse spilling to the ground at the end of his blade—

Withdrawing the sword, Revek swung again. Arching over, driving down — biting through the child's skull, a great trench bursting his nose, destroying every semblance of humanity left in his pale, twisted face. The squeals stopped abruptly.

Revek withdrew his blade, kicked the body down and spat.

Rounding back on his own men, he passed a long, vindicative glare amongst them, finding only averted eyes and sullen jaws. He strode forward, thrusting the sword back into the soldier's hand as he pushed through the throng, pressing on back towards the village, muttering the word slowly to himself.

"*Pathetic.*"

†

Chapter 47

Val Darbesh

When Markus awoke again, body aching from the motions of the wagon, he found shadows dancing lazily across the barred upper windows, and the sounds of chaos and crackling fire booming all around as if marching to the battlefields of war. He swung himself upright, head thumping, tracing every streak of light that crossed the wood-panelled walls. The other occupants in their heavy-laden chains remained upright and resolute, but they too seemed to express a growing dread at the sounds rattling at the doors – a sign that this was as foreign to them as it was to him. Only the handler and the blind man opposite appeared unphased; the blind man even continued to hum a short rhythm under his breath, at ease with a world that he could not only never understand, but also never see.

Markus shook his head. *Nothing but madness to spare.*

Their progress remained steady for some time, the wheels cranking furiously over sand-rock roads, every twinge of metal screaming as if a bone were about to crunch from its socket. The industrious machinations of the world around continued to bellow out into the desert sky – Markus found if his mind lingered on any particular place for too long, everything began to spin on its axis, and a sudden disorientation kicked in that made worse an already thundering headache. From the silent desert to the ugly vulgar refuge of the city, he found it to be an assault on the senses, especially trapped in the echo chamber of the wagon with only sweat and a lost limb to keep him company.

He thought it would go on forever – wondering how big the city was from within – until the grind of wheels stalled for a moment, and from somewhere ahead came the huge and formidable crunch of gears as a grand gatehouse slid slowly open. Rising like columns, an impervious shadow overcame the wagon's interior as they crossed the threshold. With the clatter of metal armour and the occasional hail to guards, it was clear that wherever they had been before then, in the bustle and rancour of the city proper, was nothing like the place they had entered now.

With the gateway cranking closed at their backs as the cart banked slowly left, Markus wondered with every inch of his being what manner of abomination awaited him when the call finally came for them to depart.

His answer appeared moments later, when the driver rapped his knuckles against the wood, and the winding tug of the wheels drew still. The handler, by no indication awake, rose suddenly from her stoop and clicked her eyes open like a snake, fixed at the door opposite her.

"I want all present to understand," she pronounced, "that when we leave this wagon, you will do as I command and nothing more. You will not look at anything, speak to anyone, or acknowledge where you are. You will look to the floor, and you will follow the next man... and you will do *nothing* more. Is that agreed?"

A few disparaged nods, eyes to-ground.

Markus caught her gaze and nodded once. *Don't poke the bear, for the bear has claws,* he mused to himself.

And this one has claws the length of my fuckin' arm, by the looks of her.

The door slid open to his right; Markus turned to see an open stretch of course dirt coated by shadow, some gloomy entranceway manned by blackcoat guards a short walk apart from their wagon. Rattling chains about his one wrist told him to stand, and he was again led down the causeway by the handler, shoulder-to-shoulder with a muttering blind man, into a world he did not know and wanted no part of.

Eyes to the floor, the sudden bursts of noise and intrigue made his mind wander, the instructions moments before drifting aside, the longing to make sense of the desert city around him overwhelming. Glancing up to the side, he followed a wide stretch of sand leading off to snaking markets in the distance selling their wares. Beyond that, stood the walls they had entered through: huge plates of steel, with great lengths of metal shrapnel mangled like barbed wire along the top, hanging wires stretching up toward the super-imposed structure looming above him, hardly visible for its sheer size. Eyes leering, stretching higher, guided by the crown-like spears of the city's outermost walls, up to the gilded cloth dicing the sun from the sky, and the tiny figures that worked up there suspended from ropes. As little more than tiny black dots so far above, Markus wondered of their purpose, of how the world around him revolved, trying to place voices to faces, trying to find order in the voluminous commotion all around, eyes straining to know, to see beyond—

A swipe across his left hand. Markus dropped his gaze instantly, looking sidelong to see the blind man's hand slowly retreat back to his side, the chains obediently silent around his wrist.

"This is no place for eyes, my boy," the sightless figure spoke. "Don't use them... unless you wish never to see again."

Markus nodded once, locked to the slow repetitions of his feet, trying to swallow through a bubble in his throat.

Duly noted.

They were led through the entranceway into the dark, the sandstone and metal panels sprawled across the walls reverberating every noise within: the crackle and spit of open fires; the clang of a blacksmith's hammer forging weapons and tools of iron and steel; the chime of sparring opponents, either in duel or in practice; the rattle of prison cells, with sombre words from the occupants pleading for their release – the scoffing and mockery of guards threatening to chop off fingers if they didn't step back and be quiet. Eyes to the ground, where tiles slowly formed out of the compact sand, Markus strode on with little more than echolocation and a stiff tug from the handler's chain to guide him forward. From the sounds all around, and the emptiness of the wide corridor they crossed through, he could've been anywhere from a palace to a prison – and with the growing intensity of voices and grinding metal ahead, the image of a public execution never strayed far from mind.

From madness, he mused, eyes languishing at his feet, *cometh savagery.*

They shifted left, moving onto a narrow walkway where the floor was diced with panels of light like archer slits. He lifted his right – *no* – lifted his left arm to cover his ear suddenly, and determined that the swelling levels of noise came from somewhere off to the right – out towards wherever the lights were.

"To the lights, my boy," the blind man whispered, startling him. "To the arena of the gods... to the place dead men go, just to live one more time..."

Markus swung his gaze to the right, eyes swarming with the light and colour splashing from the small windows along the wall. Adjusting, picking apart the robes and tribal dresses across rows and rows of seats down below, stretching several thousand feet across from him, bathed in glorious sunlight. It was an arena of sandstone, curling gently to the centre, a bombast of colour and life and sound at every inch, spilling down to the flags and banners that lined the central pit. Within, he spied tiny figures sparring – no, fighting – no, *brawling* in their dozens, the tiny glints of metal spinning and flashing, the spray of blood arching skyward, maimed bodies collapsing to join a handful of others already staining the white-pink sand underfoot. A furore went up, as he spied one man's head spinning off towards the crowd, hands rising to seize it from the air like the greatest prize in all the world—

The thud of a sword pommel connected with his stomach. Markus lurched, a sudden surge of vomit pulling back – catching sight of the handler glaring back at him like a child, the ripple of laughter from the blind man at his shoulder.

"I ne'er said t'look, my boy," he rumbled.

Markus ground his teeth.

Duly fucking noted.

They banked left again, descending a wide staircase where the stone had been worn through with frequent use. It was almost polished to brass underfoot – Markus found his balance sway several times before finding purchase at the bottom again, their convoy peeling off into a wider chamber elucidated by torchlight.

With a sudden echoey note, he was alerted to the call of numbers off to his right – a sharp diversion from the noises he'd heard thus far. With the throbbing in his stomach, he had little interest in looking up to see what was going on. He would just lead on as the rest, an obedient old dog with no fight left, and take his condemnation at its end with open arms.

That was until he heard the next words spoken.

"And here we have a fine female specimen... a trained fighter come all the way from Provenci!"

Heart stuttered.

Sav?

His head shot up, taking in the small crowd of brightly-coloured men and women and the small pods of money clenched in their fists. Jumping from head to head, up towards the back wall where a stage had been erected, his gaze landing on an auctioneer prostrating broadly, prancing about with all the grace of a shot pig. Hand swinging, he gestured at the thinly-clad assortment of figures behind him, each one coated in oil to accentuate shapes and muscle and form, eyes lowered to mask their bitter misery.

Markus scanned them, one over the other, in a desperate search for a face he had not long ago called friend. The person he'd dragged himself across broken hills and down through sheer mountain passes for, and through all manner of hell thereon. The journey he'd undertaken, and the pledge he'd made, and the scars he bore for it –

how I am now without an arm for my choices.

His eyes darted about, searching lost souls, until finding one stood upright, head surveying the scene before her—

With ginger hair, and polite brown eyes; two rounded cheeks blushing at the money and interest spinning the chamber floor before her. Taking it all in with a wandering gaze, the adoring faces longing for her — looking past, her eyes crossing to a thin line of six prisoners passing by with heads held low. Heads low, that was, all except one, who stared at her with such great intensity that she almost forgot where she was. Holding his gaze, trying to read what lay behind. As if she should know him from somewhere, or if he knew her…

Blinking, her attention shifted to the prisoners' handler at the head of the line, who turned to observe the auction and its goings-on, and then rounded squarely on the strange man who stared off toward the stage as if haunted. Watching the handler's face twist to a cold glare, the fingers tightening in one hand. Managing a final look at the lost prisoner before her gaze dropped away, spying the handler's fist rounding on him—

Markus took it firmly across the cheek, near-dislodging his neck with the force, a flash of spittle scattering off to the side.

Another punch caught his side, mashing his liver, a wheeze cracking from his lips. His legs failed, jarring awkwardly at the knee — falling, half-sprawled on his side.

The handler cuffed him across the jaw, drawing him up limply to eye-level. "What did I *say* to you about keeping your *eyes* to the *floor*, stumpy? I think I made myself pretty clear on that *mark*."

"*Yes, ma'am…*"

"Don't fuck with me, or I'll make that lost arm look like a *fucking papercut*. Am I understood?"

"*Yes ma'am—*"

She threw him to the ground, very roughly. "And if any of you lot" — pointing to the other prisoners — "feels inclined to disrespect me in that way… I will spare *nothing* of you when the time comes. Understood?"

Mumbled yeses; quiet nods and nothing more.

"Good." She turned back to Markus, still slumped and wheezing on the floor. "Now get to your feet, stumpy... you can cry in your cell."

As the chain began to drag at his arm, he slowly rose to his feet, helped up by the blind man and held aloft like loose scaffolding. Every wave of breath rippled as it pulled into his lungs, the exhale proving equally painful, addled by a wave of sickness – the sensation of retching, but with an empty stomach and thus none of the contents to manifest it. Only the emotion; the detachment and loss that had been numbly swimming under the surface. The burn of tears across his cheeks, red-raw round his eyes. Thinking of her, suddenly. Thinking of the lost soul he had come through hell with. The face he had not long ago called friend, lost to the world beyond.

Where are you, Sav?

†

Chapter 48

Honour Among Thieves

She watched them as they turned the corner of the stairway and filed slowly into the cold room, glancing awkwardly around like birds surveying a fresh roost: checking corners for any unwelcome guests; studying the length of the wide table in front and the four chairs at each edge; a final piercing stare, landing on the woman sat at the far end, hands clasped before her as if attending church. There were no bodyguards at her side – no sign of a weapon at her hip. Just her watchful gaze, resolute and uncompromising, alone in that quiet space – an indication, they believed, that this was her world, and that she demanded the respect of all those who entered it unequivocally.

Jinx smiled.

Of that, there's no doubt.

Three figures entered the upstairs room of the inn, sided by two bodyguards apiece, armour strapped across chest and shoulders concealed by lengths of cloth garment. They positioned themselves cautiously at each seat, guards lingering along the back walls, a weariness to each flick of the eye as they studied one another, always awaiting the first sign of trouble. And it was no fretful consideration to anticipate danger would come: there were very few places any of the four present went, where danger did not make itself known.

And to find them all in the same spot at once, well... *trouble becomes almost inevitable.*

And perhaps that's half the fun.

"There best be a damn good reason that you've brought us all here today," the man to her left announced suddenly. "With the imposition of martial law... coming 'ere is no easy business I assure you..."

He was a slight figure, all bone and no barrel, with frightfully narrow pupils and a thick swell of a beard from his ears to his nose. Observing him then in his chair, he seemed boisterous and energetic, twitches seizing across his body so he was always stirring, never still. Sheathed in a heavy spin of brown silk, cuffed at the edges with huge shoulder-guards and greaves as thick around his wrist as an oak, one would've coined him as a merchant more so than a master thief: driving caravans across foreign nations through sun and slaughter, never so much as laying a finger on a locked door. But Jinx knew, with every bone in her, that it was a ruse as best she'd seen one. That when the time came, and the hunt was on, the spasms were suddenly silenced and the bubbling seizures lapsed. A frightening transformation was made, almost from man to beast – that when the time came, the slight man became a predator of the night unlike any other.

Not the trembling wretch he seems to be now.

"Quit the whining, Shivers," a woman rustled to her right, leaning out across the table with a sly grin. "You know there's always good spoils when Jinx has a score to settle..."

She was nearly double Jinx's age, grey-brown streaks of woven hair coiling to a topknot like a beehive. There was a wicked enamour to her face, the light and bright eyes contrasting her dark features whimsically, from the bar of metal that pierced the base of her chin, down to the wires of rings spinning across each finger. She was meticulous, her palm never quite gracing the top of the table for fear of the noise her rings could make – only ever touching at things with fingertips, like the fluttering appendages of a puppet. Every motion was made with a soothing grace, even as she rolled back in her chair and eased her shoulders back at the sight of Shivers staring her down

— at ease with a world that was entirely in her grasp, as resolved as she was deadly in the field of play.

Jinx smiled her way. *I like her most.*

"Or, Shadow, this may be just another leap in the dark," boomed the voice at the far end, vibrations channelling across the table like a spider's web. "With no concern for any but her own..."

Jinx, along with the other two, found the jovial courtesy of the room dampen. Eyes crossed to the back of the room nearest the stairway, and found their gaze land on a broad, brusque-looking mammal who was more hair than face, staring them down with every ounce of displeasure.

"And who are you to judge that, Bearskin?" Jinx grumbled.

Bearskin rolled his shoulders, easing himself forward to lean against the table, a hand clasped across the ragged stump of his other forearm. "Because I've seen your treachery before... I know how this ends. Small wonder why I even *entertain* it anymore."

She had never liked Bearskin. He wore disapproval like a crown, and had a self-assuredness that most things that came out of people's mouths were not his business or in his benefit. He claimed that he had seen it all before, and had been victim to all manner of criminal blunder — one of them, so he touted, had cost him his hand. And, since that non-descript time of the past, every joint venture that had been thrown his way was dead in the water at his feet. He would hear nothing more of the sort. In that respect, it was almost idiocy to even bring him to the table that day to discuss what Jinx had in mind.

But I know the kind of prize he wants, she told herself nonetheless, *so it's never quite idiocy at all.* As much as she resented him, she needed his guile and cunning; most importantly, the syndicate he operated and those he employed. Dozens of thieves, holed up in dens across the city, waiting to do his bidding for a high reward. He was a singular piece of a wider mosaic— *and all I need now is to convince him of that.*

But even that's a leap in the dark where Bearskin's concerned.

"Let her speak, at least," Shadow countered. "If it falls in our joint interest, then we'd be fools to cast it off."

"Agreed," Shivers said calmly, "with some reluctance."

Jinx held her gaze to Bearskin, who seemed to sit straighter in his chair and produced an enormous sigh. "Have at it, then," he mumbled, waving his hand dismissively. "But keep it concise."

I'll tell it how it is, you bastard.

"Very well... to put it *concisely,*" Jinx exclaimed, "my brother has been seized and arrested by the military, on false allegations, trying to expose the murder of a fellow high-ranking official in Tarraz — a murder at the hands of people close to their inner circle. To keep him silent, he's currently locked up in the palace keep without any intention of a trial, and that is where he is destined to remain 'til the end of his days."

The room seemed to quieten; Shivers and Shadow lowered their eyes to the table. Bearskin nodded his head slowly. None of them were entirely amicable with Broska — probably cared little that he was in chains — but the story Jinx had told about the murder seemed to hold a greater weight with them, more so than any animosity they carried for the general.

"So... old porky's rubbed someone up the wrong way, hm?" the big man at the far end acknowledged, running a huge hand through his beard. "Was gonna happen sooner or later."

"You can confirm this other official is dead, an' he's telling the truth?" Shadow inquired.

Jinx nodded. "If you mean have I seen the written orders forged in Alvarez's name to kill the general in question, then yes, I have."

"How have you?" Shivers pressed.

"Because I broke in to the palace to try and steal them——"

"Bullshit you broke in," Bearskin interjected. "It's a fortress — no one *breaks in* to a place like that."

"Such was my thinking as well," Jinx countered, "until I scaled the wall, slipped through an open window, and picked my way into the bed-chamber of one General Ferreus to find the letter open on his desk."

Bearskin pulled back onto his seat, a glint of surprise in his eye. "So, where is this letter now?"

"Still in Ferreus's possession." She paused. "I was attacked before I had a chance to steal it away… they knew someone would come for it."

"So you went to steal it with all manner of heroics, and fell into their trap like a lame duck?" The big man laughed. "And now they know you are taking an active interest in trying to keep ol' Arrenso safe? Heightened security, more active patrols, increased risk." He shook his head. "With all due respect, of which I have none… it seems like I'm wasting my time being here."

Jinx ground her teeth. "I would say you are… but there *is* something I need from you – *all* of you – in this matter."

"And what might that be?"

Here it is. She clasped her hands. "Because I need you to help me break him out of the palace keep, in two days' time, because—"

"How *stupid* do you think we are?" Bearskin bellowed, matching the equal parts disgust exhibited by Shadow and Shivers. "Why would we risk our lives and our business, for your poor-fool brother? I don't care who's right and wrong, or who's died for what cause. People die all the time, and the truth is rarely clear. What makes you think we want any part in this business, knowing the odds?" He speared a finger her way. "This is a *waste* of our *time*."

Bearskin lifted from his seat, indicating for his henchmen to lead down the stairway. Jinx watched him shift away, the wavering distrust in the other two at her flanks flaring to life. Shadow sighed, grappling her chair to rise. The big man at the far end no doubt smiling, watching it all fall apart before her—

"Wait!" Jinx cried.

"Why should we?" came the holler from the door.

Here it is. "Because he knows your *name*!"

Bearskin turned back to the table with a cold glare strong enough to shatter steel. "What the fuck did you just *say?*"

"He knows your name," Jinx repeated, quieter this time. "And yours" – indicating Shivers – "and yours" – Shadow likewise – "as much as he knows my own."

Anger flared as the huge man rounded on them and pressed his arms down against the table. "What is this? What *the fuck have you done!*"

"I made a deal."

"With *Arrenso?*"

"We reached a common understanding." Jinx paused, sizing him up. "In exchange for diverting any investigations the army made into our business – doing so against his own people, I might *add* – I gave him your names and contacts to monitor... names and contacts kept in his personal possession and never revealed to anyone else. That way, we could go about our business with more freedom than we would be otherwise allowed... and he could maintain some *control* of the situation."

"Control of what, us?" Bearskin spat. "Our people?"

"If anyone overstepped *lines*, then he would have the information at his fingertips to make them *pay* for it. We are not unaccountable in this – we never have been. But every operation that happens in this city, big or small, relies *wholly* on his intervention." She speared a finger at him. "So *yes,* it *is* in your interest to help him out."

A fire raged across his reddened skull. "You told him our *names,* our *contacts,* our *operations*... our *entire* fucking *enterprise*... to save your own skin so he wouldn't arrest you for what you do?" He scoffed, fist clenching. "You really are a sly little *bitch*..."

"I did what I had to, to secure our business—"

"You did nothing of the fucking sort!" He slammed his fist against the table. "You sold us out to the people who want us dead, and you did it to save your ass, nothing more. And now that bastard, in all his whimsical skill, has landed himself in prison where he's being questioned by the enemy, and..." With a sudden presentment, the anger ducked below the surface, his face sinking solemnly like an anchor in deep water. "You son of a bitch..."

Here it is. "Now that you get it, allow me to say it *again*... I need

you to help me break him out of the palace keep, in two days' time...
because if we don't, he will be left with no choice but to exchange
your information as *leverage* to get him out of prison—"

"If you fucking *dare* have him hand us over, then we'll just tell them
every little hovel and den you operate under so you sink with *us*—"

"And I had a feeling you'd say that." Jinx smiled slyly. "So I had the
liberty of moving all of my business out of the city before martial law
was enforced. I have no permanent location that you can give them
– all you have is my name." She clicked her tongue. "And after
Arrenso rats you three out, well... I don't think they'll be
particularly bothered with a small timer like myself in the city. For
all they know, I'm no longer in the capital at all, along with the rest
of my stuff..."

Bearskin and his guards were moving towards her before she had
even finished. The huge man grappled a broad-rimmed axe from his
belt, hoisting it, ready to throw—

Shadow stood suddenly, Shivers following shortly after with that
same reluctance as before, their guards forming up with swords
raised at their side. A stand-off manifested – Jinx remained fixed to
her chair, unwavering, her eyes never swaying from the sharp, fiery
gaze of the huge man lumbering towards her, and the death-note writ
across the axe blade he wielded, intent upon her neck.

"Get out of my *way*," Bearskin growled to greying woman, but
never quite forcing his way past.

"No," Shadow said defiantly.

"Don't you *see* that she's sold us out? Don't you *see* that she's *fucked
us* in this!"

"Whatever it may be... and I don't entirely agree with the
methods used to reach this *point*" – she shot a look at Jinx for good
measure – "it is clear that it is in our best interest to keep her *alive*,
rather than gut her here and now."

"And by what fucking *logic* have you come by that?"

"'Cause if we kill 'er, where's our leverage?" Shivers said simply.
"If we kill 'er, we can't negotiate a way out o' this mess afterwards.

Then we're screwed over."

"We can organise among ourselves, sort this out without her. We don't need traitors like her among us..."

"No, we can't." Shadow took a step forward. "If we don't kill her, and do nothing, we'll be ratted out and arrested. If we kill her, and do nothing, we'll be ratted out and arrested. If we reorganise and move our shit elsewhere... it's the same. They'll have our names and our contacts, and they'll find us eventually, wherever we are."

"So we kill Arrenso and her, problem solved."

"I don't think she's that stupid." Shadow turned to Jinx. "Would I be correct in saying that?"

Here it is. "If I don't come out of this meeting alive," she said slowly, "then I have told my informants to contact the army and have Broska hand over the information before you can reach him."

The greying woman twisted back to Bearskin, nodding. "We fell into a trap, like lame ducks... do you think we're wasting our time now?"

Bearskin stood for a long, testing moment, heat coursing through his veins, flaring across his skin. It was a long moment, the henchmen on both sides eyeballing one another awkwardly, swords wavering in gloved hands. But, in all its eventuality, it was a moment come to pass: Bearskin slid the axe back into its holster and strode inelegantly back to his seat, slumping into place with a loud *thud* of metal.

He did not meet Jinx's gaze from that point on.

"Anyway," Shadow muttered, easing back into her seat and meeting the young thief's eye, "I guess you have a plan for this business? I can only hold your corner for so long, you understand."

"Of course," Jinx replied with a smile, looking between the grey woman and old Shivers, with only a passing recognition of Bearskin at the back. "As you said before, there's always good spoils when I have a score to settle..."

*

"Go through it from the start."

Jinx traced a finger along the map in front of her, skimming a thick black line indicating the outer walls of the palace keep. "In two days there is the funeral procession for the king, where he'll be taken through the city in a carriage for people to throw flowers over and say their final words. The cart will travel up from the southern districts, back along the Merchant Quarter, and swing through the central marketplace up to the keep's main gate. When it reaches the marketplace, the palace guards will be redirected to the west-facing wall and form a barricade around the podium, where the Supreme Governor is expected to speak along with a few of his cronies. As soon as they begin to mobilise for the speech, we have an opening." She swung her finger around to the south-facing part of the palace wall. "Traversing the wall and crossing the palace keep in broad daylight is suicide, as watchtowers will still be patrolled, so we're better off using the barred sewage tunnel on the southern edge of the palace. Once inside, we use the sewer system beneath the courtyard to enter the lower chambers. From there, it's a two-storey descent until we reach the prison block."

"Any chance of encounterin' guards?" Shivers inquired.

"With the procession passing through, there'll only be a skeleton crew down there, and they'll likely be on patrol so won't have a fixed location. Our best bet is to move as fast as we can down to the prison block and proceed with caution from there."

"The prison guards won't take part in the procession... they won't be on duty outside."

"This is our issue." Jinx tapped another map with the layout of the prison block – all sixteen rows – and drew a line across the red dots at the entranceway. "There are always four guards at the door, two on the exterior and two just inside, with more navigating the corridors within... providing they're on their original rotation."

"And the warden?" Shivers asked.

She winced at the word. "The warden is currently an unknown. As I said, the maps and guard rotations are several months old at

393

best... when the new military government came to power, they ousted the old warden in place of a new one. We can assume with some accuracy that the guard rotations will be the same... but the warden I cannot guarantee."

"And any idea where Arrenso might be?"

"Fourteenth row – that's where they keep political prisoners. We can safely assume he's under lock and key somewhere along there."

"That's a lot of guards to get past..."

"I understand it'll be no easy task," Jinx admitted, "but I called you three because I know you're the best." She looked to the two at her side, and tried to discern from Bearskin's expression whether he was at all interested. "And if the worst comes to it... I also have every belief we can fight our way out if necessary. With how few guards will be within the palace, the commotion would most likely go unnoticed for a while. Are we in agreement?"

Bearskin lifted his head suddenly. "So we go in, skip down the stairs, massacre the prison staff, free old porky and make our way out, all in the time Alvarez takes to finish his pretty speech about the man he hated and wanted dead all along?"

Jinx nodded. "To put it concisely, yes."

"And this comes on the understanding that, if we manage this, and get porky out of there... he'll destroy any documents about our contacts, and let us relocate in peace?"

"Through my kinship bond as his sister and family... you have my word."

The huge man stood slowly, rolling his shoulders, and slid his hand into a deep pocket. He grunted sharply. "If that's the case... then I shall at least endeavour to support this business." A pause. "But I'd like to add my *own* condition, if I am to provide my full support..."

"Name it."

Bearskin locked eyes with her. "That if this goes wrong, and we escape with our lives *without* saving your foul brother... that I will have your *head* for what you've done to us."

Without waiting for an answer, Bearskin turned like a column of stone and descended the stairway behind, the heavy creaks of his footfalls echoing brutishly, carrying off long after he had gone.

In the silence that followed, Shadow turned to her. "Do we trust him?"

"Wouldn't trust him as far as I can spit," Shivers added.

"Neither do I," Jinx said, "but we don't entirely have a choice. We need his people, and we need his skill if we get into trouble."

"And do you think we have a chance?"

Jinx thought for a long moment, rolling a ring across her thumb – by chance, a version of a ring Broska also wore, that they had crafted on a forge together when they were children. He had worked the blowpipes to keep the fire roaring; she wielded the hammer and sceptre, twisting the metal into an ugly coil and painting it silver when it'd cooled. Looking now, she saw the paint had long rubbed away, and that same ugly metal coil gleamed at her boldly. It had long lost its shine – to the common eye, long forgone its use. But the purpose still remained, as silver and glistening as ever: the bond it brought between them, no matter how far apart they had come. The memory of those childhood days; of the joy they still cherished in each other. And how she knew, beyond everything, that she would do anything to have him back again. Asking the question: *do you think we have a chance?*

"Yes," she said, smiling at the ring. "I think we do."

Chapter 49

Shackles

A white world; a pale void, growing slowly brighter. Filling at the edges, swelling at the seams. She had been here before, she knew — she had been here many times in the quiet moments, in the places lost and found, and each time she wanted to know more.

And every time, she was left wanting.

As it came to her, growing as it always does, the void began to shift. Where once there was white, then came porcelain — from porcelain came smoke, came steel and mottled graphite. Twisting, forming columns at her feet, ill-defined streaks against an unseen horizon. A criss-cross of shadow, skimming what she called the ground ahead of her. Rising all around, came spikes like knives, and with some half-expectant thought or other, she thought she saw them move. Almost as if it were a living, breathing world.

Almost as if it were real . . .

Cavara's right eye gently opened, alerted to the sound of a shutter lifting at the base of her door. She watched a metal tray slide through the narrow gap from the corridor beyond, a tiny cup of some liquid spilling over as it slipped through. The crash of the shutter closing forced her other eye open, shocked alertness capitulating within, which she met with a groan and sat slowly upright.

Into a world where she did not want to be.

She rose slowly, stiffly, a great aching chasm along her spine, and took the single step to the other side of her cell, squatting down to retrieve the small platter of food she had been left. Much of it was gruel – the kind of thing one fed the pigs in a bad harvest: a grey-green substance ladled into small portions, and a tiny slice of stale bread to compliment. What water there had been – most likely to ease down the gruel and any aftertaste that came after – had mixed with the substance to form a watery mass, almost like soup. There were no utensils, nothing that could be repurposed as a weapon or tool – there was only the tray of condensed sick, and her stomach that bubbled suddenly without any appetite.

"What even is this..." she muttered to herself, setting the tray down again and rolling against the stone base of the bed. Cheek against cold-cut rock, the urge to weep rose inside – bitten down immediately, buried to some deep-dark in her chest. She had no energy left in her for tears, especially not tears shed for herself – those had long ceased to hold any purpose, in her eyes.

That, and everything else.

She sighed. *Why am I even here?* There was a world dying somewhere; blood was spilt, and she knew nothing of it. Villages and cities in flames; the world torn apart by cannon fire. Skies burning bright, the sun falling from the sky – she knew nothing of it. She sat in squalor in a cell she could barely stand upright in, being fed gruel through a shutter on the floor, with no sunlight and no company and fuck-all wherewithal to know what was even going on outside her own door. Trying to fight the urge to cry, purely because she was lost and alone – how pathetic she found it, more than anything. That death reared its ugly head, and war blanched the horizon afar, and she sat there weeping in self-pity, wondering why the gods had abandoned her so.

And what would they make of me? Those gods high above? She lifted her hand limply, studying each blueish fingertip; watching it fall to the ground again. She sighed. *What would they make of the foolish general, locked away in her cell, with nothing but pity and regret to guide her... and that burning realisation that this might well be all there is left for me.*

Lifting her hand again, she lay it against her chest, anguishing at

397

the knots of flesh and skin that marked her there. The single, fateful act that had started it all off – the single, merciless ploy of a coward who had longed for her life to be snuffed away. From there, the world seemed to recede and abandon her; nothing she knew made sense anymore.

Cavara inhaled deeply and found the knotted wound grow tighter. *Why am I even here?*

†

"Why are you even here—"

General Ferreus landed another punch across his sternum, the verbatim of cracked ribs already seething with pain. The breach of bone made a cracking sound none too dissimilar to fire-bitten logs, the small rasps of his breath flying out his lungs as spittle. Flecks of blood followed, like tiny fish darting down the rapids of a river, speckling the officer's boot below.

Broska's head sagged, breath little more than a dishevelled wheeze.

"I'm here, because I can be, and you don't have a choice," Ferreus mused, adjusting the stiff padded glove on his right hand. "I'm here… because the sooner you die, the easier everything will be. For me, and everyone else."

Broska coughed stiffly. "That's where… you're wrong. This doesn't die if I die. The world will know… the truth of it…"

"If you're talking about your naïve little sister, I shouldn't worry… we have plans for her." Ferreus took a step closer, dragging Broska's head to meet his gaze. "As for you, well… your days are numbered, you foul pig. You will die, and there will be no funeral in your honour. Because you will die a dishonourable death" – Ferreus dropped his head – "and you will be remembered a dishonourable man."

General Ferreus turned on his heel and vacated the cell, Broska's hands suspended in shackles that longed to lunge for that grey flourish of hair as it disappeared and the door swung closed.

You are wrong, were the words he longed to scream. *You will always be wrong.* He knew the letter had escaped the city, and that the messenger had got out in time. Travelling the vast plains of Provenci in an unassuming satchel – the truth beyond the lies, signed with his hand. His final plea, the plea of an innocent man condemned to rot for the truth he held, pressing onwards to Rendevir.

Onwards to Eli, he muttered to the void, *my only beacon left in this world.*

He inhaled, deeper this time, and felt the strain of his organs press against ribs that were now little more than shrapnel. A stabbing sensation twitched in his stomach – a sign that something else had been damaged in the furore of abuse he'd taken. He wondered just how deep the wounds truly went – he wondered if this was the slow-burn realisation of fate, foreshadowing the time he would die.

The stabbing pain rekindled memories of the shoreline, in a not so distant past. The face of his only true friend, a woman of honour and good will, led pale in the sand as the life leeched from her body at the brunt of a most ruinous ploy. A death brought at the hand of the same self-serving monster who now shortened his own life, one punch at a time. And beyond all that, he knew, lay the orchestrating hands of the true culprit parading in the Tarraz wilds far away. A man who would never see their suffering, despite the orders he gave; a man who, in equal respect, would make sure no one else ever saw it too.

I've failed you. The thought came with deeper wounds than any physical one could bear. *I could not right those wrongs.* He had been deceived, guided astray; trapped away in that cell as the life sapped from his wounds with slow irreverence, and nothing to show for it but pain. To think of her, that forgotten stare on that distant shore as the end slowly came, feeling as though he could never meet her eye. That every ounce of his being, every soft touch of his soul told him the same: *you never did enough to save her, in the end.*

And that is my burden of guilt. He looked to the ceiling; a bubble popped in his throat. *That the truth may live on... but never again by my hand.*

A bloom of emotion, expanding deep within his heart.

A single tear rolled down his cheek.

I have failed you...

†

... old friend.

She wiped the tear as it touched the edge of her lip, watching as the droplet rolled down her finger, falling gracefully to the cold stone below. *You'll never know my fate was a lie... you'll only ever blame yourself, when the fault is always mine.*

A crank of hinges; the cell door swung open, spinning the tray against the wall with the gruel still untouched. The guards stepped in cautiously, frowning at the untouched food, then back towards Cavara.

"The Alderbane... he want to see you now," they muttered on slippery tongues.

She sighed at length – *so this is how it is now* – but had nothing to show for it but disdain.

With the rebellion having long abandoned her, Cavara nodded only once, and lifted her hands for the shackles to come, without even bringing herself to ask why.

†

Chapter 50

Champion's Blood

He had not slept since arriving in Val Darbesh, the unconscious world almost a forgotten memory as he lay trapped in the shadows of the holding cells below. It was a room that one could cross in a stride; at his bedside, only a single slab of sandstone jutting from the wall to imitate a bedside table. There was no sun, no solace – only an intense brownish gloom, eating at every corner and indentation. Torchlight flickered through the bars of his door from some unseen place, elucidating the corridor with an orange hue like the troubled glow of an open fire. There was nothing more, nothing less, to the sad emptiness he found himself in – Markus simply sat, eyes fixed to the rough-cut stone ahead, his skull pounding like a mallet and aches quivering from his neck to his knees. A quiet, disingenuous accept-ance, that this was all his life had come to be. In the sleepless, merciless gloom of the holding cell.

In the buried sands of Val Darbesh.

What will they do with me? came a flicker from his mind. He'd seen the arena through the openings, the huge crowds of Tarrazi souls amassed and cheering at the bloodshed below. People being auctioned; people being sold to die at the hands of new masters.

I don't wanna be bartered, another flicker acknowledged. With every bone in his body, he knew the destitution of slavery was murder most foul. To destroy one's soul so recklessly; to make animals of men and send them to the pits.

Is that all I am now? he cried to the gloom. *Is that the fate I now uphold?* He recalled proclaiming that he'd sooner die than go to slavery in what seemed like another life. Yet faced with its reality then, down in the cell below, he found things were far different.

My life is about the only thing I have left to me, came the sombre truth, *and even that is never certain... not anymore.*

In the dead silence, the sound of approaching footsteps appeared deafening. Markus was on his feet without a second thought, flinching at the crank of the lock on his cell door as the handler swung into the room, catching sight of him and spearing a finger his way.

"You, stumpy... c'mere," she muttered.

Markus approached slowly, glancing through the doorway to see if any surprises awaited. "Yes... handler?"

"It's your time... get ready."

"My time for what?"

She frowned at him viciously. "Have you been briefed?"

"I... no, handler."

Her face creased into something between anger and despair. "I *asked* them to... actually, never mind – I'll do it myself." She closed the door behind her with a wave to the guardsman who stood on the other side, and ordered Markus over to his bench to sit again.

"What's going on?" he mumbled, leaking confusion like a tap.

"You don't ask the questions," she snapped. "I tell you what's *going on,* and what you will do for me, and you will *do it.* Am I understood?"

"But I—"

"Am I *understood?*"

Markus rolled his tongue. "Yes, handler."

"Good." She leaned up against the wall, toying with a thin strand of hair at her cheek. "As I'm sure you're aware by now, you have been placed under my ownership, in a pretty little Tarrazi city called Val Darbesh. It's a place of nomads and wretches, and is generally not the place a person would long to visit – that was, if they didn't have a way of making *money.*" She flicked the hair aside. "Now, as I'm sure you're also aware, Val Darbesh has a culture of arena fighting – the city itself was originally built around an ancient colosseum... although not that I care much about that kinda shit, and not likely you'll survive long enough to care either." She took a step forward, staring through him. "All that you need to know – all that you *will* know about this – is that you are my prisoner, you are my *fighter,* and if you don't go out there at midday and start winning me the bets of each battle you fight, I will beat you to a *bloody fucking pulp* until you do..."

"So I'm made to fight, as your slave... while you earn money?"

"Is that a *problem,* stumpy?"

"No... just gettin' an old man to do your dirty work for you?"

"You'll make me a fine profit, you bastard – so help you if you don't."

"You've banked a lot on a one-armed fool."

"You're no fool and you know it," she spat. "And either way, if you die out there after a few fights, I'll at least find the entertainment in watching a Provencian be gut like a fish."

Markus ground his teeth. "And what if I refuse?"

"Why would you bother with that?"

"It isn't exactly the noblest or most *reasonable* thing to do here."

"Do you think I care about *'noble and reasonable'* in my line of work? I don't *care* for your moral qualms in this – I only care that I get paid at the end of it." Her eye twitched. "If you wanted to uphold this self-righteousness, you shouldn't have got yourself *caught* – we wouldn't be having this conversation... and you'd still have that sorry excuse for a limb to pleasure yourself in the quiet times, ay?"

"Watch your *tongue*—"

"No" – she stepped forward, a white-knuckle fist connecting with his stomach like a bludgeon – "you watch your *fucking tongue.*"

Markus curled over, his empty stomach quaking violently with the shock of it. He wheezed, rising up again to find the handler snarling his way, a veneer of disgust she made no disposition to hide.

"I'm in charge, I make the rules here – not *you*." She pressed a finger into his chest. "Now, you're going to fight, and you're going to win – I don't *care* whether you agree with it or not, or what ain't *noble* about it. Ain't shit that's noble in any of this. You'll do as I say, an' you'll do it well." She turned for the door. "Now get moving… there's blood to spill, stumpy, and a sword with your name on it."

The ancient doors slid open ahead, like the parting gates of the heavenly realm, and Markus smelt death on the sword in his hand and wondered if it was theirs or his own.

This is madness. The weapon he had been given was a short-sword – small enough to make do as a skinning knife – with a dummy wooden handle and a grip that rubbed across his thumb like sandpaper. It was awkwardly weighted, too heavy at the tip – so much so, that every practice swing he'd managed thus-far had forced him to manoeuvre as if he wielded a hammer. It was nothing close to any sword he had known.

This is my legacy. From the borders of Provenci to the Kazbak Hills, through the Nomad's Path to a viceroy's house on a lakeside, to lose an arm and the only person he ever cared about, and the mess and hell entangled everywhere between. To find himself trapped against his will in a pit-fighting sand palace, as a one-armed trophy-piece to the adulations and cheers of the masses, who hated him and everything he stood for, but longed for bloodshed nonetheless. That in the heavy sun just ahead, with a sword in hand and nothing but shame in his gut, he would die a poor fool – a fool who gave up everything to lose an arm and his life in the end.

This is where the ruined come to meet their maker, came the thought, as he began the slow march to the arena. *And now I stand among them.*

Destined to die.

Walking out from the shadows, the furore of noise and excitement was overwhelming. All around, the vast sun-baked bowl of sandstone seats erupted with colour and life, thousands upon thousands of pastel robes fluttering in the high winds, broad faces and gold-ringed hands twinkling like absent stars. The arena seemed to shudder on its foundations, a swell of brass instruments exploding through the air as flags billowed at the pit's edges, a dizzying immensity that snapped through Markus's skull like a lightning strike.

Peeling his eyes away, he found scolding sand and stone slabs marked the basin of the arena's pit, a disconcerting pinkish tinge making its presence felt as well. Metal partitions had divided the vast arena into quadrants, that he had been told would disappear into the earth by some mechanism as each battle was won. The grand pit would open out slowly, placing victor against victor, until a final bloodbath ensued to claim the crown of them all. His head spun at the thought; Markus found his resolve ebb at the diminishing prospect of success. That he would have to fight, and survive to fight two more, if he hoped to leave that wretched place alive – the certainty of which he felt was at least half, with respect to the fact he was half a fighter at best.

Imagine placing your faith in a champion with one arm, he scoffed, shaking his head at the idiocy of it all. *Here be a leper, to dance for your amusement! Watch him swing his blade.* He spat across the sand.

Bastards.

Markus was alerted to grinding gears off to the far left, and saw another grand set of doors slide open much like his own had. From within emerged a slight man – *with both his limbs* – wielding a short-sword and shield, glancing suspiciously around through the blinding grace of the sun. It seemed to overwhelm the cautious figure, much like it had Markus: watching his frightful steps forward, raising the shield to cower from the light. The crowd seemed to sense it too: their cheers became more muted, realising they were witness to the lower-end of the skirmishes that day – a brawl between a flitting bean-pole of a man, and some one-armed grandfather who looked just sane enough to stay on two feet.

It was only when the two men locked eyes, and Markus saw the other figure lick his lips like a wolf and begin a long, ambling stride toward him, that he realised it wasn't fear he saw in the man's eyes.

He's insane.

The wolfman started howling as he approached, crashing his fist against his shield, swinging gestures directed at a crowd that suddenly spurred to attention.

To mark his own mettle, Markus did likewise, striding forward, crashing his fist against his—

He felt the tug of sensation across the wound, and swore under his breath.

Really? You dumb son-of-a-bitch.

Wolfman stopped within a few strides of him – just beyond the widest arc his sword could reach – and stamped his foot like a rabbit. Markus stalled, frowning, sword swinging between his fingers nimbly, trying to make sense of the madman before him.

"Lovely day for it," Markus said facetiously. "How's about, instead of all this violence, we just call it a day and make friends here, ay? No need for all the blood."

"Hm... hm, *no*," Wolfman spluttered, fingers twitching coldly. "No... fight-time. It's *fight-time*."

"Fight-time?" He nodded. "Any chance there's a put-our-swords-down-and-let's-talk-about-it time?"

"*No!* It's fight-time. No rest-time, only *fight now*. I am hungry."

"I don't think bloodshed quite sates the appetite – trust me, I've tried." Markus held his blade up in mock surrender. "And I'm sure, in some little part that's still sane in you... you don't really wanna do this. It's all a bit misguided, and we don't have to stand for it—"

"*No talking!*" Wolfman screeched, hissing and howling. "We fight. You die. I win. *Fight-time*."

Markus sighed, lifting his arm and stretching his back out. "I was afraid you'd say that, which means the next part gets a bit messy—"

Before he had a chance to finish, Wolfman charged forward, sword swimming at his side, swinging up to cleave the old man's neck apart in one great motion—

Markus ground his teeth and struck down with frightening speed, a bone clunking in his elbow for good measure. His blade bypassed the Wolfman's entirely, and found itself connecting with the mid-section of his forearm.

And severing the hand off entirely.

Wolfman screeched like an eagle, staring blankly at the severed hand and its adjacent sword that had now fallen lame across the sand. He reeled backwards, clutching the gushing stump, stamping wildly with clenched teeth and saliva lining his gums.

Stepping back, Markus was suddenly aware of the crowds around him, and the sudden symphony of voices and cheers. Their adulation, the roar for the fight – no, for *him*. Picking apart the ruckus, he found a chant begin to rise among them, thundering some fighter's name – no, *his* fighter's name, singing it mightily for the entire arena to hear.

Blade-arm! Blade-arm!

Markus grinned, raising his sword to their cries.

I quite like that...

"You play *unfair*," the Wolfman squealed, hissing.

"I play perfectly fair," Markus exclaimed, "and I gave you a simple chance to set our swords aside and talk this out. But, as you said... it's *'fight-time'*, and with that comes a *price*."

"It *is* fight-time."

"Then fight... see how far it gets you."

Wolfman howled. "So *be it*."

He cast his shield to the ground, completely rejecting the pulse of blood still spluttering from his arm, and tore the sword from his felled hand. A current of fury ran ablaze behind his eyes; the dripping red of blood leeched across the earth like algae. Markus stepped forward to engage.

The dance began again.

Markus swung across his body, the blade knocked aside by Wolfman, who curved his own around to cut inwards. They skated in a circle, blades clashing left and right, every lean and parry igniting the shock and awe of the onlookers, waiting for one of them to slip. Markus found little strain in his motions, beyond the unrelenting crunch of his knees – a woeful testament of his age. The Wolfman was no great swordsman: he could handle a blade, and perhaps even keep himself alive, but there was no great skill to the hack-and-slash games he played. It was almost like toying with food, trying to make an even match out of him – Markus found his patience wore thin. Losing great quantities of blood had put a cold drain on the scrawny man's face, and the swordsmanship had been reduced to sudden jabs and frequent retreats. The blood that had pooled at his feet now traced a path through the sand at his back; there just came a point where the fun ended, and a man was just waiting to die.

A sudden, heavier swing overhead and the Wolfman was forced to his knees trying to deflect it. The savageness had wilted from his eyes like an autumn flower, the howls reduced to a low whimper. Markus's sword glided down the opposing blade; fearing for his arm, Wolfman dropped the weapon and withdrew his hand.

Taking command of his new fighter's name, Markus switched the blade between his fingers, spiralling about in the air, before cutting sharply across and slitting Wolfman's throat.

A gargling screech, and the scrawny corpse crashed sidelong, dying on impact with fruitless grace.

Rising to their feet, the crowd let off a thunderous cry.

A victory had been won.

Markus let out a deep sigh and raised his sword humbly toward the stands at his back. Looking up to their glowing faces, he found not a single figure was in their seat – all were standing; all were screaming his name. The chanting and the uproarious applause matched the rhythm of his heart, thundering with an uncertain proudness deep within the compact of his chest. What he was proud of – with a dead body at his feet and their severed hand several strides to the right – Markus wasn't sure. All he knew was, whatever pride he felt under their cheers and shining eyes, he certainly wasn't longing for it to stop.

So much for the leper, come to die…

Drifting back to the arena, a round-horn blasted two heavy notes somewhere beyond the cacophony, and Markus swung around to observe the metal partitions that divided the arena into four. As the final blast shrilled to a halt, a layer of sand coating the right-hand wall was shaken from its post, and the well-oiled grinding of gears cranked into life like a reanimated body.

With far greater abruptness than Markus had expected, the metal barrier slid down through the sand beneath, and revealed the quarter of the arena beyond where his next opponent was waiting.

It appeared much the same as his own, at first sight: a sand-coated quarter scattered with flecks of blood, the walls lined with spear-points and adoring crowds looking expectantly over to his arrival. But as he followed the blood, Markus could find no sign of a body, as if the land lay empty, and the earth in turn lay still.

No sign, that was, until he gazed upon the spears jutting like snapped ribs from the wall, and found what remained of a corpse there, dissected into six composite parts occupying their own stake. Like some gory shrine to ward off spirits, the head – or what remained of it – sat at the centre, with the scalp cracked open like an egg. Markus felt his stomach turn.

What sick bastard would do that…

His answer lay a few short steps away, lurching towards him like a phantom, face awash with wrath and sadism as if she was a summoning of hell. Short cut brown hair lashed across her scalp, blending with knots of tattoos coiling behind her ears and across her cheekbones. A freshly-placed scar trounced across her jaw, aligning with a similar series of strikes across her chest and wrist. As he stood clad only in a cloth shirt, Markus scowled at how much more armoured she was than he: bowls of metal plating across her chest and shoulders, straddling her thighs and knees, locked together with leather straps. Not unlike the old titans of legend, she came with a god's weapons too: two curved sabres she held neatly at her side, both laced with blood, shimmering with an aquamarine-grey hue.

Markus looked to his feet and tried to find it in him to laugh.

Fuck this.

As he strode forward, crossing the thin metal rivet in the sand the partition had slid into, he found the tattooed woman had stopped several steps aside from him, whipping her blades forward. As he met her eye, she bowed her head and lowered into a fighting stance.

"Nice to see that you have a touch more respectability than the last one," Markus mused, not daring to glance back at the corpse he'd left. "That being said" – pointing off to the spears on the wall – "it seems that doesn't carry through to the actual fighting."

"You're a *Provencian*," she grumbled, baring her teeth.

"How could you tell?"

"You *bleed* differently." Her snarl became a grin. "And I like to watch things bleed."

"I can see that," he exclaimed, nodding to the other corpse.

"I like to watch others bleed... and your kind bleeds the best. Yours will be *exceptional*."

"Well, bloodletter, I hate to say it... but you won't get the satisfaction." Markus took his turn to bow, and swung his sword forward to the stifled cheers of the crowd on his side. "Because I've bled before and survived to say it... and when I'm done with you, you won't have the luxury of saying the *same*."

She struck out, both blades chiming together. Markus swung up, his wrist grinding uncomfortably at each snap of metal, her ferocity forcing him to backstep with no opening to parry. He sensed the trepidation, the expectancy from the stands above: the swords spinning, losing ground with every strike.

The drum of death beckoning once again.

Markus dropped onto his hand, legs spinning out ahead of him, kicking through the woman's shin as she spiralled and fell to the floor. He pushed upward, lunging with his sword to strike her, but instead took a boot to the chin and collapsed backwards, as the Bloodletter rolled behind and planted back on strong feet again, snarling like a beast.

410

She moved with no hesitation, setting upon him, swords raised. He rolled to the side, watching the twin sabres plant into the sand, finding some solid earth there and wedging awkwardly.

Markus rounded, kicking out hesitantly at her arm. A grunt as her wrist buckled inwards; a moment's grace before she withdrew one sword after the other, found her footing again and swung down for another attack.

With his heels in the sand again, Markus navigated the onslaught with whatever composure he could muster. The sun proved impossibly hot overhead; blankets of sweat saturated his cloth shirt, rubbed across his groin from the circling motions he made trying to stay afoot. The barrage continued to rein down, left and right and lunging through the middle. It seemed unending, as if there was no fault to her stride.

The drum of death beckoning, once——

He knocked her left hand aside with a sudden force, and despite her best efforts of concealment, a wince of pain appeared across her scar-stricken face.

And he smiled.

Whatever I did when I kicked her hand, she's fighting against it now, he deduced, marking each strike that came his way, measuring how much she relied on each hand. *And that gives me a chance to win.*

Twisting on the ball of his foot, his blade curved inwards and struck sharply across her left. Crashing across the centre of the blade, the sabre nearly broke from her grasp, the wrist visibly bulging to keep hold.

A whimpered cry, and with almost momentous force, she took a sudden step back and lurched forward with her right blade instead.

Perhaps this is not the end, after all.

Markus brushed the attack aside confidently, no longer afraid of the left-hand blade hanging despondently in her grip. Using the skill of his fighter's name again, he flicked his sword up against his arm, and with his knuckle curled swung across and landed a solid punch along Bloodletter's jaw.

A shrill cry, like a vulture circling a fresh corpse, and the woman stumbled backwards clutching at her mouth. Her nose was broken, lips awash with blood – spat across the earth beneath with every rasp of breath she managed. With nothing but agony and the bitter taste of iron swelling across her gums, the look she cast him could have melted steel.

Markus raised his blade. "I warned you…"

She gave him no notice, drawing her blades back and charging at him yet again. He rallied forward, preparing a defensive strike, only to find her drop suddenly to a slide, skimming over the course earth, feet crashing against the broad of his shins.

His legs buckled; only the soft motion of the sand slipping out from under him saved his knees from snapping. Suddenly he was falling atop her, limbs flailing. Markus seized up, wondering where her blades were, where the danger was, the abrupt vulnerability as he squirmed about trying to break free—

A glint at the corner of his eye, and one of her swords slid through a gap and cut across his exposed shoulder.

He winced, rolling, kicking out, his own blade coiling in his hand. The sun arcing overhead, unassailable and bright; Markus twisted and speared his sword down blindly, head thundering like a hammer.

Driving it into her collar, piercing flesh and bone like butter.

Markus freed himself from her thrall, scrabbling away as she bucked and squealed, releasing a sword to try and prize out the one now wedging her against the earth. Blood spat like a fountain; her arm seemed to swim with red.

Wasting no opportunity, Markus struck out with his foot and stamped across her wrist. The other sabre slipped from her grasp, as she recoiled the arm and screamed violently. He gathered the weapon up in his numb fingers; rolling back, levelling the thin blade, striking down—

The wide-rimmed eyes of Bloodletter, finding purchase about the blade's hilt in her collar—

The two swords clashing, brushed away – nothing to show for it but faithless blood.

Markus stumbled back several steps, heaving air through his system, the barking pain of the slit in his arm begging his attention. He gazed up, watchful of the silent crowds studying curiously from afar. Their cheers were mute – what had once been joy, now swamped with anticipation. They looked on in fear at their fighter – and now at the Bloodletter, as she slowly rose to her feet, his ugly sword in one hand and the other grappled tensely over the wound.

Nothing to show for it, but faithless blood.

"Why are we even here…" Markus said aloud.

"You mus… blee… you mus… *die*," Bloodletter spewed with whatever mangled words she could force through, swaying like a drunkard.

"What's the point? You'll die from your wounds anyway – it'll be no life to live. Why bother?"

Whatever wavering consideration he had hoped for, was nowhere to be seen – the light did not prevail. Completely neglecting her other sabre buried in the sand, she levelled her sword across her chest. "You mus… *die*," she said defiantly.

Markus clicked his tongue, shaking his head.

"As you wish…"

Legs churning, she broke into a run, screaming through a bloodied mouth, sword raised overhead—

Markus inhaled deeply, eyes closed, the inner burden of his soul growing quiet and still—

Her sword struck down lazily—

Markus spun on his heel, pirouetting, sword cutting out at the last, snapping across her throat, through her neck. The howls came to an abrupt silence, as her head spun from the sabre's edge, barrelling across the sand in a thrashing mass of anguish.

Markus opened his eyes, exhaling slowly; the crowd leapt to their feet and cheered.

A victory had been won.

Markus fell to a knee and planted his blade in the ground, hissing with pain, lifting his hand awkwardly to run a finger through the slit in his shoulder. The bleeding had largely stalled, much of the wound smothered with a thin layer of sand that stung angrily. Every touch sent a shiver through his arm; every roll of the shoulder met with a throbbing unease. He wondered if he could sustain much more – *although by all accounts I've suffered worse.* Looking to the black-branded skin across the stump of his other limb, ears prickling at the calls of his name from the grand rows above, he found little joy in knowing another fighter awaited him still. That the cheers behind were for him to fight again, to fight better, oblivious to the agony he felt. Realising that his suffering had yet to end.

Some bastard life this is.

The last metal partition ahead of him rattled with motion, its great gears slowly revealing the land beyond. Markus reclaimed his sword, raising it to the crowds at his back, the joy of his place in the sun battling with the dull displeasure of the act. That he would fight again; that part of him would die again – that that was the way things would be. Stepping out onto the open ground.

It all amounts to nothing.

†

"Where came you by this one?"

"He was sold to me… by the Kazbak hunters in the south-west," the handler explained, sitting forward in her seat, watching the one-armed man retrieve his sword from the earth and amble slowly towards the arena's centre. "Said they found him camped out in an old viceroy's house near the Lake of Souls. He was accompanied by another, although I don't know much of what happened to her."

"He's a Provencian?"

"He is… with some fighting experience somewhere down the line. I thought they were joking when they sold him to me."

"And the arm?"

"Lost in the attack – they said it was almost the only way to get the bastard in chains. He's vicious... as I suppose this proves."

"Hm." He paused, considering. "You may have a *champion* in this one, don't you wonder?"

"In stumpy here?" the handler scoffed. "He'll be dead by day's end. I was under the impression he'd be a bit of a joke fighter for the crowds. The fact he's survived two fights means nothing... other than it's made me plenty of profit from those who bet against him."

"You seem to be of little faith."

"I only speak of brute realities. What use would I have for a champion anyway – even a one-armed one? Their glories are over."

"Are you certain of that?" He leaned closer, indicating her to whisper. "*Because I have reports, from a good source, that the Iron Queen is sending her most prestigious envoy to Val Darbesh to acquire a new personal champion... for a massive sum of coin.*" He reclined in his chair. "So, if you're one-armed ancient down there can survive this next one... he'll face the new rival champion tomorrow at high-sun, in a spectacle for the ages, no doubt. From there, it's a simple exchange: the winner travels to Val Azbann to be the personal fighter of the Queen herself, and the handler receives their due *reward* for the service they enact..."

The handler twisted in her chair. *The Queen's champion.* It seemed almost beyond belief. *How much money are we talking about here?*

"Mind you," he continued, pointing off to the arena, "by the look of this one, you'll be lucky if he leaves that arena with any limbs at all..."

The handler looked ahead to the great pit.

She heard the Titan roar before she saw it.

†

It was at least three times his height, a bulging mass of green-yellow skin dotted with huge cysts and red-brown blotches of rash. Its stomach stretched grotesquely, small muscular legs beneath hardly staying upright. It ambled forward with the swing of its four massive arms that hung limply at the sides, dragging huge, jagged blades of tempered stone through the sand. Welded metal was bolted to the skin, across the sternum and shoulders, around its neck like a torture device that swelled and retracted with each withering breath. Above that, skimming the uppermost edge of the arena it was so tall, the disfigured cannonball of a head was addled with growths and its six unblinking eyes – the mouth slathering, slanted and coiling across its cheek with rows of blunt teeth. It seemed unaware of its surroundings, swinging toward the crowds and bellowing, the onlookers as repulsed as they were mesmerised by its largesse. The largest of its six eyes was almost telescopic, spiralling independently of the rest, surveying the arena while the others looked off elsewhere in blind disobedience.

Landing at the puny shadow striding towards it from afar.

Markus stopped just before the metal ridge in the sand where the partition had disappeared, the cheering of onlookers echoey all around. He rolled his tongue across his teeth – the sun fell heavy across his skin. *There's no point in wasting time,* came the sad recognition. With heavy limbs, he stepped over the threshold – the Titan rose up on its back legs before him, hammering down to the ground again in threat, the sand lurching like liquid toward him. *If I'm to die, this will be it.* The Bloodletter's blade hung coldly in his hand, the rough hilt relaxing against his palm. Studying its edge, Markus wondered just how many cuts in the great beast he'd have to make, to equate the single strike it could give him to send him to the grave. *This is where fools come to meet their maker.*

Ahead, the Titan suddenly charged.

This is where we come to die.

A great stone blade lunged down toward him in an arc. Markus rolled elegantly to one side, picking up his momentum again as the huge weapon sent a flush of sand skyward. The Titan's other sword lanced through, crossing the first – a tactical dive saved him from its jagged edge, as he rose to a run skimming across the Titan's flank. Sword poised, Markus buried the pointed end deep within its taut, sickened flesh, carrying the blade through until a great gouge had ripped across its side. It seemed like merely a scratch.

But a gargling roar from above told him that he'd met a mark.

Stepping out from beneath it, he turned to find the beast had already rounded on him, the stone sword gliding across the earth towards him. Markus held his breath, dropping to his stomach as the weapon swooped overhead, hobbling back to his feet at the aggravation of his knees.

Breaching the sky, swallowing the sun, the second sword swung overhead, the Titan's wild eyes spinning in their sockets. Markus stumbled, falling backwards, the broadsword piercing the ground at the ends of his feet, inches from his aching body.

He scrambled to his feet, curling his blade and striking out towards the beast's hand. It bit down into the Titan's exposed wrist, cutting through twice, gushes of black ooze exploding from within. The lumbering behemoth howled, yet still refused to release its weapon.

Suddenly, shadows arced in the space behind him; the other sword loomed for an attack. Markus twisted, driving his blade into the Titan's other hand before letting go and dropping away at the last moment.

He watched with fearful anticipation as the incoming blade connected bluntly with the hilt of the other. The force across its thinnest edge snapped the base from its point – the entire weapon seemed to implode. Shrapnel spat through the air all around him – several indiscriminate shards lodged across his chest. Markus howled in pain, pincers like tiny bugs across his torso. Overhead, the Titan leered and loomed, squealing like a pig, its impaled hand discarding what was left of its blade.

The one-armed fighter turned to a stand, coughing blood from the chips of stone now embedded between his ribs. Each breath produced an immeasurable pain; the damage it had done was a blunt unknown. The brightness of midday now rippled into a morph of colours, his eyes struggling to focus. His sword – buried in the Titan's hand, swaying about as it regained some ugly composure –

was far, far beyond his reach. His heart drummed deep within his body; he knew a quick end was the only way he'd survive.

Looking up to the Titan howling in pain above, a glimmer of hope came to him.

Perhaps I need my sword back.

A bellow, as if the earth were shattering, and the Titan's blade sailed overhead toward him; Markus rolled to his left, the impact detonating across his side. The stone blade retracted again almost instantly, cutting diagonally towards him; he jumped forward into its inner circle, the huge forearm passing just overhead.

A moment's breath and Markus gazed up to the Titan's wounded hand wavering in the sky high above, Bloodletter's rapier still embedded deep within the bones of its knuckle. That his sword lay far from his grasp, a spear across the sun – a sword he planned to get back through a callous act of madness, and his burning will not to die.

Here goes nothing.

As the fist crossed again and pummelled down to the earth at his feet, Markus planted his heels and, with bold courage he had thought long-abandoned, jumped onto the Titan's huge knuckle, grappling a cyst on its swollen skin as the hand dragged slowly upwards again, spiralling higher and higher to the heavens above.

For a few slow heartbeats, crossing the tip of the sky, there was no weight nor sound. His hand tensed, fingers nearly piercing the skin just to hold on; his toes rammed into place behind, coursing through the wind and belting sun. All around: the ornate sandstone walls of the arena with many hundreds of expectant gazes, hands wavering, covering mouths, shock and awe and disbelief painted across every one, as colourful as the robes they wore, speckled like a painter's palette. Below him, the Titan stood looming like a statue, its small orange eyes swivelling rapidly to spy the one-armed fighter on its wrist high above, trying to work out what was going on—

The stone sword loomed from behind, rising to skin him apart where he hung desperately to the beast's arm. As the great Titan rolled backwards, the wounded hand curled closer to its body, shielding it away like a wolf and its cub, the glistening sleight of his sword twinkling on its knuckle. Moments of life crossed those of certain death with every inch the hand swayed, and every foot the stone sword swung up to carve him in two. He knew the end was near; Markus could sense it, smelt death on his hands.

Except, the scent was not his own.

In a quiet second, Markus let go — the air rushed up to meet him. Falling, down towards the mangled hand passing beneath, his own hand almost slipped as it curled about the hilt of Bloodletter's blade. The huge stone sword coiled across to meet him — Markus tore his blade from the knots of fingers he had bloodied; releasing, falling, the world spinning around him again in all its colour and life.

The stone weapon slipping past, catching Markus across the back as he fell, a serrated edge tearing across his shoulder-blade—

As he channelled the pain into anger, anger into violence, twisting through the air, switching the sabre through his fingers, the six swivelling eyes struggling to match him—

The sabre goring into the flesh of the Titan's skull, pushing down to the hilt, the momentum of his fall dragging the blade down, slashing eyes and whatever skull cavity sunk within, snapping through the top lip, biting into the bottom, carving down its chin until slipping free—

Markus fell, his back cracking against the Titan's distended stomach, rebounding from it, spilling across the sand at its feet, face down and unmoving.

The Titan staggered, dropping its broadsword, the orange pupils pulsing wildly. A single step forward; another leg refusing to follow. The exacting inevitability as it teetered slowly backwards, an exultation of black scum bubbling across its broken face, and it crashed to earth like a felled tree, a rift of sand splashing several feet outwards in a vast crater doused with broken stone and molten skin.

For long, quiet moments, the crowd stood expectantly. Mumblings cast across the bowl, fingers pointing to the lifeless body of the victor. Waiting for a sign, that life would come.

If this was do, or die.

Then came a stirring, fractional but resolute. Markus lifted his head slowly in what felt like another world, his body displaced and numb, heaving in whatever air he could manage, splattering blood across the sand below. With a near-shattered arm, he buckled his elbow and lifted himself slowly to a bridge, and then rolled back to kneel on his legs as if sat relishing in prayer.

At the sight of his face, the arena erupted. Cheers and cries roared skyward, filling the dustbowl all around him. His lungs hardly functioned; stones embedded his chest; blood drenched the sand at his feet – but even beyond that, Markus couldn't help but smile.

Perhaps a champion has come... after all.

†

"Well, how about that..."

The handler, rammed forward to the edge of her seat, was transfixed on the scene before her, disbelief and opportunism all morphed into one. The one-armed nobody she'd bought the previous morning, thinking he'd be little more than a joke fight to please the crowd... *is now my champion.* "Yes... it appears so," she muttered without much thought.

"We'll have to make the arrangements for the main event tomorrow as soon as this is settled... I guess you don't have any plans?"

A massive sum of coin. "I don't anymore..."

He clapped his hands together. "Good, excellent, we can start work right away." He rose from his seat. "In the meantime, might I recommend getting that old soul down there a long bath and some good food... he took quite a beating there, and if he's gonna be anywhere near fit tomorrow, he'll need some work done."

To fight for the Iron Queen. "Of... course."

The Champion of Tarraz.

"Drop by the main quarters this evening; we'll discuss terms of the fight and attendance. And don't be late... this is the fight of the century, and I want everything to run smoothly."

"Yes, Verlunz... I'll be there."

The great chief rose from his seat, four guards forming up ahead of him as he disappeared into the bowels of the arena, leaving the handler to stare at her new champion, the one-armed ancient who rose to his feet before them, saluting the crowds with strikes of his blade.

The Champion of Tarraz.

†

Chapter 51

Butter Knife

S tart lashing the horses to the wagons… get them moving along the road first. Keep the rest of the army in neat rows behind, no more than four abreast. I'll expect us to cross the lowlands into the Grey Plains by nightfall – we'll set up camp once we arrive, form neat clusters to secure a perimeter. Have the patrols scout the forests to the west, too… we don't wanna be crept up on with our guard down. See it done."

The messenger skittered away like a beetle fleeing an upturned rock, off to do the commander's bidding as only a reliable fool could do.

Revek sighed, running a hand through his hair, and looked ahead along the road at the motions of his army preparing to march. Skimmed with a layer of cloud shielding the sun's eye, the midday air was still bitten with cold, flushes of wind swelling up from the sea. Adjacent to the road, thick clusters of bleach-white skeletal trees formed a near-impassable barrier, growing more sporadically as the road curved off into the distance, where the pale imitations of mountains could be seen through the dull grey-blue. Everywhere else, his view was domineered by the imperial legions swelling across the wide road: armoured divisions forming rank and file, raising tents and packing them into wagons; officers enjoying a final minute's respite with clinking metal cups in hand. The draught-horses taken from the village and the fine stallions who had survived the first march were saddled and harnessed off to the side, the largest of them fitted to the carriages and sent to the front. It was an industrious business, with a dutiful professionalism that would have impressed even the most critical observer; to see such imperial prowess in motion was a sight to behold.

But all Revek could take from it, was disdain.

An army of competence, but not of ingenuity, he lamented. The two nights camped out in the ruins of the village had shown men and women willing to work their part in maintaining the army, but only with the significant oversight and direction of an officer – and in turn, oversight from him when that failed. *To be called out to address menial issues a dozen times a day is ridiculous.* Officers had come to him with requests for his advice – first taken with appreciation, but the nature of the question he was presented with soon turned to frustration. *Where are we to find food? Forage among the trees. Where shall we find materials for the road? You're surrounded by stone and wood, make use of it.* It had ebbed on relentlessly. *What shall we do with the wagons? How do you tack the horses? Where do we resupply? Where are the fires to cook food?*

By the ninth inquiry, he had simply instructed the guards to turn away anyone wishing to find his counsel. Two others had tried in vain to gain access, and after they had been dismissed a silence had endured until dusk, with Revek settling his frustration over a cold bottle of liquor he'd discovered in the chamber's cabinet. He thought then that the worst of it was over.

However, after emerging to an orange sky seeking out the army's ration-master, he had found no food was prepared, and hungry faced-soldiers sat moping in the burnt alcoves of the houses, goggling like beggars as he passed. Revek had stood for a long time, confused: why was there no food? It was procedure to hand out rations at dawn and dusk – anyone could ask. And he had thought long and hard on the issue, pondering it at length – and then his confusion had turned to realisation; and from realisation, turned to anger, until the only obvious conclusion remained: why was there no food prepared?

Because no one bothered to fucking ask for it.

Looking upon them then, even a day later, a still-burning resentment butchered his mind. *This is no army; this is a mockery. I was never like this.*

Revek blinked slowly, and saw the eyes of the young Tarrazi boy from the day before, holding the knife to the soldier's throat. *How weak they are, competent as a minimum – I was far better.* Watching how the other officers had waved their swords with such cowardice, never taking a stand, never managing something decisive. *Weakness, in its many ugly colours.* How he had strode forward, attempted to intervene – let the soldier die to kill the enemy behind without hesitation. *Don't ask questions, don't hesitate – act.* He ground his teeth. *These are weak.* An inhale of crisp air swelled his chest.

They will never be like me.

"Sir?"

No one will. "Yes, Darius."

The general appeared at his shoulder, clasping his hands behind his back, a weathered, sleep-deprived grimace worn heavy across his face. "We've had reports from our forward patrols who've been scouting the road ahead."

"What are we looking at?"

"The road stretches roughly two-dozen miles along the east coast, sir, a lot of it on open wetlands bordering the sea as the reports indicated yesterday. From there it curves sharply inland for about a mile, then opens out onto a ridge towards the Grey Plains."

"Very well – and the weather?"

"Much the same as this the entire way," Darius exclaimed. "The storm-front from the north appears to have subsided mostly... we'll only get a few showers and thunder at best."

"This is good news."

"Although, that may not play to our advantage, sir."

Revek frowned. "Why not?"

"The road, sir... it's not exactly advantageous to us in some places." He pulled his collar out. "There's subsidence along some parts from the rains a few days back... it seems the storm remained in this area for some time. And with the new storm passing through as well... the patrols described that a few patches had become *'nothing but mud and landslides'*—"

"Hopefully the soldiers have learned their lessons from our last march and know how best to guide the horses," Revek interjected. *Although I have my serious doubts about that.*

"Aye, sir." A pause. "Although, that wasn't the only thing the patrols reported."

The commander's ear twitched. "Go on..."

"When they reached the ridge banking the Grey Plains, they spotted a field camp about a half-mile west... a field camp of *soldiers,* no less."

He straightened his back like a totem. "*Blackcoat* soldiers?"

Darius nodded. "A small army, sir — upwards of three-hundred units."

How about that. "And the patrols are certain that's what it is?"

"Resolutely, sir — they couldn't wait to tell you."

"Were they spotted?"

"No, the blackcoats didn't notice them. We've got a small patrol stationed at the roadside keeping watch as we speak. I ordered relays to be set up along the main road to pass any information along to us as we march."

Because they could never organise it themselves. "This is promising news," Revek said, before gesturing with his hands. "Alert the other officers, tell them if we march strong and reach the Grey Plains tonight, we can lead an assault tomorrow and score our first victory against a blackcoat army. I want everything running in good order and in good time until then... if not, there'll be hell to pay." *By my hand no less.*

"But sir," Darius prompted as the commander made to walk off. "Are you not concerned that the road ahead may hinder our progress? With the mud and subsidence... should we not consider alternative routes—"

Revek glowered at him, the resentment of the past days suddenly finding its focal point. "No, *general*... and if you come to me with stupid shit like that again, I'll have you strung up a fucking tree. Understood?"

A wounded gaze, eyes falling to the floor. "Yes, sir."

"We don't have time to consider alternatives. The soldiers will march fast and navigate the terrain as it comes, and we will reach the Grey Plains by nightfall. Should they fail me, or our supplies become way-laid, or we are set upon by any manner of inconceivable *screw-up*... I will *personally* see that they are punished for *wasting* my *time*." He spat the demands and speared a finger at the general. "This war is *mine*... and I will not have that *stolen* from me by these *people*."

He looked out to the cloud-smoked skies, and the dull shine of an ebbing sun. Passing down across the trees, the wavering shoreline to the east, crossing to the army——

Straining, his eyes suddenly narrowing as he watched a pale head pass between them, draped in robes, unseen to everyone but him. A silent figment, passing like an absent shadow through the ranks of the army. Crossing to an opening where horses were being led to the front, it stalled for but a moment, head turning to face him slowly, the brand marks and the pale eyes——

A blink later, and it was gone.

Ten miles passed, and the effortless march of the Imperial Army prevailed on into the gloom. The thick clusters of dormant trees encompassed much of the landscape to the west, painting a myriad of porcelain white against a blue-grey sky. To the east, those same trees fell away, until much of the landscape was dominated by striking dunes of broken stone and grass, trickling out to shingle at the frothing edge of the Icebreaker Sea. Multi-legged mammals with green fur and pointed eyes leapt between the larger stones, several of them roving in packs at the shoreline picking through the surf for molluscs. Above, a murder of crows made their presence known as a shadow to the army beneath, cawing and swooping amongst the trees – it was only the sudden arrival of a four-winged land-glider, its hammerhead skull and whip-length tail twisting and diving among them, that scattered the black shadows in the end, their squawks still ringing out for some time after.

Caught in a strong cross-wind as cool air whipped up from the eastern waters, the army made steady but resolute progress, the bobbling head of a scout appearing every once in a while bearing updates on the enemy camp said to lie at the road's end. A rush of excitement would come and go at the news of their awaiting prey, and for ten well-paced miles that same momentum persisted to that great unknown somewhere ahead. The success was exactly what had been hoped for – it was exactly as the commander had wanted. Ten miles had passed like a breeze.

And then, with such abruptness, it went awfully wrong.

"Sir, they're stopping ahead," Darius addressed suddenly, sticking a finger out to the slowing ranks ahead. "Something's wrong."

Indeed, the imperial procession had drawn to a halt. Soldiers fell back into their neatly-aligned divisions, staring about blankly awaiting orders. Horses were drawn up and kept calm by tentative hands. The generals among them shifted out to the road's edge, cocking heads to each other, trying to gauge some idea of events at the head of the column.

Revek pinched the bridge of his nose; whatever resentment he harboured deep within now heated to boil again.

Why can we never seem to get this right…

"Orders, sir?" Darius inquired.

I wish everyone would stop asking me that, too. "We'll ride to the front, see what's happening. Can only hope it's nothing major."

Although with our luck, that seems to be all it ever is.

They broke left from the main column, their horses navigating the thin verge of uneven soil and crackling gravel at the road's edge. As the path ahead ridged and narrowed, officers began barking commands to provide access for the approaching generals – every man and woman donning the red-and-green sash then saluted as the commander passed, eyes expectantly following as they went. Revek found he could do little more than grimace and nod his head, barking demands for the horse to pick up pace as the road ahead crested to a small hill. Mumbling exchanges echoed from the other side: the cautious words of disagreeing, indecisive types, stumbling forward in an attempt to pick out a solution to whatever problem lay ahead.

The commander found his resent bristle even more. *Part of the Imperial Army of Provenci... yet they stand here and bicker like children.*

Cresting the ridge, the scene he was greeted with only stood to prove the point. The road bent sharply downwards, plateauing off several feet further ahead, but much of the terrain between the two points had eroded completely. By his judgement, the two front-most wagons had miscalculated just how abrupt the decline was – and by luck more than judgement, he suspected, the right-hand carriage had navigated it largely unscathed.

The left-hand one, however, had not.

"What's happened?" Darius inquired of an officer to his left.

"Misjudged the decline on this side, general – before the front two lines had a chance to stop 'em, the horses had already crested the ridge and began to slide." She gestured toward the wheel tracks skimming down to a mud-pit beneath. "The left one here got caught in all this subsidence, and one of the horse's legs fell out from underneath 'em... the cart came crashing down in the ditch right on top of him, poor boy." A pause. "That, and two of the men have cuts down their sides from the wheels... they'll need medical assistance soon if they're to make it."

"Okay." Darius took a long breath. "Get the injured men back to the command division, find the medical officers there and get them sorted. We need a single-file passage along the right-side while we attempt to recover the supply cart – I want a secondary division stationed at this hill to guide any other carts over. Make sure it's done fast." He turned to the commander. "Does that all sound reasonable, sir—"

Useless fucking people.

Revek had already dismounted, crossing ahead of Darius's horse and pushing his way through the throng of soldiers staring dumbly at the wreckage ahead.

I'll show them.

Boots submerged in mud, he steadied himself on the edge of the stranded cart. Both front wheels had all but disappeared, and the base had landed almost diagonally, threatening the cargo strapped inside. He thought perhaps the mud would have been the least of their problems, in righting the vehicle again and being off on their way.

That was until he saw the horse in question swamped in the mud, impaled by the splinter bar, its cold eyes still spinning and plumes of air still snorting from its beleaguered nostrils. Very much alive, but with a shallow grave awaiting, the wound continued to welt with thick rivers of blood that filled puddles in the mudded trench beneath. Its watchful eyes met his own, just for a moment, and it seemed to Revek that even the great beast itself knew that all there was left was to die.

"Sir, what are your—"

"*Nothing*," Revek spat, rounding on the culprit at the roadside with enough rage to split stones. "My orders are nothing. Do *nothing*. You've done enough." The soldier produced a look as if he'd been impaled through the chest; Revek paid no attention, instead drawing his gaze across to a stern, armoured woman wielding a broad-axe next to him. "Give it to me."

She frowned, looking at the weapon—

"Don't stand there and fucking gawk at it! Give it to me!"

She passed it over; the commander snatched it from her hand and heaved it forward, not bothering with the look of disdain she gave him, not caring for all the world.

He waded through the mud, sinking up across his shins, grunting with every swing. The horse writhed weakly at his approach – Revek found the axe weigh heavy and resolute in his hands. He stopped just in front of the great beast as it laboured in the mudded pit, staring

429

blankly through him with watered, blinkering eyes.

I'll show them.

"You are all responsible for *this*," he exclaimed, turning to the soldiers who watched him fearfully. "You all know procedure... you all know how to take charge. We *never* mount a ridge, no matter where we are in all the world, without *checking what's on the other side first*. You never cross that bridge, until you are *certain* you are prepared to do so. So, it is your *ignorance*... your sheer *idiocy* and neglect of procedure... that has caused this, nothing more." He stabbed a finger at the fallen, snorting beast. "You are all *wasting my time* with this stupid fucking *anarchy*! You are *all* responsible, *all of you!* And now you will watch... and no one will look away... as I show you what happens when you don't *take charge* of your *fucking actions.*"

Revek turned, swinging as he did so, the blade angling against the dull sun like an executioner's blade, and cut through the horse's neck with a deafening thud. Blood exploded across his hands; a crunch of bone, and it died in an instant, the silence echoing on.

The commander spat.

Wasting my time.

He tore the axe from the flesh with a squelch of blood, throwing it at the feet of the woman whom he'd taken it from. By her side, Darius suddenly pushed his way through, watching the scene before him unfold with a mix of confusion and horror, passing from the cart to the commander to the decapitated horse still seizing awkwardly in the mud at his feet—

"*You three*," Revek growled, stabbing at the nearest soldiers who stood sheepishly at the mud's edge. "Come to me, now."

They obeyed, wading into the mud until they stood at his side, fear-stricken and uneased by the huge carcass in the mud.

Revek grappled the nearest man and dragged him forward, the soldier sidestepping over the beast's swollen corpse. The other two followed, forming a cold, deformed line behind the body, knee-deep in the mud.

"You must take *responsibility*..." In a burning delusion, the commander unhooked the reins from the dead horse and began to loop them around the soldiers' chests, fastening them at each interval.

"You must know the *cost of it*..." Lashing the ropes tighter, a buckle apiece, tired eyes and shallow faces watching as he worked.

"This is *your fault*..." The onlookers wavered as the commander bound his soldiers, a few wary eyes looking to General Darius, who himself wore much the same complexion, knowing he had to intervene and stop this, but not knowing—

"I will not have this *stolen* from me, no one shall *steal* it—"

"Sir!" Darius shouted suddenly, over the pulsing wind and crackling waves of the sea at their backs. "What are you doing—"

"Do *not defy me!*" Revek rounded, growling through his teeth. "Do not challenge me, you *subordinate!* You will do as I fucking ask. You will *obey* me. You are nothing but a general, and you will not *challenge me*... do you *understand!*"

Darius did not answer; looking to him, the weight of disappointment in his eyes said enough.

Revek scowled back, the flame in his eyes burning bright and foul. "As for the rest of you," he boomed to the soldiers in front. "You will get this wagon out of the mud – you will drag it out if you so have to – and you will not leave this place until you *do*. And when it is free, when you have done as I have asked of you... you will drag this cart on your bare shoulders for the next fourteen miles, until we reach the next camp. You will drag it, for the mockery you have made of *this*. And if you choose to *abandon* the cart... then I will order the archers to line the roads at the edge of our camp, and I will tell them to shoot *every last one of you* that comes through without exception." A long pause: the words seemed to echo on forever. "If you do not take charge of your actions, then I *will*. And I will make you understand... that I am *not* to be *disobeyed*." He turned to look for Darius, to make his point known.

But the general was nowhere to be seen.

†

Chapter 52

The Woman in the Clouds

*L*imbo: *a place between worlds. The delicate rift between an unfortunate
life and a painful death, and whatever lay beyond that thin line she
now found herself walking. It was vacuous, for a long time deathly
silent. There was only her presence, her sheer being there. A mind, detached
from body, half-abandoned from the soul, seeking out—*

"Why am I here?"

*Her words echoed out into the porcelain vastness, but not a word was
spoken in return.*

*She wondered how long she'd been stood there, studying the nothingness,
trying to make sense of a world that didn't want her and she worried never
would. Trying to pick apart black from grey, and grey from white – shadow
from shadow, almost as life from death. Pulsing totems that were not there
anymore; criss-crossed earth at her feet and shards of landscape painted at the
edges. There were no soft sullen songs of a shadow woman; no great pits in
the ground to rise and claim them both. Only a voice, her voice – a narrow
chasm of a conscious force that she barely controlled. And beyond that, there
was nothing.*

Just the same as before.

*"Why does this keep happening?" she pleaded, or felt she should've pleaded,
had there been any emotion to plead with. "Why am I here again?"*

*The void refused an answer, or any modicum of a response. Nothing
appeared before her; nothing fell away all the same. Whatever she had hoped*

for in reaction, never came. There was only the white-grey all around her, unbroken and unforgotten — only the voice she called out with, to find a world that did not answer.

"Speak to me," she cried, muted to a whisper. "Something speak to me, please."

The void would not answer.

She wondered, for what seemed like an age but passed like a second, whether this was her fate forever. Trapped in the void with no control of how or when, to wander the vast reaches in search of a great many things, always left with no reply. That maybe one day, life and the vision would become as one, intertwining until she could not tell one from the other. A void where she was nothing, felt nothing, saw and understood even less. The effortless ticking of time passed on.

With nothing to show for it, but silence.

"Something, anything," she whispered to the void. "Please..."

Knowing nothing would come.

✝

"You want answers, don't you? Answers you think I'll give you."

"I want to know why I'm kept caged like an animal against my will," she had grumbled in her disdain.

The Alderbane had broken nothing of its composure in response, the muscles in its stretched jaw twitching coldly. "You already know the answer to that," it mused.

"I don't take 'distasteful of foreigners' as an answer — I'm not foolish enough not to question that there's more to it than that."

"How insightful of you." The huge form had rolled back delicately in its chair. "However, sometimes it is just as simple as that."

"Nothing is ever as simple as that."

A shake of its huge head. "You see shadows where there are none, general — that is all you have ever known. I expect you've run from them in the past, these shadows of yours. Perhaps with your history as an officer, you've seen plenty of good men and women ground to dust and the foul fools of the earth rise from their ashes. Or perhaps your family, in some once-forgotten time, wronged you so, and cast you aside with nothing to show for it, so you are always looking for where the motive lies, where the knife slipped past when you weren't looking. Perhaps you still feel that wound, deep within you now. Perhaps you fear the hold it has on you, and that you'll never be able to let go…"

"You know *nothing* about me," she had growled, heat biting at her neck.

"I know what I *need* to know." The change of tone had struck like a hammer; the air she had breathed seemed to turn cold and thin. "Whatever answers you seek from me, you should know, will not be forthcoming. You came to our shores – you knew of the consequences as soon as you set foot within my city. You did not obey the rules then, so I question why you think I will give you the answers you so desire now."

She had lowered her gaze, a stinging sharpness in her chest.

"That is your burden, not mine," it had proclaimed. "You will not gain redemption, or the answers you seek, from me – I have no interest in bringing you such clarity." Both hands clasped across the table. "Perhaps some lost soul may find you someday, and seek pity on you, and relinquish you of this pain. Perhaps the gods will not hate you, as much as they seem to. But until that fateful day comes, should it come at all, you spend your life *jumping at shadows*, in a void of your own making—"

†

"*Cavara.*"

She jumped, a shock ringing out through her unformed body.

Something had answered her cry.

She twisted, orientating herself, the white formlessness stretching on. Blurring, sharpening, blurring again. Head on a swivel, seeking something from nothing. Searching for the answer that had come—

A form, breaking from the pale expanse: a growing crack of grey splintering across the void, where a shadow slowly emerged, hands grappling, almost tearing itself free. There was a convulsion to it, a strange agony as if it wasn't supposed to be there. As if it was against reality, breaking the fabric of the vision at its seams. Some abandoned traveller, overwhelmed by the silence — an intruder in a lost place.

One to give her answers, she hoped, nonetheless.

With a final heave, the shadow coiled from the grey smudge and landed across whatever floor there was in a heap. The breach snapped shut at its back within moments, re-establishing the great nothingness once more — only now with its perfection blemished by the new shadow, who slowly rose to their feet and traipsed heavily over to her.

She noticed the grey impressions it left in the ground as it walked, the small dent of black where it had fallen through. The very animate, human realities of an otherwise unrealistic land — forming, shifting around, almost like it was no different than the world she knew.

Almost like they were one and the same...

"Cavara," the shadow muttered breathlessly — with lungs, and air, and strain and life. It undulated, swelling like an octopus, blacks and greys biting into each other, withstanding the void to form the dull impression of a man.

"Who are you?" she pressed, the words muffled in her ears. "Why are you here?"

"I'm here because you are here — I am here for you." The voice was masculine, guttural, but elocuting words as if being punched in the gut. From the viscous turns of its body, she saw a hand was clutched across its chest like a knot, the other pressed against one leg that seemed to swell and contract with each step. "I can't be here for long..."

"Why? What's happening?"

"I shouldn't be here... I wish I wasn't here, but I have to be."

"Why? What is this place?"

"Now is not the time," it muttered almost in fear. "She'll be here soon... I need you to trust me, I... I need to guide you."

"Who's coming? Who are you?"

A pause, a fragment of emotion churning over its face — something that

435

almost looked like a smile. "I always knew there was something special about you..." it muttered in the end.

Whatever had been her chest, suddenly dropped like a stone. From the voice, came a name.

"Brutus?"

†

"I hope you can meet him again."

"Meet who?"

"Brutus."

Cavara had placed the bowl back into the small sink and smiled, the open fire of Azura's house filling the room with warmth and the sweet scents of spices.

"And why might that be, my little friend?" she had asked.

Evelyn had shied away, rocking his shoulders side to side. "Well, it's silly really..."

"Go on, tell me..." She turned and pinched his shoulder. "I *promise* I won't laugh."

"Hm, okay." The small boy had placed himself on the stone bench at the table, swinging his legs back and forth. "He likes to tell stories, and... I think you'd like his stories. He only tells them to me, but I think he will tell them to you if you ask him nicely."

"Is that right?" she had replied. "And what are these stories about?"

"He... tells a lot of stories."

"And what's your *favourite* story?"

"The one about the special place... the world covered in clouds," he'd then exclaimed. "And every time he tells the story... he says more of the clouds disappear, and he can see more. And he goes looking, and he finds things... like an adventure. I like adventures." His face then dropped slightly. "But then he says about what else is in there, too. That there's a scary monster in the clouds, who'll catch him if it finds him. I don't like the scary monster." He seemed to trail off, then reanimate moments later. "But... but Brutus says so long as

436

we keep moving, and we know what we're looking for... then we'll be okay. And we are okay... the monster hasn't come."

She had nodded her head, smiling. "That's quite a story... I know your mother said he 'sees things' sometimes, but I didn't know he had such an imagination..."

"That's what he tells the stories about, though."

Cavara had felt her stomach knot; dropped the cloth rag in her hand. "About what?"

"About what he sees – that's what the place in the clouds is. That's where he's looking, where we... have our adventure."

She remembered her heart had stuttered. "And what is he looking for?"

"The Woman in the Clouds," the small boy had said quietly. "He says she's lost... he says she needs to be found and led to safety."

"Lead to safety?" she puzzled. "Or... what?"

"Or the scary monster will get her..."

†

"We need to get moving, come on!"

She was dragged by the arm, suddenly moving – actually moving, watching the imprints in the white floor one after the other as Brutus hobbled painfully on into the void. It was a poor pace, laborious and merely a skip for her, but from the force she found exerted across her left shoulder it was evidently far worse for the shadow at her side. For what reason, she did not know.

For anything, she did not know.

"Where are we going?" she cried out to him.

"Back through the breach... we need to get back to the other side, back to home..."

"What other side?"

"The world you know... back to the cell where you were. To safety, please..."

"But I need answers, I need to know what this is——"

The voice became more strained, tired, battling against the void. "You will, in time. You will know the truth of all things. Just please... just not now..."

"Why?"

No answer.

"Why won't you answer me!"

As she spoke, coming to a stop beside the bowl in the earth where Brutus had fallen, a ripple snapped through the expanse around them, and a piercing screech chimed in her skull. The hand at her shoulder clenched tightly; the shadow's head turned. Seizing up inside, she turned suddenly too, and lay eyes on something approaching from afar: some shadowy feminine form like the one she had seen before, striding out towards them, a flickering pulse to its movements, jarring and stuttering...

Almost as if it were on fire.

"What the fuck is that thing... Brutus?"

The shadow at her side found no response: he broke from her shoulder and began clawing at the void ahead of them, where a wall slowly began to appear.

She watched him struggling, tearing away, each breach of his hands streaking the surface with thick grey smudges, bulging and snapping with each repeating motion. Like chipping away at fine bits of stone, hoping to break free to the other side.

Behind, another screech rattled. The figure pressed forward in relentless pulses, skimming the surface of the world like the coiling motions of a snake. For a moment, Cavara almost knew it: how it was the same woman as before – the same figment that had called to her, attacked her, screamed to her before she fell away. It was discerning, even from afar, to look upon those broken, human features it manifested through the harsh veil of shadow. The motions of hands and fingers trapped away. Striding legs and planting feet. The tenseness of its jaw; the snarl at its cheeks.

The dull shimmer of something pointed and lethal snaking the length of its leg, coming to bear in a firm grip, ready to strike out at helpless prey——

"It's not working," Brutus wretched, hammering what appeared to be a fist against the granite-stained wall before him. "I don't understand..."

"What do we do now?"

He turned back to the shadow approaching, as another blasting screech ripped through the air. "I don't know... I've never not... been able to before..." As if burdened by an immense weight, he lurched forward and fell to one knee, the dull rasp and break of his breathing echoing in her ears. "I can't be here much longer... it's too much..."

"What do we do?"

"You need to tell him... you need to tell the Alderbane..."

"Why? Tell him what?"

"Tell him about this... tell him what you see... talk about the shadows, talk about the totems... he knows. The war that's coming... the end of all things..."

"What do you mean?"

Writhing under the pressure, he gave no answer.

"What do you..."

The shadow surged closer; Brutus fell to his knees, coiling over, hissing at the tenseness across his back.

Another scream: Cavara could hear the emphasis of her name breaking through. Looking back, finding the shadow woman with hands raised, a taut metal blade twisting in one hand, pleading to bite her flesh and rip her apart with each swing. Knowing she was helpless — that no answers would come.

Back to the wall, she watched as the grey strikes receded, reclaimed by the white-wash world they inhabited. Knowing that whatever lay beyond, within the grey-black shadows of the breach, meant safety, and meant something closer to home. That to do something was an unknown; to do nothing, was to die.

The scream of the shadow, drawing closer.

Death at the crease of her spine.

She swung, planting what she assumed was a fist against the solid surface, knuckles shifting across a half-imagined hand. Watching, suddenly, as a bloom of black and grey erupted from the contact point, and the breach reopened with frightening ease. That the hand that recoiled was that of her own, human and real and oddly transfixing—

A wail of horror from behind, as the shadow realised what she had done. Bundling Brutus through her arm, she pulled him up from the ground and *carried his weight through the breach — carrying her own, pushing through, jumping off whatever floor there was out into the din beyond. Twisting, coiling tightly, her vision tunnelling as the light fell away—*

The shadow woman at the edge behind them, reaching through, blade cutting out into the gloom. The electric veracity in its eyes, screeching her name, glinting grey steel in one hand—

A tiny whistle of pain, the blade slicing through, dancing across where an ankle should've been. The ground rising up to meet her...

The void swallowing her again.

†

"Wake up."

Cavara snapped awake, throwing herself to her feet in an instant, the sudden confluence of sensation rattling through her. Finding a body and a mind, and moving limbs and vertebrae. There was air, and a heartbeat, and she was blinking, and—

She was back in her cell again, the door hanging open, two disgruntled guards peering in expectantly. She had returned to the cold confines of the prison block – back to a reality she knew. Back to a silence, real and tangible, coursing all around as if nothing had ever been.

Of the void and the shadow and the echoing screams, there was nothing left to know.

Of Brutus, and the answers she had long to see, there was no sign.

"The Alderbane wants to see you," the guardsman exclaimed, stepping into the room with shackles dangling in his hand.

Absently, questioning the world, she made to stand, but hissed at a pain in her leg. Looking down, she traced the length of her body to a thin cut across her ankle.

As if done by a falling blade.

†

Chapter 53

Champion's Soul

They had taken his wounded carcass from the arena on the back of a cloth stretcher, proceeding with delicate care as if preparing a body for burial. And when he entered the cold chambers beyond, there had been no descent into the bowels of the great structure as before, when he was little more than a worthless one-armed fool: they had instead remained at the surface, skimming along tight corridors and expansive rooms, before banking sharply left at the direction of a familiar, enforcing voice who had watched his victory with great intrigue.

The room they settled him in was far larger than the former holding. They had placed him down on a thin mattress, propping his back up with pillows so he wouldn't choke on his own blood, the warming yellow glow of a three-barred window overhead bathing the room in every colour of the sun. In a half-daze, the wheezing contortion of his breath rattling through his ears, the workers who had brought him in fell away, replaced by a sudden flush of black gowns and shimmering utensils. All the while, the handler had stood bracing the iron bar at the bed's end, watching curiously as the officers went about their work.

They had offered a vial to him, that he had assumed was water and gulped down emphatically, clearing a thick lining of scum from his throat as the rasping began to recede.

Moments later, the haziness had returned with some force, and the room beyond came and went like closing shutters.

Moments again, and he was under, tiny twinges of pain tapping at his shoulder, plucking at the stones in his chest...

Markus awoke to the sound of voices muttering at the end of his bed, and stirred at a cool breeze channelling down through the high window above him. Inhaling slowly, he found the rasp that had addled his lungs was gone, and the rhythmic rise of his chest cavity no longer exhibited the pain of a hundred tiny knives. A pulling sensation tensed across his sternum – the bindings of a cloth strap he assumed, tainted with ointment, covering the tiny puncture holes flecked across his skin like pepper. Shifting the weight on his neck, he acknowledged a similar sensation pinching the ridge of his shoulder where the slice had been, now displaying no more pain than a papercut. Trying further motions beyond that to address his wounds, however, came only with numb denial – beyond the breath in his lungs and the fuzzy, entangled twitches of his fingers, all else was a half-realised nothing.

And all he had left to do, was open his eyes.

The room beyond had fallen to a dusky gloom as the sun receded outside, the white-yellow walls and cream shelves now swimming with pastel blues and deep greys. At his bedside, the light of a tiny candle flickered and danced across the table, a bead of white wax skimming slowly down its side. Its warm glow, accompanied by a lantern embedded in the wall above the door, illuminated the two figures whom he heard at the end of his bed, and whom his attention now rested upon.

Even in the fractious light, one figure he recognised distinctly as the handler, who gestured broadly to the bed where he lay. She spoke emphatically to a figure opposite: a squat, pale-skinned man adorned in striking red robes, to appear almost like his entire chest and shoulders had been skinned. A swell of piercings lined the outer lobe of his ear, quivering in the candlelight, with the deep welts of his eyes and mouth swallowed by cavernous cheeks and a heavy-set brow. Studying his gestures, and the shining rubies embedded into the skin of his hands, Markus saw there a man of lustre and interest – and a man of importance, without a doubt.

"A champion rises, Verlunz," the handler cooed, her gaze catching in the low light. "As good as new, I'm sure."

The squat man turned to him, a wry smile pursing his lips as he made a slow nod of introduction. "We shall certainly hope so… does he speak?"

"It will take several minutes to return."

As if proving the point, Markus made to ask *'why'* to find his tongue lull stupidly from his mouth, producing some odd croaking noise from his throat.

"Well, I shall dispense with pleasantries then, and get to the point." The huge man swayed up the bedside towards him and lay a hand at its edge. "I am the Verlunz of Val Darbesh – I am the leader of this city and ruler of its people, and it has come to my attention from what I saw earlier, that you are a resourceful and prodigious fighter who has already proven his ability in the arena. I believe your handler here, is very much impressed by this news…"

"It was a surprise, to be sure, Verlunz… but a welcome one," she replied with a smile.

"Naturally." He paused to provide another slow nod of approval – a gesture of respect, Markus assumed. "Now, I imagine you saw your fight earlier as little more than an act of showmanship for the crowds," he continued. "Would I be correct in that assumption?"

Markus nodded, managing a slow *'yes'* too.

"And under normal circumstances, that would be entirely the case… these, however, are not *normal* circumstances." *What do you mean by that?* "Tomorrow, an envoy of the Iron Queen arrives in the city, seeking a new champion to take back to the capital, to enter into her service as a warrior. There has not been an inquest for a new champion in nearly three decades... so this is a rare occurrence indeed. We had two contenders for champion prepared to fight tomorrow... but it seems in their practice fights today, both have been killed." A smile pinched the edge of his cheeks. "One of them, by you."

"Champion?" was all he could reply, but within Markus felt his heart twist violently. *That's where this ends? They want me to contend for champion, to serve the Iron Queen?* A sickness trounced his stomach.

The person I came all this way to help Sav kill?

"Yes... it was quite remarkable," the Verlunz continued. "And now you will fight the other contender in the arena tomorrow – a fight of the ages for all to see, no doubt – to prove that you are worthy to serve the Iron Queen. It will be quite the spectacle, I am sure..."

"Who... who do I—"

"There is no need for idle talk, good man, all shall be explained in time. For the time being, however, the handler and I must go and prepare for the events tomorrow... these things are ruinously difficult to get right, and such a prestigious fight must exceed expectations at *every* level." He turned back to the handler, who bowed her head. "Shall we, my dear?"

"Of course."

Markus tensed. "Wait... *wait*..."

A final glance back to her champion, and the handler snaked off behind the Verlunz into the corridor beyond, leaving the hollow confines of the room before him full of empty shadows – and leaving whatever pit gravitated within his soul, even emptier.

I can't do this, came the first thought. *I shouldn't do this,* followed as a second. *This is wrong.* The emptiness flickered around him.

What other choice do I have?

Without knowing, he had gone from the one-armed pit fighter to a contender for the champion of Tarraz, second only to the Iron Queen herself – whatever that meant in such a foreign, fractured land. Without knowing, he would fight when the sun rose against another contender he knew nothing about, in front of many thousands who didn't even know his name, to be shipped off to the heart of Val Azbann... *and kneel before the woman we came all this way to kill.*

A knot in his chest drew tighter: *is that not betrayal?* To fight, to survive, knowing to do so was to walk to the throne of the Iron Queen and serve by her side. To become the thing he'd travelled halfway across the known world to destroy – a betrayal of the pact he had made, long before.

But what's the alternative? What else is there?

But he knew the answer; it hardly warranted asking the question. *All that is left, is to die...*

The thought stabbed him deeper than any blade ever could. *To die a slave, or to serve against my will.*

There is no other way.

The realisation bit deep – his heart sunk like a stone. He had stared death in the face in the arena, danced the thin line it drew across the world. He knew its long gaze, knew how it lay forever waiting. Yet, as he'd known it before, it'd always been escapable: death, and its icy shadow, had always alluded him. But in the quiet confines of that chamber, knowing what awaited with the rising sun, Markus sensed its cold touch lingering about his chest, piercing through to his soul. Death knew the truth, just as much as he did.

That he'd sooner hand himself over to the blade than betray his only friend in the world to serve the Iron Queen.

Markus rolled his head back onto the pillows, a single curling tear tracing down his face. *My only friend in the world.* He didn't even know where she was – didn't even know if she was alive. His last memory of her, the person he'd trekked the Kazbaks with to keep safe and well, was her being dragged unconscious from the entrance of the viceroy's house by the same people who'd put him in chains too. He didn't know if she'd come too – he didn't know if she'd survived the journey, even if she had. For all he knew, she could've just been an etching on his mind now, a memory of a lost soul. For all he knew, she was dead and gone.

Where are you Sav? The silence ebbed on.

There would be no answer.

†

As the door to the cell fell closed, she watched the one-armed man begin to weep softly, gazing up to the ceiling with wide eyes. The latch chimed sharply as she slid it into the lock, laying a palm against the cold metal surface and looking up to the guard at her side.

"Reckon he has a chance?" the stern man muttered, arms crossed.

"Who?"

"Our new champion in there... reckon he has a chance of winning?"

She withdrew her hand from the door. "I'm not sure."

"A one-armed warrior rarely wins a good fight... but after his performance yesterday, takin' on that big fella like that... he seems to be something to be reckoned with, if anything." He pulled away from the wall. "Will certainly give the opponent a run for their money."

Yea, that he might – although she wasn't sure if that was true.

"Shiny!" a woman's voice hailed from the corridor, directed her way. "Come on, we have work to do!"

She looked to the door, a silent and solemn moment passing between, before turning her back on it and disappearing off into the chambers beyond.

A battle would be fought, come sunrise – with a victor that fate only knew.

†

Chapter 54

The Unrepentant

He's becoming unhinged.

Dusk lay fresh across a cold night sky, thin streaks of mist skimming the distant edges of the shoreline, foreshadowing the coming frost. Already the air was crisp in his lungs, a rasp like dragon's fire pluming from his nostrils. His toes remained tucked away in mud-tarnished boots, wriggling disobediently to stop them from seizing – fingers tapping the hilt of his sheathed blade, or wriggling under the tuck of his sash. Trying to fight off the rapid decline in temperature – failing at every turn.

He's becoming erratic.

Lining the edges of the road to his side, crossbowmen lined their sights out beyond the sparse trees to the south, tracing the winding gravel track as far as they could reasonably fire. They had dispensed with much of their armour, preferring instead to wear the thick undercoats from their packs, wrapping tight until they blended almost perfectly with the mossy rocks and shifting studs of grass along the embankment. It was quite an effort to pick them out from the din – the only points that marked them out in the dark were the small, shimmering bolts loaded along the crossbow shafts, twinkling like stars, ready to shoot down any foe who dared cross it. Beyond that, only the gloom of twilight remained.

He could endanger us.

Behind him, as the thick congregations of skeletal trees fell away and the road broke off into the dirt, a huge swathe of blotchy grassland dominated much of the landscape ahead. A steep incline rolled gently upwards along the horizon, the vastness of the Grey Plains stretching out beyond its peak, where the hollow eye of the night sky slowly broke across the dark above. To the northeast, where the ridge ended, a collection of small hills appeared like the ripples of a leaping fish, the indiscriminate glow of fire streaking its nearest edges. He had been sent away as they had made camp, tasked with setting up posts to watch the road while the rest of the army drunk in sweet merriment. Those who had been selected, now squat in holes awaiting the arrival of their poor comrades, had naturally complained – the commander, in his inebriated wisdom, had told them not to take it personally.

Wish I could say the same.

"When are we expecting them, sir?"

Darius sighed longingly, scanning the road hoping something had changed. "At any point now, if they've made good time." *Or if they aren't dead to some beast of the night.*

"And how long should we stay posted here, do you reckon?" the officer at his side inquired, his blonde locks tangling with each other in the wind.

"Concerned about the men getting cold feet, lad?"

"Think we're past that point, sir."

"I have a feeling you're right there."

He shrugged. "I look at it more as when an operation enters *futility*."

"A point from which we can safely assume they haven't survived the journey?"

"Precisely so, sir... well met." A pause. "I can't *possibly* imagine why they might not have made it..."

Darius smiled at the edges, picking at the ring of his middle finger. *Exhaustion, slaughtered by a predator, hypothermia... hell, they could've turned on each other 'til the last one for all we know.* He left it all unsaid, the obvious unrecognised – a silence ebbed on, echoing through the dusk, and the general could tell from the man's twitching gaze that the blonde officer had wanted him to say more.

"What say you of the punishment, sir?" he prompted eventually.

"It's not my place to say," Darius said. "It was an order given by superior command... my thoughts are of no consequence."

The officer lowered his eyes.

The general leaned in closer. *"Although I'd dread to think what logic a man can utilise if his answer to insubordination is to work 'em to death, ay?"*

A snort of laughter blew from the man's nose. "Right y'are, sir... right y'are."

Darius rose from his squat, stretching both legs, a creak of joints from hip to ankle. "That being said, I will be returning to the camp shortly to check over our supplies and check the commander hasn't thrown himself in a ditch... are you alright to keep watch and direct for now?"

"Of course, sir," came a curt reply. "Will you not be joining in with the drinks?"

Not if I can help it. "Sadly not... duty calls no matter the hour, and I think I'll be the only one not piss-drunk to do it."

"A noble cause as ever, sir."

That it is. He turned to leave, only to find the officer calling for him again.

"Sir," he said. "What should we do if the soldiers come back without the supply cart? Only Revek said..."

Darius ground his heels, turning into the moon. "You have your orders from the commander, and you know what the right thing is to do... I'll let you decide which is which."

He gave a quiet wink to the man's laughter and left for the camp.

†

"... and so I sat myself on the barstool and I asked her, I asked her 'so, how much'll it be to take you out for dinner sometime?' And she looked up from her glass and gave me one of 'em looks and said… 'you don't look like the kinda man who'd suit my tastes', all suave and sure of herself, like they all are. So… I raised my glass 'ere to her, and I said to her 'well, that may be… but I reckon I've got plenty of stuff packing that'll suit your taste, don't you worry." Revek gestured to his cock, near-enough shafting the small glass dangling in his hand, and every man and woman around him erupted with a barrage of laughter enough to shatter glass and rip oceans in two, slapping thighs and stamping boots, all manner of ale and spirits sloshing across the loose dirt at their feet.

Watching the merriments unfold in a star-studded blur, the commander swung backwards and leapt through the air onto a half-buried log, swinging back to the jeering crowd. With a toasting glass, a cheer swelled among those gathered, enticing a few of those from the other camps nearby to do likewise.

"When I was a young boy," Revek blurted, "and this was not that long ago, I'll have you know, you wicked types." A rumble of amusement in reply. "I was a middling man… with no great aspiration in the world, beyond takin' each day as it came… an' hoping I wouldn't get stabbed the next. But… but I'll tell you, with *absolute* positiveness… I would have never expected to get *this far* in all my life!"

Another cheer broke out among them, as the commander pranced across the log like a performer, gesticulating widely to the clouds streaking the skies above.

"Who'd have thought it? Who'd have ever *thought* that a measly boy like I – after all those years under someone's boot – would be leading you sorry souls out into the depths of the savage-land, to fight for these 'ere glories. Who'd have thought? Certainly not I, I'll tell you that." A pause; a sway; a swig of the glass. "Was a long time comin' though, and I'm *sure* you agree!"

A swell of *'yes, sir'* prickled the air.

"That miserable bastard of a king, denying us all this… think if he was still alive, today? Think how much of this mess would've never happened... how *boring* our lives would be. We'd still be moping about in that capital, or patrolling the villages like rotters, while the savage kind danced around on our fallen brothers and sisters... oh, so merry, so wonderful are we! Our treachery abounds, and you turn a blind eye! And I tell you" – a sway, boggle-eyed, catching sight of a rising moon above – "and I don't say this with venom... but part of me is glad that old bastard is gone. Aye?"

The affirmative left their lips.

"We've been wantin' this... *planning this...* for a long time now. And finally, we are here... savouring our glories, striking at the savage kind with all our imperial might... what a sight to *behold!*"

He raised a glass to the soldiers, bellowing the final words; the soldiers raised a glass in return and cheered out to him. A roar broke out, jumping from camp to camp, twisting across the firepits, howling like wind through the tents, soaring up across the valley's hills to either side and out onto the seafront to the east. Revek watched as the sky span and the roars continued to rise beneath him – for all he cared to believe, there was not a happier place in all the world than in that camp, drinking as if the night would never end. Singing about glories, past and to come – about the army, and duty, and the final realisation of what he'd always wanted, now beholden to him like the tight arms of a mother's embrace.

Power, he chimed with a grin. *And an army at my fingertips... a world at my dispense. Conqueror of the savage-land.* His grin widened.

What a sight to behold indeed.

Without much focus, his eyes lingered on the faces at his fire, the warm and pleasant glow of their cheeks. He raised glasses to several, gaze sliding back to the small, shadowy inlet of trees opposite, storage wagons stationary at their base. There was a rasp of wind catching at the branches, skimming the dirt path weaving at its roots – where he suddenly spied a familiar face, passing their encampment like a ghost, almost as if wishing he wouldn't be spotted...

"And would you look who it is!" Revek boomed heartily, spearing a finger ahead, all eyes turning to find what he had seen.

Stalling, lifting his head slowly with a grievous expression, Darius saluted. "Hello, sir," he said quietly.

"Please general, come and have a seat... drink with us! We are entirely endearing of new company, aren't we?"

A ripple of cheers went up, although with a notable absence of a few. Some kept their gaze fixed on the general, drinks planted at their feet in the thin mud, no longer up for the booze – it was only under the commander's prowling eye that they found some spirit to cheer too.

"A kind offer, sir, truly, but I have some business to attend to," Darius excused with a weak smile. "Work needs doing, even at this hour."

"Oh, come off it... seize up a handful of the men, set them to work. It should be no bother of yours."

"The only men we have spare currently line the roads to the south, awaiting our absent company to arrive."

Revek's mouth quivered. "And have they returned? With my *supplies?*"

"Not as of yet, sir," the general informed. "But they're due back any moment now."

"And they will be handled *properly*, should they return empty-handed?" The glass twitched delicately between his two fingers.

"They will be handled fairly sir, yes. Nothing for you to worry about... certainly not on a night such as this."

"And I charge the same to you, general! You should be here with us, not off doing meagre tasks. Come, sit, drink 'til your... heart's content."

"I maintain it is a kind gesture, sir... but as a superior officer, I feel I should be leading by example and doing my part, no matter how small the task." A few coherent eyes widened at the general's words. A few more found themselves sobering quite fast. All peered up to their commander expectantly, wondering what he had to say.

Revek stood atop the submerged log, swaying with the wind, lost in a world of his own. Whether by choice or that he was too drunk to tell, a few moments passed, and he did not rise to the challenge it. The silence seemed to trickle by, until the commander raised his glass skyward so it shimmered by the moonlight, and inhaled deeply.

"So be it, general... you may go," Revek mused.

Darius gave a nod and a salute, his stature visibly receding, as he turned to continue down the path—

"...I never liked weak men anyway."

The audible crunch of the general's heel as he drew to a halt pulsed through their ears like a strike of lightning. Several camps nearby were alerted, watching suddenly, soberly, at what came next.

"Oh, so that got your *attention*," Revek blurted, stepping down from the log, stamping his glass into the earth. "That got some *respect* out of you."

Darius turned back to the firepit, lifting his head to hold the gaze of his commander, the bristling glow of flame toying with the shadows across his chest and face, glistening across the embers of his eyes.

"Come, please... stand among us... let us *see you* for who you are."

Lumbering forward in his full suit of armour, the general was a frightening presence as he approached the fire's edge, arms folding across his chest, face awash with stern lines and darkness.

"You don't wish to sit, general?" Revek said, almost mockingly.

"With all due respect, *sir,* I am here with no intention of staying," came the icy reply.

"And why is that? Because you don't have the heart to be among your men, boosting morale? Because you look down your nose at them, and wish to be apart from them?" Revek stepped forward. "Because you do not entrust perfectly able people to do simple tasks for you... how is that supposed to make those around us now feel, hm?"

"I request my absence, because we are *at war,* sir... and because there are preparations that need to be made, that I do not wish to *drag* the soldiers from their celebrations to carry out. It is far easier to do it myself…"

"Never one to delegate, are you? Never one to *enforce the consequence*." The commander spat into the earth at his feet. "I see the look in your eye – I saw it back along the road, too. You think I act too *harshly* among my trusted people, that I punish them with too great a severity. That they deserve understanding… that they deserve *remorse*." A thin smile appeared. "As you so diligently pointed out, *general*, we *are* at war… with an enemy that is as remorseless as it is savage. Why treat the men with weakness when they will only ever need to exercise strength against such a formidable foe?"

"Because we are not Tarrazi," Darius growled. "And the members of this army, are not our *enemies*."

"And yet you treat them so." A wavering finger spearing his way. "Yet you treat them like poor, sad little children. It's why they have no great resourcefulness… it's why everyone must be guided and commanded all the time with no *thought* of their *own*. Because you plead to them, beg for them and pity them." A heavy pause. "Because you're *weak*."

No word came from the general, who stood much like a statue in the glow of the fire, his face rough as stone. Those around him appeared much the same too.

"And yet, when I try to be strong," Revek continued, spilling his words as he ambled awkwardly around the fire's edge towards him, "in all your *weakness* you still challenge me. Which is startlingly ironic, don't we think?" He hung his arms to the air, crossing the watchful eyes that sat around him. "First he is too weak to reprimand his men for their lack of order on the march…" Revek met the general's gaze and grinned. "Then he is too weak to reward them, when we finally make camp? How do you suppose they shall respect you when the time comes, if all you do is shy away from consequence? When all you do is play *weak games* and treat them as *children*…"

"I do not take my power for granted," Darius muttered suddenly. "And I certainly don't use it to belittle others."

"Oh, my dear boy, I am so *sorry*." The commander made a mocking motion of stroking his cheek. "Did I hurt your feelings?"

"I wasn't talking about me."

Revek's sly grin collapsed as he turned, catching sight of his soldiers, drinks out of hand, eyes peering up hollowly to him. Their worn faces; the inhibitions working therein. How cold and dark it was...

How they showed no love for him.

"They don't want consequence, they want fairness," Darius said softly. "They want strong mettle but a kindred mind. They want honest leadership: to be treated as individuals of a great and powerful machine... not as cannon-fodder, rank and file and nothing else. I carry out my duties while they celebrate, as that is the duty bestowed upon me as a leader... that is my care, to good and able men and women of this army, and I will never shy from that." The silence simmered for a moment, Revek swallowing painfully. "So, I say, with all due respect sir... that I am taking my absence and returning to my quarters to prepare for tomorrow. Enjoy your celebration."

The general turned, taking a single step, the rattle in his heart falling away – before he heard the quiet words of the reply.

"You are no general, you weak son-of-a-whore—"

Darius spun on the back of his heel, hand clenched like a bludgeon, swinging upwards to catch Revek across the jaw. The shockwave was deafening; the commander reeled backwards, feet swept from beneath him, clashing hard with the earth beneath, a spout of blood escaping his gob within a ream of saliva, ejecting like a fountain as the onlookers stood suddenly in shock.

"You're right: they won't follow a *weak man*," Darius thundered down to him. "So be careful which side of the line *you* fall on..."

Darius turned and left in silence, nothing more than a whisper spoken, the eyes of the mad drunk sprawled across the earth burning through his skull like a bullet. Knowing the anger that flared within.

Knowing he'd have to watch his back, come morning.

†

Chapter 55

Playing With Fire

It was an ugly side-street to behold, not that she knew any that weren't. Squat blocks of two-storey houses lined either side of the loosely-tiled path, blotching out whatever light the mid-morning sun could oblige. Every inch of the woodwork woven between the stone blocks had paint peeling, the black swell of mould creeping up the corners, spilling out onto the open drains that ran like parallel rivers at the road's edge. At the far end, a thick blockade of pale stone signalled the sharp rise up to the palace keep dominating the hillside above, etched in grey blocks and shimmering tiled pinnacles that speared the few clouds dotting the sky. Somewhere off in the wider city, the rattle and hum of the funeral procession meandered quietly, a solemn barrage of brass instruments whispering down the narrow streets. Many would leave their homes early to attend, and pay respects to their late king; some would do so in passing, or throng to the palace gates to hear their new Governor speak. Others would pay it no heed at all.

Some had different plans altogether.

"Is everything set?"

"Right as rain my dear."

"Depends on if Bearskin is as proficient as he boasts."

"Keep that shit up and I'll make you drink from that sewer."

Jinx smiled wickedly. "I'd like to see you try…"

Peering down the narrow street before them, her eye followed the trail of a small grey cat skimming the gutter opposite. Tail whipping behind absently, passing narrow alleyways drenched in a warm glow, she tracked as it turned sharply at the road's end and crossed out into the sun – her gaze stalling halfway, as she spotted a small circular grate embedded in the barricade of stone behind, its iron bars noticeably off-centre.

"You'll be pleased to hear," Jinx said, turning back to them, "that the job is as good as done… and Bearskin is not just a pretty face."

"And I'll make a pretty mess outta anyone who says otherwise, ay?" he added with a grin.

"Are we ready?"

"As we'll ever be," Shadow muttered. "Can't say I'm thrilled to stink of piss for the next fortnight."

Bearskin looked over. "Thought that was your natural scent?"

"Fuck yourself."

"Right," Jinx interjected with a flick of the hand, "let's get on with it."

They broke off from the alleyway in a thin line, hands in pockets, eyes lingering at the high towers of the palace keep above. No voices channelled the air around them; a sigh of relief passed that no other footfalls made their approach. The cat reappeared at the far end hoping to return home, but at the sight of the approaching figures draped in black cloth, the feline thought better of it and scampered away.

Bearskin pulled ahead of Jinx, not breaking pace as he swept down to a squat and, with some jimmying force, plied the grate from its sawn edges to let the others through. Jinx banked left, stooping opposite the huge man, grappling Shadow's shoulders as she hunkered down like a mushroom and shuffled awkwardly into the tube. Shivers came next, dismissing the option for help, his lean frame extending out into the stone cavern with envying comfort.

"Ladies first," Bearskin thundered with a nod toward the sewer.

Jinx rolled her eyes, hooking a hand around one of the severed bars and half-swung herself into the dark.

The huge man made a sweep of the side-streets at their backs, cautious of wandering eyes, before slipping into the putrid hole as well and fixing the grate back in place without a whisper.

As if nothing had happened at all.

†

I never wanted this.

Alvarez kicked out at the woman below cleaning his metal boots, catching her by surprise. Stood at ground level, with the Governor positioned on a raised wooden platform in front, the woman stumbled back and bowed abruptly, before scurrying off into the crush of workers still erecting parts of the stage against the palace walls at his back. The crash and hammering of metal pinged loudly in his ears; the coursing winds of mid-autumn whipped across the platform, howling violently in his ears.

I just wanted him to die and be forgotten.

The plaza ahead had been cleared of market stalls, its floors scrubbed bare until every stone gleaned like a shield wall caught in the morning sun. At the edges, blockading the narrow streets leading up the hill to the palace, the massive suits of red armour and prominent masked helmets picked out the imposing statures of the palace guards amongst the regular militias, who themselves bustled about like ants just in front. Already, people had begun to appear: at balcony windows with Provencian flags flying and blankets to keep warm; lining the streets and alleyways of the hill under the unnerving watch of the red-coats; peeling off from the funeral procession slowly coiling its way up the hill, the low thrum of brass and marching steel echoing out for many miles. Everywhere they seemed to appear, revering their dead king.

And yet we stand here, in remembrance of a coward.

Alvarez rubbed his heavy, black-ringed eyes, trying not to disturb the thin line of makeup there. There was a still-burning sweetness at the back of his throat, that coating of ethanol that was meticulously maintained each night in the sleepless gloom of his bed chamber, where he spent his time alone and pacing like a wolf shunned from its pack. Even then, he felt its tear across his skull – the lancing pain of consequence, the still-ebbing flow of the spirit biting through his veins. His stomach lurched; his legs would occasionally stiffen, forcing a misstep to hold his balance. Stood atop the platform then, the sun blaring down across his side, the stones before him like dazzling lights, Alvarez found little difference between his disconsolate body and that of the corpse being paraded through the streets below.

Death walks many avenues, he grumbled with a sigh, *but until I consider it due, it shall not dare walk mine.*

"The procession is approaching Palace Hill, sir," came the voice of General Ferreus, ascending the metal stairway to his right. "They'll be with us shortly, I believe."

"Good," he muttered. "Then we can have this over with."

"It's to give the people what they want, sir."

"And what's that?"

They locked eyes. "Answers, sir... for their peace of mind."

"My peace of mind was that he was burned and buried and forgotten and everyone took our word for it that he was even dead at all... but someone appears to have misplaced that." A pause. "I don't marvel at this pageantry... it does us no favours."

"It will at least... let the people know we honour them, and we honour the death of the king..."

"We honour *nothing*," Alvarez spat. "He was a weak bastard, sold our country off in pieces; delegating power to poor, hapless fools with no business in high office; letting Tarraz and our territories rot from the inside. Why honour such a wretch in this way? It's not good or noble of us..."

"You fear it gives the wrong idea?"

"I *know* it gives the wrong idea." His face hardened. "We've worked hard over the past few days to cement this power – to *legitimise* who we are. That we're strong, and that we mean business and we mean action. But with every *inch* that procession crawls up that hill, the king is cemented more and more like a martyr than the old fool he was. He becomes a bastion to the city's principles, even though he stood by not one of them. That we are here to do the work he never had the *guts* to do, means nothing. They will forget his past; they will forget his weakness and wrongdoing... *this*, now, will be the king they remember." Alvarez ground his teeth, lifting his head skyward to watch crows circling high above. "This will be the king they will compare with us, compare against us... and we can do nothing but watch and wait..."

The Governor's eyes lowered, skimming the wide plaza, down to the platform before him and landing at the floor at his feet. There, at the ends of his toes, a chasm between two lengths of wooden planks revealed a pitch-black void hidden away beneath.

And the eyes that lay there, watching him always.

†

A rat reared its head from a pile of sludge a few steps ahead, alerted to the sudden noise. Appearing from the tunnel at its side came a great swell of grey shadow, a head swinging side to side hissing and grunting, glittering gold rings dragging across the cylindrical walls. There were others, too: other shadows approaching from the dark, big ugly scary things with boggly eyes and mangled teeth.

A squeal of shock, and the rodent dived across the stagnant water skimming the sewer's base, half-swimming through the rotten gloom where lights began to appear at the far end.

"Lights ahead," Shadow whispered to those behind.

"What do they look like?" Bearskin rumbled.

"Holes in the ceiling, I think."

A furious scowl in reply – Jinx found her ears burning.

"A problem, Bearskin?" she teased, smiling.

"When you said that we were *'going through the arse-end of the nation'*," he grumbled, "I didn't think you meant literally..."

They approached the four openings in the ceiling and found the smell of faeces intensify. Another sewer stretched off into the abyss to the left, the scurrying of rats echoing therein. With no natural water flow – relying mostly on rainwater sweeping in from the outer sewer – the tepid fumes of urine stung their eyes, the saturating soles of their thin boots taking on less-than-pleasant liquids.

"Shall we check above?" Shadow mouthed behind her, listening out for any noises above.

"Shivers is the narrowest," Jinx replied. "Let him look."

The thin twig-of-a-man said nothing, easing his fingers over the edge of the hole above, and slowly lifted himself to a stand. A moment passed, Jinx's heart in her throat, before Shivers swung himself through the narrow gap with cat-like agility and thrust a hand back down to assist the next one through.

One after the other they filtered up into the wide lavatory, wooden benches with stone seals occupying both walls with an entrance door to the right. Illuminated by lanterns that produced a warm and inviting glow, beyond the foul smell of the latrines Jinx found it was a relatively pleasant chamber to enter up into.

"Glad to be out of that piss-'ole," Bearskin grumbled, brushing his legs down and stretching his back. "Where to next?"

"We're two floors above the prison block," Jinx announced. "By my estimation, out that door should be a short corridor leading to a set of stairs, at the base of which is our destination."

"What do we expect when we get there?" Shadow asked.

"A long passageway bathed in torchlight... and two guards who'll find us four mighty suspicious as we approach."

"Any way of getting around them?"

"There's only one way in and one way out."

"Leave it to me," Bearskin offered, raising his hand. "I have a knack for that kind of thing."

"Looking big, awkward and suspicious dressed in black?" Shadow said with a wink.

"And next time I do, it'll be at your fuckin' funeral." Stepping forward, his mouth curled into a smile. "Now c'mon... I haven't waddled in piss for nothing."

They exited into the stairway, pausing momentarily to assess any echoes above, Jinx shaking off her thin boots in a poor attempt to relinquish any residue. The swell of liquid at her feet squelched like a swampland across the stone, the discolouration of it twisting her guts. *Glad for a wash when this is over.*

Ahead, Bearskin gave a flick of his hand as an all clear, and they began the cautious descent down the first set of stairs, banking left at the base.

"You think he can do this?" Shadow asked her, trailing at her side.

"I mean... Bearskin is certainly endeavouring, but I wouldn't—"

"Not 'im... I mean your brother."

A knot in her chest formed, thinking of him in the cell, likely bruised and broken without food or fresh air, at mercy of an enemy he had once worked alongside – wondering of what strength he had left, if any, to stake a claim at freedom once more.

"My brother is many things... and tenacious is certainly one of them," she muttered, more so to convince herself than anything. "I think he'll make it out with us fine... although I imagine he'll be in a certain amount of pain doing so."

"Reckon they gave 'im a bruising?"

"If Ferreus got his way with him..."

"Is that the bastard who gave you that?" She pointed to the slit in her cheek, now healed over with a reddened scab.

"The very same."

"Then we can assume you're right... and wherever he is, your brother's probably more bruise than skin."

A pause rang out; Jinx ingested Shadow's words like lukewarm stew, fighting the urge to wretch. Thinking of her brother trapped away and chained, bleeding from the inside out – knowing it was Ferreus who'd done the dirty work.

I'll kill that bastard one day.

"Did he really do it?" the greying woman asked.

"Do what?"

"Protect us... mislead the army to save our skin?"

"It was his burden," Jinx muttered in reply. "He spent months in turmoil when I told him the business I'd gotten into. He knew with every bone in his body that he should've arrested me, and everyone I worked with, for what he knew. He should've put us all behind bars and had promotions piled at his feet... and yet he didn't. Some part of him said that he didn't want that – that he'd sooner lie to the army than betray and lock up the only family he had left. So, one day, he invited me to his office, sat me down, and made the deal: our protection, for our names. And, for every day since... he's honoured that – more than honoured it, in many ways. But it will always be his burden... and because of that, I will always look out for him, for the choices that he's made. Without him, none of us would be where we are, and doing what we do best." A lump in her throat, which she swallowed defiantly. "Doing this... coming down to free him and get him out the city to Eli and his children... this is my way of saying thanks." She blinked slowly. "This is my way of proving I'm not a burden after all."

Shadow clenched her shoulder, squeezing it twice, her gold rings rattling together like bell chimes. "Your brother is a good man... and if half of what you say is true, then our saving him is the least we can do." She stopped suddenly, drawing Jinx's face to look at her own. "And if that big bastard upfront tries to lay a single *finger* on you, for trying to free him... he'll wish he'd never been *born*."

A pat across the back and the old woman continued her descent, a wry smile crossing her cheeks as she glided deeper into the keep.

Jinx inhaled slowly, releasing air through pursed lips, and followed close behind. Thinking about her brother trapped away in a cell, soon to be a free man again.

To prove I'm not a burden, after all.

†

As the procession appeared behind the houses, and people began to filter out onto the main plaza where the guards had formed up to clear a path, Alvarez confronted his burgeoning disgust with a deep sigh and a wave of nausea.

Here it comes... the corpse of the masses.

Turning the corner, four thoroughbred horses appeared, swamped in layers of fine cloth and silks, ornamental gold masks suspended by a brace at their neck. The riders drew the beasts forward at a sombre pace, the channel through the crowds opening before them, just wide enough for the black-veiled carriage to streamline its way through behind. Catching a glimpse of its interior for a moment, Alvarez noted how the carriage was overflowing with flowers of red and green, a swarming mosaic of shifting buds and gaping petals that the crowds added to with contributions of their own. With the open-casket visible, the white-bound body of the king caught his eye suddenly, and held it there for far longer than he had intended, as if the sheer significance of the procession induced its own gravity. It was only the fanfare of brass screeching behind that eventually drew his eye away, and even then the awkward bewilderment at the sight of the corpse was only replaced by the nagging assault of a hangover.

At least I'm thinking straight, he thought, then grinned. *Probably means I need more.*

"Keeping it short and sweet, sir?" Ferreus asked from beside him, his thick mane of silver hair blushing in the wind.

"Considering my preference is to not do it at all, general," Alvarez replied, "what do you think?"

"I only ask, because I wondered if you had a hidden message up your sleeve... something about a new world order, or the glory of the nation... or perhaps a competition: see who can piss into the king's mouth from the furthest mark."

Alvarez watched his general grin; his own grin widened.

Don't tempt me.

The carriage swung into place beneath him at the very edge of the stage. Peering down, Alvarez looked over the interior and took particular note to the reimagined face that had been sculpted around the rotting original. There was an off-putting peace about it, too much smile and rise in the cheeks – the dead man almost gave the impression of laughter. It was a contentment that, upon sight, made the Governor's blood boil.

Think of how much you've left for us to clean up, he longed to scream. *The war that you left simmering for twenty-five years, and did nothing about. How we backtracked, and submitted, and had power wrought from our hands by those we were destined to control. Of how little consequence it ever meant to you... and how, in death, you laugh at us, because you escaped those consequences.*

His eyes lifted, out across the crowds amassed before him. Expectant faces and cautious eyes everywhere; grand supporters with flags held high, marked with awe at the military man who now led them; fearful mothers and fathers clutching their children, wondering about family and kin marching the vastness of the savage-land many miles away; soldiers, his own people, looking to their old commander not only as a friend, but now as a statesman too.

In death, you laugh at us because you escaped those consequences. His eyes lowered back to the king, bathed in flowers he never deserved. Alvarez cleared his throat.

What remains now is only mine.

†

Stooping low to the stairs, staying just above the bend in the ceiling before it stretched out along the corridor, Jinx spied two pairs of steel boots at the far end stood abreast to a hefty steel door, and nodded her head.

"The plans were right," she muttered, lifting gently to a stand, meeting the apprehensive gaze of her companions. "Just a single corridor with two guards at the end and a door stood between 'em."

"If there's no way o' sneakin' up on 'em," Shivers mumbled, "surely they'll raise the alarm, as soon as one o' us starts walkin' down that corridor there…"

"Indeed… although apparently, one of our number has a *'knack for this kind of thing'*, if I do recall correctly."

Turning to him, Bearskin produced a foul smile, several gold-plated teeth shimmering in the torchlight. "It's less of a knack," he admitted. "More that brute force hasn't let me down yet…"

He descended the stairway, not providing an ounce of consultation before passing into the guard's line of sight of the two guards – guards who, by the rustle of metal, were immediately alerted to his presence, and were none too happy about it at that.

Jinx watched as Bearskin crossed the stone floor in great strides, the guards hunkering down and reaching for their swords. The left man held a hand out, sword rounding in the other, demanding he stop and explain why he was there so quickly, voice wavering as the huge man refused to falter. Four strides later, and the right-hand guard issued an uneasy warning.

Four strides after that, and he was upon them.

Right lunged out with her blade; Bearskin sidestepped, grappling her around the wrist, with a single pulse of pressure crunching several bones in her hand, forcing the sword to drop.

Left swung across his body; Bearskin relinquished his grip of the other and ducked the attack, darting to the side and pummelling the man's blade against the stone – a clatter of metal, and he too was disarmed.

Right swung forward, grabbing at him; the huge man rounded with a fist, catching her across the temple, spiralling into the opposite wall, head crashing against a wooden beam. Blinkering eyes, a few stumbles, and she collapsed in the corner like a limp puppet.

Left swung with his other hand; Bearskin reeled back, the man's knuckle brushing the tip of his nose. A breath, and the huge man balled a fist once more, hooking the guard under the chin. Lurching backwards with a crunch of teeth, the guard connected sharply with the wall behind and crumpled into the corner, a near match of his counterpart slumped on the opposite side.

Bearskin stood back and rolled his shoulders, satisfied with his execution.

"Made short work of 'em," Shivers exclaimed, kicking one of their boots.

"Told you I had a knack for it," the huge man said.

"Is the door open?" Jinx inquired from behind.

"Are we not going to acknowledge what I just did?"

"I think your ego needs a pin, not more air."

Bearskin glared at her with pupils like bullets, but decided against a rebuttal, trying the door instead.

Grappling a heavy turn-bar and wrenching it upwards, veins bulged in the huge man's neck as the lock slowly eased from the stone, producing a heavy *clunk* as the bar snapped into place and the door slid a fraction their way.

Jinx stepped forward, finger to her lips, as she eased her hand round the edge and peered into the expanse beyond.

"What d'you see?" Shivers whispered, jostling for her own look.

"Nothing," she said, almost in disbelief. "There's *nothing*..."

Peeling open the door, Jinx stepped into the opening of a wide passage stretching almost indefinitely ahead. Offshoots interspersed the left-hand wall, leading to rows and rows of cell blocks locked tight behind slabs of metal. For a short stretch to her right, a long window exposed an office chamber with wooden cabinets and candles still burning – a door at the other end, reading WARDEN in bold letters. It was a still space, unnerving in its casual silence, echoey and vast yet so helplessly barren. And as for the guards, the patrols, the prison warden and about anything else the plans had outlined, there was absolutely nothing to show for it.

"I don't understand..." Jinx took several steps forward, then several more, until she stood adjacent to the next row of cells, and found yet more silent emptiness. "Where is everyone?"

"Were the plans wrong?" Shadow inquired.

467

"I don't... I don't know. It doesn't make any sense."

"Do they know we're coming?"

"They couldn't have... there were guards at the door, on watch... they had swords."

"And they were surprised... they weren't expectin' us," Shivers added.

Jinx wracked her mind. *I don't understa—*

Her heart crunched inwards, eyes darting up, short of breath all of a sudden.

"They weren't surprised," Jinx said slowly, softly, with a great volume of hurt in her chest. "When Bearskin approached, they weren't surprised to see him." She turned back to the entrance. "They were surprised he got here so fast..."

A snap of the lock; the huge man stepped away from the sealed door, a sword hanging from his grasp, a cold stirring of joy etched across his face.

The traitor in their midst.

"You should've seen it, really," he boomed. "I never wanted this – I never cared for you, or your brother, or this cause of yours. Not one *bit* of it." He raised his sword towards her. "And *you,* you conniving little *bitch...* you sold us out, made us look like fools so that you could keep your pretty little toes out of deep water. You sold us out to that fat prick and gave him *everything...* and I couldn't have *that*." A stride forward; Shivers and Shadow reached for their blades. "So, I made a deal of my own."

"What have you done?" Jinx spat, the floor opening up beneath her.

"I gave you what you deserve." The gold-plated teeth re-emerged. "I sold you out to Ferreus. I told him about your little plan – I told him everything, and I made a *deal.* To keep it nice and simple. No guards... no messy operation... all set up to make it look like an *accident.* And if Arrenso dies in the crossfire of what comes next, then so be it – my side of the bargain only relied on one thing." He strode forward, a massive titan of a man swinging his sword as if it were a toy. "My freedom... for *your head.*"

He was suddenly in motion, a goliath of muscle and steel. Scrambling back, Jinx reached for her short-sword, Bearskin lumbering towards her, mad-eyed and blood-crazed—

Shadow crossing into his path, blade raised against him.

He stopped, snarling. "This doesn't *concern* you."

"You will not lay a *finger* on her," she growled.

"Why do you protect her?"

"She's done nothing wrong."

"What do you mean she's done nothing wrong? She sold us *out!*"

"We wouldn't *be here* if it wasn't for what she did! They'd have locked us up and torn everything down years ago, but they *didn't*. I don't agree with how it's been done... but that does *not* mean I'm about to let her die by your fuckin' hand."

"If you walk away, no one has to know you were ever—"

"I made a *deal,* you bastard — and unlike yourself, I intend to stick with it. We are leaving this prison with Arrenso, whether you like it or not."

His face bloomed like thunder. "Get out of my way, *now.*"

Shadow ground her heels across the stone.

Something verging on disappointment glossed the huge man's face, before he ground his teeth and lowered into a fighting stance.

"So be it," he muttered.

"Jinx, *run!*"

A clash of blades chimed through the air; Jinx turned tail and bolted. She had no time to think, hardly enough time to breathe. A sudden flush of heat up her neck, snapping at the ends of her fingers. Corridors and blinking lanterns rose and fell away to her left; the grey-black blur of heavy stone walls stretching off to her right. The distant scrape of metal at her back, snapping and hissing, blade kissing blade — the sounds of a traitor bloodying his way to freedom.

How she so wished to kill him herself.

That bastard... I should've known. She growled through gritted teeth. *He cut the bars, secured us the equipment, has men stationed at the plaza to cause a diversion if we run into trouble... and then this.* Her sword burned at her side. *Should've seen it from the start... self-serving creatures like him can't be reasoned with, not without getting their own way.* Sweat lining her forehead; hands clenched into fists. *I should've known...*

Fucking bastard!

The corridors ticked by as she ran, the end before her rearing from the shadows at a frightening speed. Skidding to a halt, not risking a glance behind to assess the carnage, she lunged down the fourteenth row and screeched Broska's name, hammering against door after door, side to side, praying to hear some reply, some faint whisper of life that told her she wasn't too late.

Where are you, Arrenso?

A dozen doors passed by with hope fading, until Jinx ground her heels suddenly. Refusing another breath, she listened closely, beyond the distant clash of metal – and found the faint rumblings of a voice somewhere just ahead of her, so fractional and obsolete that it almost ceased to exist.

She stumbled forward, hands tapping along cold walls, passing two doors and landing on the third, where the sound came at its loudest. Laying her ear to the icy metal, all other sound falling away beyond the whisper of her breath, she lifted a fist and made a single knock.

To find a voice in return, calling her name.

A voice she knew all too well.

She slipped to a crouch, sliding a thin metal rod from her belt, pressing desperately into the lock mechanism with awkward tugs. Twisting, grinding, stalling – twist, grind, stall, twist, grind, stall, twist, grind—

Clunk.

The lockpick slid from her hand, pattering against the tiles between her feet. Her heart thundered in her chest; there seemed to be no air in the world around her. Slipping a finger around the door's edge, she stood as it slowly tipped open and peered inside.

Broken and bruised, a welt of blood still dripping from his chin, Broska looked up into the eyes of his sister and found the strength somewhere deep within him, to smile.

"Arrenso…" Jinx rushed forward, wrapping her arms around his neck, a tiny stream forming at the corners of her eyes. "Arrenso…"

"I'm okay, Alva," he spluttered, bubbles of blood popping in his throat. "Just a bit bruised, that's all…"

She stepped back. "Who did this to you?"

"Think you know the answer to that… an' he'll do it again if we… if we don't get moving. How'd you get here?"

"I'll explain that later… you're just gonna have to trust me, and do as I say."

"Just get me free… that's all I ask."

"Way ahead of you," she muttered, straining as she unfastened the lock above his head, and Broska's hands slipped free of the suspending chain.

He landed on his feet, knees buckling. Jinx swung her arm beneath his shoulder and hoisted him to standing, recognising how much lighter he was than before, how gaunt and shallow his breaths were.

"They haven't been feeding you… have they?" Jinx examined, guiding him sideways out the cell door.

"Only the scraps… and only from certain guards," he wheezed. "Mind you, it ain't the food I'm missing." Sliding from her grasp, finding his own awkward balance, his haggard face seemed to flutter at the open air. "I'd murder a bloody drink right about now…"

She gripped his shoulder. "All in good time, don't you worry."

Jinx glided back along the narrow corridor and pressed against the nearest wall, Broska ambling up behind her clutching a pink-blue dilation on his thigh. She held him back, drawing a finger to her lips, and tilted her head to survey the stone passage.

Shivers' corpse sat against the warden's door at the far end, mouth agape with a blade rammed down through his neck. The floor coursed with his blood, a small lake of it with a few stray footprints outlining the dynamics of combat, like the hovel of some abattoir where a butcher gutted his prey. But from the blood to the body to beyond, for the fourteen rows to the exit door at the end, Jinx found no living soul besides – and couldn't find any relief from that fact either.

"One of ours is dead," she said bluntly, turning aside. "There's one other somewhere around here who'll help us."

"Meaning there's a third?"

"There is… and he wants my head… for his freedom."

"He wants your… what *freedom?*"

Her words faltered. "It's… I'll tell you later." *Although I have a feeling, I'm gonna fear that conversation more than getting outta this mess.* "C'mon, let's go."

Dragging him by the forearm, they skimmed the inner edge of the wide passage, stop-start motions to survey each adjacent corridor as it came, darting to the next a heartbeat later. Their pace was slow, agonising at points, Broska forced to stop and crunch his pelvis to keep his legs moving. He pleaded for her to slow down, passing row upon row of cells, but Jinx knew they couldn't – knew that somewhere, anywhere in the intersections ahead, Bearskin was lurking, hunting them with a bloodied sadism, each step forward drawing them closer—

A roar suddenly bursting from ahead: Shadow's voice, full of anger and pain. Grinding to a halt, Jinx swung right down one of the corridors, near-throwing Broska with her out of sight as she ran…

Pacing out into the open with blood dripping down his arms, Bearskin inhaled deeply, a red-streaked blade tensed in one hand. Sensing motion, his neck snapped left, catching sight of a flash of black and beige sliding from view. Not the garments he wore – not the clothes of any others, either. Something different; someone *found*. He smiled, turning back the way he came…

Jinx hurtled down the passage, Broska finding some ounce of power to run at her tail, the rasping wheeze of his ruined lungs like trying to ring out damp cloth. Lights blistered; the metal doors shimmered as they passed. All in a daze, lost to him.

They reached the end and banked left sharply – Broska coughed blood across the stone wall and skittered across the tiles to keep pace.

The end of the corridor sprawled ahead, a mere five rows away, the back wall rising to great them—

A great shadow, emerging from the third row – a bloodied blade slicing through the air towards them.

Jinx unsheathed her own weapon, driving it upwards to meet the attack mere inches from her head.

"Why'd you never fucking *listen*," Bearskin growled, sliding the blade away and striking again. "This would all be over so much sooner if you just *hand him over* and *die...*"

"I won't give you the satisfaction..."

Jinx parried several strikes, blanching left-to-right. Fearing the strength of his attack, she swiped through suddenly, scoring a line through the black leather across his stomach, a sheen of blood splintering along the tip of her blade.

The huge man snarled. "You *bitch.*"

Bearskin grappled the back of her skull; she squealed as he lurched forward, a sudden explosion of pain as he landed a punch across her temple.

Jinx was thrown backward and slid across the tiles, a black-red bloom consuming her vision. A spinning flux of colour breaching all things; lost sensation in her legs – leaving nothing between her brother and the traitor, who stood with sword gleaming and wicked death in his eye.

"And *you!*" Bearskin snapped. "You fat foul *creature...*"

He struck down in an arc, blade sweeping lazily through to cleave open his neck—

In an unseen spur of motion, Broska sidestepping gracefully, pulling something from his side, lunging out—

Stabbing Jinx's lockpick through the slit in his abdomen, ramming it deeper with gritted teeth. Bearskin's eyes bulged like a netted fish.

"Have it, you prick," Broska spat.

He hooked Jinx under his arm and charged down the corridor Bearskin had emerged from. The huge man at their back bellowed at the top of his lungs, hands clasped around the metal point embedded in his chest, rageful in his disbelief at what had happened.

As Jinx regained her composure, she found that whatever adrenaline Broska had conjured to dodge the attack fell away almost as soon as it had come. Sudden contortions of pain lanced his face; the run crumpled into an awkward hobble. Weight shifted as they ran, Jinx taking the lead, but with the growing concern for her brother's health as he seemed to wither with each step, whatever mark she saw scored across his stomach ballooning with a ferocious agony.

They banked right at the far end, an abrupt splashing at their feet as they crossed the pool of Shivers' blood. They passed him by, no time spent reminiscing, his head eyes watching on with nervous twitches that persisted even in death.

The door reared before them; Jinx heaved forward, plastered in sweat, praying they had made it before—

The thunder of footsteps, and something connected sharply with her side. She slipped on the blooded floor, arms swinging, crashing down. Head rocking against the stone, the world a sudden agitation of colour and light and not much besides. Hands reaching out, a shadow staggering before her, silver blade in hand.

Looming towards Broska.

"You should've *died* when you had the *chance!*" Bearskin roared.

"I've done nothing wrong..." the general muttered sadly.

"*Lies!* You kept secrets of us... knowledge you had *no right* to have! We were sold out to you, all on the fragile *promise* that you'd keep your mouth *shut*. These bastards may have been lenient and taken your word... but I make *no such offering*. For what you've done, for what you *know*, the only guarantee" – he raised his sword – "comes in death..."

A twist of the hand; the blade struck down.

Jinx screamed at the top of her lungs.

From the left, metal flashed through the air above her.

Bearskin stopped.

His shadow, fixed in motion above her, stood fused in place. Jinx blinked furiously, steadied her gaze to trace the outline of his body, from the sword coiling above his head to the frightful intensity of his eyes, skimming along the nape of his neck and down the rivets in his back.

Where a knife now rested, its shining handle wedged deep between his ribs.

Bearskin took a single step forward, the sword clattering to the ground in a splatter of blood, his hands scratching at his shoulders trying to reach the knife buried between. Moments passed, as death pounded the lever at his door, and suddenly he began falling, plummeting almost, and landed along his side in a pool of blood, with life receding from his cold, grey eyes.

Treachery, now no more.

Jinx dragged herself up the wall, hands blotched with red, breath little more than a trickle staring at the felled body shivering silently in the blood. Broska rushed over suddenly, drawing her eyes away, embracing her tight. In the crush of his arms, the warmth of his body against her own, some humanity returned — stood in a pool of crimson dead, sweat-plastered and struck with fear, with only a brother left to her in all the world.

He peeled away, holding her shoulders. "It's okay," Broska exclaimed, a warm glow in his eyes. "It'll be okay." He looked to his side, out past her towards the far door. "Although you couldn't have left it any later if you tried!"

Turning, Jinx spied Shadow hobbling out from the end corridor, a huge slice across her arm and leg. "You'll have to excuse me... I was never good with knives," she said with a smile, looking across the carnage before them. "And we certainly made a god-awful mess here..."

"That we did," Jinx replied, the shock and relief all melding into one. "That we did..."

"Then let us be here no longer," Broska declared, sliding his arm through hers. "Freedom awaits... for however long it allows."

Arm in arm, dragging themselves from the blood and carnage of the prison, they crossed to Shadow and unlatched the metal door, climbing the stairs to the lavatory and the sewer, and from there, by some miracle, to the freedom beyond.

†

Alvarez lifted his hands skyward, a cool breeze whipping through his hair, the amassed below him bursting with applause.

All hail me.

The speech had landed every note, proclaiming the nation's power and the justice he would bring, befitting all and failing none in the sweep of their new regime. At the final tones, when he had pronounced their decisive power on the battlefield, and a return to long-forgotten glories, the crowd had erupted in cheers. Whatever had been, had passed – what there was now, embodied by him, they supported. With every raise of his hand, the cheers swelled louder still, carrying his vision with a grandeur unseen in decades.

The people have rallied at last.

He turned to the stage, where fellow officers were applauding, looking to him with wide eyes and fulfilled hearts. Stepping away, matching their gaze with smiles of his own, he landed on the expression of his second-in-command.

And knew immediately that something had gone wrong.

"What's *happened?*" he growled, a flush of anger rising above the pride.

Ferreus turned from the messenger, his face worn thin and pasty, as if someone had plastered it together with cement. "There's been... some kind of incident in the prison block, sir," he blustered. "Someone's broken in..."

Alvarez gritted his teeth, fists curling.

"... we've been told one of the prisoners has escaped."

He struck out, grappling Ferreus around the throat, drawing him in close.

"What did you *fucking say?*"

Tugging at his chest plate in a swamping of fear, the general squirmed in his grip like a maggot. "There's... been a *break-in...*"

Alvarez tore his grip away, swiping at the fleeing messenger, snagging his shirt collar and drawing him back. "Where are you *going?*" he boomed. "I have an *order* for you."

The fragile face turned to him. "Yes, sir...?"

"Get *everyone* on patrols, scour every street. Find me *General Broska*." Alvarez cast him away, half-throwing him down the stairway. "And bring me my *fucking horse!*"

†

Chapter 56

The Room of Shadows

He knows.
The wide doors yawned open as they approached, the dragon-horn throne stood proudly across the back wall, the ruminating shimmers of light from the windows dancing across the wide table. The great edifice was black as night, a stoic remnant of a shadowed past, revealing nothing of the towering figure in its seat except for the pair of pale, unblinking eyes buried at its centre that studied her long stride down the corridor. Always watching, always waiting.

The shadow woman.

She paid no heed to the pacing guards at her side, pushing at her arms to keep up – paid no heed to the high ceilings and broad pillars supporting the wide corridor around her – cared little for the tension that seemed to swell voluminously before her, as if entering a cloud of smoke. Instead, her eyes remained locked to the floor, tracing the rivets in the tiles; the left-right-left-right of her pale, scar-ridden feet, and the shackles dangling like a pendulum between, squeezing tight across her wrists.

The totems.

Reaching the doorway, one of the guards shoved her forward with such force that she nearly buckled over the low chair just ahead. Disconnecting their chains from her own absently, they stood back as she slid into the seat and rolled her tongue across the roof of her mouth, a great sigh echoing out as she finally lifted her head.

He knows.

"Hello again, General," the Alderbane rumbled. "Have you been keeping well?"

"If by well, you mean fed scraps once a day, cutting my feet on broken stones and spending nights sleepless on a bed of solid-cut rock," Cavara mused, "then yes, sir, I am doing *well.*"

A crooked twitch at the corners of its mouth. "I appreciate this is not your typical accommodation."

"I've been a prisoner of war and *waterboarded* in the dead of night... and have still slept more'n I have in that cell."

"And you bear the marks of a soldier sent to hell and back." A finger rose from the throne-arms, pointing to her chest. "That one says as much, wouldn't you agree?"

"That I *would,*" she growled, dismissing the gnaw of sickness as the knot of skin pulsed across her stomach.

"I see that it perhaps bears the greatest pain for you, in all this."

"It is the mark of a traitor... made worse by the fact that I will likely never get to wound him the *same.*"

Something verging on surprise crept into its hollow face. "I thought of you as many things, when I first saw you, but never the vengeful type."

"Your initial thoughts were correct" – she locked eyes with the throne – "but exceptions have to be made."

A single nod. "Then it is even more of a shame, that your initial thoughts are also correct."

"How so?"

"That you will never get the chance at revenge."

Cavara found the storm settle within her, now just a trickle of rain to cold earth. No bite left, in the end. "So, it's death then?"

"Perhaps," the Alderbane said slowly.

"There is no *perhaps* with an execution... if you'll have me die, cut the shit and get on with it – I've suffered enough as it is."

"For someone with such strength and defiance, you spin an awful lie."

"How do I lie?" she spat. "Have I not suffered? Have I not been bent to your whim, trapped in that dark abyss for long and unending days, wondering when I'd finally get that mercy of death, or the bitter cast of exile?" The heat rose in her face. "Tell me, oh *great one*... where is the lie?"

"Because if you were to die willingly, by my hand... you'd be a traitor to your cause," it said callously, "abandoning your people as they die in their thousands, leaderless and broken... and to find you, sat there like a helpless child, wishing upon that weak mercy of death because you never had the bite in you to do something about it." the Alderbane hunched over the table. "You'd be no worse than the man who gave you that mark..."

Cavara leapt from her seat, hands open like the talons of an eagle, rageful machinations painted pale across her skin. Spilling over the table, her heels had pushed away from the stone before the guards swung forward to grab her. Clawing and snapping at the faceless gaze lowering back into its chair ahead of her, she fell towards her seat again with hands braced to her back in restraint.

"I think our guest here may need some more time before she can face some bitter truths," the Alderbane commanded. "I have nothing more to say."

With a wave of its frayed hands, the guards started manoeuvring the general away from the chair back towards the door, the world slipping away before her – again, much as it had always done. Knowing this was another wasted moment, cast away so recklessly. That something needed to be done – something had to break the cycle.

Then it came to her, the striking blow of true reality.

He knows.

"I know more than you will ever know!" Cavara screeched, heels grinding across the stone. "I know about a world you will never know... I know about the shadows; I know about the totems... a white world of light that comes to me in my dreams. I know about the *shadows*—"

The Alderbane speared its hand skyward, forcing the guards to a juddering halt. "What *shadows?*" it asked forcefully.

"Another world, real yet never so... a lost place in the clouds," she proclaimed. "I've seen it... more than you can know."

The Alderbane said nothing in reply, a quiet composure twisting across its half-skull stare. Moments passed, air heavy in her lungs, watching the cogs turn in its omnipotent mind. Agonising, wrenching with the truth in all its unenviable grace, until its shoulders fell away and the withered hand lay flat across the table, and with a slow gesture Cavara was permitted to return to her seat again.

"Leave us," it boomed, as the soldiers bowed and swept aside, pulling the doors closed with a wrench of their hinges. A long silence rang out after that, the taut strings of the air lying still and subdued before the Alderbane finally spoke again.

"A land of shadows and clouds," it muttered, rolling a shrouded thumb across its fingers. "And a world as real as it is beyond belief."

"I was told you would know it," Cavara replied.

"In many ways, I do... although I have not heard it spoken about for an age."

Her heart ballooned, the air suddenly absent in her lungs. "You *know?* You know that place?" It came with disbelief, almost as a plea – someone had answers, ones she had longed to find. "What do you know? What is it... how do I...?"

"What I know is an ancient legend – I do not possess the answers you want..." it responded sharply, a moon eclipsing her newfound sun. She was about to blunder a farcical reply, begging at her knees, before the Alderbane spoke again.

"But I know where to find them."

She watched as it leaned down below the table to grapple something, and moments later, a metal wrenching sound crackled to life. With a sudden breach of motion, the slate beneath her arms began to shift. A ridge formed at its centre; two squares pulled apart like a rift valley, juddering motions taking them wider still, until they disappeared within the table altogether.

And she was left staring at five totems etched into the stone beneath, a pit opening up between them, threatening to swallow it whole...

"This has been here since the nation's founding," the Alderbane explained. "Locked away before the throne of kings, queens and usurpers alike, stretching back hundreds of generations. It was the marvel of the ancients, and the enigma of their finest scholars – none knew what it was, or what answers it hoped to reveal. According to the archives in the palace vault, the etching you see before you has not been accessed in three-hundred years." It withdrew its hand and gazed upon her curiously. "So, my question to you, is: does this look familiar?"

"The first time, in the vision... I *saw* it." The words fell off her tongue, as she stared vacantly across the carved surface. "I awoke to the sound of a singing woman... a shadow woman. I didn't know where I was, or what was happening, so I... I ran to her, followed her, and then the walls became grey and..." Her heartbeat swelled in her ears, pulsing with the vacuum that had opened in her stomach. "And then those totems appeared, and the abyss opened beneath... there was a voice in the air, and it was saying things... and then it spoke to us, and the shadow jumped." A quivering sigh. "Then everything went black."

"What did it say to you?"

"It said, *'there can only be one'*..."

"Only one of what?"

"I didn't find out." *I've never found out.*

The Alderbane gave a single nod, fingers splayed over the table edge. "Did the totems do anything, when you saw them?"

"Not the first time, no... they were just there."

"There was another?"

"I witnessed them again in a second vision... as I was attacked."

"What happened?"

She thought back to the pale void. "I tried approaching the totems, to see what they were... to try and make sense of *something* in that place. But as I ran, or so it felt, a shadow stepped out from one of them and... *attacked me*."

"Was it the same shadow as before?"

"I assume... I don't really know." *I don't know anything.*

"This woman, is she someone you know? Was there any feature to her that caught your eye?"

"She was..." Cavara closed her eyes. *She was just a shadow.* "There was nothing... I have no idea who or what she was." *I don't know much of any of it, in truth.*

"You say you were attacked – how did you then escape, this shadow woman?"

"I was confronted by her, attacked by her... I thought I was gonna die or something. But as she spoke to me, words formed and I... I said something back... and it was like a *ripple*, some shift in the world around me. She seemed in disbelief, as if what I'd done was wrong and I don't know why." A flash of a tear clicked at the edge of her gaze. "And... and then one of the totems, it seemed to respond to my voice as I spoke, matching the pulse of my heart... almost like it was—"

"Calling to you," the Alderbane finished, sliding back into the throne, a thoughtful pause as it considered. "So, the legend is true."

"What legend? What do you know?"

The eyes fell to the totems, then back to her. "There's a doorway, located deep within the palace vault beneath us, that was buried for near two centuries under rubble. Writings in the archives said it was an unopened chamber sealed shut and never opened – a place the inscriptions call '*The Room of Shadows*'."

The word seemed to resonate within her. "Who discovered it?"

"A priest, studying the ancient texts... he was only in the city long enough to see it uncovered, before going into exile."

Cavara flinched. *Brutus?*

"We knew little about it, other than that it was very old, and made of a very ancient material not known to modern craft," the Alderbane continued. "None have been able to open it – all we have gained from its discovery is the inscription across its seal."

"What does it say?"

"That only those who heed the totem's cry may enter… only those kissed by the All-Mother, may know the truth of the world."

A frozen shimmer passed over her, as the Alderbane spoke. The pit of her stomach compressed and snapped; her heart dangled from a cord, threatening to split away. *Only those kissed by the All-Mother,* she thought, the knot across her chest buckling angrily, *can know the truth of the world.*

Just as Evelyn said on the boat…

"What does it mean?" she pressed.

"I do not know – no one does," came the simple reply. She sensed its gaze pass to her. "Although if what you say is true, and the totem has called to you, then you may be the only one who can find the answer."

The room began to spin. "What must I do?"

"To survive a fatal wound by the Mother's kiss, and to hear the summons of the totem in the visions of the void… is a great unknown to us all. By our understanding, those who have forgone such things must enter the Room of Shadows, and learn why they are chosen to hear the truth of the world. That is how it must be – that is what you must do."

The truth of the world. "And then I will have answers? Then I will be free of this… whatever it is?"

"I don't know what you will find in the beyond," the Alderbane said slowly, a certain peace returned to his gaze. "No-one has known of this other world for over three hundred years – there are no answers for you to be given, except those you find yourself." It rose from the dragon throne, its huge form towering like a great tree before her. "All I know is that you are chosen by the Mother's hand, and drawn by her light… and that what you will find in that room, is a truth unlike any the world has known in generations."

Cavara took in a deep breath, lungs quivering, a silent numbness echoing from her neck to her toes. She realised she was sweating, yet strikingly cold – everything wouldn't stop spinning. There was a path, suddenly, a place to go. Answers to her questions: an answer to the visions that had plagued her every motion since that fateful day she should have died. All of it, suddenly within her grasp.

The truth of the world.

She rose from her chair on trembling legs, exhaling lengthily, and levelled her eyes at the Alderbane with all the defiance she could muster.

"Whether I am to live or die, or whether the void shall take me as its own and I never walk this land again... I will have my answers, and I will know the truth of all things." She smiled stoically, nodding her head.

"Take me to the Room of Shadows."

†

Chapter 57

Champion's Honour

When I first met you, I thought you were nothing more than a foul cripple, ready to be butchered like swine at the first turn. How some one-armed beggar from Provenci could prove to be anything more than a warm-up game for some petty criminal was beyond my estimation – beyond anyone at that. We thought you'd be sent to the grave in a single stroke... betted good money on it too. And then shit happened, ay?" The handler paused, patting his face like a dog. "Then you went and defeated a champion – ripped his face in two, at that – and suddenly we have to pay attention to you... *I* have to pay attention to you, to the foul cripple who stared down death and came out laughing." She drew a blade from her side, handing it over to him. "Whatever you were before this... whatever you *thought* you wanted from the world, doesn't mean shit anymore. None of it does. There is this fight, and your place as the new champion of a nation, or there is death. There is nothing more, and nothing less. So, you will fight, and you will win." She dragged him close by the scruff of his shirt, so their noses almost touched. "And do *not fuck* this *up*."

She shoved him away, dismissive as much as impatient, as Markus stumbled up the sanded incline towards the arena at its peak, where the gates cracked open slowly and bathed him in a warm but unruly light. Every element in his body ached; knees buckled with each labouring step; the tight slit of the wound across his shoulder hissed angrily at the weight of the sword. Sand had caused rashes across huge swathes of his chest – blistering cuts had lacerated his waist and arm. No matter how much they treated him, the handler barking orders and pressing demands to have him nursed to full force again, the ugly truth remained steadfast.

I'm old, he grumbled, tugging at his chest plate. *Old and broken, like some gnarled fucking tree.* The sword burned angrily in his hand, the gravity of its purpose dragging him to-ground. *A foul cripple... who came to death's door laughing.* Sun-streaked walls ahead stung his eyes like tiny shards of glass. *Honour and duty, life and death – forgetting everything you once were, or wanted to be.* Eyes closing for a moment, inhaling the warm air, the lights danced like shadows behind his eyelids, forming the contours of a woman's face. The ripples of hair; the harsh lines across her brow – the metal plate bound to her cheek, as hollow and foregone as she had become. *Forgetting everything you once knew... how it means nothing anymore.* He opened his eyes. *And yet, because of her, the last friend I have known in this land... there is yet still something I hold onto, even now.*

The hope that she is somehow still alive.

Markus stepped out into the arena, the full force of the sky's eye scorching the pale sand ahead. Nothing had changed within the arena as far as his eye passed, but looking up to the sweeping stands he spied newly-erected flags and beaded spinners swimming in the low desert winds. It was a vast concourse of colour, with the huge crowds seeming to have almost tripled since the previous day: some hanging from the rivets in the walkway above; others almost spilling from the arena's edge with the spears reared threateningly below. All clashing hands and drums, roaring from end-to-end – *knowing today a champion will come.*

Tracing to the right, he spied the grandstands opposite: raised stone platforms draped in rivets of red silk, white-gold canopies erected overhead to shield those inside from the heat. Within them, little more than white-red dots from afar, leaders and officials had taken their seats with servants milling between, no doubt discussing the odds of the day and where to splash their imperial gold. Although he could hardly pick out one from any other, Markus did acknowledge the traditional robes of the Verlunz seated closest to the arena – and, slightly left from him, the grey-bronze shimmer of a coat of armour also present.

And there's our envoy, he considered, raising his blade to the cheering crowds. *The one we're all here to please.*

As the thought came, the noise from the stands approached its first crescendo. Rattling echoed into the dusted air; to the left of him, the thick wooden doors edged slowly open.

His first opponent had arrived.

Emerging from the gloom, a sculpture of a man appeared, a head and shoulders taller than Markus with enough muscular profundity to wrestle a bear. With branding marks and the scorches of iron bars dicing his skin and a whisker-like dash of hair across his upper lip, he was an ugly beast to behold. Brandishing a hefty axe in one tight fist, the enormous frame swung toward Markus and paced toward him, a snarl plastered to his wide face.

Excellent. The old man spat into the sand. *A cripple like me, fighting for his life – of course you'd pit him against a titan of a man for the first round.*

Testing the weight of his sword, he growled and started walking. *Of course you would...*

He screamed far louder than Markus had expected.

The axe landed somewhere off behind them. The brute's hand came away like a knob of butter; a crimson stump remained, with pearl bone at its centre seeing light for the first time. With the screech of pain came the look of despair – the wound gushed streaks of blood like a fountain, staining the pale stone at their feet, swinging around wildly as the imposing figure fought to stay conscious. The crowd let off a bellow at the romanticised violence.

Markus couldn't have been more disgusted.

What's the point? He brought his sword to bear, gleaming with sunlight, and struck across his body with a strong hand. The brute's throat burst like a bubble; half his shoulder ripped in two, carving a trench through his chest. The stunned eyes rolled to the back of his skull, hollowing almost immediately. Falling to his knees, the unconscious sculpture seemed all but lost to the world.

Crashing across the sand, and he was dead.

Such a waste of time.

Markus kicked sand over the corpse as the stands erupted all around him, turning to them with only brief acknowledgement as he trudged towards the partition to his right. Bringing death by the sword invigorated something within him; there was a weighty satisfaction to striking a man down in his place. *Comes as second nature,* he thought with a momentary smile, *and has marked me as a killer ever since.* The new grazes across his chest came as no consequence, the nagging in his joints only a minor ripple in his mind. For the purposes he had been given – *to fight, to kill, to entertain and all the rest of it* – there was nothing but he and the blade, a swordsman and his weapon of choice, fighter and opponent.

Champion, and prey.

The barricade he approached ground its gears and fell away; the crowds on the opposing side turned expectantly to the newcomer.

Markus looked out on the arena quarter and spied a heavy suit of armour lurching around the corpse of a woman, dissected in the earth as if placed atop a surgeon's table. The circling brute was clad at every point in stalwart metal plates, the pointed dome of their helmet twisting suddenly at the sound of approaching feet. From what Markus observed, there was not a single scratch on the shimmering form, as it rose to full height and twisted a massive longsword into view. Studying the blade, by his estimation the dead woman cut to ribbons across the floor could've hardly raised her sword before she'd been struck down, the massive weapon carving through her like a roasted hog over and over again.

Markus, his own blade streaked in blood, studied his opponent with intrigue, gesturing to the corpse sprawled adjacent to them. "Made short work of 'er," he said, circling cautiously with sword levelled.

"I'll make even shorter work o' you," came a woman's voice, stamping the ground like a stag. "Don't you worry."

"I'm not worried."

"And why's that?"

A sly grin appeared. "Because with how you're circling me now… I know you didn't get out of that first fight without a scratch…"

The woman stopped in her tracks, pressing down on her right leg —watching as it buckled at the hip, weighted awkwardly to the left. Her hand wavered down towards it, longing to nurse the pain, but stopped when she caught his eye and found his grin grow wider.

"It means *nothing*," she spat. "There's no way you can come out of this alive. You're a worthless cripple and I'll gut you like a fucking fish."

Markus shrugged. "So be it." He slid into a fighter's stance, sword glistening across his chest. "But I'd like to see you *try*…"

Sun-smothered and fuelled by rage, the armoured fighter scraped the earth and charged forward, a great expulsion roaring from her lungs.

Raising blades, the chime snapped across the sun.

Here we go again.

Shock was the last thing she knew, before Markus tore her helmet from its brace with a huge fist and rounded the other to punch through her nose. In a spray of blood and bone-shrapnel, the woman teetered backwards staring into the sun, cold air rushing up through the broken plates in her armour that lay scattered across the sand nearby – all this before her leg gave in, and she collapsed onto her back like a felled tree. A cosmic blur around her, the world snapped and shrunk as an explosion of pain bloomed across her face — any attempt to scream saw her gargling her own blood, now rocketing from the wound like a volley of arrows.

Markus swayed overhead, prickly with sweat, panting like a dog through battered lungs as his opponent squirmed below. His sword lay buried in the sand nearby amongst the debris of the woman's armour, blood weeping quietly down his heel from a fresh wound. Adrenaline still rallied at his side; the bite of violence still held him close like an adoring mother, despite the blistering heat across his head, longing for him to press on into the fray.

With the crowd bellowing for a result at his back, and the woman's helmet clutched tight in one hand, he was happy to oblige.

Clutching at the leather bindings inside, he stepped over the body and swung down into her mouth with the pointed tip of the helmet.

A squeal of liquid as teeth scattered, and an explosion of bone ripped through her mouth.

Another punch shattering her cheek, carving a hole through skin, eye spinning absently above.

A third strike, snapping through the temple, piercing the cavity within — a faint whimper escaping her tired lips, and a grey sheen fell across her eyes.

Markus threw the helmet to his feet and roared up to the crowd like an animal.

Your champion has come.

Every face gleamed his way; every set of eyes lay upon him, studying the champion with awe and wonder. Fists pummelled the air; roars echoed around the bowl and through his ears. Chanting the name of the foul cripple, who came to death's door laughing. The old fighter from another land, broken at the feet of the enemy, who travelled half the known world in the name of comradeship and duty. The ancient beast with a penchant for blood, defying every expectation in the arena of the gods. The survivor, armless and broken with more shrapnel than skin, drawn to the fighting pits as a fool.

Leaving them, as its hero.

Scooping his sword up from the ground, Markus paced towards the final barricade, banking closer to the arena's edge as the grandstand boxes honed into view above. Jumping between them, every expression he found was one of entertainment and deep interest: white-robed statesmen nodding resolutely towards him, gesturing to others about the fight ahead. At the crest of them, he watched as the Verlunz rubbed his porcelain palms together, rumbling with joy at the magnitude of the day – directing to the envoy in his brass coat, whom Markus realised was already looking to him as he approached. Although the gaze he met was one of judgement and resolve – a look that said the decisive end had yet to be made.

It seems the envoy still remains undecided, Markus thought. *No matter, I suppose... I shall win this next ridiculous fight, claim that I am champion, and then watch with complete satisfaction as I tell him and his precious honour that I'm not interested in being anyone's pet. Sav would never stand for it – she'd never be involved in any of this at all.* He gave a nod to the envoy; the envoy smiled and looked away.

So why should I?

The barricade groaned to life ahead of him. Clasped in his fist, the sword remained taut and resolute at his side. A deep inhale, sun-kissed and unwavering, Markus couldn't help but smile.

The partition fell. He looked out to his opponent, who—

†

Chapter 58

Our Weight in Blood

He counted at least eighty tents scattered across the grassy bowl of the Grey Plains, with dozens of horses milling at the southern edge within the crush of skeletal trees, and a sprawling canopy at the camp's heart lined with imperial standards. The screech of a pedal-grindstone rattled somewhere deeper within, rising with the commands of officers and the low hum of crackling fires, which even from afar against a coursing wind seemed obnoxiously loud for a place so serene.

"What a rabble," Revek grumbled, adjusting his spyglass from atop a distant ridge to the east. "Nothing subtle about 'em by any stretch."

"Hard to keep quiet, sir," Darius replied from his side, "with how many of them there are in that tiny space."

The assessment was obvious, but also true: there was not an opening between any visible tent he found where blackcoat patrols were not passing, armed to the teeth in rank and file with every ounce of discipline known to man. It was a military might unlike anything he'd been expecting: even for an advancing army on the move covering great distance, each figure he found was still sealed within an impressive coat of armour. Even those tending to menial tasks – quartermasters assessing supplies, or servants dragging sacks through the crush of patrols – still bore the main force's heavy plates and barbed helmets. Like an animalistic collective, some grand hive of ants with snapping pincers and jagged carapaces, every inch of the blackcoat army pulsed with direction and force.

A formidable foe, if I've ever seen one, the commander acknowledged, retracting the spyglass and shifting back behind the ridge. Across both of his flanks, stretching back almost to the main road, hundreds of his own soldiers squat together in tight clusters with swords gleaming, hungry for the fight to come. Their enthusiasm was manifest; it weighed across his back, almost throwing him over into the sun. Every man and woman behind spoke of the battle with a lusting desire for blood – Revek knew as much because he felt it too with every sinew of his body. *A formidable foe,* he grinned.

But still no match for us.

"There's about a hundred more than were reported the other day," Darius exclaimed, dragging a finger over the horizon. "Perhaps they were reinforced overnight, using the dark to mask their——"

"Impossible," he shunned. "We had scouts on stand-by throughout the night... they would've reported any movements."

"You recalled the scouts last night, sir. They drank with you at the camp instead."

Revek cracked his jaw. "Then we best be on our toes... and keep *discipline*, general. Wouldn't want anyone falling behind and landing on their *sword*."

The venom in his words came self-evidently, but watching for a reaction, he found Darius didn't rise to the challenge: with an ebbing look of disapproval, the general slunk away from the ridge and joined the nearest cluster of officers, providing a quick brief to anyone in earshot away from the vitriol of his commander.

Revek bored through his skull for some moments, before drawing his gaze away. *I'll make short work of you, you bumbling prick.* Heat rose across his neck, tightening the collar of his chainmail. *I've done it before... I've made people disappear – I'm not afraid to do it myself.* The knife strapped across his thigh hissed its approval. *I'll make short work of you, and you won't even know what happened.*

Mark my words...

"What are your orders, sir?" the general to his right inquired, her blond flush of hair retaining the same lustre it had when they had first met at the briefing camp back home. "Are we ready?"

"As we'll ever be," he replied, dismissing the anger festering within and striking out a hand. "Pass me the signal."

From her side, she slid a concave bronze disc from a sheath of cloth and handed it over to him awkwardly. Grappling its edges, his oddly-angled reflection painted across its inner wall, Revek shuffled up the ridge on his elbows and angled the disc out across the plains ahead. With short flicks of his wrist, he flashed a beam of light across the opposing ridge, skimming the narrow edge, before sliding the signal away and retreating behind cover. With his head only just skimming the peak, he watched cautiously for a sign.

Several moments passed, before three flashes suddenly glared back at them, barely a dozen feet from the outermost reaches of the enemy camp. From his elevation, Revek watched a bobbing head move toward the trees to the south and disappear.

Time ticked on again; his heart thundered in his chest. Winds whipped up across the grass, dicing his face apart. An army at his back, watching like him, waiting for the signal. Moments passing, ears to the skies.

A thunder of hooves, growing suddenly louder.

Horses exploded from the pale wall of trees to the south, snorting and biting and tearing across the terrain in droves. Dozens of them, clad in metal plates of polished steel, the riders wielding sword and spear, roars and bellows ripping through the air. The blackcoat camp drew to a staggered halt at the sight of them, fingers pointing, an odd semblance of disbelief in the air – and in the blink of an eye, everything was motion again, the coherency abandoned for sudden formation and riotous orders to hold the southern edge. With the exquisite gleam of the morning sun stripping across the sky at their backs, the charging horses entered the camp as if summoned by the hands of gods, eviscerating any blackcoat they found, trampling everything to the sound of fatal cries and storming steel.

The commander had never seen a thing of such beauty.

Cresting the ridge with sword striking high, Revek spilt down onto the open plain with the generals at his back, howling his exuberance at the peak of his lungs. At his back, in a monumental rise, hundreds of metal boots hammered into a run, sweeping over the bank like a burst dam. All along the opposite ridge where he had signalled to moments ago, the second contingent charged with them and barrelled down into the valley below. Swords and heavy shields emerged; boots churned grass and mud beneath. From all sides, their archers formed up with loaded quivers and blitzed the air with arrows, dotting across the blue sky like steel rain, picking targets among the blackcoat ranks, loosing one after another and again. At every angle, the Imperial Army of Provenci surged forwards with hearts of hope and glory, and steel wrapped tight in white-knuckle fists ready to tally the dead. Revek drew close, voice hoarse from shouting, and grinned.

Our time has come.

†

"On your left!"

Darius caught the blade as it swung down towards the soldier's neck, pressing his mass ahead of the man and shunting the blackcoat onto the nearest tent. It stumbled, slipping across the thin cloth – Darius wasted no time, stepping over the fallen body and driving his sword through the narrow slit of its helmet. A crunch of bone and a squeal followed; any strength in its limbs evaporated, straddling across the mud below.

Another dead, among the rest.

"Thank you, sir..." the soldier heaved, sliding his own blade from another stricken corpse. "Part of me wished they'd wait in line."

"That would require common courtesy," Darius mused, "and you and I both know they're fuck-all outta that."

A scream at his back: Darius rounded in time to catch a blade mid-

496

strike, sweeping it away and snapping his elbow round to cuff the blackcoat's face. As it stumbled back, the soldier stepped forward and lunged with his short-sword, sliding under the blackcoat's helmet and piercing the throat like a bubble. A gargling mutter as the blade whipped aside, and the enemy joined his friend in the mud.

"They never know when to stop, do they…"

Another pair of boots running from behind. The general rounded, blade clasped in a tight fist—

Scaring the approaching messenger, who almost dived to-ground at the sight of his blade.

"Gods, man, at least shout my name!" Darius boomed with a relaxing smile, clapping the man across the shoulder. "How are we looking, anyway? Battle's been on for some time now."

"Revek is fighting along the southern encampments," the messenger explained, "against what's left of the wall they tried to form against the cavalry. Our archers are taking heavy ground fire to the west along the ridge – contingents are inbound to relieve them and intercept any enemy in the area. The horses have returned to the main carriage by the road to rest, and the riders should be joining us on foot shortly."

Excellent, things are going as planned, the general acknowledged. "What about the central canopy that we spied from the ridge, the one with all the flags? Any idea what it's for?"

The woman opened her collar. "That was my initial report…"

"Has something happened?"

"Rather something *isn't* happening, sir."

"What do you mean?"

"Everyone who enters the canopy never comes back out again." The words came with a blunt truth to them. "We've sent almost a dozen in… and haven't heard nor seen any sign of them since."

"Any idea of what may be in there?"

"Your guess is as good as mine, sir. Although, we can deduce it's probably human."

"What makes you certain of that?"

"Because if it were a beast that killed those twelve soldiers... we'd sure as hell know about it by now."

Darius nodded slowly – the thought of a lumbering creature tearing through the camp was a sobering one at best. *Although the thought of it being human makes it no better.*

"Well, if we're gonna move this fight on, someone needs to deal with whatever's inside." A quick glance to his blade, weighted evenly in one hand. "And as I'm the only senior officer in the vicinity... I believe that pleasure falls to me." He sheathed the weapon, a cold wind snapping through the camp between them. "So, if you please, my dear... lead the way."

They converged along a thoroughfare between two tents, the mud thick and heavy around their boots. Ahead, the walkway split like a river around the massive canopied tent at its centre, soldiers lining its edges with swords poised and ready. The slit of its entranceway lay astutely sealed, a pale river of blood leaking out from within – at the sight of it, any optimism for the survival of the soldiers who'd gone in, was fallacious at best.

"What a mess," Darius exclaimed, studying a felled tent nearby torn down by the initial cavalry charge. Several behind it were also consigned to the mud, crows hopping between to pick at any remains they found. Following one such bird, his eyes averted suddenly at the sight of a dead horse locked within the folds of cloth, broken legs hanging stiffly in the air like the branches of an old tree. Even then, the flies already circled above in a great swarm, ready to feast when the carnage ended.

Enough to make any good man wretch. The general took several steps forward, the canopy tent looming above in a wash of sunlight, and addressed the nearest guard. "Any news?"

"No activity to report, sir," the youthful face acknowledged. "No sounds or nothin'. Dunno what's in there."

"Any idea of numbers?"

"A good few soldiers went in there, sir... I'd anticipate a handful of the enemy at best. But who knows what lies within..."

"Well, wait no longer." Darius grabbed the tent fold and peeled it slightly open. "We're about to find out..."

"Will you be going in, sir?" asked another.

"Unless you're offering, soldier, I'm afraid the pleasure is all mine." Darius recoiled sharply at the scent of the dead swamping the air within. "Just, promise me one thing..."

"Sir?"

"If I don't make it out alive, burn this fucking place to the ground for me..."

He ducked through the opening into a warm, swampy room of low shadows and the grotesque smell of old blood. A slosh of liquid curled at the edge of his boots, the churned earth all around forming pits of some off-colour ooze. The pungent odour of death ate at every corner of the low ceiling, swelling in the shaded gloom – tracing the outer line of the canopy wall, he soon found out why.

The edges were lined with over a dozen bodies, sunken-eyed and lost to the world, the life bled from them litre by litre. Several corpses were rolled atop one another in places, staining its inner edge with foul fluids and murmurations of buzzing flies. The must of the air was one of onset decay and festering wounds – his nose curdled with every breath that passed.

Eyes crossing to the rear of the tent, there stood an oak table with maps and orders sprawled across its top, a potent-looking dagger fastening a stack of them in place at its centre. A hand coiled about the handle, all red-stained gloves and armoured plates, and as his gaze rose Darius locked eyes with a towering pale woman in a heavy coat of mail. She seemed almost insulted by his presence, sneering at the interruption of the enemy – yet her hand never drifted far from the jagged sword at her side, forever anticipating the next attack.

"Hope I'm not intruding," Darius said with a wry smile.

"Are you a general?" she replied, voice hoarse and brittle like snapping bones.

"What if I was?"

"You would fare a lot better than the rest." She looked absently to the piles of bodies, then over to the knife embedded in the table.

"I'd say that was evident."

She toyed with the blade's hilt. "I want to ask of you something, general of the Provenci."

"And what would that be?"

"That we may make a deal, here: that I surrender, and you let me walk *free* with no one harmed..."

"Interesting," Darius lied. "And I would say that was a reasonable request... had your soldiers not been routed... and your camp torn to pieces all around. Because I think you'll find, just by looking outside, that I hold the cards to decide your fate here... *not you.*"

"And you are mistaken."

"How is that?"

Without acknowledgement, it seemed, the woman smiled. "My surrender does not come because of the battle outside..."

"Then you're a bitter fool and a shocking leader..."

"My surrender comes so that you may walk out of here *alive*—"

The knife whipped towards him at frightening speed – anticipating the attack, Darius swung sideways, but not enough for the blade to pass him by.

A sudden strike of pain, and the general looked down to find the blade had embedded itself in his bicep, lodged in the chainmail beneath, a small stream of blood leaking across his shirt. He growled, as much by the inconvenience as the pain, and dislodged the knife—

Throwing it to the ground, turning back to—

The blackcoat leader vaulted the table with a hissing cry and struck her sword down like an executioner – Darius, bewildered, snapped his blade up to deflect the blow inches from his face.

Before he could retaliate, the woman had tackled him around the waist, her massive arms disarming any strength he had left, twisting him down into the mud. The wind blasted from his chest; the sword fumbled and fell from his grip in a flush of panic. The woman recoiled, bracing him with her legs, hungry eyes beaming as her sword spun down towards his face—

Arm free, he swung violently upwards and punched her up through the chin. The blade fell just shy of his ear, planting in the mud, the woman spitting and cursing above.

Darius wrenched himself free of the cesspit, mud plastering his back, and locked an arm around her neck. Twisting through the scum, he shoved her down into a pit of blood, her weight lurching as—

Her blade came free from the mud, swinging back across his vision—

He pulled back, the blade stabbing down, slicing through one of his fingers buried in a welt of sodden earth. He drew it from the mud, hissing, using her as a platform to push away, skittering along the floor as she righted herself again—

Hands pulling away; Darius finding the woman's knife at his side, now poised delicately in his grip—

Snarling above, the blackcoat striking down—

Pulling the knife up—

The tiny blade shattering like glass, deflecting the huge sabre. Metal shards as long as arrows flecking across his hand and wrist, embedding into his palm. A screech: biting teeth and wide eyes as the blackcoat swung down—

Darius lurching up from the mud, crossing into her circle before the blade cut him in two. Arms wrapping around her stomach – weight carrying him forward as she stumbled, toppling like a great oak, the canopy spiralling above.

They crashed through a stack of bodies, the festering stench of flesh exploding as the corpses shifted, falling away across the canopy wall. Head colliding with their metal plates, the blackcoat disposed of her blade absently, returning to the moment a heartbeat later and crushing her hands around the general's throat. Darius, pulling his hands away before they became locked under her body, met the sudden pressure across his neck with clawing hands towards her face.

They wrestled amongst the dirt and the dead, the general swiping at her eyes and nose as she clamped sharply around his windpipe. Darius blinked once, twice, again and over to find the pale face below grow hazy, dim at the edges, percolating light and colour with nothing more besides. Breathing became a rasp; veins bulged across his head. Every moment came and went, the world sinking—

Hand tightening to a fist, he connected sharply with the side of her face – followed by another, bruising across her eye socket – another, crackling across the cheekbone.

A fourth, as the lights began to give away all around, and Darius felt the cartilage in the woman's nose cave beneath it – she released her grip from his neck, screaming.

He caught himself, oxygen tearing through his system again, looking ahead at the bodies—

Reaching for a long strip of cloth trapped beneath a man's arm.

Darius grappled a knot of her hair, pulling her across, body sliding beneath his mass. On her side, he pressed down across her spine and rammed her face into the mud, screeching and flailing like a wounded animal at death's door.

The soldier's cloth drawn out between his hands, he slipped it across her face buried in the earth. Twisting a clump of it in one fist like a horseman taming a wild beast, he struggled up to his feet, pulling away as the woman's arms became trapped beneath her, head slowly lifting from the scum.

Tightening the cloth, her skull buckling back like a door hinge, he lifted a mud-coated boot from her side—

And stomped down on her neck, the snap of her spine tearing through his ears.

Darius released the cloth, staggering away from the body as it sagged limply into the mud. He drew himself up, the foul odour swamping his senses again, now accompanied by exquisite pain in his arm and the lurch of sickness in his stomach.

"*Fucking hell...*" he muttered, averting his eyes and wiping a length of spittle from his chin.

As the thick air began its slow suffocation once more, Darius swayed toward the tent's opening, ripping it open to indulge upon fresh skies and cold wind, and to be anywhere other than the abattoir gutted within that tent.

The other soldiers turned at the sound with looks of shock and horror, as their general emerged from the tent entombed in mud, bleeding in several awkward places with hollow eyes that had seen hell on earth and passed through the other end. They stepped away at his appearance, almost from terror as much as respect – they didn't want to know what lay within the canopy beyond, just from the look he held.

"Are you okay, sir?" the soldier from before inquired, sweeping an arm under Darius's shoulder to hold him steady. "What happened?"

"We're secure, my boy... that's all that matters," the general muttered despondently. "Gather some officers: salvage the bodies from inside, find places to bury them... burn everything else to the ground."

"What about you, sir?"

"A bath and a bandage will do, soldier... don't you worry." Darius managed the remnants of a smile, sighing heavily.

"There's a shallow river to the south, sir, among the trees... if you were looking to wash yourself over."

"That sounds ideal."

"That, and Commander Revek has requested your immediate presence there... to assess the battle, or something."

Of course he has. "Very well" – Darius rolled a shoulder until the joint clicked sharply – "best not waste his precious time, ay?"

The soldier smiled, mirrored by the others around him, a glimmer of admiration for their audacious leader. "Of course, sir," he said.

Darius slipped from the man's grip and, on weak legs and borrowed time, the general hobbled off between the tents toward the distant tree-line – to the commander with a thorn in his side, awaiting him there.

†

"I see you've been busy."

Darius splashed water across his face from the shallow stream that diced its way through the heavy roots of the trees. They were in a small clearing, the ground sinking away from the main stretch of grass down a clay bank to the water's edge. Apparently, somewhere in the stark vegetation ahead, a battle still raged on between blackcoat stragglers and the army patrols – but down the bank to the stretch of stream before him, there was nothing: only the tap of small fish leaping from the cool waters, and the creak of many-fingered branches swaying with the wind. A silence that perpetuated only at conflict's end – which made him wonder all the more why he was there at all.

"I had an altercation with an enemy commander," he muttered in reply, lifting his head. "Tackled to the ground and half-buried in the mud before I could finally put her away."

"Did we lose anyone in the process?"

Darius sensed the commander at his back, pacing back and forth like a wolf. "Some had already been sent in before I arrived... there was nothing but bodies inside when I engaged. Everyone'd been killed."

"And you didn't stop them from going?"

"I wasn't there to give the order, sir – I was engaged elsewhere."

"Then who did?"

"As it didn't come from me, there's only one other senior-ranking official in this army who can give an order of serious engagement." He turned back to gaze up at him. "You, sir."

In the low light, the commander's eyes were tiny pins of coal, much of his form swathed in shadow as his boots crackled the leaf litter below.

"You accuse me of making that order?" Revek eventually replied, staring him down. "You accuse me of sending those men to die?"

"I accuse no one," Darius countered. "There are only two senior officers in the army – as I didn't give the command, I wondered if you did."

"As the *more* senior officer, would I do something so stupid?"

The general sighed, knowing the challenge was there but refusing to rise to it. "Of course not, *sir,*" he muttered quietly.

"So it must've been you, who marked that order."

"It *must've been* sir... of course."

Turning away, Darius noted the edge of a snarl twitch at Revek's face. *You need to learn, you sour bastard, that I won't be taking this kinda shit from you, senior officer or not.*

"Is there a problem, general?" the commander said pointedly, little more than a few steps behind him.

Darius did not respond immediately. Instead, he cupped another bowl of water and dashed it across his wounded arm, freeing some of the dirt and clotted remnants there. "Why would there be, sir?" he said slowly, tensing his back up.

"I would say there was nothing, only it seems you and I are at different ends on some things... it seems you seek to promote a sense of *power* beyond your rank."

"I serve only the power vested in me as a general... as a *subordinate* member of this army overseeing certain decisions and engagements."

"Then why do you refer to yourself as a *senior* officer equal to *me?*"

A pause – a fraction too long. "I purely meant it, in the context of giving orders to engage, sir," Darius muttered simply, "as we were talking about earlier—"

"So a slip of the tongue, was it, *general?*"

"It was sir... merely a slip of the tongue."

"Is that so? And I would perhaps believe that" – Revek took several steps closer, until the ground shifted beneath the general's feet – "had these sort of things not happened *before* as well."

"And do you care to explain where that accusation lies, sir?" Darius questioned with the full swell of his chest, the uneasiness dissipating like a low tide. *Don't say anything you'll come to regret, sir,* came the defiant thought. *That would cross many lines you can't take back.*

"You *revolt*, general... you behave in a manner *unbecoming* of your post in this army," Revek charged. "You *defy* me, before the officers whom I posit full command of, as if I were *less than you*."

"I just find sometimes, *sir*, that we don't see *eye to eye* on matters concerning the lives and wellbeing of *our* men." Venom flung from his mouth, a heat rising across his skin.

"It is not your place to question my authority... it is your *place* to follow it. You have been given far too much leeway on that count — remember who you *serve* in this."

"I serve the army, *sir*, and the good of the *nation*."

"You serve whoever I *fucking well tell you to,*" Revek growled.

"With respect, *sir,* you cannot dictate to a general about who he serves, when you have not *placed him* there. I was placed in this army by Alvarez, *not* by you... and my rank is just the same because of it."

"You may be Alvarez's choice, but you're *not* mine... not out here."

"You don't have the authority to override a superior command... you cannot dismiss me without the permission of the Governor. Your hands are *tied,* sir, and my position remains the same. So regardless of your feelings, and regardless of our disagreements over the order of this army... I cannot be got ridden of without authority that you *do not have.*"

Silence strung out as his words trailed off, echoing out into the space between them beyond the stream and the trees and the world beyond. Silence, taut as woven string, rippling as time passed and the general's resolve ebbed and flowed. Crouched by the water's edge, studying his reflection in its water. Watching, waiting, until Revek spoke again.

"Unless we make it look like an accident."

The general frowned. "Sir, I—"

The crossbow bolt lanced through the back of his head and skittered out across the water beyond. Darius's body swayed awkwardly, the final spasms of life fading to death as he slumped forward into the water.

Revek withdrew the weapon, face awash with wrath and fire, grinding teeth and quaking hands and the bittersweet taste of fate on his tongue. He watched the body lie still and silent at last.

"None shall defy *me*."

†

Chapter 59

The End of No Beginnings

For a quiet moment, he slunk against the nearest wall, heaving and scowling at the sun's swollen eye, and every reasonable part of him genuinely believed his guts were about to rip from his stomach. Hand pressing there, fingers prodding deep within, he squirmed at the nauseating jolt of pain lancing along his ribs and snapping across his lungs like a frayed whip. Every inch was agony; the air was thin and unbelievably warm. *Whatever they've done has cut deep,* he concluded with a wheezing breath. *Don't know how much longer I can manage with it—*

"C'mon, we need to move!"

Jinx tugged him by the arm, and once more Broska found himself spinning off through the narrow alleyways and quiet passages of Casantri, the funeral procession drawing to a close somewhere at their backs. The crowds had already begun to disperse, filtering off through the city, encountering the band of three making their escape and disappearing again just as fast. Broska had caught the gaze of several: watching their frowns, conspiratorial and concerned – wondering who that huge man was, lumbering forward in little more than a plain shirt, the red-raw skin marked around his wrists, almost as if he'd been wearing shackles...

"People are getting suspicious," Shadow warned, placing her frame ahead of Broska to avert lingering eyes as they crossed another street.

"It doesn't matter," Jinx snapped. "By the time they register, we'll be out of the city and riding free. It's only a matter of time…"

He longed to tell her to slow down, to take a moment and assess the wounds, but flying through the narrow streets like a water-skate, Broska found his objections cast to the wind, the air battered from his lungs with every overburdened step. Even then, he knew there was no hope of them slowing down, no opportunity given to convalesce and take stock. He could see it in her eyes, every time Jinx looked back to him: worry and fear and confusion and adamance, fleshed out in brute colours, knowing what was at stake. The incongruous fact that his life was on the line – that her singular responsibility fell to keeping him safe.

The broken chasm, stretching out wider between the two.

"We'll make it," she said, managing a broken smile as she ran. "You'll be free… and you'll be safe, and that's all that matters."

He never found a response, and the moment passed almost as soon as it came – but even so, deep within his chest, he couldn't help but find the hope in his heart start to sing again.

Maybe there's a chance, after all…

Banking suddenly left across the main thoroughfare, Broska gazed up into the sun and recognised the tall towers and spined blockades of one of the citadels, buried unceremoniously between the bulky courtyard estates. An ugly slab of metal intertwined with huge stone blocks, it made an impressionable mark on an otherwise quaint surrounding – and one with a good vantage for the watchful eyes above.

As he thought it, the guards atop the citadel began to jostle and motion towards them, the fuzzy distinction of an arm charting their path as they slipped away again between the houses. Jinx and Shadow seemed not to have realised – either that or they knew with all certainty that time was running out.

And, within a heartbeat, it ran out altogether.

A whistle clipped the air behind them; with only its flags and turrets visible, Broska spied the sudden commotion at the roof of the citadel as orders were given and directions made to the patrols now swarming at its base. From dislocation to fear, some balance in him shifted, and by all accounts his wounds didn't seem to matter as much.

"We're two streets out!" Jinx wailed from ahead as another whistle went up. "Two streets, nearly there…"

Wherever there is…

Turning the final corner, light engulfing the street ahead as it broke open like a liquor bottle, Broska brokered the déjà vu he felt with a dissuading optimism. The same boots behind as before; the same light ahead as before. Nothing in between, nothing to stand in their way, that the enemy was so far behind. Meaning little; amounting to even less.

Hopes come and gone, so idly cast to the fire.

They emerged out onto a small plaza, surrounded by the same squat buildings as before. Birds scattered; whistles blasted at their backs. An end had come – to the common eye, as hopeless as before.

Only this time, Broska lifted his head to find steaming chimneys stretching across the bold blue above, attached to a wall of valves and plates that made up the twin-storey shape of a pumphouse. Every inch seemed to pulse as if it were circulating blood, the heat bulging through the air ahead of him. Broska scanned the wall ahead, sweat stinging his eyes, his sister lurching across his view – spying, beyond all that, the wide metal grate at the base of the wall, leading down into the main sewer that, at some point, extended out of the city and onto the wider plains beyond.

Of all the places…

Jinx rushed forward, sliding a small bludgeon from her waistband, and started to beat against the edges of the grate, the hinges screeching their disapproval as they were slowly worked apart. Watching her work, Broska was unaware as Shadow moved up alongside him and grabbed his arm.

"I cannot stay," she muttered to him. "If this goes wrong… there's no telling what they'll do to me."

Broska gave a nod of his agreement. "Do what you must. Stay alive."

"You're a good man, Arrenso... I'll never forget what you've done for us in all this."

"You have my thanks... now go, be free."

Shadow squeezed his shoulder. "I would tell your sister there to do the same, but I have my doubts that she'll——"

Her pupils swelled wider——

"*Move!*"

She shoved him back; he stepped away absently as a thunder of noise clattered across his right.

Suddenly a body appeared before him, brown and muscular, snorting and charging, the rider straddled against the heavy sun——

A connection across the side of his face, a slap of cold metal, and Broska toppled to the floor with frightening momentum, the agony in his gut wrenching him onto his side. He broke against the cobbles, twisting into the light, peeling himself up onto an elbow to see——

"Where the fuck do you think you're going, *traitor?*" Alvarez growled, rounding his horse and swinging down off its back, sword already hanging deftly in one hand. "You should be in prison." Fastened within the royal armour reworked from the king's own, the bear of a man swayed towards them, every inch of his form glistening with frightful malice. "Better yet... you should be *dead.*"

Broska drew himself back to a crawl, up to full height with agonising slowness, hand clutching across his stomach, and grit his teeth.

"Have you anything to say? Or do I have to *bleed it* out of you?"

Broska shook his head. "You're being fed lies... by a cruel man who *murdered* an officer in cold blood... a man who murdered her at the whim of the man who now *leads* your armies," the general charged. "You're being fed lies, manipulative and bitter lies... and I have done nothing *wrong.*"

"You've broken out of prison——"

511

"From false charges of conspiracy, sir! *False charges.* It's all a lie, all of it…"

"You have allied yourself with *thieves* and underlings of the state. How should I take this notion seriously?"

"What other choice do I have?" Broska took a step forward. "I witnessed Cavara killed in *cold blood…* murdered by the hand of the man you now share counsel with every day. She was never given a choice, never allowed her say before that knife was driven through her stomach and she bled to death on that *fucking* shoreline." His voice crackled. "This is my choice, to live and be free… this is the choice she *never got to make,* and the one I will make in her memory."

"You sacrifice everything, for *her?*" he spat.

"She would do the same for me… I have no other choice."

At their side, Jinx pulled away from the now-broken grate and stormed towards Alvarez with knives twisting in her hands. Broska inhaled slowly, heart wrenching, lifting his hand to stop her – Shadow stepped ahead of the thief and held her by the arms, forcing her back, a pain in the deep of her eyes.

"I know you're not a dishonourable person, sir," Broska exclaimed as Alvarez took slow steps toward him, the sword loose in his hand. "I know you mean to do what's best for us… all of us, in this… and I know that you are trusting of your general's as any good leader would be. But I am telling you… Ferreus killed her… Revek gave the order… and I had *nothing* to do with any of it. You've been lied to, sir, lied to and manipulated by one of your own."

Alvarez drew up before him, eyes to the floor, the heavy-drawn definitions of his face seizing in the light. "Perhaps I misjudged you, general," the Governor expressed shallowly. "Perhaps I have been wrong. These are trying times… people have their own agendas. I find lies as distasteful as I do treacherous, and any amount of insubordination should be reprimanded to the highest order, and with *absolute* certainty."

"Of course, sir."

"If Ferreus killed Cavara, and took the orders from Commander

512

Revek... then this could be a very serious problem indeed."

"Precisely, sir——"

"Although there is one thing, I think, that's missing from all this."

"Sir, I don't——"

The Governor leaned close to his ear. "*Who do you think gave Revek the order in the first place?*"

Alvarez plunged his sword through Broska's chest, up through the ribs, wedging it down to the hilt with a hiss of glee.

Jinx screamed, Shadow falling back in a swell of horror.

"She would do the same for you..." Alvarez rasped, "so now you can *join her in hell.*"

He slung the blade out with a streak of blood, cackling wildly; Broska collapsed to the ground in a limp pile, his body tucking up like a cocoon as his life pooled across the cobbled streets, ounce by precious ounce——

"You *prick*!" Jinx screeched, lurching forward, tears already hollowing her eyes. "You fucking *bastard*! I'll fucking *end you*!"

"You'll do nothing of the sort," Alvarez growled. "Not when I'm through with you..."

He rounded with a broad snarl, the blood-streaked blade coiling like a length of rope, tightening in his grasp, stretching out to cleave her through——

Shadow's blade snapping between, the chime piercing her ears exquisitely. Flicking it aside, Shadow stepped ahead and levelled her blade with the huge man, turning for a moment to the young thief at her back.

"Leave, *now.*"

Jinx found her heart waver, emotions spilling, the corpse of her brother sprawled across the cobbles to one side, the killer bearing down on her to the other. A protector stood between, eyes as much fear as wrath – the words echoing out to her, forcing her to move, to go, to flee and escape the world and run with her life, knowing Broska was gone and it was over.

Knowing Broska was gone...

"*Go, now!*"

Tears streaking her eyes as the blades chimed ahead of her, Jinx turned away from the carnage, managing one last look to her dying brother curled across the stone. Looking to him, the one who had protected her, and held her close every day; the only family she had ever known in the world, the only one who ever mattered – taken from the earth at the end of a tyrant's blade, never to rise again.

Slipping down into the sewer tunnel beneath the pumphouse, she watched the light grow slowly dimmer at her back.

Knowing Broska was gone...

†

Chapter 60

Champion's Fate

I'm sorry, Markus."

The weight of reality came, as if his soul were being ripped from his chest. Hanging limply in one hand, the blade he had wielded with such defiant purpose before now seemed foul and poisonous in his grasp. The heat drew in unbearably; the air rippled in his lungs hollowly. He couldn't believe any of it – *didn't want* to believe any of it. Didn't want to know…

"Why are you here?" he cried out, a knot of anger in his voice. "Why are you *here?*"

"The same reason you are… I was brought here to fight. I played their games, I defeated a champion, and now I fight for that title… same as you."

"But why?" Every word crackled in his throat. "Why you, why here?"

"It's how things have been decided."

"Why… why must *any* of this happen?" he pleaded. "Why do we have to do this? This isn't right…"

"Because we fought, and we won… and they must decide a champion from us… that's all there is."

A pinch of salt edged the corner of his eye. "I don't want this, we… we don't have to do this… we don't have to fight. We can tell them it's over, tell them we refuse… *fuck all* of this. Please… I

515

can't."

"We don't have a choice," Savanta replied coldly. "There is no other way."

"Sav, please. I can't do this – I *won't* do this. This is all wrong... all horribly wrong. We have spent *years* working together, fighting side by side... you're the only good I have in this world. After the company... after the massacre, I... I followed you through the gates of *hell* and beyond. I could've turned back, or refused, but I didn't... for *you*, and for *your* survival, I didn't." Markus dropped his sword. "We don't need to fight... we don't need any of this."

"And I commend your help in all this... I commend it always." Watching, she made no sign of dropping her own blade, clamped steadfast in both hands.

"Then put down the sword, and let's sort this."

A pause, sharp and hollow. "I can't do that."

Markus bristled. "Why? They don't own us... we don't have to give in to their whim..."

Her face steeled. "Don't make this any harder than it needs to be."

"What are you *talking about*..."

"*Redemption*, Markus!" she spat, hammering a finger against the metal plate welded through her cheek. "Don't you understand? Haven't you been listening to me, all this time? You know what I said, back in the village... you know why I'm here. It was your choice to come – you knew what was happening. I am *here* for the *Iron Queen*... I am here to *kill* that bitch for what she *did* to me, what she *took from me*." Her face contorted into a lopsided snarl. "I will have my *revenge* for what happened that day."

"And you'll go against everything you've stood for, *everything* that has meant something to you in this world... to play the game of the enemy and enter into their world, all to achieve this *ridiculous* revenge at its end?" Where there was sadness, now came anger. "Then what? Will you be *satisfied*? Will this all mean something to you, then? Once you become their puppet, bending the knee to sycophants who are killing our people every day..."

"Their fight was never mine."

"That doesn't make it right, that you choose to do this."

"What choice do I have, Markus? What *choice* do I *have?*"

"The choice to say *no*," he said defiantly. "The choice to end all this madness... this insatiable pursuit of revenge, this *insanity* just so you can feel better that the company is dead and our old life is gone—"

"Don't you want that? Don't you want an end to this?"

"I want a solution that doesn't end in bloodshed!"

"Then you should've never fucking followed me!" she screamed, spearing the sword his way.

"Sav... please... stop this..."

"*No!*" Veins bulged across her forehead. "This is how it must be – this is how it ends. My redemption... my *revenge*, as a false champion, delivered to that foul woman's arms with sword in-hand... an end to this suffering, at *all costs.*"

Markus looked to his feet, the sword shimmering beneath the sand there, and the sinkhole opening that threatened to swallow the known world away. "Is that what I am to you?" he muttered slowly, meeting her gaze again. "A tool... some asset to your revenge? That I put my life on the line for you, the only friend I have... only to be corralled to the end of your blade as an acceptable casualty, in the name of *redemption?*"

"You knew the cost, as soon as you stepped over that border line... I will never apologise for who I am, or what I want – I won't apologise for who dies and gets in my way. You *knew* the cost... and you did it anyway. Don't pin this on me." Her stance shifted. "You were expendable, the moment we left... and this, is how it ends."

His heart wrenched. "Does friendship mean *nothing* to you?"

"Friendship didn't stop this from happening" – she tapped her cheek.

"Abandoning it isn't gonna fix it, either," Markus exclaimed. "This isn't worth it, Sav... I *need* you... we're all that we have left."

"I have nothing *left* – don't you get it? This is all I have left: a plan and a death-wish. I don't care which comes first, so long as I can stare the bastard in the eye when it happens…"

"I can't fight you, Sav."

"Then you'll die willingly instead."

"I was here to keep you *alive*."

"This isn't the morally-superior choice you think it is, Markus… don't sit here and belittle me on that. The company is gone, our plans are gone… everything that once was, is *gone*. Nothing is going to bring that back, and if you're gonna stand in my way and lecture me about it… then I will not hesitate to strike you down without remorse."

Anger fell to disbelief; he looked into the eyes of a lost friend. "What have you *become?*"

"I've become what I needed to be… and you've become *expendable*."

Markus ground his teeth, anger seething, and with a powerful lunge he swiped his sword from the sand at his feet and speared it towards her like a sceptre. "Then I will say that I'm a man of honour, above everything else – so I fight with honour, as an honest man at the end of his time, and say only this to you." He slipped down into a fighting stance, sword locked in his hand, lungs swelling and skin shimmering and the world full of colour and noise. "Whether here, or in the beyond, and by whoever's hand… you will always die a coward and a traitor, nothing more."

Savanta scowled, balancing the weight across her own weapon.

"So *be it*."

A howl and she charged, storming forwards, cutting into his circle with whip-like strikes, the blade light and lethal in her hands. Markus suppressed the rancour of emotion wracking his system, as his own nimble blade parried and dismissed each incoming strike. He was nothing of the fighter she was, managing half her swing but balancing out with double her force, arcing his wrist left-right-down-right-left in sudden spasms to hold her back, heels grinding across the stone. Watching the snarl and anger in her face, that bubble of hurt aching in his chest again…

518

She ducked suddenly, driving low to the earth, a leg spinning out to axe across his shin——

Markus bunched up and rolled off to the left, up to a stand, grinding on the ball of his foot to stop. Twisting, his thin blade flashing across an open skyline, circling round to strike down across her shoulder——

Savanta sliding her blade down her back to knock it aside, twisting to a stand and pressing on with the offensive yet again, shimmering metal crossing and slashing under the ruminating gaze of the sun.

After all this, came the dumbfounded thought. He swung heavily, forcing her back an inch. *After everything we've been through.* She recoiled and lunged out, forcing him back a foot. *This is how it ends?* The attacks kept coming.

This is how it ends?

Savanta made for another lunge, but Markus stepped past it and slit a thin cut across her shoulder, scoring a trickle of blood for his efforts. Her expression became one of disgust, and from there disbelief, but then every ounce of the rage returned with an indiscriminate intensity as she made to strike again.

Markus caught the sporadic attacks awkwardly, the weight behind the onslaught forcing strain across his arm, heels sliding, a backstep inevitable but unwelcome all the same. He tried biting back, snarling and grunting with each counter as it failed to strike her, failed to meet its mark by her impossible motion – another backstep, and another following soon after.

She's lost it. He kicked out, snapping her knee backwards, forcing her to stumble. *She's been tainted by them.* He struck down, only to find her blade there ready to meet his own. *She's not herself.* Pushing upwards baring her teeth, Savanta squared a punch into his gut, forcing the air from his system. *She's——*

She snapped her blade down, scoring a long tear down his chest, catching at the tiny puncture wounds scattered there.

Markus stumbled back a few steps, his lungs heaving, tracing the shallow cut down from his collar, eyes worn with shock. The unbelievable heat bearing down from above.

She's gonna kill me.

"What were you expecting?" she spat.

"Mercy..." he said meekly.

"There is no mercy in the arena... mercy didn't get me here, and it sure as shit won't keep me alive after." The sword lashed daringly in her grip. "Don't be *pathetic*."

"Pathetic?" Markus found adrenaline rekindle in his chest, and a sudden imperative fell over him again. "*Fuck yourself*."

He stepped forward and made to lash out in rage, Savanta grinning with arrogance as she parried it—

Markus stopping the blade just short, cutting down suddenly to score a massive trench across her forearm, a splurge of blood lacing across the end of his weapon.

He watched as she reeled back and hissed at the wound, some small part of him hoping it would knock some sense into her. As if she was entranced by some spell, or under the influence of a fickle poison where her world was red and the enemy lay all around. Wishing for some glimmer of the woman he'd known from before to return: to look at his broken body and the sword in her hand, and show some remorse at how wrong it all was. Watching on, praying.

Watching... as that moment never came.

Savanta pressed forward with huge, determined strides, sword hanging low across the sand, locking eyes as if she didn't even recognise him – as if he was just a target now, and nothing had ever been.

She's gonna kill me.

A harrowing slice that he slapped aside awkwardly, never quite recovering as a fist rounded to catch him across the jaw. Stumbling, losing track of her in the blur of his vision—

A lancing pain across his shoulder-blade, streaking down his spine as the tip of her short-sword carved across him like a hock of meat. Turning back to her with bile in his throat—

Sidestepping a lunge, the blade cutting across his abdomen, as he buckled away—

A leg kicking out, ramming through the side of his knee – the sick-swelling crunch of bone as Markus howled. Stepping away, finding he couldn't balance any weight on it, the kneecap dislodged to one side—

Catching another swing of her blade, knocking it aside as he hobbled back, each motion proving more excruciating than the next, his entire leg shaking and seizing, beating back every attack that came—

One strike slipping down the handle of his sword, burying itself in the ridge of his thumb. Another squeal, pulling away as his hand ignited with pain, the sword becoming slippery in his palm with blood—

Another clash of blades, and Markus was no longer in control – parry after parry, diced at awkward intervals, with the adrenaline of before fading in his soul. Realising that he was facing down death, in all its brute realities – possessed within the eyes of his once and only friend. The absence of that now; the sheer destitution in her mind. *She's gonna kill me.*

He hissed at the pain all over, the ache in his chest.

And she won't even care anymore.

Markus dragged himself away, sickness ballooning in his stomach, his left leg numb and dishevelled. With withering strength, the infrequency of his attacks caught Savanta off-guard –tiny nicks appeared across her arms and chest, spitting blood and burning angrily like a rash across the skin. Still he fought on: fought on with the burning remnants of his life –the grim understanding that fate closed in: that one time, and only once, his sword would fail.

And mercy will not come.

Battering away, the resolve in his attacks began to collapse. Where there was once anger, came fear – where there was once hope, came bitter sadness. A well formed in his chest; his skin crawled with unease. The sky now impossibly bright, high above – almost as if the world was ending—

Savanta speared her sword towards him, an attack easily knocked aside—

Only to find her weapon snapping round, cutting through—

Embedding itself deep in his wrist.

Markus discarded his blade with a screech like a banshee and stared despondently at the huge knot of blood erupting down his arm. Agony twisted, explosive; words were lost on his tongue. Savanta struck out with her boot, a vicious kick that his faltering leg had no answer for. The arena spun, all colour and noise.

He collapsed to the floor in a heap.

As he plummeted to ground, the blue-white sky passing overhead like a comet, the fine boundary of life and death seemed to fall away all around him. There was no sensation left to his leg, no pain across his wrist or arm or shoulder – no labour to his breathing, no punctures of rock in his lungs – no cheering crowds or grand-stands or envoys or weapons. For a shallow, shattering moment, there was nothing. Nothing but the beaten body sprawled across the sand, and the impossible sun high above.

And the shadow, looming ahead, with some recollection telling him that that shadow once belonged to a friend.

"There is no other way," Savanta said slowly. "This is it."

"I just wanted to keep you safe," Markus muttered, tears catching at the corners of his eyes. "I just wanted you to make things right – to do what you had to, to feel right again. I saw the pain of the world in your eyes… and all I wanted to do was to help make that pain go away." A bubble of blood in his throat; the ugly knot of flesh tingling across his wrist. "I came all this way… so that you could be well again. That's all I ever wanted, Sav…" Finding her eyes, he saw the glimmer of sadness there: fleeting, silent, beautiful. "That's all I ever wanted…"

She blinked once, once only, and he watched the glimmer fade altogether.

"I'm sorry, Markus… I'm sorry…"

A twinkling blade like a falling star, and his world went black.

†

Chapter 61

Horizon's Fire

The time has come.

*T*he sat with his back arched, staring at his feet atop the empty throne, curtains drawn as the world ticked by outside. A few windows lay agape behind the thick silken veil, so that when a breeze mounted the palace walls, a twist of light filtered through and pierced the shadows of his inner chamber. In those moments, darkness scattered – the grey-brown smudges of stone enlightened with shimmering edges. For a moment, fractious and obsolete, life was restored in that cold recess – but, like many fleeting things the old tyrant had come to know, even that was an exercise in futility.

The time has come.

Alvarez rose from the throne, ascending to his full stature, the hollows and strain of his face greatly diminished. In the low light, only a prime, resolute glow of vitality remained – a force that burned bright in his eyes and filled his chest with resounding vigour. That he was finally the ruler he had longed to become – that the days of torment, were no more.

A half-turn right, and his gaze fell upon the far wall that had since been cleared of disused chairs, the entire area scrubbed with hard-brush until not even the cobwebs in the high coving remained. Looking there, looking to its centre, a great sweep of satisfaction held sway within him as his eyes scoured for faces only to find none were ever there. Only stone, riveted by shadow, and nothing else besides.

The haunting vestige of the Mother's curse, nowhere to be seen.

To think you could truly challenge me, he mused, scoffing into the void. *To think you sought to break me with your lies... to think you ever had any true power over my destiny.* At his side, the black veil behind the throne seemed to ripple softly, then lie still. *How far you have fallen... how wretched you had been.* A twitch of joy, edging the corners of his cheeks.

How powerful I have become.

A knocking from his door echoed through the chamber, the shadows stirring with indignation.

"Enter," Alvarez grumbled, turning to face them slowly.

At his words, a silver strike of hair appeared through the gap, a scar-laced hand edging the door open.

"Sir," General Ferreus said, closing the door behind him and bowing in the half-light. "Apologies for the disturbance."

"It is no matter... you bring news, general?"

"Word from the front lines, no less, sir."

Alvarez made a show of being interested. "Go on."

"The Fourth Division have secured key access points along the Kazbak Hills after a few bloody days fighting... estimates suggest roughly four-hundred of our soldiers have died, but certainly not in vain – a supply line has been formed through the lowlands right up to the outskirts of the Oskyme Desert."

"That's a third of Tarraz already in our grasp," the Governor replied with a nod. "What of the Third and Second?"

"Second Division took a more direct route through the lowlands and occupied small forts scattered through the forest hills, but were quickly overrun by enemy ambushes and forced to surrender three of them. Third Division, navigated down an old riverbed west of the ambush zone and formed a perimeter of camps to the north, meaning both armies have corralled a large number of the enemy amongst the trees, and are awaiting orders from high command about whether to engage."

Alvarez tugged a finger through his knotted beard. "Reorganise the border patrols, and find units to reinforce the Second along the southern flank of the forest. I want fast strikes into the trees to dislodge the enemy, and then a main force to attack anyone trying to escape. Order the Third to remain as a supporting column, but allow their patrols to scout the land to the north for vantage points and settlements."

"I'll see it done, sir."

"My thanks... and what of the First?" Alvarez exclaimed. "What of Revek?"

"They have made camp along the outskirts of the Grey Plains for the night, after an engagement with a blackcoat army of roughly six-hundred soldiers this morning. Reports indicate that sixty of our number were lost in the fray, but the enemy were decimated, with only a handful escaping into the trees to the south." Ferreus lowered his gaze. "The only dampening account of the affair was the loss of General Darius, who is reported to have died valiantly at the defence of Commander Revek before a blackcoat fatally shot him."

The Governor produced a forlorn expression. "Losses come as a burden of war... but his is certainly a shame."

"We've been in contact with his family, and a funeral has been arranged in advance, sir."

"Good work, general... a man of his quality is best honoured, for his service to the cause."

"Of course, sir." Then Ferreus seemed to squirm on the spot for a moment, as if something had bitten his tongue. "And another matter, sir..."

"Yes, general?"

A pause. "Is it true that General Broska is dead?"

Alvarez found a coldness bellow within him, ground between his teeth like ice. "Yes... he is dead, as a running and a traitor to the nation. A traitor to *the cause*, I might add."

"Then you have done me a great service, sir."

"Because you oft make a foul mess of things and can't find the guile to pick up the *pieces*," the Governor growled, Ferreus visibly shrinking as he spoke. "It nearly slipped through our fingers."

"And it was your decisive action that kept it in-hand, sir... I can only apologise that I did not enact that sooner myself."

"Your graciousness is acknowledged, and the incident may of course be forgiven." He cast a steely eye over the general. "Had things turned out differently this day, however... I would not be so *forthcoming*."

Ferreus gulped. "It won't happen again, sir."

"No, it *won't*. It shall never happen again. Because now, the enterprise of war is ours. The conduct is ours to maintain – the enemy, ours to vanquish. Of the dishonest number who dared challenge us, none remain – and their cause, their miserable *insubordination,* will never haunt us *agai*—"

A crash at the door behind.

Alvarez looked past the general, and in a volley of garbled words a young guard appeared from beyond heaving air like a blacksmith's bellows, a sheen of sweat coating her brow.

"Sir... urgent, there's—"

"Spit it *out*, officer," the Governor boomed, the quiet confidence peeling away to find hell-bitten rage in its place.

"Outside, sir, it's... please, see for yourself."

Alvarez stormed over to the curtained veil at his side, heat crackling off his skin, grappling the heavy fabric and ripping it aside, bathing the chamber in light and life...

To find the horizon on fire.

What the fuck...

Everywhere that his gaze landed, from the tiny pockets of villages and the dense flourishes of trees to the burgeoning cities and towns, a maw of flame dashed the horizon and ballooned the skies with ironclad torrents of smoke and ash. A wide line scarred across the country, as far as the eye could see, with untouched pockets sheltered among the desecration. He had never seen such devastation

— his country lay in flames. It was as if the gods had pronounced their wrath and purged the land for its sin.

As if the world had fallen out from under him, in all its twisted glee.

"What the *fuck* is going on!" Alvarez bellowed, rounding on a bewildered general and a timid-looking guard who found herself suddenly caught in the swing of the tyrant's fury.

"A rebellion, sir… a rebellion against *us*," she muttered — then, quietly: "against *you*, sir."

"*What?*" he spat. "How has this happened? How has this happened right under our *fucking noses*…"

"Reports say that it was a letter… something that got out of the city before martial law was imposed. A messenger somewhere in the city was paid off, or something — and he got through before the gates closed, to deliver a message to… *Rendevir*, I believe."

His heart tensed — the name clicked in his mind. "What *message?*"

"We aren't sure exactly, sir." She seemed to shy away. "We only know the name of the recipient."

"*Who?*"

Her eyes hollowed. "A man called Eli——"

Alvarez grappled a small wooden stand next to him and threw it across the room, screeching at the top of his lungs, the object disintegrating across the far wall and spilling out across the floor, his arms swinging white-knuckled and rageful and——

"That *prick*… that foul, fat, torturous little *prick!*" he roared, teeth grinding, shadows snapping across his complexion. "He thinks he can ruin us… that bastard. He thinks he can get the better of me… thinks he can *haunt* me now that he's dead, as if there's no *consequence*." The Governor lurched about violently, hands clenching. "I'll show him, and that bastard man-whore of his… I'll *fucking* show him, I'll show all of them what it means to mess with *me*——"

As his mind lurched, and the anger funnelled through his veins like a twisted poison, he caught sight of the wall opposite him, shrouded in shadow at the furthest edge of the room. Even with the curtain wide open, a dense shadow remained there, longing to embrace the dark. His eye hung there a few moments, and his stomach began to twist, and the flame in his eye drew cold like a candle in a storm. Studying the wall, its rivets and dark spaces.

Studying the new face that lay there, watching and smiling with glee.

†

Chapter 62

The Plague of Once Forgotten

She didn't recall how deep they had gone, descending the narrow labyrinth of stairways and corridors that intertwined below the palace keep. The darkness ebbed and flowed with torchlight, hollows flashing and fading across chiselled stone walls – fleeting shadows, rising and falling all around. For a moment, the air seemed to grow thinner; footsteps ricocheted through her eardrums, and then in another moment they were gone again. She thought it unnatural, to sense the world so acutely as she did then – and perhaps it was, for the guards at her side and the looming mass of the Alderbane at her back did not so much as flinch. Not even when the walls became like liquid around her; not even when the torches seemed to mould into a cascading river of light, gracing down the steps with them. Not even when the stairways came to an end, and all that remained ahead was a narrow corridor within the dark and hellish depths of the earth. She looked on, lost to the world, the lunging and morphing formations dancing across the walls, and found that it was an experience that the others either knew nothing of or cared nothing for. Perhaps it was an experience she alone found herself conjuring, in those recesses of the dark – perhaps this was her travelling downstream, to open waters at its end.

To the truth of all things.

Two guards stood awaiting them at the end, adjacent to a massive iron door, its shimmering surface flickering with the torchlight cast from either side. At their approach, and without a word spoken, the two guards turned from their posts and unwound the mechanism holding the door shut. Studying the thin slit between, Cavara spied huge iron rods and coiling locks pulling apart as the guards drew the levers round. Unknown to the others, she watched as patterns of light coiled elegantly across the door's face, like the shimmering manipulations of a sidewinder spinning across desert sands. She stood entranced, captivated almost, by the patterns and shapes that only she possessed the eye to see – drawn back to reality suddenly, as the levers returned to their resting place, and a final lock snapped open to shift the door ajar.

"Are you ready?" the Alderbane inquired at her back, the trance of lights fading in her gaze.

"Not even close," Cavara replied with a hint of a smile. "Now let's get on with it."

The huge figure made a satisfied nod of the head, almost as if it smiled too. "Very well... lead on."

The doors fell slowly open, and Cavara stepped forward to find a narrow precipice of broken stone rising all around, natural light spilling from some lost place high, high above. Water tip-tapped down from a deep reservoir in the rock, blossoms of green algae flourishing across sparsely-clad walls. With the ceiling coated in cobwebs as large as sails, and the fragmented slope gliding gently upwards at their feet, she came to understand what the Alderbane meant when he talked of just how ancient the place was that they had entered. From the well-kept, chiselled blocks of the chamber at her back, to the rough cavern extending all around her like a hollow spearhead, it was as if she were stepping into a forgotten world – *and by all accounts, I am.*

"The doorway is at the crest of the slope," the Alderbane explained. "We'll need the fires ignited."

At its word, the two guards pressed ahead with torches to-hand, skittering past Cavara and navigating the precarious slope like goats ascending a mountain. They reached the crest, swamped in a deluge of shadow, and stood to either side of the opening, lowering their torches into tiny shafts in the wall.

Within moments, a sudden explosion of light appeared before her, the crest of the ridge consumed with the flurry of a yellow-orange glow. It exposed an alcove of ancient carved walls and bold, scarred pillars, staggering higher and higher until crossing the back wall—

Along the top edge of an ancient doorway, the likes of which she'd never seen before.

But the image of which, I know all too well.

Like turrets on a seaboard fortress, the five totems stood towering across the door in a waning crescent, markings and etchings scrawled over each one as the vision had shown to her before. Interwoven between them lay the shimmering scales and intricate ripples of a serpent, a many-fanged jaw extending at the bottom with piercing ruby eyes, and the haunting stare of an ancient mirage locked away in time.

But Cavara found her gaze wander, and was drawn most intently to the inscription cocooned at the totems' centre. It was indecipherable, some remnant of a bygone time, but the surface seemed to twist and coil as she studied it, pulsing with a white-grey energy.

Matching the rhythm of my heart.

Cavara found a knot form at the square of her chest, watching the waves as they danced across the door, and found a tugging sensation in her stomach as if waylaid by an anchor. Only it cut deeper, flickering at the edges of her very soul, pulling her forwards toward the door and the light, seeking a new unity of the divine.

Seeking the answers that lay beyond.

"What do you see?" the Alderbane asked, an unusual imperativeness to its voice.

"A door... a very old door," she said simply. "It seems like its calling to me..."

"Calling to you? How so?"

"The inscription in the middle... what do you see there?"

A long pause – the Alderbane seemed to study it intently with the hollow eyes of its naked skull. "What inscription?" it eventually replied.

"Do you not...?" *Unless only I can see it.*

"What do you see?"

"Ancient text... it bears no meaning to me, except that whatever it is, the words there are pulsing, and match the beat of my heart. Like its... well, calling to me."

"It calls for you to enter its world – it has seen something in you that it desires."

"The kiss of the All-Mother?"

The Alderbane inclined its huge head. "For whatever purpose, the great forces in this world appear to have chosen you... the Mother gives her summons, and it is you who shall answer."

Sickness wavered in her stomach, bitten down by the magnitude of what was going on. "What must I do?" she said slowly.

"I do not know." A hand emerged, a gnarled finger extending to point at the door's centre. "But if it calls to you," the Alderbane exclaimed, "then you must go to it. There is no other way."

The pit of her heart grew wider all of a sudden. From the huge robed figure to the ancient doorway ahead; from the guards watching her expectantly to the torches burning low in their hands, Cavara found the burden of the known world lain heavy across her shoulders, and wished for it all to be gone.

There is no other way.

She approached the door, knowing it was a betrayal that had brought her there. A single act of cowardice, committed by a cruel and maniacal man, that now lay her at the foot of the gods. That without that singular moment, in what she seemed to reminisce as another life, the visions would have never come and her life would have never changed. Sevica would have remained little more than a distant land; the Alderbane, little more than an old legend. She wondered, in a quiet place in the back of her mind, whether everything that had happened would have passed her by had it not been for the Mother's kiss. That this was all some poor accident, from which she was cast into a grand narrative ill-prepared and without answer. If in another life, she may have never been summoned to the Room of Shadows.

Or whether, in the end, that had been her fate all along.

In a silent microcosm, Cavara lifted her palm and lay it flat against the cold metal. Heartbeat stuttering – moments passed with nothing to show for it.

Then a swell in her chest, and her arm seized with an electrocution of pain, and she screamed loud enough to shake dust from the cavern high above, the torchlight rippling in a sudden spur of fear.

Trying to tear her hand away, she found it frozen to the door, her entire arm locked in place like a spear. Panic flaring, she looked up to find the inscription glow brighter, and suddenly the serpent was moving, metal plates twitching, coiling out from the totems and sliding delicately down the door towards her hand. She followed its huge head, locked to the ruby eyes, its skull opening towards her, the rows of teeth angling down towards her hand. It approached in utter silence, sliding over her fingers, encasing the wrist like a glove. Heartbeat stuttering – moments passed with nothing—

Like daggers, the serpent's fangs snapped down into her hand and recoiled almost immediately, the motion so fast and abrupt that she hardly found the breath to scream, before relief overcame and her hand was released, sliding from the jaws with two huge puncture wounds just above her wrist.

Wounds, she found, that produced no blood.

What have I done?

On quaking legs, she stood back to find the door had formed a seal at its centre, striking the middle totem in two, and as the inscription began to fade it drew slowly open, the rubies still watching on from the eyes of the metal serpent.

What have I done?

"What do you see?" the Alderbane called from behind.

Cavara struggled for words. "A wall of shadow..." she replied.

Rippling like water, the black void beyond seemed to shudder and rebound like water: some impassable wall of obsidian liquid that consumed the space from corner to corner. An intense nothingness, darker than she thought dark could ever be, trapped away behind a cursed door with no answers to be seen.

"There is no shadow – we do not see as you see. We see an antechamber, but it stands behind something – a wall of glass, almost. There are lights there, and what appear to be ornaments. Do you see the room as well?"

Confusion bubbled within. "No… I see nothing," she muttered. "There's just this wall… I can't see past it…"

Stepping forward, taken by an inquisitiveness, Cavara reached out towards the rippling black waters, until a cold lick of waves splashed against her fingertips…

Suddenly she was falling, spilling forwards, the light of the torches slipping away behind, screams lost to the silence of the void.

And darkness rose to meet her, yet again.

†

Like the pearlescent waves of rolling clouds, streaked by grey shadows and the leaking strands of dusk, she returned to the white world as if flung from a catapult, a new life and energy pulsing all around.

Stretching out at her feet as the world stopped its sudden spin, veins of grey-white liquid meandered through the void like tributaries, carrying off from every angle she could see. Pulsing with the rhythms of her heart, the energy flowed away from her, meeting other convergences as it pulled gently away, sliding off into the distance. She followed them with her eyes, those delicate meanderings in the ground, tracing them until they swept together in a neat pool some several dozen feet away.

At the base of five grand totems, stood dormant just ahead.

Carved of an ancient stone, lined with tiny grooves like the bark of a tree, each one bore a complex mixture of finely-etched engravings and the painful desecration of scars. Yet, beyond the imperfections, every twist and scrape across the totems' faces swelled with the same effluvial energy as what laced the ground beneath, bulging and contracting like air through the lungs, steady and resolute as if it were a living thing. Bastions of reality, in an otherwise forsaken land.

Studying them intently, but with the fear that she was witnessing the same illusion as before, she took a defiant step forward, and found the five forms remained steadfast in their place. Another step, and nothing moved again. Another, and she was striding purposefully forward, crossing between the pipelines below, closing the gap ahead.

A few steps more, and she was before them.

Looking down to her black-shadow feet, she traced the tiny streams of liquid as they buckled up and over what appeared to be steps, rising to pool across some platform that supported the ancient stones. She ascended them slowly, never aware of where the steps were until her foot fell, as if she conjured them by her presence alone.

As she did so, the pool of liquid at the platform's centre seeped away into the ground, and a spiralling inscription of blue light formed in its centre much like the one she'd seen on the door. She drew level with it, and with a blunted hiss of life, it branded itself to the platform, stark black lines and snaking letters emblazoned harshly against the white below.

Standing there, the weightless soundless nothing consuming all around her, she closed her eyes and centred in on her soul for a moment. All was senseless, within her — there were no limbs or blood or bones or anything between. She was little more than a shadow detached from its post, gliding through an empty world, so that the only point of sensation came from the anchor-point at the square of her chest, hooked to her soul and lunging forward into the void.

A sensation, she found, that grew very suddenly stronger.

The force of it came without warning — a recollection of nausea came and went. She wavered on lifeless legs, an inner turmoil ravaged by the void, straining as it pulled her deeper, beyond her control—

Opening her eyes, guided by the revolutions in her chest, she gazed upon the centre-right totem just ahead. It pulsed angrily with the grey-white energy, pulling at her chest, a voice catching in the hollows of her ears — the

535

voice of a woman, she discovered, and the sweet melodies of song.

Much like the one from the first time, where it had all begun.

She approached slowly, stifling the surge of her soul that longed to connect with the ancient stone. Drawing closer, the markings it bore became more defined: interwoven spirals and snaking rivers; the antlers of wild stags and the claws of great bears locked in combat – the unusual lines and formations of buildings and walls, sprawling out from the centre.

If she'd known better, it almost looked like Casantri...

Crossing the platform and standing just before the totem, she wondered what lay beyond for her. She wondered whether there, in the unassuming marks of the stone's carved surface, the answers to her questions lay waiting. That the void, and the totems, and the shadow woman and everything between would unravel before her.

The truth of all things.

With slow certainty, she lifted her shadowy arm to the totem and lay her palm flat against its centre, the structure and realness of it sending a shock through her system. Holding it there, she waited for a response. Moments came; moments passed. The void remained caught in its rapture. She blinked once.

And the hand became human again.

She snapped her arm away, studying fingernails and knuckles and joints in her wrists. Tracing an arm, up to a shoulder, down to a chest and legs. A body and a mind, and moving limbs and vertebrae. There was air, and a heartbeat, and she was sweating, and—

"It's real," she muttered, studying her palms, the sheer humanity of it all. "It's all real..."

"Yes, it is."

A voice from behind. She lurched round to search the white-grey world beyond, the rivers of energy through the earth grown faint and still, shadows dancing at the edges defining a distant landscape, some far land in a forgotten place. All quiet, still as before, nothing to show for it, no sign of a voice—

And then she emerged, appearing from the shadows like a wraith.

Some great evil, conjured from the unknown.

Crossing the base of the steps, the striking dark skin and white markings across her shoulders accentuated her slender form, her bare scalp shimmering like a cannonball with deep pale eyes and a row of impossibly-white teeth. A tattoo of a serpent snaked up her neck and cheek on the left side, coiling about her brow with bared fangs and a haunting gaze. Her chest-plate seemed to be carved of purest steel, dashes of purple silk lining the edges, guarding the bindings at her waist and the two terrifying rapiers sheathed at her side. Every motion she made was one of elegance and grace, as if she were harmless to the world — but there lay a cold flame burning behind her eyes that betrayed a greater potency within. There was a power to her, the general found, a gravitating strength that never faltered.

As if she were in the presence of a god.

"Who are you?" Cavara exclaimed, her voice hollow, fading away with every inch it expanded.

"I am known by many names," the woman said softly. "To you, I am the shadow woman... the one who's been here all this time." The thin lips pursed into a smile. "But my true name, known to the world beyond, is Gaza Minesk... the Iron Queen of Tarraz."

Cavara found the terror take on a new purpose in her soul, snapping and crackling like a bitter flame. She physically recoiled from the woman as she skated the edge of the steps — there was a self-certain wickedness tracing her fair skin. Realisation and its malcontents bit poisonously through Cavara's mind: that this was the enemy, stood before her — the one enemy above all else.

And she'd been there the whole time...

"You're supposed to be dead," Cavara muttered, flushed with disbelief. "You're supposed to have died in The Collapse, cast from a thousand-foot cliff... you're supposed to be dead."

"Bedtime stories and tales of legend often have a terrible habit of exaggerating the truth," the Iron Queen replied. "If possessing any truth at all, that is."

"But, how are you alive? How are you... here?"

"Because I survived, when your leaders cast me off good-as-dead. Twenty-five years has not robbed me of that foul memory."

"How?"

She scoffed. "You wish to know the truth? How quaint."

"Don't toy with me," Cavara pronounced. "I want answers... I want to know what happened. I want to know why you're here in this void, and I want to know why my country bleeds at your hand."

"You want to know the truth? You want to know who has blood on their hands? Then I'll tell you the truth." She drew herself up, a coiling snarl biting across her nose. "Twenty-five years ago, your people took up arms against Tarraz, because of the lies and unbridled hate fed through by your officers: that we were savages and murderers, all of us, and we needed to be put in our place. All of it unfounded, yet unquestioned... and we fell into war and chaos because of it with nowhere left to run." She speared a finger at her chest. "Tarraz fought, day and night, and we fought with the honour of a people fighting for their very lives... and all your people left was a trail of blood... bodies in piles at the roadside... right up until that final, decisive battle where we had nowhere left to turn." The Iron Queen studied her sword for a moment. "And when they cut me down, your pathetic leaders... and their backward notions of right and wrong... they left that battlefield while I still breathed, and never had the guts to finish the job. So I survived... and I crawled my way back to the mountains, back to the high peaks of Val Azbann... and I made a deal with our Mother as she lay dying." Every word came with venom, ancient burdens finally told true. "A soul... bound to a soul, so that we may both live on into the world. She knew her fate, as much as any other... she knew the Mothers were dying, as you also now do, and knew in all her ancient wisdom that I was her only hope at redemption. So I made a deal... that her soul would pass on to me..."

"...and that you would survive to finish what you started, in her name."

"Precisely so," the Iron Queen acknowledged. "All I wanted was a people of my own... a nation of my own, not bound to your principles, to that high-handed brutality you dispose of so callously. I wanted a Tarraz for my people... and your leaders, in all their piety, ripped that from us with blood and steel." A pause, a machinating flare in her eyes. "And now, we shall take back what you stole from us... and we will wipe the earth of your greed for what you've done."

"You wish to exterminate us..."

"I wish to reset the balance... I wish to right that which has been wronged. The Mother has granted me this power... and with it, your people shall fall."

Cavara strained against the void, a bubble of emotion catching in her throat. "Is the King's death not enough for you?" she cried. "Is the humiliation not enough of a revenge?"

"The King did not spill our blood. The King did not burn our villages and ravage our fields. The King did not slaughter the innocents." The Iron Queen speared a finger out. "You... and your people, were the ones who tore us to the ground. Your people subjugated us as slaves and puppets... exploited us, and took everything of our way of life from us. The King was a single blade, an unfortunate by-product of a malicious war... but it was your people who wrought our end and bled our suffering, so it is the people, who must pay as a whole."

"You are wrong... the people are not part of this——"

"They were always part of this, even as we speak. Look at them now: it is no one person who wages a war against us... it is the army and its cronies, with the support of the people, that demand its operation. Now, as before, our extermination and ruin is paraded through your streets with such joy... even as the truth lays hidden, and my people die in their droves. When will that come to an end, as I watch twenty-five years of pain come full circle again? Tell me, when will it end?"

"When there is peace... when the people know the truth," Cavara said quietly. "That is when wrongs can be amended."

"They have never known the truth... they've looked to the stains on their palms and shrugged for decades; they will not know the truth for fear of the reality it brings."

"With peace, they can learn."

"And when will this peace come? With your armies already burning through a third of my country, where will that line be drawn? On our maps... or at our throats?"

"In the right way, whatever that may be... the way that lets bloodshed end, and our nations come to terms."

She scoffed. "Your leaders wouldn't know fair terms if you strung them up by their necks."

"They can…" Cavara grappled at nothing. "They can learn… we can put differences aside, come to a common understanding—"

"And those are pretty words for an outcast betrayed by her own to quell dissent," the Iron Queen spat. "I've heard it all before. This bravado of peace and trust and good will… no wonder the Mother picked you. Bold yet spineless, as ever…"

Cavara stalled her thoughts, the nature of the void fluctuating all around her. "How do you know that?" she asked.

"That the Mother picked you? It's how you're here… in the Rapture."

"What's… what's the Rapture?"

The cold woman seemed bemused. "You really don't know, do you?"

"Why am I here?" The pain in her voice leaked through.

"Now isn't that interesting…" A hand slid down her side, gracing the sword hilt at her waist. "Well, I suppose that makes my life easier…"

"Why? What's going on?"

"There's no point in offering explanation, my dear." The Iron Queen drew her blade out from its sheath with a shimmer of light, twisting menacingly towards the general. "You'll be dead before it's worth knowing… so I'll just kill you, and take what's mine…"

She took a step forward; Cavara found her heart seize up and her legs slide back beneath her. The Iron Queen ascended the steps—

"You shall do no such thing."

Both figures stopped, frozen in place, turning to the voice—

Laying eyes on a huge, pale figure draped in black robes, forming from the white of the beyond.

Skin, pale as dragon-fire. Branded below the eyes, black and bloody like a raven's. A pale scalp like the moon, with a great trench cutting through one side like a mountain ravine. Sliding deep into the skull, through the brain itself, a rotten knot of flesh coiled within. A wound, that in all sense, would've seen any mortal man dead. But whatever this thing was, this creature of the darkness stood before them, it played by no such rules.

Only those of blood, and terror.

"Who are you?" the Iron Queen growled. "Why are you here?"

"I am a redeemer," the mysterious figure boomed, without emotion or

540

humanity.

"Don't play games with us, creature... what are you?"

Its eyes centred fully on her, cold and all-seeing. "You know... what I am."

A wry smile crossed her face suddenly, recollection rising to the fore. "You're a Forgotten One... aren't you? One of the All-Mother's great champions of the world... I've seen your kind before, walking the lands of my people. Except, last I recalled... your kind chose me as their leader, and chose me to enter the Rapture." She turned back to Cavara. "So I'm sure you have no quarrel in me ending this poor wretch here..."

She lifted her blade again.

"You shall do no such thing."

Irritation flashed across the Queen's face. "And why should I not?"

"Because I am here, with the All-Mother's dying wish..." Its eyes passed from Gaza to the general. "To protect her chosen successor..."

"Her?" the Queen spat.

"What?" Cavara gasped, the pit of her stomach falling out beneath her.

"You have been chosen," it rumbled slowly. "That is why you are here, why all this has happened to you. The death of your King was no accident – from that point on, you were chosen as the All-Mother's successor... it cannot be undone."

Suddenly, there was no air in the void around her. "Why me?" she spluttered. "How do you know? How do you know it was no accident that he died? He was murdered by the Tarrazi––"

"He was not."

"And how do you know?"

A long pause, the eyes burrowing through her. "Because I was the one who killed him."

Her head spun like a swivel, an anxious breach of anger and betrayal bubbling in her chest, reeling against the shock and fear of the truths she had been told into one crush at the base of her soul. The urge to scream beckoned within. "Why?" she questioned. "Why would you do that?"

"It was the All-Mother's final wish... a successor had to be found. With the death of your king, the balance of your nation would be reordered and a new leader would be found. From there, they would be embodied by the

Mother; they would enter the Rapture and fight for the mantle of successor. The balance of the world would be restored when the victor prevailed." A slow nod of acknowledgement. "Only rather than the leader of Provenci... the All-Mother has picked you."

"But why? Why me?"

"Because the All-Mother has found you worthy... and it cannot be undone. You have been chosen as her successor, the first in three centuries, and you must take up the mantle and fight in her name within the Rapture and beyond." The pale figure's face seemed to shadow over. "This is no mortal war of common people... this is a war between gods, for the survival of the world as you know it. And your enemy, the one who stakes claim to that same mantle you fight for... stands before you now."

Cavara glanced frightfully towards the Iron Queen — and found her eyes already locked to her, burning through her, twisting anger glaring across her skin. Hatred, vengeance, malice and ruin painted bold across her complexion — the truth of the world on her shoulders, biting like the snake at her cheek.

"But I'm no leader," Cavara exclaimed, turning back to the Forgotten One. "I'm nothing... why would she have chosen me? It makes no sense."

"I was only ever asked to protect you, and bind you with the Mother's kiss so you may enter the Rapture as you are now."

"Why? What even is this place?"

"A world within a world... a mirror of reality. Only those blessed by the Mother may enter this place, and walk in a world of white shadow."

"That makes no sense," she charged. "Why were you asked to protect me?"

"Because without it, you would never have made it here." A pale finger extended towards her, pointing to her abdomen. "Who else do you think could have saved you from death on that distant shore, when the end was most inevitable?"

She drew a hand across the knotted wound on her stomach and blinked heavily. "You did?"

"By the All-Mother's hand and her final wish, I saved you... so you may be her champion. That was the choice I made when others would not."

"What others?"

Its face shifted, almost to sadness. "The others... the Forgotten Ones your

542

opponent spoke of... place their faith in the people of Tarraz, and their champion to the Rapture stood before you." A glance to the Queen, blade still clenched tightly in one hand. "They act by their own gain, not by duty, and defied the All-Mother's wish to seek their own fate. I went against their unanimous choice, and carried out the All-Mother's command as they sought to destroy it..." The hand lifted, tapping the deep wound in its skull. "They almost killed me for it... but now, I am here to serve you, as the successor of the All-Mother... to help you bring balance back to a breaking world, as its new champion——"

"You fucking traitor!" the Iron Queen growled, sword flashing dangerously in one hand. "Enough of this! You lie and you betray — you're kind made their will known to me, and you wish to cast them aside."

"I've done nothing but uphold the highest order——"

"You deny me the right of successor... when within me lives the very soul of the Mother herself? You choose a pathetic wretch like this to take up that mantle, and let her slaughter my people once more? The rest of your kind have made their choice... they march among my ranks and have marked me as the champion of this world — they support my people against their common enemy. What gives you the right to defy that?"

"I speak for the All-Mother, and I do as she commands — it is the Forgotten Ones who stand marked with defiance. You are no champion... you are a usurper. This was meant to be done peacefully——"

"There is no peace, while war rages and my people die!" Her voice rattled through the void like shattering metal. "I have waited a quarter of a century for this... all these years to mark my ascent and claim the mantle of All-Mother myself. So you will not stand against me... as I take what I have survived twenty-five years for, and will now take as my own." She unsheathed her second blade and snarled towards them. "With the Mother's power, and with the death of this poor wretch who stands before me, I will tear this world to the ground... and none shall defy me."

The Iron Queen charged forward suddenly, crossing the platform with staggering speed and swords bearing. Cavara slid back, an all-consuming fear tearing through her system. A snarling face, the enemy cut across; the general raised her hand——

And caught the blade with one of her own, conjured from nothing — a blade of purest light, dazzling like a thousand tiny stars, shimmering immaculately in her hand.

The pale figure smiled.

"The chosen one, has come."

With a roar of hate enough to shake the walls of the void all around, the Iron Queen lunged out and struck for her again, both swords pirouetting in her grasp like the reins of a chariot. Cavara, still reeling from the sudden appearance of the blade in her hand, whimpered like a pup at the threat of the attack and thrust her arm forward lamely in defence.

The luminescent sword snapped round, catching both swords with impossible speed, the force so great that the Queen forced a backstep and ground her jaw with anger. A moment of joy, that Cavara found wavering as the blade sent shockwaves up her arm, catching along the bone as if someone had burrowed nails into it. Almost like the weapon was fighting her — as if she was worthy of it, but untrained in its art.

The Iron Queen began her assault once more, a relentless execution of strikes that Cavara's sword turned to match, but at the great price of whatever pain now lanced through her arm. With every consecutive blow, the general became aware of her unmatched skill — that this was a fighter imbued with the soul of a god, and she was but a lowly fighter far out of her depth. She was no match for her usurper threat — the sword at her hand was, but only at the expense of her strength, as her forearm seemed ready to shatter altogether. Her shoulder burned, skin crawling with a prickly sweat that seemed wholly unnatural in such a displaced land. Fighting back, attempting to tame the ignited blade coiling in her fingers — falling foul of its disobedience, the pressure across her knuckle too great.

A strike to her left; Cavara coiled about, with the sword stretching further again to meet it—

The Queen's other sword rounding, forcing a sharp half-turn to catch it, the general's elbow crunching with the strain—

The wrath of a god flaring before her in the eyes of the Iron Queen — the creeping agony of defeat pulsing stronger with each moment that passed.

Still the onslaught came.

"I can't..." Cavara strained into the void, to anyone who'd listen, sword lurching back and forth to match her opponent. "It's too much..."

At the corner of one eye, she caught the gaze of the Forgotten One from afar, a determined intrigue in his expression, demurred by a growing uneasiness that the game had gone on for long enough.

Dicing left and right as the strikes became more erratic, the general assessed the strength in her arm and found the blade begin to falter. Suddenly she was backstepping, the blade's impressive lustre fading, the rapiers crossing in vicious arcs far faster than she could counter.

The panic returned, ugly and unnerving, the weight of everything bearing down like the crushing force of a landslide. That at any moment, the blade could give out. At any moment, she would miss a strike. At any moment, she could die——

A snap in her hand, and the sword slipped away from her like a falling star, fading to the void with a contraction of her heart——

Seizing the moment, the Iron Queen lunged out——

A pale hand appeared at Cavara's side, catching her arm, swiping her away as the sword skimmed across her, drawing a thin streak of red across her waist.

A screech of anger, enough to topple mountains.

"Do not interfere, creature!" the Queen roared, turning on the Forgotten One, the general now shielded away within its arms. "She is mine to kill!"

The Queen struck out, blade sliding through the void towards them.

Like a deafening blow, the pale figure flashed its hand out and repulsed the sword with a strike of energy, an unseen force gravitating through the void, ripples bending the air between like paper. The Queen stumbled back, the anger tame but resolute behind her eyes, snarling like a wolf brought to bay.

The Forgotten One adjusted its huge robes, hands recoiling back into their sleeves. "The time will come when the successor is chosen... and you shall both fight for the mantle of All-Mother," it proclaimed, greys and blacks twisting in the aura around it. "But by the power vested in me by the Mother upon her death, I say to you only this: a usurper may attempt to take that which has been destined for another, but if you wish to tread that path and *raise your sword against the balance of the world as we know it... know that your end will come, and you'll have to go through me to get there."*

Cavara caught a final glimpse of the Iron Queen of Tarraz, grinning pointedly, sheathing her blades with a slow certainty that made the general fearful for her life. That someday they would have to fight again — for the mantle of successor to the greatest being of the known world. That even with the Forgotten One as her protector, the final engagement would come down to her.

And would the weapon return, when she did? Would she control it? Would she be able to fight? Would she be a match? How would the pale figure intervene? Would they fight in the Rapture, or in the real world? Could she choose when to fight? Would she embody the All-Mother's power? Would she fight with it? Could she control the Rapture using it? What even was the Rapture at all?

She didn't know...

Shielded within its robes, the Forgotten One stepped away from the totems, out from the void of white that surrounded them, and then a darkness came to claim all things with the truth of the world beyond.

Its shadow rose to meet her, once again.

†

"Wake up."

The next thing she felt was the cold touch of stone against her cheek, tingling at the palms of her hands.

Eyes flicking open suddenly, pulling herself up from the ground, she found herself in a torch-lit chamber streaked with ancient markings of ash and gold. They formed like roots, taking hold at the room's corners, spreading out and drifting between the cracks in the chiselled stone, stretching down to a wide floor pooled with water from the rippling natural springs. Upon carved stands scattered absently around the edge, ornaments stood dormant, their faces laced with gold inscriptions and images of battles long-forgotten. There was an archaic temperance to everything she laid eyes upon, from the floor at her feet to the dark ceilings high above – a lost part of a lost time, realised in the world before her.

Alerted to a disturbance behind, Cavara twisted to discover the doorway from before, now without its liquid barrier, where the Alderbane stooped slowly into the wide chamber and studied her intently, several questions rolling at the tip of its tongue.

But another sound from ahead drew its attention away, and a graceless fear melded across its skull at the sight of it. Turning back, Cavara gazed up to find the pale figure looming large in front, the gravity and weight in its expression commanding the room beyond.

"Who are you?" the Alderbane asked, keeping the guards at its side at bay.

"I am the messenger of the All-Mother, protector of her mortal successor," the Forgotten One exclaimed. It looked down to her, a slight smile catching at the edge of its cheeks as it offered a hand. "And you and I have a lot of work to do... if we're going to save the world from ruin."

Cavara looked to the Alderbane, a certain satisfaction in the shock of his face, and turned back to the Forgotten One.

She found a smile, took his hand and got to her feet.

Yes... yes we do.

†

The Fangs of War

A frozen breeze swept up from the shoreline to the east, the Grey Plains stretching soundlessly before them, rippling with every dice of the wind. A hollow glow caught the skies, bleeding hues of red and orange as the sun dipped below the distant mountains, dashed with clouds and the slow spirals of smoke still rising from the remains of the camp.

What could be salvaged had been bundled into wagons and sent back along the main road, destined to reinforce columns marching to the west. Already, small camps and staging posts had been erected all across the lowlands, as the armies had swept through with blood and steel to spare. The victory won that day on the plain – routing the enemy with such clinical brutality – had been repeated ten-fold across the front lines. By the time the moon poked its head over the mountains to the south, a third of Tarraz flew the red-and-green standard.

And come the morning, they would march for more.

Revek raised his glass, offering toasts to the officers gathered before him in a quiet inlet of the ruined camp, cool air sweeping through his body and a quiet song humming in his heart. He stood at the edge of greatness – he stood as an envy of gods and kings. The might of imperial Provenci had been realised.

And still greater times are yet to come.

"My fellow officers," the commander exclaimed. "My fellow victors in this fine war of ours." A few smiles and jeers passed around. "This is, as ever, a time to celebrate. Our enemy are routed, in chaos and beaten back across this savage land by our forces far and wide. Although our dead are many, and our journey has been... *quarrelsome* to say the least... our suffering is far from that of the humiliation our enemy has been served by our hand and by our blades these past few days. And it is to that, I salute you all: your work is stellar, and our victories are grand by your collective skill." He lifted his glass to catch the dying sun. "A toast... to our effortless fortune, and *long may it last*."

Glasses rose to meet his own; a cheer of joy caught the air as if they were back in a quiet tavern back home: with bright eyes and slaps across the back – the glow of honour painted in every inch of their gaze.

"It is your good will that brought us to this time," Revek continued, taking a long sip of liquor that burned down his throat. "It is your strength that has served us – it is your duty and command and your *subordination* that mark you as survivors." A pain bit through him, images of the riverbed crossing his mind – he ground his teeth and took another swig. "As a man who honours the diligence of his army more than anything else... you not only have my respect, but my thanks too."

All around, the admiration proved almost tangible.

"And tomorrow, we march again," he declared. "Tomorrow, we drive north onto the Grey Plains, following the eastern mountains into the beating heart of our enemy. We shall strive forward, marching our ranks dawn 'til dusk... and we shall kill anything we find that stands in our way. This enemy, who we stand amongst the ruins of now, was the first... but I assure you it shall not be the last. And when we find that next enemy, and the one after that, and the one after that... we shall fight, and we shall fight to the last man, and we shall win. Because *we* are *victors* and *we* are *gods* of this land. And when we march to the heart of Val Azbann... we shall do so with our swords gleaming, and none shall stand in our way!"

A roar of exuberance claimed the crowd, joined by passing patrols who had stopped to listen, clattering armour and jostling arms swinging skyward in a chant of their glory. Revek simply smiled, watching over them like a father, the commanding officer of a grand cause and the new order of the world. He danced between their eyes, out to the tents behind them, a bleeding horizon stretching from afar.

And the black shadow slowly forming at the ridge.

Everywhere he looked, he discovered suddenly row upon row of dark smudges, swamping the ridge for miles across from the valley to the mountains at their right. The lancing shapes of spears and standards stood defiantly against the wind; mounted figures on huge stallions bore down at the flanks. An open circle of armoured guards massed at the formation's centre, with a single entity stood within them bearing force against all.

A black-robed figure, pale as the moon, watching him from the shadows.

Revek felt the glass slip from his hand.

Fuck...

Printed in Great Britain
by Amazon